S0-ACS-469

Also by Mike Stewart

Sins of the Brother

mike
stewart

G. P. Putnam's Sons New York

dog
island

This is a work of fiction. Names, characters, places, and incidents either are the product of the author's imagination or are used fictitiously, and any resemblance to actual persons living or dead, business establishments, events, or locales is entirely coincidental.

G. P. Putnam's Sons
Publishers Since 1838
a member of
Penguin Putnam Inc.
375 Hudson Street
New York, NY 10014

Published simultaneously in Canada

Library of Congress Cataloging-in-Publication Data

Stewart, Mike, date.
Dog Island / Mike Stewart.
p. cm.
ISBN 0-399-14645-8
1. Gulf Coast (U.S.)—Fiction. I. Title.
PS3569.T46544 D64 2000 00-037014
813'.54—dc21

Printed in the United States of America

10 9 8 7 6 5 4 3 2 1

Book design by Lynne Amft

For my parents

From the beach the child holding the hand of her father,
Those burial-clouds that lower victorious soon to devour all,
Watching, silently weeps.

WALT WHITMAN
On the Beach at Night

prologue

THE MOTOR STOPPED. Cool rain glanced off the windshield and side windows in gray needles and disappeared into the dark sheet of water stretched across the parking lot. Inside the car, a sinewy boy with sun-bleached hair leaned across the center console and pushed his mouth against a teenage girl's lips. She put her hand on the back of his head, and the boy began to fondle her breasts with his left hand. Pulling away, the girl popped open the passenger door and stepped out onto wet pavement where she spun in a circle, her arms extended, her palms cupped to catch the rain. Even at night, her face glowed from warm days of Florida sun. Thick black hair bounced against her shoulder blades as she danced.

The boy said something from inside the car. The girl stopped and ran across the pavement and onto the sand toward the surf, where she disappeared into the night. The boy muttered something; then he stepped out and followed.

He found her sitting on a scattered path of gray and white shells at the high-tide mark, kicking at waves with her toes as they lapped against her feet and calves. He sat down on the sand behind her, encircled her hips with his legs, and reached around from behind to hold both of her breasts in sunburned hands. She seemed not to notice. She sat and watched whitecaps roll across the rain-splattered Gulf.

Growing restless for a response, he pulled her over backward and rolled on top of her. His hands met behind her neck, and his legs intertwined with hers. Their mouths worked together while her hands slowly kneaded the sand beside her hips. Without warning or finesse, the boy's clumsy hands shoved her windbreaker, shirt, and bra up to her neck, and the sun-bleached head moved down to kiss her breasts. The girl lay still for seconds while his mouth moved over her nipples. Her hands squeezed pockets of sand. Tears filled the corners of closed lids and rolled down her cheekbones and temples, mixing with the salt spray and cool raindrops in her hair.

"Stop."

The boy didn't respond, except to press harder against her with his hips and to work more frantically with his tongue.

"Stop, please." She pushed him away and stood up. He watched her breasts until she had untangled her clothes and pulled her shirtfront over the cotton bra. She looked out again at the whitecaps. Behind her, the boy walked back up the beach and climbed into his Mustang. The girl turned and walked away down the shoreline. In the distance, she could hear the car drive away.

She carried her sandals dangling from two fingers and squeezed the sharp, cool sand with her toes as she walked. The rhythms and the scents of the Gulf echoed the rhythms and scents of childhood; they reminded her, in a softer, easier way, of the Atlantic shore. There was still the throb of distant hurt in the waves, but she needed the sound. Maybe she even needed the hurt. She hugged her windbreaker tight. All around her, swirls of fog hugged the beach above rippled shadows in the sand.

She had hoped the boy in the Mustang would walk with her along the sand and softly kiss her and maybe tell her something about the stars, but that wasn't life. She had known that when he asked her out. Now, she had no way to get home.

The girl walked until creosote pilings marking the end of public access beaches materialized out of the night. Turning her back to the water, she moved up the beach and found a lounge chair on the patio of a pastel beach house. There was no car on the oyster-shell driveway and no sign of life inside. She pressed her fist against the flesh between her stomach and chest, closed her eyes, and tried to sleep.

Voices floated out of the beach house, and she sighed. Moving quietly out of the chair, she walked around the corner of the house opposite the driveway and headed for the road. A few paces ahead, a jagged rectangle of light fell from a window onto a tangle of sea grass, cockleburs, and dirty sand. She turned toward the beach, but the sound of something or someone falling brought her back. Crouching to the side of the window, she peered through the slats of a bamboo blind that hung against the inside of the glass. She saw four men in the room. One lay on the floor and seemed hurt. The others were standing. Two wore tank tops, cutoffs, and caps. One of the two had tattoos on one arm. The fourth man was larger than the others—over six feet and bulky, like a weight lifter or an ex-jock going to fat. He wore tan dress pants and a red short-sleeved shirt.

The big one seemed to say something, and the other two picked up the injured man by his armpits. Someone was talking—a baritone hum floated into the night. She saw the big man pull a pistol out of the back of his waistband and put it in the hurt man's mouth. A loud *thoump* bounced against the glass in the window, and the hurt man's cheeks flashed iridescent blood red like a kid shining a flashlight into his mouth on a summer evening. At the same time, the man's head popped back and he sagged between the two men in cutoffs.

The next instant, all three men swiveled their heads to look at the window. She may have tried to say "no," but what came out was shapeless and guttural—not something so precise as a word. The big man started out of the room. The other two dropped the dead man and followed. Within seconds, all three were outside searching the beach.

They found nothing to account for the sound.

chapter one

SPRING RAINS EAST of Baton Rouge had poured fog across Mobile Bay. A cool breeze, stirred up by warm days and cool nights, swept down the beach and across the second-floor deck where it tugged at my robe. Inside, through French doors, red dots hovered in the dark over the bedside table, showing that it was a little after four in the morning.

Glenfiddich scotch and Umbérto Eco had finally put me under a little after midnight—about three hours before I woke and wandered out on the deck. I was getting used to it. You can get a lot of thinking done if you aren't able to sleep.

The bedroom phone was ringing. A greenish-white glow pulsed next to the red dots on the clock. The answering machine was off, and I watched the telephone ring for most of a minute before walking into the bedroom. I picked up the handset and cleared my throat. "Hello?"

A woman's voice said, "Tom?"

"Yeah, this is Tom."

"Tom, this is Susan Fitzsimmons. I apologize for calling in the middle of the night."

I felt for the switch on the bedside lamp, and yellow light jarred the backs of my eyes. "Are you all right?"

Susan said, "I'm fine. Something bad has happened though."

"What do you mean by 'something bad'?"

"There's someone here with me who needs to talk to you. We need some legal advice on how to handle a disturbing situation."

I had known Susan for six months. We met in early October when fall was just starting to cool the Gulf Coast. She was smart and graceful and striking, and I had almost gotten her killed. Or, at least, I was one reason among many why Susan found herself limping through the holidays recovering from knife wounds. One set of reasons was that her artist husband had gotten greedy, crossed my little brother, and ended up with his throat sliced open. Another was that I stuck my nose in and figured out what happened and, along the way, managed to bring an impressively dangerous person into Susan's life. Now she had only fading memories of her dead husband and, apparently, a friend in trouble. I had a dead brother and a long line of sleepless nights. And I was not blind to the possibility that, over the past few months, I might have been wallowing in it a bit.

I reached for the pen and pad on the bedside table. I asked, "Where are you?"

"We're at the beach house on St. George. The girl who needs to talk to you is," she paused, "a friend of mine here on the island. She thinks she may have seen someone get killed. You know, murdered. Earlier tonight on the beach."

I thought, *damn*. I said, "I'm assuming she wasn't involved."

"No. Well, only to the extent that she saw it happen."

"Then the advice is easy. Call the cops."

"She wasn't involved, but it's more complicated than that." Susan sounded unsure of what to say. "I think she needs to talk to a lawyer."

"What's complicated about it?"

Susan didn't answer.

"It's okay to talk on the phone. No one's listening."

"You're right. I guess it's silly, but I am uncomfortable talking this way. Part of the problem is, well, you know how it is down here on the coast. Somebody disappears or you see somebody flashing a wad of money or somebody looks like they're up to no good, first thing that pops into your head is it's got something to do with drugs. And you never know whose brother or cousin or friend might be involved, so you don't know who's safe to talk to."

"She thinks she saw some kind of drug hit?"

"Tom, she doesn't know what it was. Just that somebody got killed right in front of her, and she's scared out of her mind. And here's the complicated part. She's a runaway, and she's a minor. She's absolutely terrified that her family's going to find out where she is and come get her. You know, if she goes to the police and they check her out and find out she's a runaway."

"Susan, maybe her father or mother coming to get her is the best thing that could come out of this."

"I don't think so."

"What do you mean, you don't think so? You can't decide something like that on your own."

"In this case, I can."

"I guess there's something you're not telling me."

She didn't answer.

I gave up. "When did it happen?"

"When did what happen?"

"The murder. When did this friend . . . What's her name?"

"Carli. Carli Monroe."

"When did Carli see this happen?"

"About three hours ago, I think."

"Shit."

"Yes, I know." Susan hesitated, then said, "She needs to talk to a lawyer, Tom. I hate to ask, but could you come down here?"

"Susan, I know she's scared, but I'm not a criminal attorney. Hell, I'm not even licensed in Florida. And I'm supposed to be at a meeting in Tuscaloosa this afternoon. My advice is to find a good local attorney, somebody who's down at the courthouse every week drinking coffee with the prosecutors and bailiffs, and work through him or her."

Susan lowered her voice. "Tom, it's taken me two hours to get her to let me make this call." She had cupped her hand over the mouthpiece, and her muffled words buzzed around the edges. "Carli doesn't know who to trust down here and neither do I. If you don't help, she's just going to leave here and try to deal with it by herself. And she's not really capable of doing that." I didn't respond. Seconds passed as faint static filled the earpiece. Finally, Susan just repeated my name with what sounded like a little shame sprinkled over it.

My mouth tasted bitter and smoky from last night's scotch and three hours sleep. I breathed deeply to clear my head and looked out at the night. Light from the bedside lamp had washed out the view through open French doors, merging sea and sky and clouds into one black sheet. Susan waited some more while I decided to do the right thing. I said, "I'll be there around mid-morning."

"Thanks. I'm sorry to do this to you."

"Don't worry about it. I should have said yes right away."

Puffs of clean air rolled through the open door and across the bed. I walked into the bathroom and splashed water against my face and neck before going back to the phone and punching in a seven-digit number. A deep voice, wide awake, answered on the second ring.

chapter two

"WE'VE GOT TO check out something on St. George Island."

The best investigator on the Gulf, maybe one of the best anywhere, said, "You know what time it is?"

"It's twenty till five."

"*I* know what time it is." Joey didn't call me a dipshit, but it was there in his tone. "What's on St. George Island that's worth me hauling my ass out of bed this time of the morning?"

"Somebody's dead."

"Anybody I know?"

"Got no idea. That's what I need you to find out. You got any contacts over around the Appalachicola-St. George area?"

"Nope. Hang on a second." I heard some rustling and a few clicking sounds, and Joey came back on the line. "Okay, go ahead."

"I just got a call from Susan Fitzsimmons."

"She okay?"

"Susan's fine. But she's got some friend on St. George who thinks she saw some guy, or maybe some woman, get killed tonight."

"You're kidding."

"No. I'm not."

"For one hell of a good person, Susan's got some bad karma or something junking up her life."

I was thinking the same thing. I said, "Yeah, well, she needs some help. So, I was hoping you could sniff around the cops in Appalachicola and see if anything's been reported. I could do it, but . . ."

He interrupted. "But they aren't going to tell some lawyer shit. You'd just start 'em beating the bushes." Joey paused, then went on. "Yeah, I can do that. Don't know anybody down there in the fucking boonies, but I got a couple of boys on the Panama City force who'll fish around for me. Cost a couple of bills. That okay?"

"Sure. Fine. Thanks."

"Give me the details."

I looked at the pad on my bedside table. Exactly seven words were written on it: *Susan*, *St. George Island*, *Carli Monroe*, and *Murder*. I said, "I don't know any."

Joey sighed and hung up.

Before stepping into the shower, I called the office and left voice mail for my secretary, Kelly. I told her to call the prospective client I was supposed to meet that afternoon and make something up.

A few minutes later, as hot water began to sting my chest and shoulders, I thought about the timber tycoon in Tuscaloosa who—after receiving Kelly's call—would be seeking legal advice elsewhere. And I realized that it was all part of my grand plan. A year ago, I had bailed from a fat six-figure job to start a solo practice. And now, blowing off wealthy, paying clients was the next logical step in my strategy to avoid worldly distractions like money and success and solving legal problems for people who could actually afford to pay me.

I squirted shampoo into my palm and rubbed my hands together.

Maybe Carli would turn out to be a runaway heiress.

A few minutes after six-thirty, a blue Ford Expedition crunched onto the white gravel drive. I stepped out onto the porch. Heavy dew had darkened the tops of the weathered banisters. Smudged swirls of orange and pink glowed in the east beneath a light gray sky.

Joey stepped out of the car, and I said, "Good morning."

Joey said, "Morning," as he climbed the front steps and turned sideways to navigate the entry hall on his way to the kitchen. It was a tight fit. I'm six feet tall, and I could look Joey squarely in the throat if I concentrated on my posture. He was about six six and two hundred forty pounds of muscle and bone. He looked like a lost Viking: short white-blonde hair, ruddy sun-creased skin, and hard gray eyes the color of a new tin roof. That morning, the Viking wore pleated olive-green khakis, a cream-colored rugby shirt, and Hush Puppies without socks.

I followed and found Joey standing in front of my open refrigerator drinking out of a half-gallon carton of Tropicana Pure Premium orange juice.

"Help yourself."

"That's what I thought I was doing. Been up half the frigging night looking for a dead guy who probably ain't even dead. You got any of those sesame seed bagels you had last time I was out here? Found 'em."

"Want some breakfast?"

Joey ignored the question. He found a knife, cut two bagels in half, and popped them in the toaster oven. I poured two cups of coffee and gave one to Joey. He smeared cream cheese on the four toasted bagel halves and put all four on his plate.

When he was seated at the kitchen table, I said, "No dead guys. Is that the story?"

Joey said, "That's the story."

"Well, did you find out anything from your Panama City contacts besides the fact that no murder has been reported?"

Joey talked over a mouthful of bagel. "Like what?"

"I don't know. I thought maybe you got the lowdown on the cops in Appalachicola, or you fished around for some general information about whether they've had any trouble down that way."

"No cops. Just a sheriff's office. Sheriff Todd Wilson."

"Todd? They got a yuppie beach sheriff?"

"From what I could find out, Wilson wouldn't know a yuppie if he ate one. Word is, though, he's a good enough guy. Probably as honest as most small-town sheriffs along the coast." Joey paused to drain the rest of the orange juice from the carton he had lifted from my refrigerator.

"What's that mean?"

"What's what mean?"

"What do you mean he's as honest as most sheriffs along the coast?"

"It means he keeps the peace. You know, keeps the streets safe for old ladies and tourists. But the rumor is that he also takes a little money every now and then to ignore the Bodines."

"The what?"

"Kind of a redneck mafia. The cops down there call 'em 'the Bodines.' You know, like Jethro on *The Beverly Hillbillies*. Lots of jokes about this bunch of rednecks 'ciphering' their profits and that kinda shit. But they run the coast down there. And they're organized—half of 'em are related to each other."

"And that's all you know right now?"

"That's it. No murders, no bodies, nothing."

I asked Joey to lock up and left him sitting at my kitchen table drinking coffee and reading my morning *Mobile Register*. By seven, I was in my Cherokee cruising down Scenic 98 toward Appalachicola and the causeway to St. George Island. I flipped on the radio to drown out the whine of mud grips on blacktop. National Public Radio out of Mobile lasted through Foley and Pensacola, across Pensacola Bay, and into Navarre.

Outside Ft. Walton, static drowned out NPR. An oldies station out of Panama City filled the Jeep with a different noise as 98 wound next to Choctawhatchee Bay, past the new-money, Easter-egg villas at Seaside and the old-money resort at Grayton Beach, and then cut through the spring-break motels, neon signs, and giant water slides that pollute Panama City Beach.

East of Panama City, used car and mobile home lots with hand-painted signs, boxy fast-food joints, and staccato stoplights dissolved into pine forests that sporadically separated the pavement from a clear view of the Gulf. After an hour of nothing, the road bumped into the quick-mart-and-fast-food outskirts of Appalachicola and then eased into that quaint seaside town's Victorian architecture and palm lined streets.

I killed the radio and tried to think about what I would say to Susan and her friend about witnessing a crime and the best way to handle involvement with the police.

I couldn't think of anything.

Without music, the mud grips whirred again on the causeway that stretches from the east end of Appalachicola to the bay side of St. George Island. I drove to the ocean side of the island, turned right away from the state park, and cruised between rows of stilted, hurricane-ready vacation homes. As the road moved away from the center of the island, the houses grew generally newer and larger until I turned away from the ocean and then left into The Plantation.

An overstuffed guard's uniform shuffled out of the gatehouse and asked my business. I asked for directions to Susan Fitzsimmons' house. He found my name on a clipboard, handed me a green tag to hang from my rearview mirror, and told me how to get where I was going. Back over on the Gulf side of the island, I found a two-story Caribbean-plantation-style beach house with the right numbers.

Latticework and tropical plants camouflaged the hurricane stilts. Above the crisscross pattern, weathered gray siding contrasted with white trim work around windows and doors and highlighted an oversized round window suspended beneath a gable's point above the back entrance. A banistered crow's nest stretched twenty feet across the apex of a green copper roof, providing what had to be one hell of a view of the water.

I smiled. Sticking out of the carport beneath the house was Susan's antique step-side pickup. I parked on oyster-shell paving behind Susan's truck and climbed wooden steps to the main door. I pressed the doorbell. Someone was moving inside the house.

chapter three

SUSAN FITZSIMMONS OPENED the door and smiled with perfect white teeth and sun-crinkled eyes. She stepped out, gave me a quick but exuberant hug, and stepped back to look at my face.

I said, "You look great." And she did.

The last time I had seen Susan, she had been lying in a hospital bed with clear plastic tubes looped into her arms and nostrils. She had been pale and tired and frightened. Now Susan looked like Susan again—sun-streaked blonde hair worn short and shaggy, tanned cheeks, and intelligent blue eyes.

Susan is from the Midwest and has never had the penchant for small talk that Southerners think is part of good manners—or, as she describes it, talking until you can think of something to say. Now, all Susan said was, "Come in. Carli's inside."

The door opened into a cavernous room featuring a large circular staircase made of polished aluminum that swirled upward against the left wall. Twelve feet up, metal stairs connected to a wooden catwalk that hung from the left and right walls, wrapped around the back wall that held the door we had come through, and, apparently, provided access to bedrooms on the second level. On the right wall, a six-foot oil painting of nothing but dozens of beautifully detailed seashells flooded the room with color. Glass stretched across the front of the room, showing huge rectangles of ocean and sky framed by rough-cut beams.

Susan's kitchen lay to the right and against the back wall. It was separated from the main living area by a long, antique butcher's table surrounded by brushed aluminum chairs that echoed the staircase. Next to the table sat a striking teenage girl with blue-black hair, dark brown eyes set in a pretty oval face, and suntanned legs that she displayed beneath blue jean cutoffs with slits up the outside seams that ended high enough to show just a hint of where her panties curved around her hips. Above the jeans, four inches of skin and a very attractive navel were on display beneath a green knit shirt designed to show off young navels. She sat with her ankles crossed and her legs extended toward us as we entered. She wore black sport sandals with blue Aztec designs on the straps, and her toenails were painted pink. A yellow windbreaker hung across the back of her chair.

"Tom. This is Carli. Carli, this is the friend I told you about."

She uncrossed her ankles, recrossed them with the other foot on top, and smiled a strange, somehow inappropriate smile. Her pelvis seemed to rise up in the chair as she moved her legs. She said, "Nice to meet you." She had some kind of working-class Northern accent.

I was suddenly a little irritated. I said, "Can your friend excuse us for a minute?" Carli stopped smiling. Susan asked her to please step outside for a moment, and Carli stood and walked out onto the deck. I said, "What was that about?"

Susan said, "A brave front."

"That didn't look like a brave front. That looked like plain old *come and get it*, which I guess is fine and maybe she's old enough to advertise if she wants to, but don't you think the Lolita routine is a little out of place considering what she says happened to her last night?"

Susan studied my face. She was thinking, and I was standing there waiting for her to do it. It's her way. Some time ticked by, then Susan spoke softly. "Carli's a good person, and she's a lot smarter than you'd think when you first meet her. She waits tables at the Pelican's Roost. I eat there a good deal when I'm down here, and I've gotten to know her. Carli doesn't know I know this, but she used to switch tables with other waitresses so she could wait on me whenever I came in."

"What's that, some kind of mother complex?"

"No. At least, I don't think that's part of it. She wants to be an artist, and somebody told her Bird Fitzsimmons had been my husband. We started talking, and she knew all about him. Carli was kind of proud of the fact that she was once thrown out of the gallery in New Orleans that handles Bird's paintings because she hung around there for half a day just looking."

"Why would they throw her out for looking? I thought that was what you were supposed to do at galleries."

Susan smiled. "You're innocent. You're supposed to *buy* art at commercial galleries. Looking is only foreplay for people who can afford to consummate. And, as Carli said, she had 'broke runaway' written all over her. I'm telling you, Tom, Carli's got a lot going for her. But however smart or artistic or sensitive she can be, for some reason, what you just saw seems to be the only way she knows how to act around men."

"Well, nothing has been reported to the authorities that supports her story, which could just mean the killer is either lucky or good. But, take it all together, and you have to wonder if we're wasting our time here. You have to admit, she doesn't exactly look traumatized and desperate for help."

Susan said, "Go talk to her."

I walked out onto the deck and closed the glass door. Carli was leaning against a weathered railing, staring down the beach to her left. I asked, "How old are you?"

When I spoke, she turned to face me and propped her left hip against the rail. Tears had drawn dark wet trails across her cheeks down to her jawline, but I couldn't decide whether she was upset or angry. She wasn't wearing makeup. She didn't need any.

She said, "What difference does it make?"

"Susan says you're a minor."

She repeated the same question.

"Look, Carli. Susan asked me to help you. And she says the reason you can't just go to the police and tell them what happened is because you're a minor and you're a runaway. So, I'd like to know how old you are. It could make a difference, a legal difference, as to whether your family has any right to come get you. Also, if I'm going to help you, you've got to trust me enough to answer some questions. And we don't have time to argue about whether everything I ask you makes a difference."

"Sixteen. I'm sixteen."

"When's your birthday?"

"What diff . . . It's in May. The fifth."

"So you're going to be seventeen in May."

"No. I mean. I guess I'm not really sixteen yet. I'll be sixteen in May."

"You look older than fifteen."

"Yeah. They let me serve beer at the restaurant. Nobody's said anything." She seemed to focus on the pupils in my eyes. "I guess I'm more developed than most girls my age." As she spoke, Carli began to stroke her bare stomach with her index finger in a calculatedly absentminded way. She noticed that I noticed, and her expression changed. She looked like maybe she knew a secret that I didn't.

"What happened last night?"

"I was down on the public beach with this guy I met."

"What's his name?"

"Bobby. Anyway . . ."

I interrupted. "Bobby what?"

"Oh, uh, I don't think he told me. He's a local. Works at the Chevron station in town. Anyway, he picked me up at one after I got off at the Pelican and we drove down to the parking lot at the public beach. After a few minutes, we got out and walked down to the beach. I like it at night. Anyway, we stayed there awhile and Bobby left."

"He just left you there on the beach when you two were done?"

Carli's face flushed red. "We weren't *done* the way you say it. I don't just *do it* like that."

"No offense, Carli. I'm not judging you. It just sounds like the guy acted like a jerk."

"He left 'cause I wouldn't do it. In case you're wondering."

It had been a long time since I'd talked to a fifteen-year-old girl about her sex life. In fact, I had never talked to a fifteen-year-old girl about her sex life. I said, "Let's talk about what happened after Bobby left. How did you get from there to witnessing a murder?"

Carli told me she had walked on the beach, tried to crash on the patio of a seemingly empty beach house, and ended up witnessing a murder through a bedroom window. She described the men who came out and searched the beach while she darted from one dark house to another, finally making her way to Susan's door.

By the time Carli finished her story, tears had overfilled wide brown eyes and begun rolling down her cheeks. Susan was right. As Carli talked, she had become the adolescent she was, and she looked genuinely frightened. Carli rubbed the tears away with her palms while I stood there feeling impotent and wishing I carried a handkerchief in my back pocket the way my father always did.

When she was composed, I asked, "What is it you want to do here, Carli? I checked this morning, and nothing has been reported to the police. They have no idea that a murder even happened. So I want you to consider that the easiest thing—the safest thing for you—would be for you to walk away and forget the whole thing."

Carli focused hard on my pupils again, but this time the look wasn't seductive or affectionate. "You're telling me it doesn't matter if somebody got the back of his head shot off?"

"Hell, no, Carli. But I'm here to look after *your* interests, and I'm telling you the safest thing for *you* to do. If you want me to report the crime, I think I can protect your identity from the police. But if you step into the middle of something like this, there's always a chance somebody's going to find out who you are. And, if they do, you've got to realize that being a witness in a murder trial is dangerous under any circumstances. Plus, if you're that scared of being sent home . . . Well, that's one more reason to just walk away."

Carli turned to look out over the water. "Mr. McInnes, would you run away and hide if it were you?"

"It's not me." It was a lawyer's answer.

Seconds passed as my young client scanned the curving blue horizon where ocean met sky. "I want you to tell the police about the murder and get them to . . . to investigate it. Just don't tell them who I am. Can you do that?"

Tough kid. I said, "Yeah, Carli. I can definitely do that."

While we were outside, Susan had piled brunch on the long butcher's table next to her kitchen. We all ate and made polite conversation. Afterward, Susan walked me to the Jeep. We were back on the driveway, well away from Carli, when Susan simply said, "Well?"

"I'm pretty sure *something* happened," I said. "I don't think she's just looking for attention, but, if she is, she's got me fooled. Maybe she's that good. Who knows? Anyone who claims they can tell if a truly dishonest person is lying is full of it. You just can't."

Now it was Susan's turn to sound irritated. "Carli's got some problems, but I told you she's basically a good kid."

"I'm not calling her a liar. Like I said, I think she saw something, and I think whatever it was scared the hell out of her. It's exactly what she saw that's in question." Susan started to argue, and I held up a hand to stop her. "Just hang on. I'm only saying eye-witness testimony is the most unreliable evidence you can have, particularly in a murder trial. Emotions take over and color and distort perceptions and memories. Jurors love to hear somebody say they saw what happened, but lawyers and judges know how shaky that kind of testimony usually is." I scratched at the oyster-shell paving with my shoe. "Look, you and I don't know for certain what happened last night. Only Carli knows, and she wants me to go to the cops. So, that's what I'm going to do."

Susan just looked at me.

"Let's say I stop by the sheriff's office in town and tell him I have a client who saw some shady-looking guys up to no good last night at this particular beach house, and we're just concerned that someone may have gotten hurt. If the sheriff checks it out and it's nothing, then Carli probably need never come forward."

Susan said, "That's fine if it works out that way, but what if it's not nothing?"

"Well, if we find blood splattered all over the walls then we'll negotiate some kind of deal to keep her identity secret. She's a minor, so that's possible. Maybe we could also get you appointed Carli's guardian *ad litem* until this mess is over."

"Is that the best you can come up with?"

I smiled. "No. There are other things we can do, including just telling them that my client refuses to testify. The DA can't compel her testimony if he doesn't know who she is. And, as her attorney, I don't have to tell them. But first we need to find out if . . ." Susan raised an eyebrow. "Okay, first we need to find out *what* actually happened last night. Don't worry. If the cops find blood all over the place, then I'll either negotiate a deal to keep Carli's name out of it, or we just won't let her talk to them."

Susan told me the name of the house in question—in resort towns every little hovel has a desperately cute name—and I prepared to dance my jig for the sheriff.

chapter four

I DROVE INTO Appalachicola and found the sheriff's office—a squatty yellow-brick building wedged between two Victorian homes that had been converted into offices for a few lawyers and accountants and a couple of real estate agents.

Inside at the front desk, a pleasant young woman wearing a telephone operator's headset and an overbite asked if she could help. I said I was hoping to see a deputy. She pushed a button, waited, and spoke into her headset. A few seconds later, a friendly red-headed guy came through the door. He looked like he smiled a lot, and that's what he did as he introduced himself as Deputy Mickey Burns. He looked strong, and he had a scattering of faded-blue, Marine Corp tattoos competing for space among a few hundred freckles and a carpet of reddish-blonde hair on his forearms. I told my rehearsed story. He smiled some more and said, "Let's go have a look."

Twenty minutes later, we pulled onto the driveway of "See Shore Cottage" in the deputy's patrol car and parked behind a white truck with a chrome toolbox installed behind the cab. Two five-gallon, plastic paint buckets lay on their sides in the sand and clover that made up the front yard. The deputy said, "Looks like they're having some work done." I agreed that it looked just like that. He thought for a few seconds, and asked, "You think maybe your client saw some construction workers horsing around and got the wrong idea?"

"I guess you never know, but I don't think so. That really doesn't fit what my client told me."

Deputy Mickey Burns exhaled through his nose, looked out at the water, and said, "Well, let's go look around." We both stepped out of the car into a bright spring day.

The cottage was a classic Florida beach bunker—concrete block, aqua-blue exterior, white asphalt roof, and, running along one side, a privacy wall constructed of decorative cement blocks turned on edge so that you could see through the inside pattern. A pair of mirror-image, oversized plaster casts of seahorses flanked the front door. The cottage sat at ground level and would violate every high wind and water damage construction spec on the books if it were built today.

Local law enforcement took the lead, and I followed. After banging on the aluminum doorjamb, the deputy pulled open the screen door and walked inside. "Yo! Who's here?"

No one answered, but I could hear what sounded like an old Lynard Skynard song bouncing around some other part of the house. We walked down a short hall and into what seemed to be a bedroom. Drop cloths were draped over the furniture, the carpet had been pulled up, and two guys in shorts and sandals and not much else were working hard at brushing white paint onto white walls. The deputy said, "Can't y'all hear back here?"

At least that's what I think he said. All I heard was, "Can't y'all he . . . ," before one of the painters yelled, "Shit," and spun around, slinging a thick streak of white across his buddy's shoulder. The deputy held up both palms and said, "Whoa. Nothing to get excited about here. We're just looking around."

The jumpy painter smiled now and said, "You scared the hell out of us."

The deputy said, "Sorry about that. We knocked, and then I yelled for you in the front room there. I guess you couldn't hear over the music."

The painter with a new white stripe on his shoulder didn't smile. He did walk over and flip off a paint-speckled boom box. The talkative one said, "What can we do for you?"

The deputy introduced me to the two painters by name, which, even then, seemed like a bad idea. The one who was doing all the talking said "Hey," and gave their names: Tim and Sonny. My escort then explained that someone on the island had called me the night before and reported that they had seen some guys up to no good at See Shore Cottage. Tim, who was apparently the only one of the two with the gift of speech, laughed and said, "Me and old Sonny here are generally up to no good alright."

We all laughed a little, everybody except Sonny. Tim laughed because he thought he was funny, and the deputy and I laughed to be polite. The bare-chested, paint-spattered Sonny glanced furtively around the room while paint dribbled from the brush in his hand onto the bare concrete floor. Deputy Mickey said, "I don't know if anything happened around here last night or not. And I don't think Mr. McInnes really knows either. He just had somebody . . ." The deputy turned to look at me. "Was it a man or a woman? I don't even know whether to call 'em him or her, here."

I stared at him for a couple of seconds while trying to decide why he would ask that in front of Tim and Sonny, whether it really made any difference that he had, and, finally, how much of a schmuck I would look like if I refused to answer. I said, "A man. The client is a man." And I said it after just enough pause and with just the right emphasis to look like I was completely full of shit.

The deputy looked a little confused, said, "okay," and went on talking to Tim and Sonny. "Mr. McInnes' client says he saw three guys hauling a fourth guy around who looked like he was hurt. Said it was late last night sometime."

Tim fixed his face into a look of concern, Sonny glanced around the room some more, and I was beginning to regret giving too many details to Deputy Mickey. Tim said, "Me and Sonny worked here pretty late last night. We had to get the carpet up and out before we could start painting this morning. So we just kept at it until it was done."

I asked why.

Tim said, "Whatcha mean?"

"Why pull up the carpet? I mean, if the owner's going to keep it, you could just cover it with drop cloths like you did the furniture. And if you're planning to throw it out and put in new carpeting, why not just use the old carpet for a drop cloth and tear it up later?"

Tim looked theatrically puzzled. The deputy scrunched up his face in thought and said, "Yeah. I don't know why we're that worried about the carpet. But what he says makes sense, if you wanted . . ."

Sonny, the mute painter, blurted out, "It stunk." We all looked at him. He had stopped glancing around the room and focused his eyes on mine. I liked it better when he couldn't focus. He looked a little nuts. "We got it outta here 'cause it stunk. The roof musta leaked or something and got it wet. All I know is it smelled like . . . it stunk when we come in to do the job. I told 'em I wasn't going to paint nothing until that rug was gone."

Tim joined in, "That's a fact, buddy. First thing we did was rip it up and get it out of here."

Sonny continued to stare into my eyes. I asked, "What happened to it?"

Tim said, "Took it to the dump. Probably buried under a few tons of garbage by now. Don't know why you'd care, though."

The deputy said, "We're getting off the point here. All I want to know is if either of y'all saw anything last night or this morning that didn't look right, and if anybody else came with you or stopped by yesterday."

Sonny resumed his wandering eyes act, and Tim said, "Nope and nope. Just another job, Sheriff."

"Deputy Sheriff."

"Sorry. Nobody got hurt around here that we know about, Deputy."

Deputy Mickey thanked them and then, as if it were an afterthought, asked, "Have you two got a contract or a work order or something like that from the owner for this work?"

Tim said, "Yessir, we sure do. Out in the truck."

The deputy asked if he could see it, and the rest of our little group left Sonny alone to continue his eye exercises. Outside, Tim lifted a metal clipboard off the truck seat, flipped open the cover, and handed it to Deputy Mickey. I read it over his shoulder. The only page in the clip was a work order from Dolphin Rentals, authorizing carpet replacement and new paint in the bedroom of one See Shore Cottage. The work order was dated two weeks earlier and signed by Billie Timmons, Agent.

Back at the sheriff's office, Deputy Mickey walked me to my car. I got in and rolled down the front two windows. He bent down, leaned two furry, tattooed forearms in the driver's window, and peered inside the Jeep. He smelled faintly of sweat and citrus aftershave. He said, "Well, that looked like a wild-goose chase, but chasing wild geese is mostly what the job is about. You happy?"

I wasn't a damned bit happy, but I just shrugged and said, "Sure. At least I can report back to my client. I'm sure he'll be relieved no one was hurt."

Deputy Mickey said, "Yeah, we can all be happy about that. Anyway, I was glad to help." He fixed a reassuring smile on his face and turned to walk away.

I asked, "Does your department keep ownership records on the houses on St. George?"

Burns stopped and turned back. "We probably got that information around somewhere. But, if you're a lawyer, you can find it as easy as I can by going by the courthouse."

"I just thought you might be able to save me some time."

Deputy Burns smiled again. Very nice. Very friendly. But we both knew he was done with me. Then he turned and walked inside the sheriff's building. I backed out and, once again, turned southeast toward St. George Island.

Back at the beach house, I discovered that Carli was gone. Susan had given her a ride to the restaurant so she would be there to help set up for the lunch crowd. In light of my unsettling encounter with Tim and Sonny, I wasn't happy about my new client running around the island unescorted. But Susan assured me that she had impressed on Carli the need to keep her mouth shut. Susan added, "It's hard anyway to get Carli to say much of anything except just making small talk or, if she's really comfortable, maybe talking about being an artist one day. I think you learn early to keep secrets when you grow up in a family like hers."

I asked, "What kind of a family does she have? You've mentioned a couple of times that she's *terrified* about going home, but you've never said why."

"I really don't know exactly. And I don't know why I tried to sound dramatic and sage about 'keeping secrets.' The whole thing sounds a little Barbara Walters, doesn't it?"

"It sounds like you're making it up as you go. If that's what you mean."

Susan gave me a look. "I just know that Carli's scared to death of having to go back. *And* I know it's not just some high school angst thing. *And* I know that she won't talk about it." Susan paused and said, "What did you find out at the sheriff's office?"

I told her. I recited my morning adventure and jotted down notes while the whole mess was fresh in my mind. Later, I would transfer the notes to my laptop, just as I did with every case, so they would be available for word searches and for preparing a chronology of the facts. While I was writing out a summary of my meetings with Deputy Mickey Burns and the painting duo of Tim and Sonny, Susan pulled out her yellow pages and looked up Dolphin Rentals, which turned out to be a small real estate company in Appalachicola. She punched in the number and asked for Billie Timmons. Ms. Timmons was not in the office and would not be back for another four days, but she did handle See Shore Cottage and had full authority to authorize normal repairs to the property.

Susan and I sat in her living room and looked at each other for a while. Now she was thinking, and I was watching her do it. Finally, she said, "Okay, what about the paint? They can't just slap some paint on the walls and cover up all traces of blood. I mean, I know real life isn't like cop shows on TV. But the police are more sophisticated than that, aren't they?"

"Sure they are. The cops could probably peel the walls and find some bloodstains between the paint layers. But they'd need sufficient probable cause to get a search warrant that would allow them not only to search the cottage but to also strip the walls looking for bloodstains. Which sounds like a good idea, except that a warrant that allows destruction of property is pretty hard to get. At a minimum, any judge would want an eyewitness before he allowed something like that to happen." I stood and stretched out my back. "I'm afraid something like that would take Carli coming forward and making a sworn statement." Susan started to speak, and I said, "And, even if Carli did that, we couldn't be certain the cops would find enough evidence to do anything. A little blood on the wall doesn't mean much without a body."

Susan looked disappointed. "We should be able to do something."

I said, "We will. We just don't know what it is yet."

A few quiet seconds passed before Susan's head snapped up from the impact of a sudden thought. "Tom! Shouldn't we be over there to follow those painter-guys when they leave?"

"Nope."

"Why not? They've got to be connected some way with the murder. If we followed them . . ."

I sat up and put my elbows on my knees and looked at Susan. "If we followed them, they'd probably spot us a mile down the road. Neither of us is qualified to do that kind of thing well. And, if Tim and Sonny did spot us tagging along behind their pickup, we could count on one of two things happening. *One*, they would know we were on to them, which would cause them to take off down some swamp road to the middle of nowhere and hide. Or, *two*, they would know we were on to them, which would cause them to turn around and attempt to do us bodily harm. In either case, we've announced that I didn't buy their good-old-boy routine at the cottage. And, in one case, we could end up hurt or worse."

"You're sure about this?"

"I've got the tag number and make of the truck, their descriptions, and the names they gave us. This is a small place. If we need to find them again, I imagine Joey can do it in an hour or two."

Susan and I wandered out onto the deck. Frustration and feelings of impotency seemed to be working on her, and I felt pretty much the same way. Maybe I was handling it better because, for a lot of reasons, the feelings were less foreign to me. Finally, we decided to load into my Jeep to go have another look at See Shore Cottage.

We made a reconnaissance trip past the cottage and saw that Tim's truck had departed taking Tim and Sonny and the plastic paint buckets with it. I turned around in a driveway three doors down, backtracked, and pulled onto the now-familiar parking pad of Carli's nightmare house. We got out. For the second time that day, I approached the giant-seahorse-guarded door of See Shore Cottage with the intention of conducting some sort of investigation. Through the front bedroom window, we could see that the paint job was lousy but finished, the drop cloths had vanished, and the bed and other furniture had been shoved back into place. Susan said, "Poof."

"Yeah. Like magic." I walked around to the side window to peer inside the way Carli had the night before.

Susan said, "Look at the floor." I cupped my hand against the glass to block the sun's glare and looked down at bare, paint-splattered concrete. "You think they're coming back later to put down new carpet?"

She was being sarcastic. I said, "I wouldn't count on it."

I drove Susan to her beach house. Along the way, a running debate streamed through my mind—should I stay on St. George with Susan and the girl or head back to Mobile? On the one hand, I didn't much like the idea of leaving Susan and Carli alone on the island. Emotionally, it felt like I was deserting them. On the other hand, my surprise meeting with Tim and Sonny had turned my presence into a liability. As we turned into Susan's driveway, I decided that putting some distance between my clients and myself seemed the smartest way to go.

I explained my reasoning to Susan. She agreed and promised to keep an eye on Carli. I promised to try to think of something useful to do.

It had not been a successful day, and the drive home seemed endless. Back at my place, I checked in with Kelly, my secretary, and made a few business calls before wandering down the beach to the Grand Hotel for dinner. I thought a good meal might make me feel better. It usually does. It didn't. Back snug in my living room, I checked my answering machine, turned the recording volume and the ringer all the way down, and spent a couple of unfocused hours with Umberto Eco. *The hell with it.* I started getting ready for bed. Maybe I'd wake up smarter in the morning.

Twenty minutes later, I heard a fist banging on my front door. I trotted downstairs, flipped on the porch light, and peeked outside through a narrow column of windows. Joey stood there glaring at the door, looking angry and excited all at once. I opened the door.

"Where the hell have you been? We called Susan. She said you left there hours ago."

"I've been here. I just turned the sound off on my machine. What's wrong?" In the half second before he could answer, I had a sickening thought. "Is Carli okay?"

"Carli's fine. Everybody's fine. But Kelly's been trying to get you for over an hour. Somebody broke in your office. Kelly says the security company called her. She's down there now with the cops, and they need you to come down."

I said, "Hang on," and went inside to get my shoes. Two minutes later, I was seated in Joey's huge four-wheel-drive, and he was speeding toward Mobile. I looked out the window and watched pine trees and underbrush spin by in the dark. Joey asked about my trip to St. George, and I filled him in.

As we entered the city's neon outskirts, talk turned to the break-in, and Joey said, "One more crummy thing in a crummy day, huh?"

"Maybe not."

"You like having somebody break in your office?"

"Not much. But at least something's happening. I sat around all day down at Susan's drinking coffee and wondering what to do next. I did learn a few things from the painters. But now, at least, the coincidences are starting to pile up, and we can begin trying to make some sense out of it."

"That all sounds real good. But somebody still busted in your office tonight and probably took some of your favorite lawyer stuff."

"Lawyer stuff?"

Joey didn't elaborate.

We were on city streets now, close to the Oswyn Israel Building where my violated office and, I hoped, some answers awaited. I said, "I'm going to call Susan and tell her to get hold of Carli, maybe bring her to the beach house and lock everything up tight until we can think this out."

"Probably a good idea. Susan got a gun?"

"I have no idea."

I used Joey's cell phone to get Susan. She promised to pick up Carli from work and keep her at the beach house. Susan reminded me of the guard at the gate to The Plantation and said she also had a .38 revolver. I hung up as Joey turned into my parking lot.

Upstairs, Kelly was waiting in the reception area. She said, "Looks like they got scared off."

A pair of blue uniforms lounged on the sofa drinking coffee that I guessed Kelly had brewed for them in my new Krups machine. One of the officers started to stand. I said, "Let me look around first, okay?" He nodded and sat back down. His was not a controlling personality. As I walked back to my office, I asked Kelly, "Nothing's missing?"

Kelly followed. "Almost nothing."

I made a quick inventory of the desk drawers, the small wall safe, and the few expensive odds and ends on my walls and shelves. I sat down behind my desk to think. Joey strolled in holding a mug of steaming coffee in each giant paw and put one down in front of me. Then he plopped into a leather guest chair and sipped his coffee. Kelly sat in a chair that matched the one Joey was overflowing, looked across the desk, and said, "The policemen want you to sign some kind of report. They couldn't find any fingerprints or anything like that, by the way."

I said, "What do you mean 'almost nothing' is missing?"

"What? Oh. It's creepy. Right now, it looks like whoever broke in just grabbed the appointment calendar off my desk and took off."

"Your appointment calendar? Are you sure that's all?"

"I've got to look around some more, but, like I said, right now that looks like it."

A shapeless, but vaguely disturbing, thought was worming around the back of my mind. I let it work through, and my stomach began to squeeze into a knot.

"Kelly, did you put Susan Fitzsimmons' name in the appointment book today?"

"Sure. I put all your appointments in there."

Joey cussed as he and I jumped up and ran out of the office. As we rushed through the waiting room, the two cops looked surprised. They didn't move, but they did appear to consider the option.

chapter five

JOEY WAS A former shore patrolman, former Navy Intelligence officer, former Alabama state trooper, and former Alabama Bureau of Investigation agent. In fact, *former* would serve as a pretty accurate one-word description of his career in law enforcement, all of which sounds worse in some ways than it is. Joey was never unreliable, unless you were counting on him to follow orders or to treat an employee handbook like the Word of God. And, when things get serious, attitude and obstinance and confidence are what I want. Boy Scouts scare the shit out of me.

Now, on the highway east of Mobile, Joey was driving like the cop he used to be, going ninety-plus on two-lane roads. And, like a cop, he seemed to be in complete control behind the wheel as trees, houses, shops, and other traffic whirled by as varying shapes and colors in the night.

"She's not there." It was the fourth time I had punched in Susan's St. George number.

"Shit. Can you call that deputy from Appalachicola?"

"What am I supposed to say? Hello Officer. Somebody kicked in the door of my office in Mobile tonight, and now my secretary can't find her appointment book. So, I was wondering if you'd mind driving back out on the island there and checking on a female client who I told you earlier today was a man. And, by the way, I know I wouldn't tell you the client's name today and I'm still trying to keep it a secret because it might put her in danger, but . . ."

"You got a better idea?"

I didn't like it, but I dialed up North Florida information and then the sheriff's office in Appalachicola. Deputy Mickey Burns was off duty. "We have a deputy on patrol. Is this an emergency?"

"I don't know. Probably not. I just asked for Deputy Burns because he helped me earlier today. I'm a lawyer in Mobile. I've got a client on the island who may be in trouble. It'd be a big help if your patrolman could just ride by and check on her." The operator agreed to have a deputy do just that. I gave her the address and said goodbye.

Joey said, "You know if you don't say it's an emergency they'll take fucking forever to get there."

"Yeah, I know. But I'd have to do a lot of explaining to call in an emergency on St. George from a car phone in Alabama."

"We're in Florida now."

"Thanks for the update. But to make it an emergency you usually have to say someone's inside your house or you're in some kind of imminent danger."

"I know all that. I used to be a cop."

"Then what are you bitching about?"

"I just don't like it."

The truth was that we were both worried and irritated and feeling impotent and, in general, acting pretty graceless under pressure. I asked, "How much longer?"

"If we don't run into any blue lights, we'll be there in less than two hours."

I glanced at the digital clock on the dash. *10:33.* Yellow-tinged high beams swept gray pavement ahead of the Expedition as it lunged and swayed and rocked along Highway 98 northwest of Panama City. Every ten or twenty miles, bright eyes stared and fixed on the headlights as whitetails froze along the roadside. "It'd be hard to miss a deer at this speed if it was in the road."

Joey said, "Fuck 'em."

More road. Joey turned on the radio and played with the search button until he found a soft rock station. I put up with Mariah Carey for a while, then reached over and turned it off when an old Journey song came on. Joey didn't complain. I don't think he realized I had done it.

We had been outside of cellular range for some time. As we neared Panama City, the in-service light flashed on, and I tried Susan again. She answered on the third ring.

"Where have you been? Are you okay?"

Susan sounded surprised. "I'm fine. You knew I was going to pick up Carli from work."

"You've been gone a long time."

"She didn't get off till after ten. I had to wait. What's wrong? Has something else happened?"

"I don't want to scare you."

"Then that's not a good way to start."

"Sorry. Look, somebody broke into my office about three hours ago. All they took was Kelly's appointment book. It probably doesn't mean anything, but the book had your name in it. And, you know, after everything that happened today."

"We're fine, Tom. Carli's here. We're locked up in the house, there's a guard at the gate, and I put the .38 in my purse. Go back to sleep. We can figure all this out in the morning."

I said something like, "Uh."

"Is there more to it?"

"Kind of. Joey and I got worried when we couldn't get you. And, we're most of the way there. We'll probably be knocking on your door in about an hour."

"Tom, that's sweet." Now she sounded amused. "Like I told you, we're fine. But you're almost here now, so you may as well come on. I'll put some coffee on."

"It was Joey's idea."

After I ended the connection, Joey said, "Everything okay?"

"Yeah."

"What was that about something being my idea?"

"She was thanking me for coming."

I looked over at Joey's face in the glow from the dash. He looked like he was thinking about that. "Want to turn around and go home?"

"No. We've come this far. I'll feel better if we go have a look around."

The dash clock glowed *12:18* as we pulled onto Susan's driveway and a motion detector light popped on. Susan met us at the door.

We were sitting at the butcher block table drinking decaffeinated coffee when Carli descended the dark staircase and walked into the downstairs light. She wore a maroon Florida State football jersey for a nightgown, and a huge white towel wound around and covered her head like a turban. Wet black curls peeked out from beneath the towel. Susan said, "Feel better?"

Carli just smiled and sat down next to Joey. Susan introduced them.

I said, "Did you tell Carli why we're here?"

"I told her about your break-in. I also told her there's no reason for her to get worked up over it. Right? We don't have any reason to think the break-in was connected to Carli in any way, *do we?*" As she spoke the last two words, Susan gave me a meaningful look.

I'm not stupid, or, if I am, I can at least take a hint. I looked at Carli and said, "No reason at all. Joey and I are only here because we tried to call Susan to tell her about the burglary, and we couldn't get her. If we had known she was just out picking you up from work, we would have stayed in Mobile."

I wasn't the only nonstupid person at the table. Carli said, "But your office got broken into after I talked with you today about those guys on the beach. And Susan told me what happened with those painters at the beach house where it happened."

"Carli, it's easy to tie unrelated problems together when you're scared, but, like Susan says . . ."

Carli kept going. "You called here right after you figured out Susan's name was in that book they stole. And you drove all the way here at midnight when we didn't answer the phone." Silence hung in the air above the table. "Isn't that right, Mr. McInnes?"

"You can call me Tom." Carli sighed and lowered her eyes to stare at gnawed, glitter-pink fingernails. "Carli, you really *don't* need to worry. Not about my office break-in, anyhow. You have to understand my and Joey's history with Susan. I got her into a pretty nasty mess about six months ago, and she ended up getting hurt pretty badly."

Susan interrupted with surprising force. "That was not your fault." She held my eyes for a few beats and then turned to face Carli. "My husband was killed last summer. They found Tom's younger brother a couple of months later on the bottom of the Alabama River. It wasn't easy and it cost him, but Tom found out what happened. While he was doing it, I got attacked by someone involved in both deaths, but that wasn't because Tom did anything wrong or messed anything up." I opened my mouth to interrupt without really knowing what I wanted to say, but Susan kept talking. She was still looking at Carli. "I just want you to understand that Tom feels some misplaced duty to me because of what happened. That's why he and Joey drove down here in the middle of the night, and, as much as I hate to admit it, even to myself, that's how I knew he would drop everything and help *you* if I asked him to."

Carli looked up at me for a moment. The towel on her hair had tilted to one side, and the insides of her eyelids, the part just inside her lashes, had turned red. I tried to smile reassuringly.

Carli's brown irises seemed to have grown larger, and, when she spoke, her voice was soft and unsure. "I was up all night last night. I gotta go to bed." And she got up and climbed the stairs.

I looked at Susan. "You're right. She's not stupid."

Susan nodded slowly. "More there than meets the eye."

"Yeah, but well-adjusted she's not."

Susan shrugged. "Who is?"

It was past one in the morning, and suddenly I was bone tired. "It's been a long day. We better go and let you get to bed too."

Joey said, "I don't know where you're going, hoss. But I'm tired, and I'm staying right here if it's okay with Susan."

Susan said, "It's perfect. If you're as bushed as I am, you don't have any business driving anyhow. I was up most of the night last night with Carli. And I know Tom's wiped out, because I called and woke him before sunrise."

"And he woke me up to tell me about it," Joey said.

"Well then," Susan said, "I suggest we all hit the rack and think this through in the morning."

The house had exactly four bedrooms, which was exactly how many we needed. Upstairs, Susan showed us past Carli's closed door to the empty rooms. Joey said good night and walked down the hall to find the bathroom. Susan walked me to my room, clicked on the bedside lamp, and turned to look at me.

She sounded tired and a little hoarse when she spoke. All she said was, "Thanks." I looked down into her upturned face. Missed sleep and tension showed around her eyes, but they were still beautiful eyes. Very quickly, Susan rocked forward onto her toes, kissed me lightly on the lips, and left the room, closing the door behind her. I stripped down to boxers, switched the light off, and stretched out on top of the covers. I smiled up at the ceiling. My mouth still tingled where her lips had brushed against mine.

I didn't think I had been asleep when Joey shook me awake. He was whispering. "Wake up, bubba. Wake up. We need to look around."

I rubbed my eyes and looked at my watch. I was too groggy to focus on the glowing dots and lines that were supposed to show me what time it was.

"Whatsa matter?"

"I thought I heard something a couple of times, then the bedroom clock went out."

I was too tired for this. "What're you talking about?"

He sounded exasperated. "The power's out. You understand that?" I sat up. He went on. "The phone's dead, too. Something's going on, and I'm gonna go look around a little. I need you to keep an eye on Susan and Carli."

I swung my feet onto the floor and felt for my pants. I said, "Go," and Joey moved silently through the door and down the hallway. I managed to pull on pants and loafers. My shirt and socks had disappeared on the dark carpet, and I left the room bare-chested.

Out in the hall, I found Carli's door and stuck my head inside. A shadowy shape, surprisingly small and childlike, breathed beneath the covers. I eased the door shut and moved to Susan's door, which swung open without a sound. On the wall opposite her bed, open double windows welcomed moonlight and a cool breeze into the room. I crept over and looked outside, wondering who might be out there in the dark with Joey. When I turned to look at Susan, she was looking back.

She still sounded tired but wide awake. "You scared me."

I walked over and stood by the bed. As I approached, Susan sat up, holding the sheet against her breasts. She appeared to be naked beneath the covers. I held my index finger against my lips and then leaned down to whisper. "The power and phones are out. Joey's outside checking on it."

To her benefit, Susan hesitated only a few seconds before saying, "Turn around. I need to get dressed." I walked back over and looked out through the open window. Night air flowed into the room, sprinkling chill bumps across my chest and shoulders and making me wish I had been able to find my shirt. I scanned the shore and the sand dunes and listened for strange voices or the sound of feet on the wooden deck or . . . something. Everything just looked and sounded and smelled like a spring night at the beach. Behind me, I could hear Susan walk barefoot across the carpet and open dresser drawers. She asked, "Have you checked on Carli?"

"Yeah. She's fine, but I wanted to get you first." I heard Susan slipping her legs into jeans.

"Afraid you'd scare her?"

"I though it'd be better if you woke her. But we need to hurry. If somebody's out there, she needs to be up and ready to move."

Susan told me I could turn back around. When I did, she was sitting on the bed in jeans and a dark T-shirt, pulling on running shoes. She made loops and knots in the laces and stood up. We moved down the hall. Carli's door was closed. Inside, the delicate shape I had seen breathing under the covers was gone.

chapter six

FINE LINES OF moonlight angled through mini-blinds and faintly streaked Carli's empty bed with light. Visibly shocked, Susan said, a little too loudly, "Where is she?"

I shushed her and made a quick search of the closet and the floor beneath the bed, thinking, hoping the girl had heard something and tried to hide. I looked at Susan and said, "I don't know. Come on." The hall was preternaturally dark—no windows, no electricity, just black. I ducked into my bedroom and Joey's and then checked the bathroom. Back in the hallway, I leaned in close to Susan. "She probably heard something and got up to look around. I think we would have heard some kind of scuffle if something worse than that had happened."

"Maybe she heard Joey."

"Where's that thirty-eight you told me about?"

"In my purse. I think it's on the kitchen table." I looked at her. She said, "You know, downstairs."

I wasn't that sleepy. I knew damn well where the kitchen table was. I just wasn't happy about it. I thought about asking Susan to stay upstairs, but decided I didn't want to take a chance on losing someone else. I also realized that, with Carli missing and probably in trouble, Susan wasn't likely to take instructions from me and hide in the closet while I ran around doing manly things.

I said, "Stay with me, okay," and led the way to the circular aluminum staircase. Three steps down, I heard a soft hiss and froze. Susan heard it too. She stopped as still as death.

A sharp whisper from the kitchen, "Tom!" The glass wall along the front of the living area allowed a diffused fog of gray light into the room. Joey stepped out from a shadow and whispered, "Carli's here."

Thank God. I started down the stairs and was quickly stopped by another hiss. I looked down and back toward the kitchen where Joey stood in the shadows. He appeared to be holding up three fingers, waving them back and forth like a kid saying bye-bye. Then he pointed at the glass door leading out onto the deck. I looked but saw nothing. I looked back toward Joey and still saw nothing. He had disappeared. I glanced at Susan. She was looking past me toward the deck.

I whispered, "What?"

She held up an index finger, telling me to wait. I watched her pale eyes scan back and forth and stop. She tapped my shoulder and pointed. The glass wall overlooking the Gulf was made of ten-foot squares of tempered glass separated by thick cypress beams. Silhouetted against the outside of one of the vertical beams was a very human shape. I held up one finger. Susan nodded. She shook her head when I held up two. I pointed to where Joey had been and held up three fingers. She nodded and raised her palms in the air.

We agreed. Joey said three. We saw one. Another hiss.

Joey's hand and arm materialized out of kitchen shadows and motioned us back upstairs. We watched the silhouette outside run from one beam to the next. He held a long, thick gun at an angle across his midsection. Maybe a shotgun. When he flattened against the second beam, Susan and I tiptoed back up to the hallway.

She asked, "Has Joey got a gun?"

"Joey's always got a gun. But one pistol against three rifles or shotguns is a real bad idea. And Joey's got a scared fifteen-year-old girl to take care of."

"Can't we help him?"

I tried to slow my breathing and think.

She was scared and talking fast. "What do you think he wants us to do?"

"Joey waved us up here, so it's probably safe in the house for now. But if there are three of them with guns and they come inside, there won't be much we can do but hide. Look, everybody but you and me and Carli has a gun, and Carli's with Joey. We've got to trust Joey to look after her. He's going to expect me to do the same for you."

"I'm not fifteen, Tom."

In fact, Susan was a few years older than I was, even if she didn't look it. I said, "We can get politically correct later. Right now, we need to figure out how we're going to get out of here if that guy on the deck comes inside."

"The stairs are the only way down, but we can go up."

A lightbulb went off. "The crow's nest?"

"Yep. But there's no way down from there either, unless . . ."

"Can we . . ." A shotgun blast shattered the quiet. Glass exploded downstairs, and footsteps crunched across broken windows.

Susan gasped and yanked my arm by the elbow. I turned to look, and she was hauling ass. I caught her as she hooked a left and charged up a short flight of steps that dead-ended into the ceiling. She twisted some little knob I couldn't even see and pushed open a hatch. Stars filled a three-by-four foot hole in the roof. Susan shot through, and I followed. Up on the catwalk, I quietly fitted the hatch back into place.

We crouched on narrow strips of teak that made the banistered catwalk look like a miniaturized deck. We had a space about six feet wide and twenty feet long and nowhere to hide.

Susan breathed hard. She said, "Do you think we'll be able to stay here?"

I looked around. "Do we have a choice?"

"There's a palm over there at the back corner. The roof's steep, but if we could figure out how to slide down at an angle somehow, we could get hold of it and climb down to the driveway."

"What?" She started to explain again, and I stopped her. "Listen." The house was quiet. "What the hell? Susan, come on. Stay low. Get over here. We better sit on the hatch."

"They might shoot through it."

"And they might just try it and move on. It's better than leaving it open so they can pop through and shoot at us."

As Susan started to edge over, she glanced through the banisters toward the shoreline. She said, "Look," and pointed down at the beach. We saw a figure in dark clothes kneeling on the sand. And he saw us. A black shape moved in his hands, and a sharp rap sounded a split second before something small and hard and deadly hit the copper roof below us.

I said, "Let's do it. Stay low, and go through the banisters. Don't go over them." Susan wiggled through a repeating diamond shape in the banister and began inching down the side of the steep metal roof opposite the beach. Easing my head to the far edge of the catwalk, I looked for the gunman. He was motioning to someone in the house. He was motioning at the roof. *Shit.* Belly crawling to the other side, I found Susan flat on her back, butt against the roof with both feet wedged in the rain gutter. She was eight feet away from the palm fronds and inching her way there not nearly fast enough.

Just in case, I tried to fit my shoulders through the banister. It wasn't even close. Taking a deep breath, I came off my knees at a full run and hand sprinted over the railing. I expected to hear, or maybe even feel, another gunshot. The guy on the beach just stood there. He probably couldn't believe his eyes. For all the world, it had to look like I was leaping into a full gainer over the driveway.

It felt that way too. I hit the copper roof on my right hip and bare shoulder blade and started sliding like a downed skier on a patch of ice. I managed to get my butt under me and my head up in time to nail the gutter with my heels. The jolt jammed my knees and ankles, knocked a section of gutter loose, and flipped me forward into a face full of palm tree. It hurt like hell. I hurt everywhere, but I managed to grab fists full of spiky fronds and hold on.

The world scrambled for a second. When it fell back into place, I looked around for Susan. She had fallen sideways trying to grab me before I flipped off the roof, and she was almost gone. Her feet were on the roof's edge. Her right hand had a death grip on the piece of gutter I had slammed loose, and her left hand was reaching out for me. Clenching a thick frond with my right fist, I bent my knees, swung to the left using the frond as a pivot, and grabbed Susan's hand. Her grip on the gutter came loose, and I swung her into the tree trunk with a painful thud. She held on.

"Go, Susan. They know we're back here."

She started down the trunk and, with me shinnying behind her, had made it to within six feet of the ground when three gunshots snapped the night air. Susan dropped.

Joey yelled, "Move. They're coming. Move!"

Susan scrambled to her feet and ran. I dropped ten feet, executed an unplanned and painful backward somersault, and sprinted down the driveway. Up ahead, Susan veered left into underbrush and I followed her. Out of nowhere, a hand grabbed my wrist and spun me into the ground. As I landed in sea grass, Joey said, "Stay down." I did. Joey sat crouched in a shooter's stance with his .45 automatic leveled at the house. Susan lay on the ground next to him.

"Susan? Susan, did you get hit?"

Joey said, "Nobody got hit—none of us anyhow. That was me shooting. One of 'em came around the corner while you two were monkeying around that tree, so I fired three rounds. Think I hit him." Susan reached over and squeezed my hand to let me know she was okay. Joey said, "Here they come. We better go."

Tearing through sea grass, cockleburs, wild azaleas, yucca plants, and a thousand species of lowland brier bushes, Joey ran full out ahead of us for what seemed like a couple hundred yards. Next to a wooden walkway that stretched from the road to the beach so normal people could avoid the brush and thorns we had just run through, Joey stopped, motioned with his head and said, "See that big, funny-looking bush?"

I looked, and it was kind of funny looking. "Yeah."

"Carli's over there. I'll be back. If I'm not, stay away from the house and figure out some way to get Susan and the girl out of here."

I started to say something, to tell him I'd come with him. But he was gone.

Susan walked toward Joey's bush. I followed. We found Carli sitting in a fetal position on the dark side of the bush away from the moonlight. She didn't cry. She didn't speak. She hugged her knees and rocked and looked impossibly small.

Susan sat on the sand and put an arm around Carli's shoulders. I found some shadow nearby where a big, funny-looking bush wasn't blocking half the world from view. I peered into the dark and watched for nameless, faceless men who had come to murder two women in a house on the beach.

Minutes crept by. In the distance, sirens swirled through the night air. Two shots popped almost quaintly farther down the coastline. More time passed. The sirens grew louder as Joey emerged out of the underbrush. I met him at his bush next to Susan and Carli.

I asked, "What happened? I heard a couple more shots."

Joey said, "That was me. When I got back to the house, they were loading one of 'em into a pontoon boat on the sand. So I *did* hit him. Anyway, when he was in, one stayed with him and the other one jumped out and looked like he might come back for more. I took a couple of shots, and he jumped behind the boat and pulled it in the water. They took off."

Susan said, "Did you shoot to scare them off?"

"Hell no. I shot to kill the sonofabitch. He was just too far away for me to hit him with a pistol. They were getting ready to haul ass, anyhow. One of 'em was shot, and you could hear the cops coming."

I asked, "Are the police there now?"

"Probably are. I didn't stay around to find out." He wedged his .45 in the back of his waistband, looked at me, and said, "So, Counselor. That's what I do. Now do what you do. What's the plan?"

Susan and Carli were silent. The teenager was still now, but she still hugged her knees tightly against her breasts. Susan stroked her hair.

I said, "You got a license for that gun in Florida?"

Joey said, "Nope. Licensed in Alabama. Not here."

"Okay. Susan and I are going back. You look after Carli. Take her wherever you need to to keep out of sight, but," I pointed at the street end of the wooden walkway, "be on the path next to the road in, let's see, it's about two-twenty now, be there at three-thirty."

"What are you gonna say?"

"Don't worry about it. You and Carli were never there. See you at three-thirty. Susan? You ready?"

Susan hugged Carli and whispered something I couldn't hear.

On the way back, I briefed Susan, telling her to stay as close as possible to the facts with only the changes we specifically discussed. Twenty yards from the house, I led her out onto the pavement so we could approach along the driveway. Jumping out of the bushes at a bunch of nervous, heavily armed deputies seemed like a bad idea.

As we neared her drive, a deputy stationed to keep people out said, "What the hell?"

Susan's now filthy T-shirt was ripped across her stomach where she had snagged it on the palm. Cuts and scratches covered her arms, and dirt smudged her face. I was worse, having scrambled down a palm tree, rolled around the driveway, and torn through Br'er Rabbit's playground without a shirt. A grapefruit-sized strawberry covered my left nipple. From the waist up, I was pretty much one big stinging scrape.

I said, "I'm Tom McInnes, and this is Susan Fitzsimmons. This is her house." The deputy seemed to think about that for a second before he pulled out a nickel-plated revolver with a six-inch barrel and pointed it at us.

He said, "Walk up to the house," and that's what we did.

chapter seven

WE HAD ROLLED into Mobile as the sun rose in our rearview mirror. Now it was dark again, and the faint sounds and peculiar aromas of breakfast cooking pulled me out of a hard dreamless sleep and into a tangle of covers.

It was an old house and elegant, but nothing seemed to fit quite right. Warm light from the hall shone through an inch-high crack under the door, spotlighting ball-and-claw feet on an antique dresser and softly illuminating the room like a night-light. Without thinking I rolled to the right, found the floor with bare feet, and straightened up. Pockets of pain erupted in every joint and muscle, prodding me with memories of sliding down roofs, jumping from trees, somersaulting on oyster shells, and running through picturesque coastal thickets.

I stood there for a while and hurt. Eventually the pain subsided, and I was able to walk over and switch on the overhead light.

When we arrived, we had taken turns with the shower and the Bactine. Now I was surprised that the sandy-headed, scratched-up guy in the mirror looked better than I felt. Beneath the mirror, neatly folded squares of someone else's clothes were set out on the dresser. I put them on and went in search of fellow victims.

The place was a maze of oak floors and crown molding. After visiting an empty living room and wandering twice through the same study, I found the kitchen by locating the dining room and then following the sound of voices through the butler's pantry.

"Good morning."

An ex-stripper named Loutie Blue, who was our hostess, said, "It's seven o'clock."

"Oh."

"At night."

"Oh." She handed me a cup of coffee, and I sat in a chair at one end of a table with food on it. Joey sat at the other end eating thick Belgian waffles. Susan perched on a bar stool next to the center island where Loutie was working.

"Where's Carli?"

Susan said, "She's still sleeping."

I said, "Oh," and drank some coffee.

Loutie said, "With everybody just waking up, I decided to make breakfast for dinner. You hungry?"

I realized it had been twenty-four hours since I had eaten. I told her I was starving, and she poured batter into a waffle iron from a stainless steel pitcher.

Loutie Blue was tall, exceptionally tall for a woman, which, I thought, might be one reason Joey felt so comfortable around her. Standing next to Loutie, he would have looked almost normal. She had shoulder-length chestnut hair and greenish-brown eyes that grew harder the longer you looked at them. She wore black jeans, white tennis shoes, and an oversized blue polo shirt with the tail out. And, even in that domestic outfit, standing over a steaming waffle iron chatting with Susan, you could see how she had retired from stripping in her twenties with enough money to buy that house. Loutie Blue was beautiful—in a thoroughly intimidating kind of way.

She and Susan seemed to enjoy each other's company. They weren't really saying much. They just looked comfortable together.

I looked at Susan, "How long have you been up?"

"I don't know. I guess I've been up and down."

Joey said, "Checking on Carli."

I said, "Oh." It was becoming my trademark. I looked at Loutie. "I hope it's not out of line to ask, but would it be all right if Susan and Carli stayed here with you for a couple of days? I need to get back to the office in the morning and try to figure out what to do about all this. And, in the meantime, you know, after what happened at my office and at Susan's beach house, I'm not sure yet where else they'll be safe."

Loutie said, "Joey already asked. Glad to have them."

Loutie Blue was resourceful and intelligent and, under the right circumstances, a disturbingly dangerous woman. I knew from past experience that, as far as the statuesque woman cooking waffles was concerned, if Joey wanted something, he got it. She felt an extraordinary and intense devotion to my giant friend.

I turned to Joey. "I don't know what you're working on right now, but I could use your help on this."

Joey said, "You mean *more* help, don't you? In case you missed it, I've been buried ass deep in this case since about two this morning when I started shooting people."

"I didn't miss it. But, unless you've got a better idea, we need someone—you—who can hang around St. George and Appalachicola and bang on doors or bang on heads, or whatever it is you do, to get a lead on who might be trying to kill our client. And I'm guessing it's going to take more than a day or two to do it."

"So you're not really asking if I can do it. You're asking if I can do it for free."

"More or less. I can cover expenses, but Carli's going to have trouble coming up with seventy-five an hour for your time."

Susan interrupted. "I'll pay."

Joey looked embarrassed. "Shit, Susan. I was just jerking Tom's chain. I damn sure wasn't trying to get you to pay. You know if you're in trouble, I'm gonna help you."

Susan stepped down from the bar stool and pulled up a chair at the table. She said, "Thank you. But I asked you and Tom for help."

Joey said, "You asked Tom for help. I just showed up."

Susan said, "That's right. You showed up last night and saved our lives. You don't need to be noble here. A lot of things have been hard for me since Bird died, but with our investments and Bird's life insurance and a studio full of finished canvases, my crazy artist husband left me pretty well off."

Loutie walked over and poured fresh coffee in Joey's cup. He watched steam curl off the surface. "Okay. I'm hired," Joey said. "But, look, we're gonna be dealing with a bunch of crooks. And crooks, if they're making a living at it and they got any sense, generally keep a wad of cash stashed away for emergencies. So, let's say you're paying the tab for now, but we can renegotiate if I stumble across any free money along the way."

I said, "I didn't hear that."

Joey said, "Kinda late in life to be turning into a Boy Scout." And I agreed that it probably was.

Whether she was sleeping the whole time, I don't know. But when Joey and I left around ten, we hadn't laid eyes on Carli.

After Joey had departed for his place, Susan loaned me her snub-nose .38. I drove home to Point Clear where I half expected to find my burglar alarm blaring. Everything was fine. Maybe an unlisted number had spared my house the same fate as my office, or maybe the burglars had already stolen everything they needed. I managed a few more hours' sleep in my own bed, then drummed sore muscles under a hot shower before dressing and driving in to the office. Building maintenance had nailed a square of unfinished plywood over my broken window. It was not a look designed to impress clients.

Inside, Kelly was in her office, and a fresh pot of coffee warmed the kitchen. Kelly heard me rattling around for a mug and came in as I was adding sugar to my coffee. She looked anxious, "Is Susan okay?"

Oh hell. I had forgotten all about Kelly. I said, "I'm sorry. Susan's fine. Three men with guns did come after her and the teenager last night when we were there, though."

She asked what happened, and I told her. When I was through, she said, "Loutie, huh? I should have thought of that. I called Susan's after the police left and I got back home, but by that time her phone was out. I guess I called you and Joey about twenty times this morning."

"Kelly, I'm really sorry. You shouldn't have had to think of calling Loutie Blue's house. I should have called you."

"You were busy." She paused. " I thought of something. You said when you and Susan went back in the house after the cops, or I guess the sheriff, got there that that deputy who took you to meet those painters was there." I said she was right. She nodded and went on. "And you said the sheriff was the only one out of uniform, which means that that deputy . . ."

"Mickey Burns."

"It means that this Deputy Burns was in uniform, but when you called earlier the operator told you he was off duty."

"And the other deputy, the one who met us in the driveway, was on duty that night because he got the call about checking on Susan. Even though he never got around to doing it."

"So, the sheriff and Deputy Burns are both off duty. It's two in the morning, and Burns shows up in full uniform. Isn't that strange?"

"Yeah, it is."

"Do you think it means anything?"

"I have no idea."

Four uneventful days passed. I made some calls, practiced a little law, and learned that See Shore Cottage was owned by ProAm Holdings Corp. Apparently, the same company owned a number of beach properties scattered along the Panhandle, in addition to substantial real estate investments in one of the agricultural regions located in the north-central part of the state. Also, finally, on Tuesday morning I spoke with Billie Timmons at Dolphin Rentals about the painting duo of Tim and Sonny. She refused to "divulge information" about the property, but did offer to let me rent the place for a nice vacation with my wife and children. I told her I didn't have anyone who fit into those particular categories but that I knew a private cop with an ex-stripper girlfriend who might be interested, and she thanked me for calling.

On Wednesday, I received a fax of two clippings from the weekly *Appalachicola Times*. One described an attempted burglary on St. George Island that Sheriff Todd Wilson said had resulted in no harm to anyone and no theft of property. (No need to scare the tourists.) He did mention that a window had been broken. The second clipping was a short notice placed by the management of the Pelican's Roost restaurant. It requested help in locating a missing employee named Carli Monroe.

Scribbled on the bottom of the fax was a note from Joey.

Tom,
I had a little trouble the first night here. Tied up with a couple of locals in a bar parking lot. Have their ID, etc. Will be in Mobile late this afternoon. Meet me at L.B.'s place around 4:00. We need to discuss my progress and this stuff from the local paper.
Joey

A few minutes before four, I turned down Loutie Blue's historic, tree-lined street and parked next to the curb. Joey's Expedition was in the driveway.

chapter eight

SHIPPING MERCHANTS SETTLED along Monterey Street in the late 1700s, building rambling clapboard houses with impossibly high ceilings and wavy glass in their tall windows. Like most historic districts, the place went to seed in the fifties and sixties when prosperous World War II veterans were making everything newer and, they thought, better; and, like some of the lucky places that dodged new lives as parking lots or turnpikes, the neighborhood around Monterey Street started a gradual comeback in the seventies. Joey once told me that Loutie bought her place about ten years ago for eighty grand. Now she could sell it for four times that.

The house was built when friends actually walked to see each other. So, instead of a modern-America concrete strip curving from the driveway to the front steps, a wide herringbone-pattern brick walk started on the shaded sidewalk and led visitors through twin rows of impatiens and up the steps to a covered porch.

I bumped a brass knocker against the door. Loutie appeared and led me back to the kitchen. It was a replay of my last visit to that room. Loutie leaned against her counter, and Susan and Joey sat at the table. No coffee this time. They were all sipping Abita wheat beer. At least Susan and Loutie were sipping theirs; Joey was taking his in mouthfuls.

I asked, "Is there some reason Carli's not here?"

"She's just outside. My flowers are the only thing she's shown any interest in since she got here. So I put her to work this afternoon planting bulbs I've had in the refrigerator. Unless there's something she shouldn't hear, I can call her in."

I said, "Nothing from me. Joey?"

He shook his head and took in a swallow of Abita. Loutie stepped into the mudroom and called out for Carli. We heard Carli say, "Just a minute."

I asked, "How's she doing?"

Susan said, "I'm not sure. She seems fine on the surface."

"She's a long way from fine," Loutie said. "She just doesn't show it."

I asked, "How can you tell?" But, before the conversation could go any further, a screen door slammed, and Carli walked into the kitchen. She was barefoot and wearing the same blue jean cutoffs I had seen before. This time, though, her shirt was one of those flimsy tank-top undershirts that everybody's grandfather wore. And it was soaked through, concealing nothing, clinging like a second skin, and plainly displaying an exceptional pair of gravity-defying teenage breasts with tan, erect nipples. She looked sweaty from yard work, but the shirt seemed a little wetter than the rest of her.

While Joey and I sat there looking and trying not to look at our young client's knockers, Loutie said, "Carli, go put on a decent shirt."

Carli said, "I'm fine," and started to pull out a chair at the table.

Loutie caught Carli's eye and gave her what was, for me anyway, a sphincter-tightening look. When Loutie spoke again, her voice was an octave lower. She said, "Do it."

Carli dropped her eyes to the floor and walked quickly out of the room.

I said, "What's wrong with her? That's the second time she's pulled something like that. And it's not like she's just your basic high school tease driving the boys crazy. To her, Joey and I have got to look like a couple of old men."

Joey looked up and said, "Speak for yourself."

While we were talking, Loutie had moved to the doorway to make sure Carli wasn't within earshot. She turned toward us and said, "It's probably more pronounced because you're older. I think some older man taught her early, probably in ways you can't imagine, that her only value to men is sexual. She's been abused, and she's scared. And she's acting out when you're around because she wants your help and probably your approval."

Susan said, "I knew she was afraid of her father, but that's all. Did she tell you about this?"

"No, I've just been watching her. That child has been sexually abused by someone. Probably her father from what you're saying." Loutie turned to me. "Tom, I think it also explains why Carli *insisted* on reporting the murder on St. George to begin with. If Carli's father was the abuser, he's already killed that child inside a hundred times over. Carli didn't want to walk away from this murder the way her mother or her family or friends walked away from her abuse without helping."

I said, "How can you be so sure? The way you explain it, it seems to make sense. But people are screwed up for a lot of different reasons."

Joey piped in. "This isn't a deposition, Tom. Just take her word for it." He sounded angry.

I was taken aback. "What's wrong with you?"

Loutie put a hand on Joey's shoulder and squeezed to quiet him. She said, "Joey knows my history."

I thought for a second and said, "Oh."

Loutie said, "You know I used to strip. I'm not ashamed of it. It's how I got this house, in a roundabout way. And it set me up so I can work with Joey to make ends meet, and I don't have to go to some office every day and blow the boss to keep my job."

Joey interrupted to tell her she didn't owe anybody any excuses.

She said, not unkindly, "Hush Joey. I'm not making excuses. I'm explaining how I know something." Loutie faced me again. "A therapist told me once that ninety percent of exotic dancers have been sexually abused, and, from the girls I knew in the business, that seems low.

"I grew up mostly in foster homes. Some of them were okay. Some were bad, and some were awful. At thirteen, I looked eighteen, the way Carli looks twenty at fifteen. Anyway . . ." Loutie turned away to look out the window as she continued. "I was thirteen when I started having problems with a forty-year-old asshole who was suppose to be taking care of me. No one believed me, and no one helped. And I ended up probably more screwed up, for a few years, than Carli is now."

Loutie's eyes looked soft and tired when she turned away from the window to face us. She took a long pull from her beer.

I said, "Sorry."

"There's nothing for you to be sorry about. You didn't do anything wrong. Neither did I, and neither did Carli. The only difference between me and Carli is that she doesn't understand that yet." Her voice sounded husky. She took another long swallow of beer and cleared her throat. Then we watched as Loutie pushed more hurt than most people ever deal with back down where it had been for twenty years. In the space of a few seconds, her eyes turned as hard and cool as glass, and, through pure force of will, she became the old Loutie Blue again. The level of self-control we had witnessed was amazing and sad and a little frightening.

We were quiet until Carli came back into the room wearing a washed face and her Florida State football jersey.

Carli looked at Loutie and said, "You happy?"

"Thrilled," Loutie said and turned to look at me. "Who's got something to report?"

I pointed a finger at Joey. "He's done all the work, but before he gets started, I want to talk about this fax Joey sent me this morning." I reached inside a leather folder, pulled out the fax, and put it in front of Carli. "This is a problem. The newspaper story about the break-in is pretty weak and doesn't present any problems on its own. The problem is that it appeared in today's paper. And the notice that you are missing was in the same edition. Now Carli, I may be giving these people too much credit, but it wouldn't be impossible for someone to connect the timing of your disappearance with the break-in at Susan's house. Particularly, if they ask around a little and find out you and Susan are friends." Loutie put a Coke in front of Carli. She ignored it. Her lips had turned pale. I went on. "This is not something to freak out over. It's a stretch to think they'll put this together. Even if they did, no one outside this room knows you're here with Loutie. You are completely safe, Carli. But, I wouldn't be doing my job if I didn't tell you about this and tell you that we can no longer assume that no one has figured out that you were the witness on the beach." I turned to look at Susan. "That's the long shot—that somebody has put all this together and decided the witness was Carli. The reality, the thing we know, is that they found your name in my appointment book, and three men came to your house with guns.

"I know none of this is a news flash. But I want you to go on taking it seriously. Stay here, stay out of sight, and, for goodness sake, don't call anybody. And that goes for you too, Carli. With caller ID and star-sixty-nine, calling somebody these days is like announcing your address."

I tried to sound more confident than I felt. "Joey and I will get you through this, but we can't do it if we're having to worry every minute of the day about whether you're safe." Carli's lips had returned to their natural color, and she was sipping her Coke. Good. "Carli. We're working for you. Do you have any questions?"

Carli drank some more Coke and studied the table in front of her. She said, "What happened at the house the other night? You know, when you and Susan went back to talk with the cops, and me and Joey waited for you by the road. What did you tell them?"

"First Carli, let me explain something I should have told you already. Everything we're talking about here is privileged. That means you don't ever have to tell anyone on earth about anything we say here, and I'll never tell anyone any of this. I would go to jail before I would tell anyone anything you tell me as your attorney.

"Do you understand all this?"

She nodded her head.

I said, "Carli, please look at me and answer me out loud. This is important. I don't want to hear later that you weren't really sure what I was talking about. Do you understand everything I've told you?"

She said, "I understand what you said, but . . ."

"But what, Carli?"

"That stuff about going to jail to protect me. Is that true? Would you really do that?"

I smiled. "Don't worry, nobody's going to throw me in jail for doing my job. But yes Carli, if it came to it, I would definitely go to jail to protect you and what you tell me."

Our fifteen-year-old exhibitionist client actually blushed. She said, "What about the other night at Susan's beach house? You still haven't answered my question about that."

"I'm getting to that. I wanted you to understand privilege before I got into it with you.

"After Susan and I left you and Joey on the beach, we talked about how to handle the sheriff. I told her to tell the truth about everything except you and Joey being at the house that night. Normally, I would never lie to the police." Joey cleared his throat. I ignored him. "But the sheriff and his people were just treating it as an attempted burglary anyway, so I didn't see any reason to argue with them.

"When we got back to the house, the sheriff and two deputies were there. We explained who we were, and Susan asked to go upstairs to take an aspirin. No one had been up there yet, so Susan quickly made up your and Joey's beds and came back down.

"The only sticky part was explaining about multiple gunshots that had been reported to the sheriff's office. But, with glass blown all over the living room, it wasn't hard to convince the sheriff that the intruders shot up the house for fun."

Joey said, "And that wouldn't be unusual. Teenagers who break into a house are usually drunk or stoned and spend more time trashing the place than looking for stuff to steal. And Sheriff Wilson would know that. Also, while I was down there this week, a couple of people I talked to said something about 'all the trouble we've been having with these young guys,' or something close to that. I'm guessing that the break-in at Susan's wasn't the first local crime glossed over so they wouldn't upset the tourists."

I asked Carli, "Is that it? Do you have any other questions about anything?" Carli shook her head. I looked at Joey.

Joey reached down, lifted a brown paper shopping bag off the floor, and dumped its contents on the kitchen table. Most of it looked like stuff you'd find on someone's dresser: keys, cash and change, one billfold, and three Churchill-sized cigars. A couple of less routine items rounded out the collection: a switchblade with a yellow handle and a half-smoked joint.

He looked at me. "You see my note on the fax about getting jumped by a couple of locals the first night down there?" I nodded. "Well, this is what they had on 'em.

"The first night there, I'm driving around, getting the feel of the place, and stopping in any bars I come up on to have a drink and ask a few questions. Around eleven, I stop in a place called the Shrimp Boat, buy a glass of whatever's on tap, and tell the bartender I'm looking into the break-in the night before on St. George Island." Joey stopped to drain his beer. "Somebody my size doesn't get told to fuck off as much as your normal, run-of-the-mill loudmouth. But this bartender—who must have weighed about a hundred forty soaking wet—gave me that instruction. So, I take a couple more sips of lukewarm beer and move on, figuring, you know, that the Shrimp Boat had future possibilities.

"Outside, I get in the car and, two hundred yards down the road, I know somebody's following me. I keep going. Looking for somewhere with lights and people. Over across the bridge, I see a place called Mother's Milk."

Susan laughed and said, "That's impressive, Joey. Between the Shrimp Boat and Mother's Milk, you managed to hit the two sleaziest places in Franklin County, Florida, in one night."

Joey smiled and said, "Thank you. I didn't think I was gonna find three killers at the yacht club or at one of those yuppie restaurants they got stuffed into the storefronts there. Damnedest thing I ever saw. Places that used to be diners and feed stores, they got filled with pasta restaurants, cappuccino shops, shit like that.

"Anyway, getting back to my story, I pull into the parking lot of Mother's Milk, figuring whoever's tailing me will probably hang back and maybe follow me if I go inside. But I park, and these two assholes in a red pickup pull in behind me and block me in. To make a long story short, they ask me why I'm asking questions about the burglary. I decline to provide information, and they come after me with that little yellow knife there and a baseball bat. I took the bat and tapped them with the small end."

I said, "Tapped them, huh?"

"Yeah, I tapped 'em. It ain't what you saw on the Rodney King tape, but it's the way cops are *supposed* to use a nightstick. You don't wail on somebody with one, unless you want 'em dead. You just pop 'em on the knees and shins and shoulders and maybe across the nose. Hurts like hell." Joey stood and retrieved another Abita from the refrigerator. He leaned against the counter next to Loutie and twisted off the cap. "They were a couple of tough boys. Prison tattoos and one of 'em with three or four teeth missing from other fights. They weren't talking.

"I thought about calling the sheriff, but any cop would have just thrown us all in jail for brawling outside a bar. So, I emptied their pockets, went through the truck, got the tag number, that kinda stuff. Before I left, I popped the hood and yanked a few wires off the distributor so they'd stay put."

"What have you found out from the things you took out of their pockets?" I asked him.

Joey told us that the only one with ID—Thomas Bobby Haycock—also owned the truck. Mr. Haycock had a record going back twenty years and featuring drug dealing, battery, and attempted murder. Haycock's friend had no ID and wouldn't talk, but he had a dagger tattoo on his left forearm with R.I.P. over it and the initials R.E.T. under it. The two had almost seven hundred dollars between them, not to mention a bat, a knife, a joint, and three cigars.

Susan picked up one of the huge cigars, looked at the label, and rolled it between her fingers. She said, "Mr. Haycock has pretty good taste for someone with prison tattoos. This is a Cuban, handmade Cohiba. Legally, you can't get them in this country. But every now and then Bird used to get a few from his gallery in New Orleans. The gallery owner picked them up in Canada when he was up there schmoozing some wildlife artist. These things cost about thirty-five, forty dollars each even up there."

I said, "Where'd some Franklin County hard-ass come up with three forty-dollar, imported, contraband Cuban cigars?"

Joey said, "Interesting, ain't it?"

I nodded "Yes, it is. You had this Haycock's name and tag, his criminal record, and some kind of address. What happened when you checked out his address? He wasn't there, was he?"

"You think you're smart don't you?"

I just looked at him. It was a rhetorical question.

"No. He wasn't there, and he didn't come home for two more days. I found a comfortable place in the brush nearby, and caught up on my reading. He showed up Sunday night at his little house, stayed inside until just before daybreak, and came out with a stuffed sports bag and a half-full, brown grocery bag like this one." Joey held up the bag he had used to hold his attackers' possessions. "I followed him down the coast to a marina in Carabelle. He waited around there until seven and got on the ferry to Dog Island."

"How close is that to St. George?" I asked.

Susan said, "It's just southeast of St. George. Less than a mile. It's about half as big, and it doesn't have a causeway. You've got to either take the ferry or take a plane. They've got a little landing strip in the middle of the island. Or, of course, you could always go by boat if the chop's not too bad and you watch out for oyster beds.

"It's a lot less developed than St. George, too, because it's harder to get to. The last couple of years, though, a few people with big money have started building some major houses out there. Still, for the most part, it's pretty undeveloped. There's just one small motel and mostly a lot of old-fashioned, wooden beach houses."

"And our friend Tommy Bobby Haycock is in one of 'em." Joey added, "This ferry he got on ain't exactly the Staten Island Ferry. It's a little pissant boat, where everybody sees everybody else. So I waited for the next one and went over. Like Susan says, there's not much on Dog Island, so I was able to find him pretty quick.

"Last night, I tailed Haycock when he went out on a little adventure. And, Tom, if you got a few days to kill, I think I can show you where those Cuban cigars come from."

chapter nine

SEASONS NEVER CHANGE smoothly along the coast. By Thursday morning, winter had stuttered forward again into March and dropped the temperature on the Panhandle from high seventies to low fifties. A steady rain fell from gray cloud cover, drenching the morning in melancholy tones.

I reached over and clicked off the high beams as a scattering of weekend houses began to transition into boat shops and real estate offices. Joey directed me through downtown Carabelle, over a curving bridge, and into a marina that looked like a transplant from Buzzard's Bay in Massachusetts. Row upon row of oversized yachts lined a maze of concrete docks, and, everywhere, gray-haired couples roamed about, sipping coffee and talking boats.

We were expected at the marina office, and, after dropping ten twenties on the counter, my Jeep got the one vehicle slot on the seven-o'clock ferry. Back out in the morning drizzle, I drove around a bunker and down a concrete incline to the ferry. One of the less promising delegates from Generation X stood on deck and waved us forward. I rolled onto the boat and stopped next to a guy with three gold hoops piercing one eyebrow and a large blue dot tattooed across the bridge of his nose.

Joey said, "You don't see that every day."

I smiled and poured some coffee from a steel thermos into a plastic cup. And we waited. The FSU station out of Tallahassee was rerunning a segment from "Car Talk." Joey and I listened to middle-age guys in New England act silly until the ferry left the dock and moved toward the mouth of the harbor; then Joey reached over and turned off the radio. Enough was enough.

The view began to open up, and smooth water turned choppy as the ferry beneath us moved out of the harbor and into Appalachicola Bay. I flipped up the hood on my windbreaker and stepped out into the morning mist to get a feel for the place. I guess Joey got out because I did.

Bumpy, steel-gray water reflected the rain-filled sky. Diesel fumes swirled in the air, raising whispers of nausea in my stomach and making me wish I had eaten breakfast. We climbed back in the Jeep.

An hour later we chugged into a wide, sandy inlet on the bay side of Dog Island. The ferry ploughed a straight line through a jumble of anchored sailing yachts and docked alongside one of two wooden docks. According to a carefully painted sign on shore, we had arrived at the *Dog Island Yacht Club*. There was no building or facilities; just the sign.

Near the docks, a collection of plywood rectangles on two-by-four stakes held a laminated assortment of maps and charts and set out a list of island rules. Joey poked me and pointed to one. *Do not clean fish on the dock. Alligator Hazard Area.*

I turned the key in the ignition and looked for the off-ramp. There wasn't one. Cost or environmental concerns, or maybe ambivalence, had kept the shoreline unblemished by concrete or asphalt. If you wanted a car on Dog Island, you drove it off the ferry, down into a foot or two of salt water, and up onto the beach. I guess it kept out the riffraff. It also seemed to have a startling effect on the kind of vehicles people brought over. The sandy ruts leading away from the ephemeral Dog Island Yacht Club led us between rows of junkyard Americana. On each side, thirty or forty decrepit, rusted-out vehicles formed precise queues of mobile scrap metal. Ancient VW vans sat next to geriatric Jeeps with winches bolted to their front bumpers, and those sat beside *Brady-Bunch* station wagons with faded-plastic wood grain peeling from their doors. A dozen boxy Fords and about as many tail-finned Plymouths were mixed in. Several had been hand painted with rainbows and flowers.

I said, "Looks like the parking lot of a Grateful Dead concert from 1978."

Joey nodded at a shiny new Range Rover parked in among the rust buckets. "That's embarrassing."

"What is all this?"

"Most folks with houses out here bring over old clunkers to use while they're on the island. They'll keep a heap here until the salt air turns it into a block of rust; then they'll haul it away and bring over another one. With the ferry just carrying one car at a time and at two hundred a pop, I guess it's easier and cheaper than trying to bring over the family car every time you wanna come out."

"Looks like hell."

"Yeah. Supposed to be some big controversy. The old residents think it's . . . I don't know."

"Droll?"

"Yeah, I guess. Kind of atmospheric. Some of the new ones who came out here in the last couple of years and built mansions think it looks like shit. That's probably what the Range Rover's doing here. Somebody trying to make a point."

"Or just somebody with more money than sense."

"It happens."

I lowered my window and put my hand out with the palm up to feel the rain. "How do you know all this?"

Joey sighed. "I been talking to people. You know, *investigating*. That's what I do."

I pulled my hand back inside. It was wet. "I thought you just beat up people and shot holes in them, that sort of thing."

"That too."

Up past the rows of rusted junkers, the sandy road dead-ended into the main island highway, which was nothing but a couple of slightly deeper ruts in the sand. Joey told me to turn left, and we followed the tracks of countless tires past Captain Casey's Inn and along the backbone of the island before turning off onto an even fainter roadway.

Finally, we parked; we found a spot near our prey; and we waited.

Hours passed. Thomas Bobby Haycock sat warm and dry inside his island bungalow. Not far away, Joey and I sat, wet and cold and miserable, huddled under a few scrawny pine trees and drinking coffee from a steel thermos. My Jeep waited nearby on an undeveloped piece of beach hidden from view by a half dozen sand dunes topped with undulating tufts of sea grass.

"Tell me again why we're sitting in the rain, staring at his house."

Joey had a pair of binoculars trained on Haycock's bungalow. He said, "In case he goes somewhere."

"And the reason we can't just wait down the road in my Jeep—with a heater, out of the rain, maybe listening to a little jazz on the CD player—and wait for his pickup to drive by is . . . ?"

"We're on an island. All he's gotta do is take a walk on the beach and not come back. In twenty minutes, he could be at the ferry or climbing into a buddy's boat or just be somewhere on the island where we aren't."

"That explains why you're doing it. Why does a highly trained attorney like myself have to sit out here with you?"

"The bonds of friendship."

"I knew there was a good reason."

"And Susan and Carli."

"Even better."

Joey leaned back against the trunk of a wind-tortured pine and squirmed his butt in the sand to try to get comfortable.

"That little girl's got herself fixated on you, you know? All that wet undershirt stuff and waving her tits around."

"Fixated?"

"Fuck you. You know what I mean. It's just something to watch out for is all. Loutie says it's kinda sweet. Says she's glad it's you and not some asshole who'd take advantage of her."

I lay on my back, closed my eyes, and let the light rain sting my face. I said, "I'll say one thing. You can't bullshit her. She's going to need some counseling or something when this is over, but she's not stupid. If we can give her the chance, she's going to be okay. And Susan says she's got some talent. Draws and paints a little. Knows the difference in good art and bad."

"Something there worth saving."

I said, "Everybody's worth saving," but thought better of it and added, "Almost everybody."

"You know what I mean."

"Yeah," I said, "I know."

A little after noon, I hiked over dune and dale to fetch Cokes, sandwiches, and Oreos from a cooler in the Jeep. Around six, I made the same trip.

These were the highlights of my day.

At ten that night, I found a slab of my left buttock and thigh with no feeling in it. Nothing, not even needles. Two hours later, our quarry emerged from his house in darkness. We saw him when he opened the driver's door on his pickup and stepped inside.

Joey said, "Let's go," and my dead hindquarters and I humped along behind Joey as he sprinted to the Jeep. I unlocked the doors with the remote, jumped in, and got the thing cranked and turned around in time to see Haycock's truck zoom by on the dirt roadway. Joey had pulled the fuse responsible for lighting the Jeep's interior. It was my job to remember not to turn on the headlights and, of course, to drive that way down a curving dirt road at midnight without crashing and without losing sight of Haycock. All of which I somehow did.

Haycock led us to a deserted stretch of beach, where he drove across the sand, pointed his front bumper at the water, and killed the headlights. I hid the Jeep in a pine thicket diagonally across the road, and we circled around to the beach on foot. My reward for my first successful tail was another forty minutes cramped against a rain-soaked dune, watching Haycock's motionless pickup.

Finally, Joey tapped my back with a knuckle, pointed out at the ocean, and said, "Look."

"What?"

"Straight out from here. Don't look at the horizon. It's about halfway between the horizon and the beach."

I still hadn't seen anything when Haycock flashed his low beams three times. Almost immediately, a single blue light flashed three times on the water. If we hadn't been looking for the signal and we had noticed it at all, it would have looked like nothing more than a reflected star.

I whispered, "You saw this before?"

"Yeah. It's what we came down here to see. Now watch. If it's like the other night, a boat's gonna pull up here in a few minutes with a couple of men and some boxes." I moved up on the dune for a better look. Joey said, "Keep your head down. The men on the boat the other night were carrying what looked like AK-47s."

I put my head down.

An outboard motor rumbled in the distance. Minutes passed. Twice there was a triple flash on the water that Haycock answered with his headlights. I said, "The guy in the boat is checking his course on the way in."

Joey said, "Looks like it."

Thirteen minutes after the first set of blue flashes, an arrowhead-shaped pontoon boat puttered onto the sand. A figure in the bow jumped out to pull the boat up onto the beach. Haycock stepped out of the truck's cab and walked down the beach to help.

Joey whispered, "I count three left in the boat. And two on the beach, including Haycock."

"Four and two. There's a kid in the boat."

"I'll be damned."

With a quarter moon and cloud cover, the passengers' features were impossible to see. But we could plainly make out the dark outlines of Haycock, two armed men, a plump, unarmed man, a woman, and a small child. Voices floated on the night air. The plump man helped the woman and child out of the boat, and the woman led the child to Haycock's pickup and climbed inside, placing the child on her lap. When the interior light came on, we could see them both plainly. She had straight dark hair and black eyes. The child had her coloring and his father's pudgy build—assuming the unarmed man was his father.

While this was going on, the armed man in the stern sat still with a rifle across his lap. When mother and child were safe inside the truck, he stepped over the gunwale and stationed himself halfway between the truck and boat, holding a serious-looking firearm at the ready. The other three men formed a fire line. Pudgy Poppa knelt inside the boat and handed large cardboard boxes and small wooden crates to the second, formerly armed man, who, in turn, stacked the cargo above the high-tide mark and out of the surf's reach. Haycock carried the boxes and crates to his truck and stacked them in the bed. This was not the first time Haycock and friends had done this. In less than fifteen minutes and with minimal communication, they had filled the truck bed with cargo and the two armed men had departed in the pontoon boat.

Haycock secured a tarp over his truckload as Poppa climbed in the cab with his family. Illuminated by the overhead bulb, Poppa's coloring was, if anything, darker than his wife's. The kid hadn't gotten anything from Mom. He was a curly-headed clone of his father.

Joey tapped my leg and started to move away. I closed a hand on his arm to stop him. "Wait." I motioned for Joey to stay put and then crawled to a point ten yards behind and a few paces to the left of Haycock's pickup. Something was going on inside the cab. Haycock had a highway map unfolded and propped against the steering wheel. Poppa craned his neck and leaned across his wife and child to see. Haycock held a metal cigarette lighter to illuminate and trace a path across the map.

The lighter snapped shut. Haycock flashed his low beams twice and then twice more. The same pattern repeated in blue on the water, and he turned the ignition key. Tires spun in the sand, and the back bumper arced backward, thumping into the small dune I was hiding behind. Haycock changed gears and dusted me with a cloud of sand as he drove off the beach and turned left onto the dirt road.

Scrambling to my feet, I sprinted to the Jeep. Joey met me there. By the time we were back on the road, Haycock was out of sight. I pointed the Jeep in his direction, flipped on the headlights, and floored it.

Joey sounded a tad judgmental. "That was interesting."

"Yeah, it was."

"He's gone."

"Maybe."

Parallel white ruts stretched out in front. Sand and dark thickets and an occasional vacation home whirred by in the night. Joey said, "We lost him."

"You said that."

"Where are we going?"

"The motel."

"Why?"

"Haycock's got to do something with that family. The ferry doesn't run at night, and he's headed away from his house. And I'm guessing they're not going to another boat. If they had planned to reach the mainland tonight by water, they would have just landed there to start with. It doesn't make sense to risk two landings when one would do. So, that leaves two possible destinations—a private home or the only motel on the island. And I think it's going to be the motel."

"How do you figure that?"

"Because," I said, "if they're going to a private home, I lost them."

Vapor lights bathed the roadside ahead in ugly light. I slowed and cruised past Captain Casey's Inn. There in the parking lot, big as life and butt ugly, was Thomas Bobby Haycock striding toward his truck. Mom, Poppa, and junior were gone. We cruised on past and, a hundred yards down, hung a "U." I waited for Haycock's red taillights to disappear around a curve so we would be out of view and switched off my headlights. We were able to tail him back to his bungalow, unnoticed.

I turned to Joey. "Is that it?"

"That's pretty much it. In the morning—if he does the same thing he did a few days ago—he's gonna catch the early ferry and transport his truck to the mainland. Where he goes from there, I have no idea."

"And even if we could get on the same ferry without being noticed, the Dog Island Ferry only hauls one car at a time."

Joey nodded. "Yep."

"So, there's not much else we can do for now."

"Not much. If you think it's worth it, I'll hang around a few more days and try to catch him coming off the ferry one morning with a truckload of stuff. He knows my Expedition, but I can rent a car and follow him. Try to see where he's taking it."

"Yeah. I think it's worth it. I'll double-check with Susan to make sure she thinks it's worth the money, but it looks like the next step to me." My mind wandered over what we had seen and formed a picture of a chubby little boy crossing the Gulf at night in an open boat. I asked, "What was the deal with the kid in the boat? You told me Haycock was involved in what looks like a smuggling operation. You didn't say anything about smuggling people."

"That's cause I didn't know it. The other night, it was just boxes."

"Oh. Okay. What now?"

Joey said, "We go get some sleep. I've got a room at Captain Casey's."

I turned the Jeep around and, a quarter mile down the road, clicked the headlights back on. I said, "How did you know Haycock was going to meet that boat tonight? Don't tell me he does that every night."

"Nope. That's just the second time in a week. We got lucky."

My backside hurt. I had been drenched, chilled to the bone, and nearly run over. I said, "Yeah. I guess we were."

Captain Casey had thoughtfully placed a clock radio on the chipped Formica nightstand in lieu of providing wake-up service. I set the alarm, and Joey clicked off the lamp at 2:56 A.M.

Having caught up on missed sleep at Loutie's, I was back to my usual three hours. I woke Joey a few minutes after six, stumbling to the bathroom to brush my teeth and rinse with motel mouthwash. The first ferry from the island to the mainland was at eight. Joey turned over. I pulled on yesterday's damp jeans and a windbreaker and went out for a walk on the beach.

As I've said before, you can get a lot of thinking done if you aren't able to sleep. You also get to see things that people without night demons never get to see. That morning, I saw a bleary-eyed but exuberant Hispanic family watching the sun rise over the Gulf of Mexico. Plump Poppa sat on the sand, presiding over mother and son as they fashioned a drip castle from handfuls of sopping sand. As I approached, the mother seemed to have tears in her tired eyes. I said, "Buenos días."

The little boy, who looked to be about six years old, smiled up at me, and said, "Buenos días."

Mom froze with her pretty profile outlined against the pale, early morning beach; then she turned to her husband. Poppa gave me a hard look and said, "Good morning," in cultivated English that, despite its precision, had an alien, equatorial inflection. And for the first time—maybe because he had spoken or because anger had flashed across his delicate, puffy features—I seemed to recognize him from some half-remembered news story, from a faded newspaper photo or one of the hundreds of video clips that wash across the television screen every day. And the faint gray-tone memory cast a brief but unsettling shadow over my thoughts.

As I walked away, the mother gathered up junior in her arms and the two parents walked quickly toward the motel. I could hear the little boy start to cry and to beg his parents for something. My only Spanish is what I remember from high school. But even I knew that the sweet child who had smiled and wished me a good morning only wanted to stay on the beautiful beach and finish building his castle in the sand. And I knew I was the asshole who ruined it for him.

chapter ten

OUTSIDE THE OFFICE window, tender new growth flecked the dark ivy that framed my view of the docks. Sinking deep into my chair, I sipped coffee-flavored milk foam. It beat the hell out of crouching in the rain for sixteen hours. Kelly had brewed cappuccino, in her words, to celebrate my presence in the office. There seemed, I thought, to be a work-ethic message or reprimand in there somewhere. I was thinking about that and about Carli and about sand castles.

Kelly sat in a client chair blowing gently to make a hole in her foam. She asked, "How's the coffee?"

"It's wonderful. It does, however, seem to be encouraging sloth on my part."

Kelly smiled, and, like every time she smiled, I remembered how much I liked her. Kelly stood about five foot two and weighed in at maybe a hundred pounds after Thanksgiving dinner. She wore her black hair short, too short in my unsolicited and unexpressed opinion, and she looked out at the world through bright blue eyes. For years, she had run five miles a day, and she looked it.

She said, "What happened to the little boy on the beach?"

"The whole family got on the eight o'clock ferry with Tommy

Bobby Haycock and his loaded pickup. Joey and I had to wait for the next ferry, and, by the time we got to the landing, Haycock and the family had cleared out." Kelly blew her foam some more. I said, "Are you going to drink any of that or did you just make it so you could play with the suds?" Kelly smiled, and a thought occurred to me. "Who do we know at the state docks?"

She looked out the window and wrinkled her forehead with thought. "No one. We've got a couple of clients whose families were in the shipping business a hundred years ago, but no one at the state docks. And really no one who's in shipping now."

"I need to find out what ships or boats were in Appalachicola Bay on two specific dates. And, if there's any way we can find out, I'd like to know if any of those boats arrived recently from South or Central America."

"Good luck."

"Thank you."

Kelly thought some more and said, "I go out sometimes with a guy in the Coast Guard. I don't think he'd break any rules for me. We're not that close. But if it's public knowledge, he should either know how to dig it out or how to find someone else who can."

"Do you mind asking him?"

"Nah. What're the dates?"

"Yesterday and last Tuesday. The twentieth and twenty-second."

She said, "Gotcha," and walked out of the office. Ten minutes later, she was back. "Looks like he's out guarding the coast. I left a message with the operator, or whatever they call people who take messages at the Coast Guard. And I left a message on his answering machine at home."

"Thank you very much."

"You're welcome very much."

I turned once again to look out the window. Over Mobile Bay, the sun lasered yellow beams through white clouds. I did not feel like dictating or drafting or planning legal strategies. And, for better or worse, my workload was such that there wasn't all that much of that sort of thing to do. I swiveled my chair around to look at Kelly. "It's Friday. Why don't you take off early?"

"Because I've got work to do."

"Can it wait until Monday?"

"Probably."

"Then you can probably go home. Take off. I'll see you next week."

A few minutes later, I heard her leave by the front door. I flipped through pink message slips on my desk and tried to return a few calls from fellow members of the bar. No luck. Mobile may be a bustling international seaport, but then it's also a seaport. People don't kill themselves with work and worry. And most lawyers play golf on Friday afternoons. It's one of the things I always admired most about the city.

I had finished off my coffee and was ransacking the kitchen for a lost bag of double-chocolate Milano cookies when a thought occurred to me. Back behind my desk, I flipped on my laptop and searched Lotus Organizer for the phrase, "natural resource." Elmore Puppet popped up. Elmore was one of my father's contacts at the Alabama Department of Natural Resources and Conservation. My father owns a small sawmill, and Puppet had helped him solve minor political problems over the years. And, a few years ago, he had helped me find a job for an out-of-work client with a forestry degree and a bad attitude.

It was a few minutes past three—a problematic time to find a state employee in his office on a Friday afternoon. I called. After getting passed around by a succession of pleasant female voices, I heard Puppet pick up.

"Mr. Puppet. This is Tom McInnes in Mobile. Sam McInnes in Coopers Bend is my father."

I had forgotten how unreasonably happy the guy was. "I'll be damned. Sure. It's Sam's hot-shit lawyer son. How you doin'?"

"I'm fine Mr. Puppet."

"Call me Elmore, Tom. I may be old as hell, but your old man is family."

To Elmore, everyone he ever met was family. I said, "I've got a problem. I remember seeing some aerial photos of the sawmill and some timberland on Sam's desk."

"You call your daddy Sam? My old man would have kicked my ass."

I turned to look out again at the bay. The truth was that I didn't much care for the man who begat me, and I sure as hell wasn't going to call him Daddy. Even as an adult, I never could figure out why so many people seemed to like him. The closest I could come is that my old man had made a lot of money over the course of his life, and too many people seem to like saying some old rich guy is their friend. And it occurred to me that that cynical conclusion probably said something about how nice a guy I was too.

I took a deep breath. "Elmore, I've lost track of everyone who wants to kick my ass." He laughed too hard, and I resumed my effort to elicit useful information. "Anyway, I know Sam got the aerials from you, and I need some photos of the Panhandle."

"Oh. Okay. Well, you see, we don't take the pictures ourselves. We get 'em from the federal government. Either the Air Force or the Interior Department or NASA. There's several places that do that."

"Are they detailed enough to see a particular boat anchored off the Panhandle and identify it?"

Elmore paused to think about that. He said, "Let me put it this way. No. But, if you knew the exact location of the boat, you could hire a guy I know in Marengo County to fly over and get any kind of pictures you want."

"All I know is that the boat's probably in Appalachicola Bay, but it could be anywhere within a dozen miles of Appalachicola."

Elmore laughed. "Well then, get out your checkbook. To get the detail you want, you'd have to hire the pilot to fly up and down the coast all day taking a series of overlapping photographs."

What I had really wanted were photos from the day before. I had gone ahead and asked about the pilot because there was some possibility that Joey could let me know the next time the smugglers made a nighttime landing, and I could take that opportunity to call the aerial photographer. Which was a pretty stupid idea, since, if I were going to do that, I could just hire a pilot or even a power boat and make the rounds myself. I said, "What about NASA? I heard they had close-ups of Saddam Hussein having breakfast before the Gulf War."

Elmore laughed some more. He was one happy guy. "Saddam Hussein ain't hanging out on the Panhandle, Tom. Most of the time, NASA has their satellites shut down when they're not over something they're interested in. I mean, I don't mean to make you feel stupid. I just know 'cause I've been doing this for forty years."

"Any suggestions?"

"Check with the Coast Guard."

"It's in the works. Thanks, Elmore."

"Any time. Any time at all. And tell your father I said howdy."

I said I would and hung up. State employees. Some hold on to their jobs through shifting administrations by digging up dirt, some by never being noticed, and some, like Elmore Puppet, stayed put for forty years by liking every miserable s.o.b. they ever met.

I couldn't think of anything else useful to do, and the thought—or more precisely the absence of thought—was making me antsy. I called Susan and invited myself over for dinner at Loutie's house.

Susan said, "Joey's already coming over to see Loutie tonight. Why don't you pick up some pizza, and we'll make a party of it?" I agreed that that sounded like one hell of an idea. I called ahead for two deep dish pizzas with everything, then drove to Blockbuster and picked up *Rear Window* and *Get Shorty*, figuring that between Hitchcock and Elmore Leonard there would be something for everyone. On the way to the pizza place, I reached Joey on his cell phone.

He said, "I hear we're having a party."

"Looks like it." I asked, "Why aren't you on Dog Island watching Haycock?"

"I thought I'd come home and talk with Susan and Carli about what happened and go back down on Monday with a fresh perspective."

I said, "Wanted the weekend off, huh?"

"Basically."

I told him to bring beer and soft drinks and pushed the *end* button on my flip phone.

When *Get Shorty* ended, Carli popped in Hitchcock and made an effort to get into Jimmy Stewart and Grace Kelly. Susan asked me to give her a hand with the leftovers, and we carried cardboard pizza boxes, tomato pasted plates, and sticky glasses into the kitchen. Susan scraped cold crust into the disposal and loaded the dishwasher while I searched out trash bags and stuffed one with boxes and napkins and other trash from the plastic receptacle under Loutie's sink.

I finished with the trash and walked through the mudroom and out the back door with the intention of finding an outside garbage can. The flat lawn reached back to a brick wall that separated it from the service alley. The cans hunkered against the wall on the alley side. I reached over the brick wall, stuffed my black plastic bag in an empty Rubbermaid can, and pressed the lid back into place. When I turned around, Susan stood in the doorway framed by light from the kitchen. I started walking back, and she came out to meet me, carrying a fresh beer in each hand.

She handed one to me, and I thanked her. She said, "It's nice out, isn't it?"

"Yeah. It is. It's funny. Joey and I nearly froze in the rain yesterday on Dog Island."

Susan walked away from the house and leaned against a slender magnolia tree that looked like a relatively recent addition to the two-hundred-year-old yard. I followed and stood in the shadows looking at her. She asked, "How much longer before Carli and I get our lives back?"

"I don't know, Susan. We know a lot. We might be able to go to the cops now and get Haycock arrested, but I don't think it would stick. It's just our word against his. I guess we could report the beach rendezvous and shut them down on Dog Island for a while, but they'd just pick back up somewhere else. And then we wouldn't be able to keep an eye on them. Right now, I think it's better to know where the Bodines are and what they're doing. And, as far as I can see, shutting down one little smuggling operation wouldn't do much to keep Carli safe."

Susan's features had disappeared into a dark silhouette, but I could feel her eyes moving over my face like fingertips as I talked. My thoughts turned liquid, and I had to concentrate to bring my mind back on point. "I'm . . . I'm open to suggestions. But it looks like we've just got to stick it out until we can figure out enough about what's going on to completely shut down whoever's after you and Carli." Susan shifted her weight from one foot to the other. With only a sliver of moon in the night sky, she was nearly invisible beneath the tree's shadow. I said, "I'm going back down there tomorrow to see if I can find out who was anchored offshore last night."

Susan's voice dropped to just above a whisper. "I really appreciate everything you and Joey are doing." I tried to say something about the others wondering where we were, but she kept speaking quietly. "After the comments you made to Carli about getting me hurt last fall, which you didn't, I want to make sure you're not doing all this because you still feel guilty about something."

"I don't think I feel guilty. It's more like I feel responsible. It was my brother who . . ."

Susan interrupted. "There's plenty of blame in what happened, but none of it is yours. You helped me through a very hard time. I am nothing but grateful for that and for what you're doing for me and Carli now." As Susan spoke, she leaned forward and hooked her finger in the front of my shirt and bumped me gently on the chest for emphasis.

When she tilted forward, she came out of the magnolia's shadow, and I could see her face in the moonlight. Her small hand felt warm against my chest, and my mind filled with the image and sensations of our brief kiss at her beach house. Without really thinking, I leaned forward and kissed her lips. I stepped back, and she smiled. I took a sip of beer, because I wasn't sure what else to do right then, and felt her hand on my shirt pulling me toward her. I put my arms around her waist, and her hand slid up my chest and neck to the back of my head as our lips met again. Her lips parted and our tongues touched.

Slowly, I found myself pushing deeper into her mouth and pulling her body close against mine. Minutes later, when we stepped apart, the night air held too little oxygen.

Susan said, "I haven't made out like that in years. Jeez. High school at the drive-in."

I was glad she couldn't see my face. "Is that good or bad?"

"Ohhh. That's good." As she pulled me to her, she said, "I liked high school."

We kissed again, and I pulled back to look at her eyes. The pupils were dilated, which could have meant she was interested or even aroused if we hadn't been standing in the dark. But, interested or not, I thought I saw a few too many emotions playing across her face. I realized it had been years since she had kissed anyone but her husband, and, if my guess was right, it had been eight or nine months with no one to kiss or hold since he had died.

I turned and led her across the moonlit yard to the back door.

When we entered the kitchen, Susan said, "Come on. I want to show you something," and led me away from the living room and toward the back of the house.

"What is it?"

"Just follow me."

Susan led me down the hall to a bedroom door. She pushed it open and reached inside to flick on the light.

I asked, "Why are we going into a bedroom?"

Susan gave me a look and said, "You wish." She stepped inside. "I want you to see something Carli did."

I followed Susan into the room and looked around. Taped to the vanity mirror, scattered on the bed, and stacked on the bedside table were a total of maybe twenty drawings. I walked over to the vanity and looked. My charcoal image looked back from a piece of lined notebook paper taped there.

I said, "This isn't a stalker thing is it?"

Susan shook her head. "We really do think a lot of ourselves tonight, don't we? No. She's done drawings of all of us. And some of the house. And some of Loutie's flowers. I wanted you to see how good they are."

I walked over to the bed and picked up a pencil drawing of one of the trees in Loutie's backyard. "They look good to me. But I'm not much of a judge. How good are they?"

Susan had walked over to squint at Carli's picture of me. "Well, they're not professional. She's not the next Picasso or anything. But they're good. Probably on the level of an undergraduate art student."

Suddenly I felt uncomfortable. "Should we be in here? This is her private stuff."

Susan looked around. "Probably not. I just wanted you to see what your client can do. That she's not just some little tramp in a wet T-shirt."

"I never thought anything like that. Or, if I did, I understand why she's the way she is."

Susan just said, "Well, you're probably right that we're invading her privacy here. Let's go," and we left Carli's bedroom.

Back in the den, Jimmy Stewart spied on Miss Lonely Hearts as she served dinner and made conversation with a make-believe date. Joey sat on the sofa massaging Loutie's feet. Carli sat cross-legged six feet from the television screen. She said, "This is a good movie. It's got Princess Grace in it. She was like the first Princess Di."

Joey grinned at us and said, "Did you two get the dishes cleaned up?"

I said, "Yeah. Susan did."

He kept grinning. "Take the trash out to the alley?"

I said, "Uh-huh."

"Mmmm. You find anything else interesting to do out there in the yard? Under the stars, moonlight bouncing off the flowers, soft spring breezes blowing through your hair . . ."

Loutie said, "Shut up, Joey."

He was chuckling. "Yeah, I was gettin' a little misty myself. And I gotta go anyway. It's been four or five days without much sleep. I need to get home and hit the hay."

Everyone but Carli was tired, so Joey and I thanked Loutie for having us and wandered out into the night. As we walked between rows of purple flowers toward the street, I said, "You're a real asshole. You know that?"

Joey was still laughing to himself when he climbed into his Expedition and shut the door.

chapter eleven

BRIGHT SUNSHINE POURED through French doors and tilted a warm rectangle of light across the white sheet where it covered my legs. I squinted at the alarm clock, rubbed my eyes like the fat kid in "The Little Rascals," and squinted some more. It read *7:18.* For the first time in months, I had slept for six straight hours, and I felt like kissing someone. Again.

Since late fall, the red-dotted numbers over my bedside table had become more of a gauge than a reminder to get up and face the day. They were a gauge of how long I had dented sheets and tossed covers without sleeping. Then they were a gauge of how long I had slept before waking up more tired than when I went to bed. More than anything, they had become a gauge of how screwed up my life had become since my difficult—some might say criminal—younger brother caught a thirty-aught-six round in the neck one September night on the Alabama River. I had been too busy to deal with Hall's bullshit when he was alive, which meant that—for the past six months—I'd been lying awake every night feeling like a jerk for failing to salvage a life that was ultimately unsalvageable.

But something had happened now. And I guessed it had a lot to do with the widow Fitzsimmons and even more to do with some sort of absolution that my subconscious seemed to have tied to Susan's playful intimacy. Whatever the reason, for the first time in six months, the sun was up on that bright Saturday morning before Tom McInnes was.

I decided to lie there and think about making out under a magnolia tree and smile.

Around nine, Kelly called to let me know her Coast Guard captain had phoned. She got a date out of it. I got bupkus. According to the boyfriend, all vessels leaving foreign ports must go through customs when arriving back in the United States. But, between ports, they can pretty much wander around the Gulf of Mexico—or anywhere else they want—without telling a soul. The young captain explained that a private yacht, for example, could have left Brazil, sailed along the Central American coast, and cut over to Appalachicola Bay without filing a report or leaving any record of its route. Also, that same yacht could pull into Tampa two days later and no one would ever know where it had been—only that it left Brazil and then entered the United States a certain number of days later.

After saying good-bye to Kelly, I padded downstairs and scrambled three eggs, which tasted better than I remembered eggs tasting. Later, as I swirled orange juice in my mouth like wine, I punched in Joey's number on the kitchen phone. We spoke briefly before I hung up and called Loutie's. Carli answered. I said good morning, made polite conversation about Hitchcock and Grace Kelly, and asked for Susan.

When Susan picked up, I said, "Good morning."

Susan, I thought, sounded pleased. She said, "Good morning to you. Is this call one of those Southern things that Midwestern girls like me don't know about?"

"What are you talking about?"

"You know. Calling your conquest the next day to let her know you still respect her."

"Cute. Unfortunately, it wasn't much of a conquest, which is not to say that I will not always think fondly of emptying the trash." Susan laughed. I said, "The reason I called is that I've tried every way I can think of—short of going to Appalachicola and renting a boat—to find out who may be cruising from South America to Dog Island with merchandise and refugees on board. Monday morning, Kelly's going to start checking customs in Panama City, Mobile, and Tampa to see if anything jumps out at her, but that's really a hope-we-get-lucky tactic. I think I'm going to have to head down to the islands and ask a few questions and maybe rent a boat or a plane."

"Yes. Last night, you said you might do something like that. Do you want to stay at my house while you're down there? It's a little shot up at the moment, but I've already had the real estate company—you know, the people who handle renting out the place when I'm not there—I've already had them clean up the mess and nail plywood over broken windows and that kind of thing. So, if you're interested, you're welcome to it."

I said, "I think I'd rather stay someplace where the Bodines haven't already tried to kill us."

"Good point."

"I think I'll try to rent something on one of the islands. Probably on St. George, since Joey already has Dog Island covered. He's going to keep watching Haycock and let me know when he goes out to meet another boat. That way, I can check around with some of the local fishermen or maybe rent a boat the next morning. If I can get out there before our smugglers weigh anchor, I should be able to get a name or a registration number off the boat."

Susan was laughing again. "Weigh anchor, huh?" I didn't answer. She gave me the name of her agent so I'd have someone to help me find a rental, and asked, "Are you going to come by before you leave?"

"No. I hadn't planned to. Do you think I should see Carli and explain what I'm doing?"

There was a brief silence. "No. No, that's okay. I think she's fine."

Now there was a short silence on my end as my sad little brain kicked in. "I slept like a baby last night."

She said, "Okay," but what she meant was, *Why are you telling me this?*

"Since my brother died last fall, I haven't been able to sleep a whole lot. Hell, I see the sunrise so much I've gotten tired of looking at it." I said, "I just wanted you to know that last night, for the first time in months, I slept through the night and didn't wake up until after seven."

"If you're this happy about sleeping in till seven on Saturday morning, you *must* have been having problems. So, I'm glad. Whatever the reason." She hesitated and said, "For whatever it's worth, last night had the opposite effect on me. I tossed and turned for an hour before finally drifting off."

I thought of how I had pulled her against me in the moonlight, and I recalled the emotion in her eyes. I decided I had gone too far. She obviously missed her husband and wasn't ready for another relationship.

"I'm sorry, Susan. I know it must be hard."

She giggled, which was something I had never heard her do. I had heard her laugh, chuckle, and even guffaw on one occasion, but I had never heard Susan Fitzsimmons giggle. She said, "Tom? You really don't get it, do you? For me, the only hard thing about kissing you was *stopping*. And, oh yeah, then trying to go to sleep in what I can only *politely* describe as a thoroughly unsatisfied condition."

"Oh."

Susan repeated back, "Oh."

I promised to call from the beach and to come by the minute I got back in town. I put the receiver in its cradle and found myself sitting at the breakfast table, smiling idiotically at an empty glass of orange juice.

The house Susan's agent found for me was not in The Plantation. Based on past experience, I decided that the fat guy at the gate was not an insurmountable obstacle to people who wanted to kill me. And there was always the consideration that Susan was footing the bill. Unless I stayed in Susan's house, which seemed like a monumentally bad idea, I would be looking at a couple-thousand-plus a week for a rental house inside that gated community. But just a few hundred yards away, on the low-rent side of The Plantation's guarded gate, I found a beachfront Jim Walter home on hurricane stilts for a mere eight hundred.

Inside the little house, pastel upholstery, pastel curtains and blinds, and pastel prints filled the house with faded ocean motifs. There was a "master bedroom," which meant, if you were careful, you could actually walk around the bed without bumping into the wall or the dresser, and there was a "guest bedroom," which meant, in there, you couldn't. The kitchen occupied a back corner of the living room, which boasted two double sliding glass doors that provided the requisite Gulf view and led out onto a weathered deck.

I threw my canvas duffle on the guest bed and rummaged around until I came up with running shorts and shoes and a Grand Hotel T-shirt with a faded nautilus shell on the front. After stuffing my new house key and two fifty-dollar bills into the inside pocket of my shorts, I left through the roadside door, circled back under the house, and walked out onto the beach.

Small whitecaps lapped the sand ten feet below a wavering line of gray and white shells that marked high tide. A hundred yards offshore, a striped-sail catamaran skidded across blue-green swells. Seagulls hovered over my head like graceful beggars, and, as far as I could see in each direction, no more than a dozen bodies interrupted the soft flow of sandy beach.

The island was between seasons. The end of spring break had emptied the beaches of young, nubile bodies; winter had fled New England and the Midwest, pulling hoards of not-so-young and not-so-nubile snowbirds back to their native climes; and the summer vacation trade had not yet begun to flood the beaches with sun-blistered families. I turned toward the center of the island, in the direction of a cluster of buildings that serves as the island's downtown, and began walking. With every step, pockets of powdery sand squeaked like baby seals beneath my feet. I could feel the muscles in my thighs and calves and a thousand tiny fibers in my ankles and knees stretch and work and warm. I started to run.

Twenty minutes and a little more than two miles later, the mustard walls of the island's only motel jogged by on my left. I slowed to a walk and turned toward the restaurant-slash-bar just east of the motel. A wooden walkway stretched over grassy dunes and connected to an outside dining area furnished with plastic tables and chairs and a freestanding bar roofed with palm fronds and surrounded by four huge Tiki masks. I tried to imagine why Hawaiian kitsch had been used to decorate a bar in North Florida. If nothing else, the Seminoles should complain.

I ordered iced tea and fried crab claws and struck up a conversation with my blonde, nut-brown waitress. Summer sun had bleached her as white and burned her as brown as a person can bleach and burn in the tropical sun. A yellow metal button on her left breast told me her name was Lauren. In fifteen years, when Lauren turned forty, she would look fifty. But, for now, she looked pretty damn good.

It was midafternoon, and the restaurant was as deserted as the beach. Lauren took my order, and we talked. After she put a basket of steaming crab claws on the table, I asked her to sit.

Lauren told me about life on the island and about the fishermen and about the pleasure boats that anchored and dropped speedboats full of yachtsmen who dined and drank and tipped like nobody's business. And, most interesting of all, she told me about an old fishmonger—a local legend named Peety Boy who had known everything and everyone on the island since the dawn of time.

Lauren went back to work, and I trotted over the walkway and down the beach to the waterline, where I pulled off my shoes and shirt and dropped them in the sand. Cold surf swirled over my toes and ankles and then my legs. A deep breath, and I dove into a wave. I didn't wait thirty minutes after eating, but then I didn't plan on deep-water swimming. I just needed cold water on my face. I needed to think.

A few laps back and forth parallel with the shoreline, and I staggered out covered in chill bumps. I donned shirt and shoes and walked back up along the wooden walkway and past the restaurant. As I passed, Lauren waved and flashed a friendly smile.

It was time to find Peety Boy. According to my new friend Lauren, every day of the week the old man parked his wagon next to the public basketball court near the center of the island. She said I couldn't miss it, particularly since Peety Boy's rolling store bore the logical name of "Peety Boy's Seafood." I was assured that word on the island was: If Peety Boy didn't know about it, it didn't happen.

I hung a right on Gorrie Drive, the main road along the Gulf side of the island. The public beaches' parking lot where Carli had parked with her date that fateful night came up on the right. Across the road, a basketball hoop protruded at a downward angle from a dejected backboard. The goalpost sprouted from a slab of sand-powdered pavement that sat in the middle of a small grassy field. On the far back corner of the grass sat Peety Boy's Seafood. The boxy trailer looked homemade but well built. It was the size of one of those pop-up things that retired people haul from state to state, but this one was square and white, with a long service window cut into the side. Painted plywood hung down by chains to form a counter that, come nightfall, would swing back into place and close the window. Above the opening, Peety Boy had stretched a striped awning. Above the awning, he had painted the name of his business.

As I approached, an elderly man with thick white hair, sun-wrinkled skin, and a paucity of teeth, said, "Good day to be alive!"

I said, "Yep. This is a beautiful place."

Peety Boy turned to toss a couple of fresh fillets in the icebox and stepped back up to the window. The store sat on truck tires, so he looked down at me. "Most beautiful place on God's earth. Been here my whole life. Never moved an inch, 'cept for World War II. Helped whip the Germans in France. Then came on home and thanked God for gettin' back and bein' back."

I said, "They trained around here somewhere for D-Day, didn't they?"

Peety Boy looked pleased but, probably because of his missing teeth, smiled more with his eyes than his lips. "Not many folks know that nowadays. Yessir. Down close to Carabelle, at Lanart Village, six divisions, 'bout forty thousand troops, got what they called amphibious trainin'. A couple dozen drowned tryin' to learn it. Walter Winchell, he called Carabelle 'Hell by the Sea.' But it ain't. Everywhere is hell when you're trainin' to fight a war." Peety Boy wiped fish blood on his white apron, and changed to a businesslike tone. "So. What can I do for you today? Got some beautiful jumbo shrimp. Got the prettiest oysters you ever saw. Come right out of Appalachicola Bay. Just got 'em in this mornin'."

"I'm trying to get some information."

Some of the openness faded, and Peety Boy looked doubtful. He said, "Well, I guess that's all right."

"I'm trying to locate someone who would know whether the boat of a friend of mine has been around here recently. I don't think my friend came ashore. But I'm pretty sure he laid up off Dog Island for a few days last week."

Peety Boy put his hands on the counter and leaned forward. Fish blood stained his thick nails and work-scarred fingers, and, as he put weight on his hands, hard cords of muscle jumped and strained beneath thin parched skin on his forearms. He said, "You say this is a friend of yours?"

Peety Boy's watery black eyes drilled through my face and into my thoughts. Country isn't stupid. Uneducated isn't stupid.

Peety Boy had my number. I said, "No. It's just easier to say a friend than to tell everything I know to everyone I ask. I'm looking for a large boat, probably a yacht, that was in the area last week. It's for a real friend. A young girl who's in trouble."

The old man's face relaxed. He straightened up and reached over to pull a wooden stool up to the counter. He perched his thin rump on the stool, poked a Camel non-filter between a pair of dry chapped lips, and lit the end with a Zippo. Through a cloud of gray smoke, he said, "That's fine. How long you been lookin'?"

"A few days. But this is my first day here on the island."

He chuckled, but there wasn't much pleasure in it. "You go around askin' questions like that 'un, and it'll probably be your last day here too." He paused and looked out across the basketball court and the parking lot at the Gulf of Mexico. "Tell you what. I'm gonna fill you in, and I'm mostly doin' it 'cause you're gonna get messed up if I don't. And, the way I see it, if you're lookin' after a friend, that's the right way to go. So listen up. Don't ask nobody else about this stuff, and don't tell nobody you talked to me. If you promise that, I'll tell you who I think can help you out."

"I can do that. I'm not looking for trouble."

Peety Boy looked out at the water some more, then he said, "Get in your car and drive over to Eastpoint. You just go back across the causeway and take the first right. There's a line of little seafood houses over there. Places where they buy the catch off the boats and sell it to tourists. Same thing I do, only they ain't as particular about how old some of it is. You go to a place called Teeter's and ask to talk to Billy Teeter. Tell him I sent you. Don't tell nobody else. Just tell Billy. If he ain't there, you ask when he'll be back. You got that?" I told him I had it and thanked him. He said, "Well, that's all right."

I pushed two fingers inside my waistband and fished out a wet fifty from the inside pocket. As I looked up, I noticed a bumper sticker over Peety Boy's cutting board for the first time. It read, *God is love.* I said, "Can I pay you? Believe me, it's worth it to me."

He looked down at my wet money and said, "No, sir."

I thought for a few seconds and said, "Can I buy fifty dollars' worth of shrimp from you?"

Peety Boy looked doubtful. "Yessir. You can do that. How you gonna get it home?"

"I'll come back for it." He didn't look like he believed me. I said, "I'm going to be on the island for a few days. If there's any way possible, I'll stop on the way home and pick up the shrimp. If I run into trouble or I have to return home in a hurry, then next weekend I want you to give fifty dollars' worth of seafood to the next young couple who comes by. Is that a deal?"

Peety Boy thought a bit and said, "Yessir. That's all right."

And I felt good—for about ten seconds.

chapter twelve

As I stood there trying to convince Peety Boy to take my money, I had unrolled the soaked fifty and pressed it against my T-shirt with my palm. I had squeezed a rectangle of water into my shirt and managed to flatten the bill back into shape before pressing it into Peety Boy's hard palm. That felt good. Seeing Deputy Mickey Burns cruise by when I turned to leave did not.

Burns' cruiser moved at that intimidating snail-pace cops use to make you feel like you're under surveillance and like you've done something wrong, if only you could remember what it was. I waved and got the universal cop nod in response. I decided to jog back to my pastel palace along Gorrie Drive where I would be in plain view of the island traffic, which, as it turned out, consisted of one four-wheel-drive convertible with two dark-suited, Hispanic-looking businessmen inside, what appeared to be an old lady trudging along deep inside a straw hat, dark glasses, and a flowing dashiki, and three dogs. Two of the dogs barked and growled and chased me for a few feet to spice up their day. Otherwise, the trip was uneventful.

I had reached the top of the wooden steps and was fishing inside my waistband for my rented key when I saw him step out from the tall space under the house. Sonny, the almost mute, eye-jumping painter walked up the stairs behind me. When he was four steps away, he hung back like someone who had been kicked down stairs before. "Go on inside. It ain't locked."

As Sonny spoke, he swiveled his right hip toward me and showed me the butt of a handgun sticking out of his pocket. The movement looked a little effeminate. I decided not to tell him.

I pushed open the door and stepped inside my own little pastel hell. A familiar-looking man sat in a rattan chair padded with green and peach puffs of printed seashells. Carli had given me a pretty good description. He did in fact look like a weight lifter or an ex-jock going to fat. My young client didn't know it, but she had seen a pretty famous guy shoot another man in the mouth. Leroy Purcell, former All-American running back for the University of Florida, used gridiron-scarred, oversized hands to push out of the chair. If I hadn't known he'd taken out a knee his last year with the Cowboys, I don't think I would have noticed that he favored it getting up.

Purcell seemed to be trying for a Florida resort look. He wore a blond crew cut—waxed straight up in front—and an expensive set of golfer's duds. His problem was that the wardrobe didn't much go with the scarred gash across his chin, or his twenty-inch neck, or the overwhelming sense of controlled violence that seemed to radiate from every pore.

He rose to his full height and said my least favorite sentence in the English language. "Do you know who I am?"

I said, "You used to be some kind of jock, didn't you?"

Purcell looked disgusted. "My name is Leroy Purcell. And, yeah, I was some kind of jock. I was the kind who played tailback for Florida and spent five seasons with the Dallas Cowboys."

I really did not like this guy. "Congratulations. What can I do for you?"

He turned deep red. "I'm not used to being talked to that way."

And, I thought, I'm not used to entertaining murderers. I said, "I didn't invite you here. You and Harpo here broke in because you wanted to see me, and you think I'm supposed to be impressed by who you are. Fine. I'm impressed. Now tell me what you want."

This, I thought, *is not going well.* Over the past week, I had been shot at; Susan had been shot at; her house had been vandalized; my life, Susan's life, and Carli's life had been turned upside down; and a frightened, abused teenage girl had been traumatized beyond description. It all came pouring in on me. I breathed deeply and tried to regain control.

I repeated, "What do you want?"

I was not the only one starting to lose it. Leroy Purcell said, "You're not exactly impressing the shit out of me either, McInnes." I looked at him. "I came here to talk business."

"So, talk."

"Are you this big an asshole with everyone, or do you think you know something about me in particular?"

"I'm this big of an asshole with everyone."

"Well, asshole, we're going for a little ride."

"I don't think so. You want to shoot me, then shoot me. But I'm not going to get in a car and go anywhere with you two."

"I could have Sonny make you."

I turned and looked at Sonny. His eyes were bouncing around the room, never really looking at me but keeping me in view somehow. I said, "I doubt it," and Sonny's eyes stopped ricocheting and focused.

Purcell said, "I know about you, McInnes. I've taken the time to know about you. I hear you're some kinda minor league hard-ass. But old Sonny here is major league. You might say he's a professional." I shrugged. Purcell smiled, but it wasn't pretty. "You need to come with us. If you do, you'll be fine. We're just going up to The Plantation. If you won't come, Sonny's gonna put a bullet in your ass."

"I guess I'll come then."

Purcell said, "I thought you would."

"In case you're wondering, it was that 'bullet in the ass' line that did the trick. That sounds like it would hurt."

No one thought I was funny.

Purcell drove my Jeep—he already had the keys—while Sonny and I sat in back. The back windows on a Jeep Cherokee are tinted dark. Sonny had drawn his hip gun and was keeping it leveled at my rib cage. As we approached the gate, Sonny took off his cap and placed it on the seat. Then he used his free hand to pull an old-fashioned switchblade out of his left hip pocket. He pressed the point of the blade deep enough into my side to just break the skin and then put the gun away and placed his cap over his knife hand. Behind tinted windows, no one outside would be able to tell I was a flick of Sonny's hand away from a punctured lung. Purcell was right. Sonny seemed pretty professional.

The guardhouse came up on the left, and Sonny said, "Don't say nothin'."

The overstuffed guard's uniform shuffled to the car, was visibly and loudly impressed with Leroy Purcell's presence, and waved us through. I assumed Purcell or one of his capos had a house on the island and that was where we were going. I was wrong. We went to Susan's beach house, and I was relieved not to see an old Ford pickup sticking out of the carport.

We trudged up the wooden steps single file, and Sonny kicked in Susan's front door while Purcell and I watched. When the door splintered and swung open, Sonny limped to one side, and Purcell strutted in ahead of us like an African chieftain at a war council.

Sonny said, "Inside." He had his gun out again, and it was pointed at me. I sighed and followed Purcell.

Purcell said, "This is more like it. Where does she keep the liquor?" I didn't answer, which seemed to upset Sonny because he rapped me on the shoulder with the butt of his revolver. That was enough. I turned and hit Sonny on the bridge of his nose with a straight right that had six months of anger and frustration and wanting to hit someone behind it. Sonny went down. Then he came up again with blood pouring from both nostrils and every intention of killing me where I stood. Purcell yelled, "Stop!"

Sonny looked pleadingly at Purcell, who said, "Did I tell you to hit him?" Sonny shook his bloody face and dripped red on the carpet. "I told you I wanted to talk to this man, and I wanted to impress him that we are serious. When I need your help impressing him, I'll tell you. You got that?"

Sonny nodded this time and dripped more blood on Susan's rug.

I said, "Can he sit up and beg?"

Purcell looked pissed. "Shut the fuck up, McInnes."

"It's your party."

Leroy Purcell walked over to the kitchen, snatched a roll of paper towels out of its holder over the sink, and tossed it to Sonny. While Sonny put pressure on his flowing red nose, Purcell located a bottle of bourbon and mixed it with ice and Coke from the refrigerator. He walked over and sat in a chair with its back to Susan's bright view of the Gulf. He said, "Sit down." I didn't see any reason not to, so I sat on the sofa and looked out at the beach. Purcell said, "Now, this is more like it. That fucking place you're staying is for shit." He gestured at the room. "These people got some goddamn taste." He sipped his sweetened bourbon. "Tell me, McInnes, what do you think you know about me that makes you so pissed off?" I looked at him. "What does Susan Fitzsimmons tell you about me?"

I said, "Who is Susan Fitzpatrick?"

"Funny." He said, "Susan Fitz*simmons* owns this house, and she's a client of yours. And I think that you think she and that white trash waitress from the Pelican's Roost may have seen something last Wednesday night at a house down the beach from here." He stopped for me to agree with him. I picked up a throw pillow and put it behind my head. He said, "I'm here to work something out. I really don't know what your clients saw or didn't see. I'm just here for some friends who don't want any trouble. What I want is to meet with Fitzsimmons and the girl and straighten this out."

"Explain the problem to me. What are you going to straighten out?"

"Then she is your client."

I repeated, "What are you going to straighten out?" He didn't answer. I said, "You know what I think? I think you're scared shitless because you think someone saw you up to no good, and you don't know how to find them. Look, I admit Susan Fitzsimmons has been both my client and my friend for a long time. If you've got half a brain, you could find that out in an hour anyway. But she's never laid eyes on you, and, if I have anything to say about it, she never will."

"So you're not going to let me meet with her?"

"Nope."

Purcell rose up out of the chair. "Maybe I should convince you."

"Maybe you should kiss my ass."

He walked toward me. I sat still. The former football hero stopped a foot from the sofa and took in a deep breath. "McInnes, all I want is a meeting. And all you gotta do is say yes. It'll save your client a load of grief down the road. And it'll save you an ass whipping right now. Think about it." He smiled. The man was thinking about hurting me, and it seemed to put him in a better mood. "Hell, McInnes, I can see you're a pretty good-sized guy. Probably push around the Nautilus machines pretty good. Probably in a spinning class down at the fags-are-us sportsplex. But you caught Sonny by surprise. If I hadn't stopped him, you'd be dead now. And you need to understand that, even if you think you're tough, I got fifty pounds of muscle on you and Sonny."

I said, "You've got fifty pounds hanging over your belt," and, as soon as I got the words out, I realized I might have gone too far.

I could feel the violence arcing like static electricity between Purcell and Sonny over my head. I could see him breathing hard, trying to regain control.

Purcell raised his glass and downed what was left of his drink in one swallow; then he turned and threw the empty glass at the kitchen sink from across the room. The crystal tumbler hit dead center on the stainless steel sink and exploded on impact.

Purcell's eyes moved around the room and over Susan's things. He was thinking; he was breathing deeply and thinking. Finally, he said, "You don't understand what the fuck you're in, McInnes. You may not believe it, but me and Sonny are about the most reasonable people you're gonna meet on this thing."

"Yeah." I said, "You and Sonny got *reasonable* written all over you."

Purcell huffed and shook his head. "Boy, there's tough and there's bad and there's just plain evil. Old Sonny there is tough. I'm tougher, and I got a Super Bowl ring to prove it. But we can bring somebody into this thing who—believe me—would scare the living shit out of the toughest sonofabitch I ever saw on a football field. I make a phone call and say it's out of my hands, you're gonna get to meet a mean-ass spic who'll slice you open and play with your guts while you're still alive and watching. Crazy fuck'll do the same and worse—perverted sex stuff with knives and spikes, shit like that—to the Fitzsimmons woman *and* that trailer-trash girl." He paused before he said, "This is your last chance to settle this normal."

Purcell paused again to let me think about that. And I did, but the whole thing sounded like a lame horror story concocted to scare me into bad judgment—not to mention my concerns with Leroy Purcell's definition of "normal." The threats were over the top. They were ridiculous. But . . . Purcell said this alleged boogeyman was Hispanic, and the cold puffy stare of the fat guy on Dog Island kept haunting me.

I shook it off. "Bedtime stories."

Purcell looked surprised. "Huh?"

I explained. "You're full of shit."

Leroy Purcell pulled a nickel-plated Colt .45 out of his waistband and chopped at my face with the barrel. I ducked and he missed, and it occurred to me that maybe I should have let him hit me. Maybe it would have been better to let him vent some violence without pulling a trigger.

Purcell raised the .45 again but not to swing it. He pointed the muzzle at my face and cocked the hammer. The room grew still. Purcell breathed hard against an adrenaline rush, and in the short eternity between his breaths—when I waited for the bullet aimed at my eyes—the only other sound was the soft hum of Susan's refrigerator.

The room faded. I was focused on the gun in Purcell's giant hand, and my only conscious thought was to wonder why I hadn't noticed the refrigerator noise before.

The moment passed, and a dark mist seemed to lift. The battle-scared ex-jock rolled his shoulders to relax the muscles in his thick neck. He said, "Sonny?"

"Yessir." Sonny sounded excited now.

"You got the lighter fluid?"

"Yessir."

"Use it."

Sonny appeared in the corner of my eye. I kept looking at the volcanic muzzle of Purcell's .45. Sonny moved to the wall opposite Susan's circular stairs and stopped in front of Bird Fitzsimmons' wall-sized painting of seashells. Now I looked. Sonny pulled a yellow and blue squeeze can of lighter fluid from his back pocket.

"That painting's worth a fortune. The artist is dead." It was a stupid thing to say, but it was what I said. I looked up at Purcell. He had backed off a step and lowered the muzzle to point at my chest. The Saturday cookout smell of charcoal lighter fluid filled the room, and I looked over to see Sonny squirting the painting in big dripping circles.

Purcell said, "We're done here. You can leave if you want to." I sat still. He walked over to the painting and pulled a Zippo from his pocket like the one Peety Boy had used to light his Camel. "Just remember, all you got to do is set up a meeting with the Fitzsimmons woman and the waitress. We'll work everything out, and they'll be safe." He spun the little black wheel on the lighter with his thumb and turned the flame all the way up. "You tell 'em. Nobody's safe. Nothing they got is safe until we work this out."

And Leroy Purcell, former All-American tailback for the University of Florida, set fire to Susan's most cherished remnant of her dead husband's talented life.

I shot off the sofa and ran toward the deck, and they let me. Sonny and Purcell were already on their way out the back when I got the double doors open.

Behind me, flames shot eight feet in the air, scorching the walls and threatening the house. The painting was engulfed in fire. Unable to grasp it bare-handed, I grabbed a lamp and swung it in a hard upward arc against the lower edge of the painting. The flaming square flew off the wall and crashed onto the carpeted floor as I jumped out of the way. The top left corner was untouched. I gripped it and ran across the carpet and through the doors and swung a double handful of flames over the railing and onto the sand below.

Back inside, the carpet smoked, and the wall was too hot to touch. I splashed pans of water on everything and called the fire department.

Then I called Susan.

chapter thirteen

THE FLIRTATION WAS gone. Susan sounded dead inside. "I know it's just a painting, Tom. And I'm so thankful that you're okay. But . . . oh God, Tom. What do we do now?"

"Well, we damn sure don't agree to let you and Carli meet with him. I'm going to put Joey on it. We'll bug Purcell's house and where he works and every other damn thing we can think of to find out what he's up to. And, if he even gets close to hurting you or Carli, we'll kill the sonofabitch." Susan didn't respond. I was mad and getting carried away, and Susan understood and let me do it. It's what angry, overwhelmed males do instead of crying. I took a few breaths. "Susan, I know and you know you're reacting to more than a ruined painting. Even if it was one of Bird's best. So go ahead and feel bad for a while, and let me take care of this. I know it doesn't look like I'm doing much of a job so far. But every time I stumble into a mess, we know a little more." I stopped and tried to focus. "I'm going to get off and call Joey now. Take care of yourself and take care of Carli. I'll see you in a few days. And, by the way, I'm going to take you up on your offer to stay in your house here on the island. I don't seem to be especially invisible in my little house down the beach, and it'll save us eight hundred a week for me to stay here." She agreed, and we said good-bye.

It was past five, so I decided it was okay to locate a bottle of scotch and pour some in a glass. I sat on the sofa and waited for the Appalachicola Volunteer Fire Department. Thirty-two minutes after I dialed 911, half a dozen barbers, merchants, and mechanics came rushing through Susan's kicked-in door in full fireproof regalia. We talked. A couple of them felt the wall. One checked out the electrical system, as best he could. We talked some more, and I almost told them about Leroy Purcell. But I realized it would be my word against his. And it occurred to me that the worst he'd face was financial responsibility for what he would almost certainly claim was an accidental fire.

Whether it made sense or not, I decided to hold off inserting the law into my relationship with Purcell. So I told the part-time firemen of Appalachicola that I'd been trying to remove a smudge from the frame around the painting with some cleaning fluid I had found under the kitchen sink. I said I'd stopped to light a cigar and the whole thing went up in flames. That seemed to satisfy them. They got to give me a lecture, and I got to keep my run-in with Purcell private.

After the firemen departed, I sat and sipped my scotch and realized that maybe I didn't want anyone to know that I wanted Leroy Purcell dead. Right then—at that moment—I wanted and expected something terrible to happen to Purcell in the future, and, when it did, I didn't want anyone looking too closely at me.

Joey answered his cell phone on the second ring. "Yeah?"

I said, "It's me."

"What's wrong?"

"How'd you know something was wrong?"

An edge had crept into Joey's voice. It was as close as he ever got to sounding panicked. "Are the women okay?"

"Oh. Yeah. Yeah, Loutie and her guests are fine. I'm over on St. George at Susan's house. I had some trouble."

"You sound like your puppy died. And I thought you were gonna stay away from Susan's house. Hell, you should've known they'd be looking there, Tom. I mean, shit, I'm guessing you're okay, or I wouldn't be running off at the mouth. You are okay, aren't you?"

"Yeah, Joey. I'm fine. I'm about as pissed off as I've ever been in my life, but I'm fine."

"As pissed as you've ever been is pretty pissed."

I didn't say anything.

"What do you need?"

"Is our boy Haycock in his cottage?"

"He's there, and he's got a little stringy-haired woman in there with him. I sneaked up to the house and checked on 'em a little while ago and was sorry I did. The two of 'em were buck naked and tangled up, banging away like a couple of stray dogs. I'm telling you, after seeing that, I need to go watch some hogs humping to put the romance back in my life."

"So it looks like he's staying put for a while?"

"Yeah," Joey said. "I don't think he's going anywhere tonight."

"Come over, then. We've got a lot to talk about."

I hadn't thought about the ferry and whether Joey could even get off the island. More than an hour after Purcell's and Sonny's exit, I was still pumping too much adrenaline to think about much but murder. So I wasn't surprised when Joey walked into Susan's charred living room.

I was sitting in the chair Purcell had used. Joey stopped in the middle of the room and surveyed the black mess where Bird Fitzsimmons' painting had hung. "What the hell happened?" I raised a glass of scotch, tipped it at him, and took a swallow. "Damn. When you told me you had some trouble, I figured you got your ass whipped or something. What'd they do? Try to burn the place down?"

"You ever hear of a prick named Leroy Purcell? Used to play for the Cowboys."

"Yeah. He's a scumbag." My giant friend paused and looked stunned. "Purcell was here? He did that?"

"Yeah. He was here, and he set fire to Susan's favorite painting by her dead husband. And came real close to burning the whole place down. It's supposed to be a lesson about what he'll do to everything Susan owns if she and Carli don't meet with him to discuss the guy he murdered in front of Carli."

Joey stood and walked to the kitchen. When he came back he had a glass full of ice cubes, which he covered with amber whiskey from my half-empty bottle.

"Shit, Tom. I've been hearing rumors about Leroy Purcell ever since he left the pros. It's pretty much common knowledge he likes to hang out with hoods and gamblers and that he's gotten ass deep in a lot of shady deals down here in Florida." Joey stopped to turn up his glass. He was not a sipper. Joey drank scotch the way he drank beer and orange juice and everything else. He swallowed a mouthful of whiskey and said, "The guy had about a million opportunities to make an honest living when he came back from the pros. They love the bastard down here. But, word is, he likes the action. Likes the dangerous reputation." Joey clinked the ice in his glass and looked out at the night. "So it was Purcell who Carli saw shoot that guy in the beach house?"

"Yep."

Joey cussed, and shook his head, and drank more scotch.

I asked, "Can you let go of watching Haycock for a few days?"

"I can do whatever you need me to do."

"I want to know what Purcell's doing. I want to know who he talks to, where he goes, and who he's sleeping with. I want to know everything I can about what he's up to. Because we've got to know if he's getting close to finding Susan and Carli."

"I'll bury him in bugs. Get his house and his car. Tap his phones. But I'm gonna need to pull Loutie off guard duty to help with this if you want me to keep covering Haycock. I can put another man on Susan and Carli if you want."

"Yeah. Do that. The whole point is to keep them safe. In the meantime, we've got to find a way to stop Purcell for good."

Joey looked up. "Short of killing him." I didn't say anything, and Joey noticed. He seemed to think about that, then he asked, "Did you report him setting the fire?"

"No."

Joey thought a little while longer. "Does anyone know you two had this run-in?"

I said, "Just the guy who helped him set it," and Joey slowly nodded his head. Joey knew that Susan didn't need or deserve any more pain in her life. If it came to it, Joey would snap Purcell's neck without thought or regret. Now, though, as the *idea* of murderous revenge turned real, I began to hope it wouldn't come to that.

Joey shook his head. "Ain't this some shit?"

Joey was eloquent, and he was right. This was indeed some shit. I said, "You think your buddies on the Panama City force could tell us whether Purcell is mixed up with the Bodines?"

Joey stood and walked to the kitchen phone. He punched in a number and spoke quietly into the mouthpiece.

A fresh whiskey and I walked out on the deck. Bird's seashells were ash, but their charcoal frame drew a black square in the sand where it had landed and burned. Small flaps of charred canvas ruffled and skitted down the beach ahead of the breeze and disappeared into the dusk. Leaving my drink untouched on the railing, I wandered back inside as Joey was thanking Detective Coosa for his help.

I looked at him. "Well?"

"The rumor is Purcell *runs* the Bodines up there around Panama City. Coosa didn't know anything about Appalachicola."

"Okay, then see if you can find out who runs the Bodines down here. We need to know whether Purcell is *the* King of the Jethros or just one of several. I want to know if he's messing around in somebody else's backyard. Can you do that?"

"Probably. One way or another." Joey sat back on the sofa. "Look, I got something else to tell you. I got a name on the fat guy Haycock smuggled in." He paused to drain his drink. "It took a few tries to get to the desk at Captain Casey's Inn without somebody around, but last night I checked out the card file—they ain't even got a computer. It's gonna turn out to be some kinda alias, but the guy's name on the card was 'L. Carpintero.'" Joey spelled the last name. "Mean anything to you?"

"Nope. But I'll make a note. It may fit in somewhere if we find out something else."

Joey got up to leave, and I walked with him to the door. He asked why he hadn't seen my Jeep outside when he drove up. I told him about Purcell commandeering the vehicle, and he offered to get me a car. I shook my head. I could have one brought over in the morning.

At the door, Joey hesitated. "It never would've entered my head that Leroy Purcell would be blowing people away. I thought he just liked hanging out with hoods. Trying to look tough."

"Murder and arson with Sonny the Psycho to back him up. Not to mention him threatening teenage girls. Not exactly what I'd call tough." I said, "A real All-American, huh?"

Joey said, "Yeah, a real All-American asshole."

Susan had abandoned her house in a hurry. The bathrooms were ready for the morning shower she took instead at Loutie's house after fleeing killers in her own home. I lay on Susan's bed and breathed in the smell of her and tried to think. Outside, through the windows I had stood before while Susan slept, the sunset splashed the horizon with oranges and pinks and purples and streaked the ocean with jagged ripples of molten silver and gold. I rolled off the bed, stripped, walked into the bathroom, and turned on the shower. As the water began to heat and steam clouded the ceiling, I looked at the guy in the mirror. I wasn't impressed.

The shower felt good, and it kept on feeling good until Susan's water heater was drained and tepid. I found a box with some of Bird's old clothes in it and put them on. My stuff was back on the guest room bed at pastel hell, and I didn't feel like hiking.

Back downstairs, I found my unfinished drink and poured it over the weathered banister and into the sand below. Sharp white pricks dotted the eastern sky above a smudged black horizon, and the approaching night washed the sky with charcoals that faded overhead to the soft gray tones of summer flannel. In the west, the last thin blue tint of daylight hung in a crescent-shaped curtain above the horizon.

I went in search of a hammer and nails, which I found in a combination laundry and storage room under the stilted house. After nailing Sonny's kicked-in door shut, I went to bed. Susan's pillow held the soft feminine scents of her shampoo and cologne and makeup and some other girl smell I couldn't identify. An overwhelming loneliness enveloped me like a physical presence, and I fell asleep.

I was up before the sun with more than four hours sleep, but less than I'd had the night before. It was as if my mind were signaling that my level of screwed-upness had digressed, but not to the depths I had occupied before finding some sort of redemption in helping Susan and Carli.

I washed my face, ate a few bites of a hard aged croissant from Susan's refrigerator, and stuck out along the bright morning beach in the direction of my pastel palace. Purcell had returned my Jeep to the parking space beneath the house. Inside, I half expected the place to be stained somehow with Purcell's intrusion, but everything was the way it had been since I arrived. I changed out of Bird's clothes and into a pair of jeans and a faded red pullover. I traded sandy running shoes for New Balance cross trainers, packed up, and left. My plan was to drive over to Eastpoint and look for Peety Boy's friend Billy Teeter.

I tossed my duffel in the backseat. The keys were in the ignition, and an envelope had been snapped under the windshield wiper like a parking ticket. I was inside the Jeep when I saw it. Stepping out, I pulled up the wiper and lifted out a white business envelope gone floppy with salt spray from a night facing the waves. The moist envelope tore easily and unevenly. It held a single sheet of copy paper.

Report on Carli Monroe (alias)

Name: Carli Poultrez *Age: 15*

Hair: Black *Eyes: Brown* *Approx: 5'4", 110 lbs.*

Poultrez is a runaway minor from Gloucester, Massachusetts. (Address: 2128 Cleaverhead Road.) She has a record going back three years as a repeat runaway. Her father, Russell (Rus) Poultrez, owns and operates a fishing vessel out of Gloucester.

Rus Poultrez - Contact Report

That was it. Before making the copy, someone had placed two large Post-it notes over the rest of the page, including, I guessed, the name and signature of the investigator. Also, I could see the outline of a smaller Post-it at the top covering a letterhead.

I removed my keys from the ignition and went back inside to call Susan with more bad news. When she answered, she sounded a little better than she had the night before.

I asked, "How's Carli?"

Susan said, "She seems fine. But then, she always does. This has to be wearing on her, though."

"How are you?"

"A lot better. Thanks. I'd kind of like to see you, even though I know that's not really in the cards right now. But I wanted you to know that I want to. Losing 'Scattered Shells' was difficult for me because I'll always love Bird. But that doesn't mean I'm not ready to see you and enjoy being with you." She hesitated. "Unless I'm taking too much for granted."

"You're not." And she wasn't, but, for some reason, she was making me uncomfortable. I retreated into the business at hand. "I'm sorry to do this to you, but I'm afraid I have some more disturbing news. Purcell knows who Carli is."

"Yes, you told me that last night. You said he's looking for both of us."

"No. You don't understand. He knows who Carli *really* is." I told her what the report said. I also suggested that I'd rather deliver the news to Carli in person, so I could advise her on how to proceed.

"Are you coming back then?"

"Probably tomorrow. Today, I've got to go find an old shrimper named Billy Teeter."

"There's a seafood shack over in Eastpoint called Teeter's."

"That's the guy."

"You may as well go get some breakfast then. The places over there that open on Sunday don't open until one. You know. Church."

I told Susan again I'd see her Monday or Tuesday, and hung up.

The island had five restaurant-slash-bars, and they all had signs advertising Sunday brunch. I chose the Pelican's Roost, where Carli had worked. Susan said it was good, and I thought that I probably needed to look around the place sooner or later anyway. So I turned in and parked in the gravel lot and stepped back out into the warm morning air.

A pair of plateglass windows stared blankly out at the parking lot from either side of the front door. I turned the knob and stepped inside. The waiting area was the bar, but there was no wait. Another nut-brown waitress—this one with long brown hair and crow's feet—led me up narrow steps to the second floor, which was furnished with a dozen or so round tables and two long picnic benches hidden beneath plastic, red-and-white-checked tablecloths. Wide, crank-out windows lined both long walls, and a door in the short front wall led out onto a small balcony or deck overlooking the parking lot and a crowded queue of beach houses across the way. Ocean breeze wafted in through open windows on one wall and out through matching windows on the opposite wall.

All in all, the place was simple and more pleasant than it sounds.

Seven or eight people were scattered among the tables. My suntanned waitress smiled and patted my back in a mildly flirtatious way and suggested that I might want to eat out on the deck. I said okay, and she led me out and deposited me near the right front corner where I had a narrow view of the water between two rows of anorectic, architecturally strident sliver-houses.

After she left, I looked out at the distant wedge of water for a while. I moved on to an examination of the skinny vacation houses and the mostly deserted street. I watched a bouncing, tube-topped jogger until she was out of sight. Finally, I glanced down at the parking lot.

This was not going to be an enjoyable meal. There, in the driver's seat of a Cobra convertible, sat gun-toting, knife-poking, paint-dribbling Sonny. And he was watching me with those jittery, psychotic eyes of his.

chapter fourteen

EITHER SONNY WAS scaling new heights of incompetency, or I was supposed to know he was following me. The Cobra's top was down, and he had parked only ten or twelve feet from my Jeep in an otherwise empty section of the lot. So, considering how rattled I guessed I was supposed to be by Sonny's blatant disrespect for my privacy, I had three obvious alternatives. One, I could get mad and beat him about the head and shoulders, which would net me either an arrest or an ass whipping. Two, I could respect his wishes and panic, which was what Purcell was counting on. Or, three, I could decide to mess with him.

Sonny may have been a professional thug, but he still looked like a dumb-ass to me.

When my waitress returned, I ordered steak and eggs with an English muffin and a double order of cheese grits on the side. Contrary to popular belief outside the South, if properly prepared and eaten while steaming hot, cheese grits are actually pretty damn good and almost identical to polenta, which every pseudo-sophisticate in the country likes to see piled next to grilled medallions of veal. But in this instance, I didn't much care whether the grits were well made, and I purposely let them chill into a thick glutenous mass while I forked beef and eggs into my mouth.

I was full. Time to make grit bombs. I pulled four paper napkins from the dispenser on my table and put three large dollops of cheese grits on each napkin. My waitress came out and gave me a concerned look. I said, "Saving them for later." She smiled the way people smile at paranoid schizophrenics in Central Park and went back inside.

As I pulled the napkins' four corners up and around each grit wad and twisted the ends together, Sonny looked up and gave me a self-satisfied grin, and, for the first time, I noticed the blurry prison tattoo Joey had described. On Sonny's left arm was a large, deep-blue dagger with three letters above its handle and three more beneath its point. I couldn't make out the initials, but they had to be the *R.I.P.* and *R.E.T.* Joey had seen on Haycock's partner that violent night in the parking lot of Mother's Milk in Appalachicola.

I smiled back at him. *Good to see you too, asshole.* Something seemed to catch the corner of Sonny's eye, and he turned toward the bike path running next to the street to check out a plump blonde in a thong. As he turned away, I completed my first package by dunking it in ice water just before I stood, took aim, and literally creamed him behind his left ear.

The man said some really bad words.

While he screamed, I dunked the second grit ball. He ducked. *This*, I thought, *is fun.* I let him duck. This sticky handful was headed for the center of his shiny black hood. It hit with a deeply satisfying thud and splattered like a baseball-sized wad of pelican droppings. Sonny jumped up from behind the dash to see what had happened. I was waiting. *Damn.* I missed him and sent a thick schmear of cheese grits across his leather seats.

Sonny went nuts. The car door flew open, and he jumped out onto the gravel parking lot, screaming, flailing his arms, and generally cussing a lot. His sentences were liberally sprinkled, I noticed, with the words "kill" and "dead" and seemed to be directed at me and those I hold dear. I dunked the last grit ball and let it fly. He tried to catch it—no doubt intending to send it back my way—but you can't really catch a wet paper napkin full of grit paste. It exploded in his hand, splattering a nicely formed pattern of cheese grits across his face, neck, and chest. That just about did it. Sonny charged the restaurant through the front door downstairs.

I had already dropped twenty dollars on the table. No reason to stick around now. I picked up my steak knife, stepped over the railing, and carefully dropped eight or nine feet to the ground. My knees would pay later, but now I was too pumped to care.

Pulling keys from my pocket, I sprinted over to Sonny's forty-thousand-dollar Mustang, plunged the serrated steak knife into the side of his tire, twisted with all my strength, and left it there. I had turned back toward the Jeep and had just shot the doors open with the remote when I heard a murderous yell from the restaurant deck. I caught a blur of Sonny jumping as I scrambled into the Jeep and jammed the key in the ignition. *Good Jeep.* It cranked and, flooring the gas even before I found reverse, I spewed a dusty semicircle of bleached gravel and broken shells across the parking lot. As I dropped the transmission into drive, I hazarded a glance at what I was sure would be Sonny crouched in a shooter's stance, unloading a full clip in my direction. What I saw instead was Sonny rolling on his back in sand and gravel, holding his left knee in the air and gripping it with both hands. His mouth gaped open, his face burned red, and tendons strained beneath the thin skin on his neck. He seemed to be screaming, but by then I was gone.

I was looking at maybe forty-five minutes to an hour before Sonny reported my escape to Purcell. First, the pain and the anger would have to subside to a point that would allow rational thought, or whatever Sonny used instead. Then Sonny would have to think of a way to explain to his boss that I got away by attacking him with an arsenal of cheese grits.

Hell, it might take more than an hour.

Only a hundred yards down, I swerved right onto the causeway and backed off on the gas. I didn't think Sonny would or even could follow, but, whether he could or not, a two-lane road with deep, choppy water on each side is no place to play chase. Better to be caught, I thought, than wind up breathing salt water with my headlights buried in the sandy bottom.

But he didn't catch me or, as far as I could see, even try, and after four miles of glancing back and forth from the wide pavement ahead to the narrow strip of blacktop in my rearview mirror, I rolled onto the mainland—tailless. Less than a quarter mile in, a county road angled off to the right. I followed it through stands of scruffy coastal pines into the quintessential shrimping village of Eastpoint.

The right side of the road was perfect—jumbled, rusting, ramshackle, and everything a seafaring town should be. Tin-roofed seafood shacks and shrimp-processing plants fronted the street and backed up to long, concrete docks that reached out into Appalachicola Bay like gray fingers separated by oily water and a scattering of white shrimp boats with red and blue trim.

Unfortunately, across the road from the local shrimp entrepreneurs, the place got ugly fast. A plastic orange Citgo station squatted next to a new brick-and-plateglass Piggly Wiggly, which led to a blue plastic gas station that offered a free car wash with each fill-up. I decided Peety Boy's friend Billy Teeter would have a place on the water—as much because that's the direction I wanted to look as anything—so that's were I concentrated my search. Although, considering that one can drive completely through Eastpoint in less than five minutes, "search" may be a more impressive description than the process warranted.

Maybe two minutes after leaving the causeway, Teeter's came up on the right. I wasn't much worried now about Sonny. Even if he had recovered from his hurt knee and stabbed tire, he would assume I had turned west toward Appalachicola, Panama City, and Mobile. Just to be sure, though, I checked the mirror once more for his psychotic presence before pulling up onto a sandy parking area just deep enough to hold the Jeep without donating a bumper to passing traffic.

Teeter's seafood shack was just that—unpainted, weathered boards beneath a rusted tin roof and a sagging front porch made for sitting. Two aluminum patio chairs flanked the door. A youngish woman sat in one. An old man suitable for casting in *Captains Courageous* lounged in the other.

With miles of sapphire waters, distant islands, and endless blue skies stretched out behind them, these locals spent their days watching traffic pass in front of a Citgo station.

I cut the engine, stepped out onto the sandy yard, and walked two steps to the bottom of Teeter's three wooden steps. The woman spoke. "How you doin' today?"

I told her I was just fine, and that seemed to genuinely please her. I said, "Peety Boy sent me over here."

The old man perked up. "Me and Peety Boy grew up together." He smiled, and a mouthful of tobacco stained teeth peeked out shyly from the thick brown and gray brush that obscured his face from the nostrils and cheekbones down.

I asked, "Are you Billy Teeter?"

"Yessir, that I am."

The young woman said, "You got the right place. Peety Boy sends folks over all the time when he ain't got something they want. You just come on inside, we got fresh shrimp off the boat this morning. Fresh oysters. Crabs. Crab legs. And we got some frozen crab cakes that taste like something you got off the menu at a restaurant."

I smiled. The old man looked happy to sit and talk, but this young one was looking for a sale. I said, "I might be interested in looking at that in a minute, but Peety Boy sent me over here because I need some information about who might have been out on the bay the other night. He said Billy Teeter would be able to help if anyone could."

The old man looked at the younger woman and said, "Go on in and shuck some of them oysters. We're gonna have plenty of folks coming by after church." But, before he had even spoken, the woman was on her feet and headed inside. I couldn't decide whether she intended to confer privately or just didn't want to be part of what we were going to talk about. The old man said, "What'd Peety Boy volunteer me for?" As he spoke, Billy Teeter sat forward in his chipped metal chair, pulled off his *Bubba Gump Shrimp* cap, slicked a few long strands of gray hair back over his spotted bald pate, and resettled the cap.

"Mr. Teeter, Peety Boy didn't volunteer you. He just said you were somebody I could ask about boats in Appalachicola Bay without getting into trouble for asking.

"My name is Tom McInnes, and I'm from Mobile. I'm trying to find out if any boats just up from Central or South America might have been laying off Dog Island one night last week." Teeter harrumphed. I've always read about people harrumphing, but never knew exactly what that was until that old shrimper did it. I was losing him. When I had become nothing but a memory for the old man, he would have to go on living there on the Gulf. He would have to keep living among men and women who might work in a little contraband when the fishing got slow and who wouldn't appreciate Teeter discussing that embarrassing sideline with an outsider. From his viewpoint, there was no reason on earth to tell some rich-looking city guy about things that weren't anybody's business. I decided to get very honest. "Peety Boy sent me because I'm trying to help a young girl in trouble. Leroy Purcell's mixed up in it, and he's got some crazy looking sonofabitch named Sonny following me around. Now, I know all that sounds like a really good reason to go inside your place there and leave me alone, but I need help. I can take care of myself, but there's a teenage girl in a world of trouble, and I don't know how else to get her out of it but to figure out what's going on down here."

Billy Teeter leaned back in his chair and studied me. I shut up and let him.

Teeter shifted his weight to one hip and fished a mashed pack of Kools out of the back pocket of his khakis. He shook two brown filters out of the pack with a practiced flip of his wrist and extracted one with small nicotined teeth. Then he winked at me and motioned with his hand at the door the young woman had gone through. "Julie don't like me to smoke these." Teeter paused to fire the end with an old-fashioned chrome flip lighter. As he clicked the lighter shut and pushed it down inside his hip pocket, I glanced a worn brass Marine Corps globe-and-eagle insignia on its side. He said, "What she don't know ain't gonna hurt her, is it?"

I thought about the absurdity of a still hard-as-nails World War II marine having to sneak a smoke on his porch, and, without really wanting to, I thought some about getting old in America. Oddly, I thought about it quite a lot in one of those autopilot flashes of connected thoughts that race through the brain in the midst of doing other things.

I agreed with him. "It won't hurt her a bit."

He asked, "What night?"

"Last Thursday."

"Off Dog Island, you say?" I nodded, and he thought some. "No way to know where somebody's coming from. See a fancy yacht anchored out there, you don't know if it's coming from Tampa or Timbuctu. So, there ain't no way to know if a vessel that might've been out there come in from where you're talking about." Teeter put the soles of his salt-crusted work boots up on the two-by-four railing and rocked up onto the back legs of his chair. He was killing the flattened Kool a quarter inch at a time, pulling thick lung-fulls of menthol smoke down into his chest and shooting them out through his mouth and nostrils. "Yessir, I was out on Thursday, and there was one of them fancy fiberglass motor yachts out off Dog Island. Couldn't tell you where it come from, and it didn't have no name that you could see."

I was quickly becoming a big Billy Teeter fan. I motioned at the empty chair on the porch and said, "Mind if I sit down?"

"Don't mind a bit. Take a load off." Teeter lowered his voice to a conspiratorial level. "Want a cigarette?"

I smiled. "No. Thank you." Then I asked, "How can you remember so much about a no-name yacht you just happened to see one night last week?"

"'Cause of just what you said. It didn't have no name. My grandboy, Willie, named for me, he seen this hellacious big motor yacht laying up off Dog Island when we was out last Thursday. We had pretty much called it a night. So me and Willie made up our minds to cut over close to the thing and get a good look at it. You don't see many like that around here. Down around Tampa and Miami, sure. Hell yeah, you see 'em all the time. But not too many up this way, if you see what I'm saying. Anyway, we cruise over thinking maybe we'll look her over, maybe see some rich guy drinking champagne and lookin' at the stars." Lowering his voice again, now. "Willie, he's only nineteen, he thinks he might see some little rich girls in bikinis, you know. I told him it was too cold, but hope springs eternal, as they say." Now, Teeter raised his voice back to its normal level. "Anyhow, me and Willie pull up pretty close alongside, and, once Willie figures out there ain't no half-naked girls running around the deck, he sees that the vessel ain't got no name painted on it. I look, and he's almost right. Now, what it was was that somebody had taped a sheet of white plastic or something over the name."

Billy Teeter flipped the butt of his Kool out into the sand. Then he looked back over his shoulder at the door, and whispered, "Reckon I'll smoke one more."

I waited while he got it going. "You said the yacht had its name covered?"

"Yep. That's right. Had it covered right up. So, you know, we figure they're up to no good, and Willie says we better get out of there. So, I take a turn around the thing and head home."

I was thinking this was all a little too neat. I said, "I guess Peety Boy sent me to the right place."

Teeter pulled hard at his Kool and let the heavy smoke puff out of his mouth and nose as he spoke. "Peety Boy already knew all this. Him and me talked about it last week the morning I got in. I reckon he just didn't figure it was his business to be telling you about it. He done the right thing by sending you over here, though."

"Mr. Teeter, I appreciate your telling me this. I don't know how it'll help my young friend yet, but every little bit helps." I stopped to think and said, "Can you describe the boat to me. I know it'd be a long shot, but I need to try to identify it if I can."

He smiled. "Sure. I can do that, but it ain't really necessary. What with the name covered up and all, I copied the registration number off the hull." He motioned inside. "I got it in the back there with the records of the catch that night."

I said, "You're kidding."

"No, sir."

I asked, "Why on God's green earth would someone cover a boat's name and not its registration numbers?"

" 'Cause of the Coast Guard." Teeter said, "Everybody names boats, but you don't have to. It ain't a law. People just do it. But you gotta register a boat, and you gotta have its registration numbers prominently displayed, as they say, on the hull. That's the law. So, a fella could get by with covering over the name, if that's what he wanted to do. But you cover over the registration numbers, and you're pretty much gonna get yourself boarded by the Coast Guard, if the ATF or the immigration folks don't get to you first."

"Will you give me the number?"

"I reckon. But listen, I know you say you're helping a little girl, and I believe you and all. But it wouldn't hurt my feelings none if you thought that number was worth a few dollars."

Strange. Peety Boy wouldn't take money when I offered it, and Billy Teeter had come right out and asked for it. But, if pressed, I couldn't tell you which was the better man. Different people have different rules and different needs. I pulled out my wallet and found a fifty-dollar bill. Teeter put his calloused hand out, and I pressed it into his palm. He said, "I appreciate it." Then he stood and walked inside. When he came back, he handed me a scrap of brown wrapping paper with a dozen numbers and letters written on it in ballpoint pen. He said, "I copied it off for you. I need to hold on to the paper I wrote it on the other night. Got other stuff on it I need."

"How much money do you make in a good night on the water?"

Teeter looked guarded, but not offended. All he said was, "Depends."

I said, "If I paid you, say, two hundred dollars, would that be enough to get you to lay off shrimping for a night and take me out?"

"It'd be enough, depending on what you wanted to do when you got out there."

"Same thing you did last week. Just get a look at whoever's out there."

Teeter's eyes narrowed. "Two fifty."

I laughed out loud and walked over to shake his hand. "It's a deal. I'll give you as much notice as I can, but it may be a last-minute thing."

Teeter took the brown paper from my hand, pulled a ball-point out of his shirt pocket, and jotted down a phone number. He said, "Just call me. If I'm here, I'll do it. If I ain't, that means I'm probably out working, and you'll have to get up with me when I get back in."

I thanked him again and trotted down the three wooden steps to my Jeep. As I pulled open the door, Teeter called out. "Mr. McInnes!" I stopped and looked at him. "You said a couple of names when you first got here."

"Leroy Purcell and Sonny?"

He nodded. "I don't mean to be talking out of school. But you be careful of them two. You hear me? You're messing around with people who'll cut your throat for looking at 'em wrong. And if you're getting in their business, you're asking for a heap of trouble."

"Why are you helping me then? Aren't you scared of them?"

Billy Teeter—seventy-something ex-Marine and secret menthol cigarette smoker—smiled the smile of the toughest kid in the

Franklin County class of '42 and made two knowing syllables of one short word. "She-it."

The drive to Mobile was excruciatingly, perhaps unnecessarily, long. Visions of Sonny lying in wait along the Panhandle's famous Highway 98, holding—in my imagination—a scoped sniper's rifle, encouraged me to find my way home along a network of interconnected county and state roads until I was out of Florida. Pelting Sonny with grit bombs had been stupid, but fun. This scurrying along back country roads to avoid his wrath was even dumber, no fun at all, and more than a little humiliating.

It was nearly nine when I finally parked beneath a thick-branched water oak on Monterey Street next to Loutie's brick walkway. Stepping out into the spring night, I breathed in the old neighborhood smells of azaleas, bougainvillaea, wisteria, and the first grass clippings of the season. Aromatherapy. All thoughts of Leroy Purcell and psychotic Sonny dissolved and floated away on the soft mix of nostalgic scents as I walked across the bricks to the front door and rang the bell. I felt wonderful, right up until I felt the metallic press of a gun barrel in the small of my back.

chapter fifteen

"PUT YOUR HANDS behind your head, please."

It wasn't Sonny. It wasn't Purcell. I did as instructed.

A hard hand clamped my fingers together behind my neck as another hand moved quickly and expertly down my sides, over my pants, and inside my waistband. The hand lifted my wallet. Five seconds later, my fingers were released, and the voice said, "Sorry, Mr. McInnes. Joey described you, but he also told me not to take any chances." I turned around. "Here's your billfold." The man who had pressed a gun into my back was little more than twenty. He stood about five six and had the spare muscular build and close-cropped hair of a military man.

I asked, "Who are you?"

"Randy Whittles. I work for Joey when he needs somebody protected. I do some investigating sometimes if he needs me, but I'm mostly just protection." I smiled at the idea of this mighty mouse working as hired muscle. But I knew that if Joey thought someone was tough, they were by God tough.

I asked, "Can I go inside now?"

"Yes, sir. Sorry, sir. Here." He slipped a key in the door and opened it. I stepped inside. Randy called out, "It's okay ma'am," closed the door from the outside and, I guessed, went back to his hidey-hole.

Susan and Carli walked into the living room. I looked at them and said, "That was interesting."

Susan said, "Loutie says he's a Navy SEAL. Our Mr. Whittles is one very serious young man."

Carli said, "I call him G.I. Joe."

"Good. That he's serious, I mean. Not that you call him G.I. Joe." I said, "Joey says he needs Loutie to handle some, uh, surveillance I asked him to do."

Susan said, "Carli knows Purcell paid you a visit."

I asked, "Does she know about the investigator's note?" Susan shook her head. I said, "Come on. Let's go back to the kitchen where we can get comfortable and talk."

Carli asked, "What's going on?"

I said, "We've got a lot more information now. A lot of it's helpful, and some of it's disturbing. Come on. I need to fill you in."

We sat at the table, and I talked. Susan had steeled Carli for the involvement of Leroy Purcell, and my young client had, it seemed, come to terms with Purcell knowing about Carli Monroe. She was less prepared to hear that Purcell knew about Carli *Poultrez*. As I described finding the investigator's report under my windshield wiper, blood drained from Carli's lips. When I placed the report on the cream tablecloth in front of her, the rest of her face lost color. Her small ears, visible because she had swept her dark hair back in a ponytail, turned fiery red and made her face look even paler.

She said, "What's this mean at the bottom? 'Rus Poultrez—Contact Report.' There's nothing after it." Carli's voice caught in her throat. "It means they found my father and talked with him, doesn't it. Isn't that what it means?"

"I think it means Purcell wants us to *believe* his investigator met with your father. It could be nothing. Just something to make us nervous. To make you do something stupid."

She shook her head from side to side as I spoke. "The name's right. The address is right." I couldn't think of anything useful or comforting to say about that, so I pushed on and reported my dialogue with Billy Teeter. It didn't help.

Carli's eyes grew larger, and edges of her eyelids turned bright red. "What's that stuff got to do with me? I don't care if Leroy Purcell is smuggling drugs or people or anything else. I just want him to leave me alone." Tears were streaming down her cheeks now. Her voice cracked as she spoke. "Tell him. Tell him I don't care about what he does. Tell him to just leave me alone. I'll go away. I'll go out west somewhere and forget I ever heard of him."

Susan put her hand on Carli's back to console her, and Carli pushed it away. My young client thought we had failed her. And, at least for the moment, punishing Leroy Purcell—doing the right thing—became far less important to her than staying alive.

We were quiet for a while. I tried to think. Carli's movements grew less frenetic. Her shoulders relaxed. She wiped away the tears. The central air cycled off, and the quiet hum fell away to reveal a chorus of crickets beneath the kitchen window.

When the tears had stopped, I said, "The reason you can't just tell Purcell you'll leave him alone is that—the way he looks at it—he never knows when you'll show up and blackmail him to keep quiet. And, Carli, the fact that you'd never blackmail him is irrelevant. He'd do it, so he figures you would too."

Carli looked down at the tablecloth, but her eyes were focused a thousand miles away. I glanced up at Susan and went on. "Carli, even if we somehow got Purcell to say he'd leave you alone, you couldn't trust him. He's the kind of man who'll make a deal, and then stick a knife in your stomach while you're shaking on it." Carli began to cry again, and Susan gave me an angry look. "I'm sorry, Carli. I'm sorry to say it that way. But you have to understand who you're dealing with. You cannot convince yourself that you can end this with a phone call or a meeting. And, right now, we don't have enough evidence to get Purcell convicted of the murder you witnessed. We could get him arrested. Maybe. But he'd never go to jail based on what we've got. Now, under normal circumstances, we could report the crime, put it on the record that you witnessed the murder, and make it hard for Purcell to retaliate without getting in more trouble. But Carli, these aren't normal circumstances. I'm afraid Purcell would worry about getting rid of witnesses first and how to deal with your obvious disappearance down the road somewhere.

"Remember, Purcell is a violent, explosive man. He's where he is because he's crazy enough to do things that even other criminals won't do. Sooner or later, it'll catch up with him. A man can't go on forever killing and setting fires to settle disputes. But for now, he's kind of bullet proof because he is so damn crazy."

Carli had stopped crying. Tears had drawn dark trails down her cheeks to her jawline, just as they had the first time I spoke with her. She said, "You said he's bullet proof, but he's not. I know what you mean, but he's not. A bullet would kill him."

I looked at Susan, who raised her eyebrows as if to say, *Who can blame her?* I let the subject drop.

Carli left to wash her face. I found bread in Loutie's wormwood cupboard and roast beef, mayonnaise, mustard, and farmer's cheese in the stainless steel refrigerator. Susan said that she and Carli had eaten. I built two sandwiches for myself and had eaten one and started on the second by the time Carli came back in the room. It was a few minutes after ten now.

Carli said, "I'm tired. This is a lot. I mean, it's a lot to think about. I'm just gonna go to bed." And she left Susan and me alone in the kitchen as the air conditioner cycled on again, deadening the mating calls of the crickets who lived in Loutie's shrubbery.

"She does that a lot."

"What?" Susan said.

"When things get bad, she goes to bed. Nothing wrong with it. I just noticed it. People in prison do that."

"Go to bed early?"

"No. Not just that. They sleep all the time because they can't stand where they are. It's like temporary suicide. If you're not conscious, you don't have to feel bad. I read about it for the first time after Watergate. Ehrlichman, I think it was, commented in an interview that all these white-collar crooks in minimum security slept their time away." I asked, "Has Carli been sleeping much during the day?"

"Some. Well, come to think of it, she takes a nap every afternoon. I just thought she was bored."

"Maybe she is. I'm just armchair shrinking to avoid some unpleasant thoughts of my own." I motioned at the door Carli had gone through on her way to bed. "It must be tough for her."

Susan said, "It's been a tough couple of days for you too. What do you say we go veg out in front of the TV? We won't even watch *Nightline*. We'll watch Leno or Letterman."

"It's Sunday."

Susan grabbed my hand and pulled me up and toward the living room. "Then we'll find a great old movie and forget the real world is even out there."

Rear Window and *Get Shorty* were still on top of the VCR from two nights earlier. Susan said, "Loutie was saying the other night when you rented *Rear Window* that she already had it. Apparently, she's a Hitchcock nut." Susan opened a narrow painted-pine cabinet next to the converted antique chifforobe that held Loutie's TV and said, "Look." Every Hitchcock I had ever seen, along with a few I didn't know existed, was lined up on rows of shallow shelves. Hitch had his own ordered space on the top three racks. Loutie's other videos were there, but they were out of order and clearly subservient to Sir Alfred's body of work. Susan said, "What about *Dial M for Murder?*"

I said, "Pop it in," and she did.

Instead of previews, the tape started with a film lesson on Alfred Hitchcock and his penchant for upper-crust-looking blondes. Susan disappeared. I watched Janet Leigh, Tippi Hendren, Grace Kelly, Doris Day, and Kim Novak take turns looking horrified. Three or four minutes of that went by, and Susan reappeared holding a cold bottle of Chardonnay, two tulip-shaped glasses, and a corkscrew. She said, "All part of the program. Watch what's-his-name, um, Robert Cummings, and Grace Kelly smooch, drink a little wine, and see where it leads."

"You do know that there's kind of a grisly murder in the movie too?"

She said, "I can take it if you can," and sat on the sofa next to me. I performed the oddly satisfying job of cutting and peeling foil from the bottle's neck. The cork came out in one piece, and the slightly greenish spirits flowed into both expectant glasses with minimal mess. We settled back and sipped some of the buttery Chardonnay. I'm not much of a white wine drinker, but you don't tell a woman who has surprised you with a romantic gesture that you'd just as soon have red wine, or maybe even a little scotch if she has it. We settled into the cushions as an oversized finger began to dial an old-fashioned rotary phone. Hitch showed the mechanical telephone machinery jump and shudder in response to the movements of the finger. And there she was. Grace Kelly. And she was kissing Robert Cummings of all people. I said, "Now, explain this to me. She's got this dashing former-international-tennis-star husband at home, who's a prick, but she doesn't know that—not to mention that she could get pretty much any other man she wants—and she decides to go after Bob Cummings. What the hell is that about?"

Susan cleared her throat, and I turned to look at her. She gave me a sidelong look that said, *you're ruining the mood, dummy*, and took in a small sip of wine. I turned back to the movie, and, for the first time, noticed the warmth of Susan's thigh and knee against my leg where she had turned ever so slightly my way and ever so casually rested her leg on mine. *Oh.* And she had been resting her empty hand on my shoulder in what I thought was a friendly and comfortable way. *Oh, again.* I can take a hint, so long as it's sufficiently obvious and prolonged.

Susan was wearing a simple white pullover with short sleeves, a crew neck, and a squared shirttail that hung untucked over blue shorts that sort of looked like a miniskirt until you realized they were shorts. I shifted the glass to my right hand and casually, I hoped, placed my left hand on Susan's leg in what I also hoped was an intimate, as opposed to a blatantly horny, gesture. When I did, she lifted her hand from my shoulder and began to stroke my hair. It felt wonderful. It felt relaxing. And I felt sleepy. *Yawn now and you're a dead man.* Instead, I leaned toward Susan, and she took away any chance of awkwardness by folding into me so that our lips met perfectly and softly. I wasn't sleepy anymore. Time floated as we kissed gently. We parted, and I looked for any caution or concern on her face. She looked happy.

Susan hummed. "Mmmm."

I put my glass on the coffee table and smiled. "You're pretty vocal, aren't you?"

As Susan leaned her face in close to mine, she said, "You have no idea."

This time our mouths and tongues melted together. We pulled closer, and I moved my hand over her thigh just to feel the silkiness of her legs. As I did, Susan reached down and placed her hand over mine.

I said, "Sorry."

Susan smiled. She pulled my hand up and inside her shirt and cupped it over her left breast.

I caressed her through a thin layer of cotton and, as we kissed again, slid my hand down and then back up inside her sports bra. Her breast felt hot and firm, and I could feel the tiny, rhythmic thuds of her heart beating. I desperately wanted, even needed, to move my mouth down and across her neck and collarbone and shoulders, to kiss her breasts and hold her nipples inside my mouth. I kissed her throat, and she pulled away just enough to click off the lamp on the end table, pull her shirt and bra over her head, and toss them aside. She lay back against the pillows and pulled me on top of her. I pushed into her mouth and moved my hands over her breasts.

Susan shoved gently against my chest and tugged at my shirt and dropped it on the floor. Skin to skin now, I kissed her mouth and her nipples and every inch of skin in between. We lay there on the sofa with *Dial M for Murder* playing in the background and made out and touched and breathed in each other like teenage sweethearts with no bed to go to.

Susan guided my hand again, this time to her legs and over her impossibly warm smooth inner thigh and inside the blue cotton shorts. As I pushed her panties aside and my fingers found the silky places where she wanted to be touched and I wanted to touch, Susan began to unbutton my jeans.

Suddenly, she pushed away. "Come on."

I sat up, and whispered, "Is something wrong?"

Standing now next to the sofa in nothing but a pair of miniskirt-looking shorts and framed by Hitchcock's glow, she said, "Let's go to the bedroom." My brain's usual blood supply was otherwise engaged, and I was a little dazed by the past half hour and by the sudden interruption. I looked at her and blinked. She said, "Hurry."

And I did. Then I didn't.

Someone, somewhere out there, rapped on a door. It went away, and then started again. This time, the rapping pushed sleep away and grew louder. Susan called out. "Carli?"

Randy Whittles' voice said, "It's me, Mrs. Fitzsimmons."

"Yes. What is it, Randy?"

"I gotta go home and catch a few hours' sleep. Loutie's supposed to be back around eleven. And, with Mr. McInnes in the house, I thought it'd be okay." He hesitated and said, "You guys must have had a late night. Nobody's up yet."

I looked at my watch. 10:24. I smiled and showed it to Susan. She moved her eyebrows up and down like a lascivious Groucho Marx, and spoke to Randy. "Go ahead. We'll be fine."

Randy yes-ma'amed her and departed.

I said, "Wow. I haven't slept this late in six months."

Susan said, "I haven't slept this well in longer than that. This is delicious. Lying in bed on a Monday morning, enjoying the . . . the what, maybe the afterglow if that doesn't sound ridiculous."

"Sounds perfect to me."

Susan leaned over and kissed my lips. Then, as she turned and reached to click on the bedside lamp, she said, "Nowhere to be and nothing I have to do. And you absolutely deserve a day off."

When she had leaned over to turn on the light, the sheet had fallen to her waist, and I was conducting a thorough and thoroughly satisfying study of her breasts. I said, "You know what we could do?"

Susan gave me a look. "We could go check on Carli to make sure she's all right."

"Yeah. That's what I was going to say." Susan laughed and rolled off the bed and, from my perspective, made a very nice job of walking to the bathroom. I sat up, swung my feet to the floor, and pushed up. My jeans were in a tangle against a baseboard ten feet from the bed. I pulled them on and went to the living room with the intention of retrieving my shirt and Susan's bra and shirt before Carli found them.

Randy said she wasn't up yet. I still had a chance to be discreet.

The faint hum of Susan's shower dissipated as I moved down the hallway. On through the hall and the study and then into the living room, I found nothing but quiet. I had gathered up our clothes and started back when, for some reason, I stopped in the study and listened. And there was nothing. Almost too much nothing, and I was overwhelmed by the feeling that Susan and I were in the house alone.

I trotted across the study floor, turned away from Susan's room, and hung a left down a second hallway. Carli's paneled door was on the right. I knocked. Nothing. I knocked again and called her name. Still nothing.

"Carli? Carli! Answer me! I'm coming in now. So, cover yourself up or whatever you need to do."

The knob twisted in my hand, but the door stood immobile. I called out again and remembered my own pseudo-shrink comment that constant napping and sleeping like Carli had been doing was a form of temporary suicide. I thought about kicking the door in but decided that might be an overreaction. And I wasn't even sure I could do it. That was two inches of antique oak between me and Carli. I ran to get Susan.

Thank God, the bathroom door was unlocked. Inside, Susan sloshed in the shower, and I could barely see through all the billowing steam stuffed into the small tiled room.

I said, "I need the key to Carli's room. She's not answering."

Through fogged glass, I could just make out Susan scrubbing suds out of her hair and rinsing foam off her face. Two beats passed while she washed away soap and shampoo, and she said, "Maybe she's just sleeping hard." But, even as she spoke, Susan stepped out of the shower and grabbed a terry cloth robe off a hook on the door. I am ashamed to say that, even then and even under those circumstances, I was struck and aroused by all that beautiful wet skin. I am pleased to say that I did not pause to enjoy either the view or the fantasy.

Susan wasn't running, but she was moving fast. She said, "Go back and try again. Loutie keeps all the keys on hooks in the kitchen. I'll be right there."

I didn't have Susan's self-control. I sprinted, as much as anyone can sprint in an old house full of antiques, back to Carli's door.

Still, nothing but quiet.

I banged and called and banged some more. And, out of nowhere, Susan was beside me, pushing an antique skeleton key into the lock. She swung the door wide, and we stepped into the room

The bed was made. The window was open. And Carli was gone.

chapter sixteen

WE STOOD, STUNNED. When we moved, Susan ran to the window, and I performed the same lame searches I had the last time Carli's bed had been unexpectedly empty. She wasn't in the closet or under the bed this time either, and neither were any of her things. But there was a penciled note on the vanity. I called Susan over, and when she turned to face me, white showed all around her bright blue irises.

The note was on the same notebook paper Carli had been using for all her drawings. On the top half of the page, Carli had sketched a picture of Susan's antique step-side pickup with tall grass all around and what looked like a rosebush covering the front wheel. On the bottom half, she had simply written, *Thanks— Sorry— Carli.*

When Susan spoke, her voice fluttered just above a whisper. "It looks like she took off last night after she left us in the kitchen."

"Probably. But after Randy left this morning would've been the best time to get away unnoticed, and she could've gotten up and made her bed before slipping out." In contrast to Susan's strained syllables, my voice sounded loud and uncouth in the abandoned bedroom. I self-consciously lowered and calmed my voice. "It had to take some time to draw this, assuming she drew it at the same time she wrote the note. She may have just picked up an old drawing and written on it." I said, "Go out front and check the sidewalks. I'll check in back."

Susan turned and flew through the bedroom door. I pushed the note inside my hip pocket, put my feet through the bottom half of the tall, open window, and sat on the sill. Turning and sliding, I caught the sill with both hands and dropped the last few feet to the ground. A teenage girl could easily have done the same thing. And she had. The mud-grip tread of Carli's sport sandals was pressed neatly into the soft earth of a flower bed. She had barely missed stomping the freshly planted tulip bulbs Loutie had assigned to her care when she first arrived.

Textured footprints moved off the bed at an angle. The few, diluted drops of Creek blood flowing through my veins didn't help me track her steps. I followed the angle but, after that, couldn't really tell what she had done. It seemed likely, though, that Carli had moved parallel with Monterey Street, crossing three contiguous back lawns, before being forced by a tall privacy fence to turn back toward the street and hit the sidewalk. If Randy had been focused on the street and alley, he never would have seen her scurry away.

Following my guesswork route, I circled around to the street and met Susan trotting down the sidewalk. She halted in front of me. Her wide eyes had narrowed with focus. I asked, "Have you got your pickup around here somewhere?"

Susan's voice was clear now. "It's parked around off the alley out of sight."

"You'd better get it. She's probably long gone, but it'd be stupid not to split up and cover the streets around here." We turned and walked hurriedly toward the house. Inside, Susan got dressed in less than a minute, shedding her robe, pulling on panties, jeans, and running shoes, and sliding a green T-shirt over wet hair which she didn't bother to brush. I put on last night's clothes, grabbed a mouthful of Scope, sloshed a little, and spit in the sink.

As Susan turned the key in Loutie's front door, I said, "Just drive up and down the streets looking. And take a good look at any parks you come across. I'll cover the bus stops and work my way toward downtown." I asked, "What's the code on Loutie's answering machine?"

"I don't know. Why?"

"I'm trying to figure out how one of us can let the other one know if we find her." I handed her my cell phone. "Here. I'll find a phone and call you in an hour. If one of us hasn't come across her by then, it'll be time to get Joey on it."

Susan said, "Tell me his number. I'll call him now." And she was right, of course. I told her Joey's office and cell phone numbers. As I climbed into my Jeep, Susan strode through Loutie's side yard toward the alley. Her face was pale and concentrated as she punched buttons on the tiny gray flip phone.

An hour later, I called. We agreed to keep going. An hour after that, even over cell phone static, I could hear defeat in Susan's voice.

Randy Whittles and Joey were inside Loutie's house when I arrived. The air crackled with tension, and Randy's ears burned as red as Joey's face. I could have sworn there had been yelling in that room.

I sat and explained everything I knew about Carli's disappearance. Randy added nothing. He hadn't seen anything.

After Susan arrived and joined us in the living room, Joey leaned forward in his chair and propped his elbows on his knees. He looked at the piece of hardwood floor between his Hush Puppies for a few seconds and then up at me.

"Letting a teenage girl slip out of here under our . . . under *my* nose is . . . shit. Anyway, after I got Susan's call this morning, I called Randy and then got a few men out looking. I told Randy here to fix his fucking mess. But, hell, it's my fault. I should have been here myself."

Susan scrunched up her eyebrows. She looked at me and then at Joey and then back at me again. I rolled my eyes and said,

"It's nobody's fault, Joey. And nobody—not even you—can be everywhere.

"Now, about little Randy here." I noticed that Randy Whittles sat up a little straighter and glared at me when I called him "little." Any man who has gone through what it takes to become a SEAL deserves not to be insulted. I said, "No offense, Randy. It's just that you look like a kid to an old man in his thirties." Randy's chest unswelled a little, and he turned the bass down on his glare. "Joey, Randy was assigned to keep people out of this house, not keep them in. And you know as well as I do that those are different things. And, on top of that, Carli may have taken off this morning after Randy was gone."

Joey said, "Except that Randy had no business leaving here without my okay."

I said, "Well, Randy works for you, not me." And Joey nodded, as if to say, *Damn right he does*. "But I'm not blaming you for anything, and I'm sure Susan isn't either."

Susan piped in on cue. "You're the best. Anyone else would be making excuses or covering up, but you're here pointing out nonexistent mistakes and taking full blame." She walked over and squeezed his huge hand.

Joey said, "This turned touchy-feely all of a sudden, didn't it?" Susan laughed and slapped him lightly on the top of his head.

I said, "Now that everything's cuddly again, we need to figure out where our client is."

Joey said, "I've got somebody at the bus station. And I've got someone at the airport, even though I doubt Carli's got the money to take a plane to the nearest hub. By the way, how much money *does* she have?"

Susan knitted her eyebrows again and shook her head. "I don't know. Carli probably had some tips from her last night at the Pelican's Roost, but I never asked her. Loutie gave her some clothes and bought her a few more."

Joey asked, "Have you checked your purse?"

Susan said, "I don't think Carli would ever . . ."

"I'm not saying she's a crook, Susan. The girl was scared. Scared shitless of Leroy Purcell from what Tom tells me. Just go check your purse."

Susan pointed at an antique sideboard against the back wall and said, "It's right there on the table." She walked over and looked inside. "My whole wallet's gone." She sounded tired.

I said, "Call MasterCard and American Express and whatever other cards you've got. Check on recent purchases. Tell them your daughter sneaked off with your cards. Say you don't want the police involved, but you want to know if someone tries to charge anything."

"Will they do that?"

Joey said, "Sometimes. Not always. How much money is missing?"

"I don't know. Somewhere between two and three hundred dollars."

Joey stood. "I'm gonna go call my man at the airport. On Southwest Airlines, that little girl could fly just about any-damn-where Southwest goes for three hundred bucks." As he stood, he added, "Randy. Go fix this mess." Joey walked out, and, in quick order, Randy stood and marched out the front door without uttering a word.

Susan said, "Testosterone poisoning."

"That's more than a little insulting, you know." Susan looked taken aback. I said, "If a man, every time a woman acted stupid or vain, said she was suffering from estrogen poisoning, he'd be drawn and quartered by every woman and half the men in the room."

Susan said, "Okay. You're right. But why are we arguing about this?"

I said, "Because I'm ticked off about Carli and Sonny and Leroy Purcell, and I want to argue with someone."

"Feel better?"

"Yeah."

"Good. What now?"

"I think I'm going to go mess with Leroy Purcell."

"Why on earth would you do that?"

"Because it seems like the only time we learn anything in this case is when things get stirred up. And I'm tired of the other guy doing all the stirring. This is something I've been giving serious thought to. I want to give Purcell something to think about besides looking for you and Carli. So, I'm going to try to mess with his mind a little and see if I can split his attention and maybe even get him to make a mistake."

Susan said, "Can I help?"

I said, "Yeah. I think you probably can."

chapter seventeen

I AWOKE TUESDAY morning in a strange room in Seaside, Florida. A pale blue ceiling floated over the bed. Two sandy yellow walls angled together and formed a square with another right angle of walls painted the blue-green color of shallow Gulf water on a summer morning. The bed's driftwood headboard swirled with hand-painted shells and fish and mermaids. Found-object sculptures decorated only one sand-colored wall. All other walls were left blank to catch the sunshine and the changing shadows of outside vegetation projected through oversized windows. The room, in short, was horribly and expensively whimsical.

A soft tangle of brunette hair lay on the pillow next to my own sandy head. The covers had fallen away to reveal one perfect female shoulder and a strong, firm rib cage that flowed into that wonderful woman place where narrow waist meets the beginning swell of hips. I ran my hand over the exposed, cool curve of her hip and circled her waist with my arm. My hand moved over the dimple of her navel and stopped at her ribs to pull her warm back against my chest and stomach and her rounded bottom against my thighs. I kissed her shoulder. She stirred and yawned, and Susan turned on her back to look at me.

I propped up on my left elbow, rested my head in my hand, and said, "Good morning."

Susan said, "Morning." Her voice came out soft and husky with sleep.

I studied her. A friend of Loutie's had visited the house on Monterey Street Monday afternoon and dyed Susan's hair a surprisingly realistic dark brown. The petite, frizzy-haired magician had even tinted Susan's eyebrows to match.

Susan pulled the sheet up to her neck and laced her fingers behind her head. She smiled. "What are you looking at?"

I've never quite known what to say when a woman asks that. So, I just said, "You."

Susan said, "I think you're enjoying this."

"You're right."

"No. I mean sleeping with a blonde one night and a brunette the next."

I sat up and put my feet on the floor. Smiling, I said, "Yeah, I knew that's what you meant." I heard her weight shift on the bed, and I should have gotten out of the way. Susan swung a playful but solid fist into my right shoulder blade. I yelled, "Ow," more from surprise than pain and jumped up.

Susan was laughing and looking inordinately proud of herself. She said, "Watch it."

I said, "Jeez. Consider it watched."

Susan sat up, hooking the sheet under her arms, and looked at me. "Most people over thirty look better *with* clothes than without them. But you happen to look very, very nice naked."

As I walked toward the bathroom to take a shower, I said, "Then I guess you'd better watch it too. It'd be a shame to have to deny you all this."

Susan smiled, it seemed, with more indulgence than amusement.

Twenty minutes later, I was showered and outfitted in clean jeans and shirt. After finding my way down an open teak staircase, over nubby carpet and Mexican tile, and through an oversized hexagonal doorway into the kitchen, I found Loutie sipping tomato juice and fiddling the knobs on an impressive array of electronic equipment that had been spread out on an artistically chipped slab of granite the owners had intended to be the breakfast table.

"Good morning."

Loutie frowned at a graphic readout and held a black foam rubber knob attached to one side of a tiny headset to her ear. She said, "Hey," and tossed the headset on top of a graphite-colored box.

I asked, "What's Purcell up to this morning?"

"Sleeping." Loutie motioned at the refrigerator with her thumb. "There's muffins. Orange juice and tomato juice. Coffee's still okay. Been on the burner awhile, though."

She wasn't exactly testy. But Loutie had become very . . . focused. I asked, "Is anything wrong? I mean, anything I don't know about?"

"No. I'm just keeping tabs on Purcell. Joey's back on Dog Island watching Haycock."

I said, "And Carli's out there alone somewhere, and Joey's pushing everyone because he thinks he's supposed to be perfect." Loutie shrugged and sat in an awkward, designer dining chair made of four sticks of chrome and two swatches of mauve leather.

Susan walked in, running her hands through damp hair. New, dark mascara made her eyes appear bigger and an even lighter blue than usual; earth tones powdered her eyelids; and dark lip gloss and blush gave her tanned complexion a decidedly olive cast. Together with her new dark brown hair and eyebrows, it was a pretty amazing disguise.

I said, "Who the hell are you?" And Susan smiled.

Loutie told her about the muffins and juice. Susan found a glass in the cabinet next to the sink and poured some orange juice in it. Loutie turned to me. "Joey said to tell you he's still working on who runs the Bodines down around the islands."

I asked, "Does that mean it's not Purcell?"

"No. I think it just means he still hasn't found out who runs what. Could be Purcell. Could be somebody else. All the cops could find out is there's a rumor that the young Turks, as Joey put it, may be trying to take over from the old guard. But Joey says that's not exactly earth-shattering news since somebody's always trying to edge out somebody else when business is good. You know, criminal business."

"And that's all?"

"That's all."

So much for that. I came back to the task at hand. "Anybody else in Purcell's place?" Loutie shook her head. I asked her how to find it, and she told me. I gave her my cell phone number. As I tapped a series of four buttons on the tiny gray keypad, I said, "I'm turning off the ringer and setting the phone on vibrate. If Purcell wakes up or somebody else shows up, give me a call. I won't answer unless I'm clear of the house, though. So don't worry if you can't get me."

Susan frowned. "You sure you know what you're doing?"

I said, "Nope. But, I'll be careful." I lifted my shirttail to show her the butt of a Browning 9mm automatic I had gotten from my father in the aftermath of my brother's death the previous fall. The sight seemed to scare her more, not less. I found a khaki cap with a blue visor and *Seaside, Florida* stitched across the front, and put that on along with a pair of overpriced, purple-mirrored, Revo sunglasses a client had given me.

Quaint pathways passed beneath bright sky and beside white picket fences, perfect pastel vacation homes, and decorator bird-houses that seemed to be the object of some kind of cuteness competition. If my Jim Walter house on St. George had been pastel hell, then Seaside, Florida certainly was pastel heaven—if banal, architecturally angular homogeneity is your idea of heaven. Seaside is, in the best and worst senses, a planned community. Mostly, it was planned to provide new-rich Chardonnay-Southerners a tidy—some might say sterile—place to vacation far from the unwashed throngs who sunned and sloshed and guzzled Budweiser along the rest of the Redneck Riviera.

The place looks so unreal and unlikely that Hollywood used Seaside as the fantasy town that could only exist on television in the Jim Carrey film *The Truman Show*.

It's a small place. Nothing in Seaside is very far from anything else. And no more than a hundred yards from our modestly ostentatious rental, Leroy Purcell's beach palace occupied a sandy, picketed lot just one left and two rights from our own canary-yellow front door. I was not surprised to see that our all-American hero owned one of the larger chunks of aqua blue siding in Seaside, which is saying something. Neither was I surprised that parked behind his house was one of the longest, reddest Cadillacs I have ever encountered.

Spring break revelers had trudged back to class, and the arthritic flocks of sun-browned snowbirds who took up winter residence on the Gulf had pointedly migrated north even before the spring break crowd had arrived. So, as I moved among the clapboard canyons of Seaside, I had encountered only a few lonely, sandy-bottomed souls. Now, standing outside Purcell's million-dollar beachfront, I saw no one.

I waved and jogged across Purcell's lot as if attempting to catch up with a friend. *Acting 101.* As I came up on his fiery Caddy, I stumbled and knelt down to retie a perfectly tied Reebok. *More acting.* From inside my hip pocket, I pulled out a small black box with a tracking device on the inside and magnets on the outside. Following Joey's earlier instructions, I reached under Purcell's Caddy, felt for the steel frame, and clicked the box into place.

I stood and squinted into the western sky before jogging out to look longingly down the beach at my departed, imaginary buddy, whoever he might be.

Turning away from the surf, I had started up the beach on the way back to Susan and Loutie when my flip phone vibrated, not unpleasantly, in the hip pocket of my jeans. I hesitated before realizing I would look suspiciously out of place on the beach at Seaside only if I *didn't* occasionally confer with unseen minions by cell phone. I pulled up the tiny antenna and opened the phone.

Loutie said, "Joey called. He needs you in Appalachicola."

"Is he all right?"

Loutie sounded surprised. "Joey's fine. He has somebody he wants you to meet."

"Who is it?"

"He just said somebody with information about Purcell. Call him, okay?"

I said, "okay," and ended the call.

A recorded female voice full of misplaced emphasis told me the cellular customer I was calling was unavailable. I looked around some and tried Joey's number again with the same result. I walked back along manicured, sandy paths to Susan and Loutie and the rented house with the canary door.

Long morning. Loutie listened to Purcell listen to ESPN; Susan read the complimentary copy of *USA Today* she had found on our steps that morning; and, between unsuccessful attempts to return Joey's call, I glanced at whatever pages Susan wasn't reading. I was absentmindedly looking at a four-color pie chart with a line of Zorro masks next to it—something about crime going down—when the phone rang.

Joey sounded excited. He had been tailing the guy he wanted me to meet, trying to decide whether the man really wanted to talk or maybe just wanted to do us bodily harm.

I asked, "So, what do you think?"

I could hear Joey's radio playing softly as he spoke. "I think we ought to meet with him. Coosa—the cop in Panama City I've been working with—says he's okay. I mean, he's a fucking snitch, which means he's basically human shit, but, for a snitch, he's okay."

"How'd you find out about him?"

"Like I said. Coosa. I guess he figured we weren't getting much for our money, so he just called me up and gave me the guy's name and address and stuff."

Joey was happier about this than I was. I asked, "Does that seem strange to you?"

"Yeah, a little."

"But you still want to meet with him?"

"Sure. It's better than sitting around waiting. And the only trap I'm worried about is one I don't see coming. I figure we're gonna learn something whatever happens. The boy's either gonna tell us something useful 'cause he wants to or 'cause we make him. Doesn't make much difference to me."

I said, "You do know that you're not *actually* immortal?"

"Mother's Milk at ten tonight."

"Mother's Milk?"

He repeated, "Mother's Milk," and hung up.

chapter eighteen

MOTHER'S MILK WAS a cinder-block edifice deposited on a stretch of stunted timberland north of Appalachicola. A mercury light hanging from a tall creosote post cast an ugly bluish illumination across the parking lot where, days before, Joey had relieved Haycock and his accomplice of the tools of their trade. Halfway down the light post, the proprietor had suspended a Coca-Cola sign—the kind country stores get for free—with the bar's name painted in green across a lighted white panel. I pulled into the lot and found a place among the pickups, Z-28's, and Firebirds.

As I clicked off the headlights on my newly rented Bonneville, Joey startled me by tapping loudly on the passenger window. I jumped hard enough to bang my knee on the steering wheel.

I popped the locks, and Joey climbed into the passenger seat.

He said, "You're early."

"Wasn't sure I'd be able to find it."

Joey nodded at Mother's Milk. "Pretty, isn't it?"

The rusted metal roof drooped, and once-white paint had flaked off the concrete exterior in irregular patches, revealing a soiled pea-soup color. In addition to the lighted Cola-Cola sign hanging from the light post, the bar's name had been painted in red script across the front wall, which bore the pockmarks of a hundred rifle and pistol shots fired over the years from passing cars.

I said, "It looks like a good place to get killed."

Joey looked thoughtful. "I don't guess we'd be the first."

"You think that's a possibility?"

"Hell, it's always a possibility. It's a possibility you're gonna get creamed crossing the road. It's a possibility you're gonna catch a cramp one of these days while you're out swimming in Mobile Bay."

"Yeah." I said, "That's just what I wanted. I wasn't worried about somebody sticking a knife in me tonight. I wanted to have a philosophical discussion about life's inherent uncertainties."

"Just trying to put things in perspective." He looked over at me. "You ready to go?"

"Yeah. But, before we go in, mind if I ask why you chose this particular establishment?"

"I didn't. The snitch—Squirley McCall—he picked it."

I smiled. "Squirley?"

"And Detective Coosa says it fits him like his momma knew he was gonna grow up to be a snitch. Anyway, he wanted to meet here. I guess it's his usual watering hole."

"So I guess he'll have some buddies around in case something goes wrong."

Joey shook his head. "Snitching ain't a team sport. Boy's taking his life in his hands every time he sells some information. So I don't think we gotta worry about him having backup. He probably just wants lots of people around." Joey reached over and put his hand on his door release. "You ready?"

I stepped out onto the dirt parking lot. Joey led the way as we mounted the small porch and walked in through the open front door.

At six foot six and two hundred forty pounds, Joey is used to other men getting out of his way, and that's what they did as we entered the bar. Unfortunately, I'm not quite so intimidating a presence. And, as I stepped inside, a patron with a black, mountain-man beard, a yellow Caterpillar cap, and rolls of cellulite hanging from his exposed underarms put a hand across the little entry hall, blocking my way.

"You haven't paid the cover charge."

I looked at him. "My friend didn't pay either. Neither did the two people ahead of us."

The cellulite mountain man smiled and looked around to make sure his buddies were watching. "Shit. I guess they snuck in when I wasn't looking." He tried to mock my voice. "Let's see that's two people ahead of you, your friend, and you." He cut his eyes back to check out the appreciative laughter of his friends. " I guess you're gonna have to pay for all of 'em. Let's see. It's a ten-dollar cover. Ain't that right, Louis?"

One of his buddies laughed and said, "Hell, Jimbo, I believe it was twenty."

Jimbo said, "Naw. That'd be greedy. Tell you what. You just make it a even twenty for you and your boyfriend there."

I could see Joey over Jimbo's shoulder. He caught my eye, and I shook my head. I said, "Excuse me," and pushed Jimbo's arm out of the way.

Jimbo didn't know when to quit. He grabbed the front of my shirt and said, "Goddamnit, boy. Don't put your fucking hands on me."

I brought my right hand up fast, clamped his trachea between my thumb and fingers, and shoved him hard into the wall. Jimbo hit with a thud and lost balance. I pinned him to the wall by jamming my fingers into his chubby neck and squeezing hard enough to make him wheeze and squeak trying to breathe. I heard cussing and caught movement out of the corner of my eye as his friends started to move forward.

Joey stepped in front of them, and cussing turned to mumbling.

I looked into Jimbo's eyes. He let go of my shirt and aimed his right fist at my head. I blocked the punch by spearing his forearm with my left elbow and slapped him hard across his ear in the same motion. A high-pitched squeal came through his pinched throat.

I said, "You want some more of this?"

He shook his head, and I let go. Jimbo staggered out onto the small porch holding his throat. I stepped outside and spoke quietly to him, then came inside and walked with Joey to a small table covered in plastic with wood grain printed on it.

When we were seated, Joey said, "What'd you tell him outside?"

"That he asked for it, and embarrassed is better than dead."

"You be a dangerous man, huh?"

"Actually, I'm pretty much full of shit. But Jimbo doesn't know it. Or, at least, I don't think he does—choking makes you feel pretty helpless. Anyway, I was just trying to keep him from waiting for me out in the parking lot with a gun."

"He may do it anyhow."

I said, "Yeah, well, you can get killed crossing the street."

"Wish I'd said that." Joey said, "You know why he messed with you, don't you?"

"Yeah."

"You got on a diving watch costs more than most of these boys make in a month. Polo shirt and L. L. Bean khakis. You were asking for it."

"I believe I told you that I knew why he did it."

"Just making sure."

We were sitting in the back right corner, well away from the plywood bar that ran half the length of the wall on the left side of the room. A spring training game out of South Florida flickered bright green across the televison behind the bartender. Next to the TV, a Playboy centerfold that someone had blown up into a poster stretched four feet across the pressed-paneling wall. As our eyes adjusted, we could see a sampling of thirty or forty other centerfolds from the past thirty years taped to the walls, and, on the backs of the draft beer taps, the owner had glued a series of life-sized plastic breasts.

I pointed at the plastic boobs and said, "Mother's Milk."

Joey said, "Lot of thought went into that."

I nodded.

Joey looked around the room. "Something else I was thinking about. There aren't a hell of a lot of bars where you can half choke a man to death at the front door and nobody seems to notice."

"Probably happens too much to worry about."

"Probably."

A dishwater blonde came over and asked what we wanted. We said we wanted beer, and she went away.

I said, "I guess you don't see Squirley."

"Nope. Told him to look for me."

"You stand out in a crowd."

Joey nodded.

I had been studying the centerfold for March '77, trying to decide what she probably looked like twenty years later. The waitress brought our beer, and I drank some.

Joey said, "You notice on these centerfolds how the old ones were photographed without any nookie showing. Then they started showing it. Then they started shaving the stuff they started showing. It's like we thought we wanted to see it, but we really didn't."

I closed my eyes and rubbed the bridge of my nose.

I heard a new voice. "Joey?"

I looked up at a man standing next to our table.

Joey said, "Squirley. Sit down and have a beer."

The man nodded his head by repeating a birdlike ducking motion, like someone trying to swallow peanut butter.

I noticed that Squirley wobbled a little as he sat. I also noted that he hadn't been squandering his hard-earned snitch income on soap or razor blades.

Joey looked irritated. "You already drunk?"

"Working on it." He held up his hand and snapped his fingers at the waitress. She flipped him a bird and walked to the bar. Squirley jerked his thumb at me. "Who's zis?"

"I'm Tom."

"You buying, Tom?"

I said, "Sure," and motioned to the waitress.

She came over with a fresh beer balanced on her tray. "Somebody gonna pay for this? I ain't giving it to him till somebody pays for it."

I put three ones on her tray, and she put the glass in front of Squirley. He drank half of it and said, "I don't usually do business here."

Joey said, "You picked it."

Squirley nodded gravely and drank the rest of his beer. "Gimme another three. I'll just get me one more beer, and we'll go outside and talk."

I looked at Joey. He nodded, and I counted out three ones. Squirley McCall gathered them up and wove his way to the bar, where he pushed his way roughly through a small group of Latino men. Squirley waved at the bartender, who pretended not to see him. Squirley almost shouted. "I got the goddamn money. Gimme a beer, Leonard. I say I got your goddamn money."

Joey sighed.

When Squirley finally got his draft, he turned his back to the bar and leaned one elbow on the edge while he took in the first gulp. He looked around at the small band of Latino patrons and said, "Lucy, you got some *splaining* to do," and began to laugh uncontrollably. One of the men said something I couldn't hear. Squirley grinned and said, "How do you get 148 Cubans in a shoe box? Tell 'em it floats." And he laughed so hard he gave himself hiccups.

I decided to go fetch our snitch while there was still enough left of him to snitch with. As I stepped through the men Squirley had just insulted, I said, "Excuse me," and grabbed one of his arms.

One of the men stepped in front of Squirley. "We are not Cuban. We are Peruvian. Not everyone who lives south of this country is from the same place."

Squirley smiled. "Who gives a fuck?"

The man turned to me. "Does your friend *want* to have his heart cut out?"

"He's not my friend."

"He should leave."

I said, "Sounds about right."

Joey had wandered over in case my rescue of Squirley turned into a war. Now he grabbed the snitch's other arm and we started for the front door.

Squirley said, "Other way. Other way. Go out back and talk."

Joey looked at me. I said, "Guess he's got his reasons," and gently steered him as he staggered to a doorway in the back wall and then led us through a filthy kitchen and out a back door. Once outside, Squirley walked over and leaned against a particularly foul-smelling Dumpster.

Joey looked disgusted.

I said, "You really think this idiot knows something?"

Joey shook his head. "You never know. Almost every snitch is a drunk or a junkie or both. You pretty much gotta find somebody who'll sell out his friends for fifty bucks if you want information, and that usually means somebody who needs a bottle or a fix." He motioned at Squirley with his hand. "That, unfortunately, is your basic professional snitch."

"But who would tell that dumb-ass anything?"

Joey said, "I don't know. But Coosa says he's pretty reliable."

Squirley perked up. "I can hear you talkin'. You don't want help? Fine. Fuck off. I got better stuff to do." Joey and I walked over and stood in front of Squirley. He was still mad about being hauled out of the bar in front of the Peruvians. "Bunch of fucking Ricky Ricardo spic assholes. Buying up the whole fucking coast. Motherfuckers coming up here outta South Florida. Already ruined it down there for real Americans, and, much as I care, they're welcome to it. Fucking Margaritaville. We don't need that shit up here."

I said, "Who's buying up the coast?"

Squirley seemed to sober up a little. He shifted his eyes from side to side, checking for spies, signaling that he was about to impart confidential information. He said, "I'm gonna tell you, just to let you know that old Squirley knows what he's talkin' about, you know, that old Squirley got his finger on the place."

His breath fogged the air between us, competing with the Dumpster's aroma—stench layered on stench. I nodded encouragingly.

"There's a buncha rich cigar spics, call themselves 'Pro-Am,' like that golf show. They own all kinda shit around here. Houses, boats, some of the businesses in town. Most people don't know that shit."

Joey said, "They got a leader?"

"I guess they do. Don't know many names, though."

Joey just looked at him.

Squirley seemed to shrink a little inside his skin. His husky, alcoholic voice cracked when he said, "I thought you was bringin' some money." Joey handed him a twenty. Squirley turned it over in his fingers, examining both sides like he wasn't used to dealing in such small denominations. "Not much."

I said, "That's just for starters. To see if you know anything worth paying for."

Squirley raised his eyebrows, dropped open his mouth, and held his palms in the air with the twenty protruding from trembling fingertips. He tried to look hurt, to look put-upon. The snitch said, "You called me. So you know . . ."

Joey said, "Give us the fucking name."

Squirley stopped to think. As he did, he popped the knuckles of his right hand, one at a time, snatching them with his thumb. "Martillo is one." He pronounced it *Marr-til-oh*. "And another one I heard is something like Carpet Hero, but I think that one's a nickname."

Joey sounded disgusted. "Yeah. I bet that's it."

Squirley looked at us and blinked puffy, bloodshot eyes.

I said, "What's Leroy Purcell doing down here?"

He grinned. "You know a little somethin', don't you? I'll tell you what Leroy's doin'. He's pissin' in the wrong pond. That's what he's doin'. And I reckon you know he's the one brought the spics in here."

I asked, "Whose pond is this down here?"

"Well, you see, that ain't exactly clear."

Joey said, "What's that mean?"

"Could mean lotsa things, couldn't it? I reckon it mostly means I wanna see some more green before I tell you what it means."

I said, "A hundred. If we don't already know what you know."

"I don't do business like that. You hand over the goddamn money . . ."

Joey stepped forward and hit Squirley with an open right, and the putrid little bigot spun and hit the wall behind him face first. He hung there a moment, as if hurt or dazed. Joey's .45 auto appeared, and my giant friend pressed the muzzle behind Squirley's left ear.

I jumped. "Whoa, Joey . . ."

Joey kept looking at our drunken snitch. "Drop the knife." Squirley hesitated, and Joey cocked the hammer on his Colt.

Slowly, the drunk's right hand moved out from the space between his stomach and the wall. It held a hunting knife with a six-inch blade. Squirley lifted his blade to the side and dropped it in the gravel.

Joey said, "Put your hands on the wall and spread 'em. That's right. You've done it before."

Joey patted him down and told him to turn around.

Squirley looked scared. He said, "Do I still get the hundred?"

Joey shook his head and laughed.

I said, "Tell us what you know."

Squirley licked dry, cracked lips, then snorted hard down deep in his throat and spit on the gravel. He was getting ready to talk.

"There's a hell of a mess goin' on. On the one side, you got old men been running things down here—some of 'em since after Korea. On the other side you got a buncha mean-ass kids tryin' to take over. Startin' to get bad, too. These young 'uns, they don't give a shit about nothin'. Kill you for nothin', for fun. Don't give a shit about jail. Nothin'."

I said, "Where's Purcell come in?"

"Old Leroy thinks he's gonna come in and take over while there's a war goin' on. But he's fuckin' up. Shoulda picked a side and cut some kinda deal. But, hell no, fuckin' football hero wants it all. Word is he wants to set up one of them cartels like they got down in Spicland. Old Leroy wants to be king shit of smugglers. Kinda do for guns and military stuff what the spics did with coke." He paused to turn his head and spit into the gravel. "Shit. You ask me, Leroy's fuckin' up big time. Now, he's got the old boys pissed—and they been doin' this shit a long time—and he's got the young 'uns pissed—and, like I said, they just don't give a shit. Kill your momma for a dollar."

I said, "We need names."

"You're asking shit that's gonna get me killed if anybody finds out I talked."

Joey said, "How about if we give you our word that we'll be as careful with your reputation as you are?"

"You tryin' to be a smart-ass?" Joey shrugged, and Squirley flinched. He turned to me. "Your boy here don't know how to do business. Now, you look smart."

I said, "Uh-huh."

"All I'm saying is, if you want names, I gotta see that hundred."

I pulled some folded bills from my hip pocket, peeled one off, and handed it to Squirley.

He smiled. He beamed. It wasn't pretty.

Our inebriated informer pushed the bill deep inside his pocket, and a dark shape hit him flush in the mouth. Squirley McCall fell back onto the wall and slid to the ground. I spun around.

Joey already had his .45 trained on a group of three men. The one in the middle was casually tossing half a brick into the air and catching it.

Joey said, "Put it down."

The man caught the brick, turned his hand upside down, and let it drop. The same man looked up and said, "Time for you two to get on out of here."

Joey said, "I was just gonna say the same thing to you. Seeing how I'm the one with the gun and all."

The brick thrower smiled and walked away followed by the other two.

Joey said, "Let's go."

I grabbed Squirley's elbow and said, "Get the other arm."

"Why?"

"Because they're going to kill him if we leave him here."

Joey said, "They're gonna kill him anyhow for talking to us," but he grabbed the other arm and helped me get Squirley to my car.

After dropping Squirley at the emergency room, I took a few minutes to talk over the night with Joey. Then I headed back to Seaside. I needed to spend some time in front of a laptop while my little adventure at Mother's Milk was fresh in my mind.

For the first time, the loose ends were beginning to weave themselves into an indistinct but vaguely recognizable fabric.

chapter nineteen

I SHUT DOWN my new Dell laptop a little after one, trudged up the rented teak stairs of our Seaside cottage, and climbed under the covers beside Susan, who stirred and murmured *half words whispered low* and found sleep again. I lay there listening to the widow Fitzsimmons' rhythmic breathing and let panic take hold the way it does when it finds you exhausted and unsettled and uncomfortably awake in the hours between midnight and dawn.

I got up and drank some water. Got back in bed. Got out again and straightened the covers. Again Susan stirred, and I lay still. Much less time went by than it felt like, and I drifted into a fitful sleep.

That morning, I slept late but not well.

Downstairs, Loutie was manning the listening equipment. Susan was on the phone; she put her hand over the mouthpiece and said, "It's Joey. He needs to talk to you."

I took the phone, and said, "Kind of an interesting night."

"Yeah. That's one thing you could call it. Might've been more interesting if Squirley had turned loose of a couple more names before eating a brick."

I walked over to the cabinet and found a glass. "Go see him in the hospital. We left him the hundred. He still owes us the names." As I spoke, I filled the glass with ice and water.

Joey said, "Too late. Squirley McCall's a goner."

"He died from getting hit in the mouth with a brick? That doesn't make sense."

"Hell no. He just hauled ass. The orderly took in his breakfast, and old Squirley had taken a powder. And his clothes were gone. So it looked like Squirley just got dressed and slipped out. I wouldn't put it past him to just be trying to stiff the hospital, but, considering last night, I'm guessing he's hiding out somewhere for a while. You want me to try to find him?"

"No, I don't think so. Tell me if I'm wrong, but I think you need to watch Haycock, and I need to keep an eye on Purcell."

Joey agreed and got off the phone. I made a detour upstairs for a quick shower and clean clothes and, after donning my cap-and-sunglasses disguise, strolled over and loitered on the beach outside Purcell's pastel mansion.

Everything looked the way it had the day before. The sky was blue and the Cadillac was red.

I had just gotten there when my phone vibrated. It was Susan. "He's up. Get out of there."

"I didn't know he was down."

"Yes. He was still in bed."

"I'm on the beach. I can see the house, but I'm nowhere near it."

I waited, feeling a little silly, while Susan conveyed my position to Loutie. Susan repeated, "He's up. He just got a call from a man who didn't identify himself. And Tom, the guy said he was, quote, 'bringing in Poultrez.'"

"Shit!"

"They've got her, Tom. The only good thing is they're bringing Carli here, to Purcell's house."

"That's strange. I've been operating on the assumption that Purcell would want to maintain a veneer of respectability around here." I thought. "Another good thing is that if they're bringing her here she's probably okay. I don't think they'll let her come in kicking and screaming, but I don't think they'll want to unload any unconscious teenage girls in broad daylight either."

I heard Loutie speaking in the background, and Susan said, "Loutie's coming over. She says stay on the beach side of the house. She'll hang around in front. She says if you see her move, to come running and to have that gun of yours ready."

I said, "Let me talk to her."

Loutie came on. "Tom. Just stay where you are. The man who phoned Purcell said he'd be pulling into Seaside in fifteen or twenty minutes. Like Susan said, I'll stay on the side of the house away from the beach. If a car comes up, I'll be in sight. Just follow my lead."

"You're kidding. You want to have a shoot-out in the middle of Seaside at nine in the morning?"

Loutie's voice was tense with the strained patience of an older sister explaining life to her none-too-bright sibling. "No, Tom. I don't want that, and neither will Purcell. He lives here. But if we want any chance of getting her back, we better do it now. They won't be expecting an ambush outside Purcell's driveway. And we'll all be in the open and in clear view of the neighbors, and they won't want to shoot. No. This is as good as it's going to get, Tom." She paused and said, "Are you with me?"

I didn't like it, but I said, "I'm with you."

"Good."

"Have you talked with Joey?"

"Yeah. I called while Susan was on with you. Looks like something's happening with Haycock, and he couldn't get here in time to do anything anyway. He said to handle it."

I said, "Then I guess that's what we'll do," and pressed *end*.

I walked down to the surf's edge and looked both ways. The closest humans were little more than distant dots on the beach. Facing the water, I eased the 9mm out of my waistband and held it close against my stomach while I chambered a round and checked the safety. I put it back.

Suddenly the breeze and the sun were irritating, the sand in my shoes ground uncomfortably into tender, sockless feet, and I noticed seaweed and dead jellyfish marring the beach. *Shit, shit, and shit.* I walked up the beach to a small dune behind Purcell's place and pretended to collect driftwood. As seconds and minutes ticked by, I walked back and forth along a small section of startlingly white beach collecting smooth brown sticks one at a time and placing them on a neat pile next to the dune, also one at a time. I was trying to stretch a two-minute job into twenty. Finally, when I had exhausted the stick supply, I took a minute to walk up and look for Loutie. Nothing wrong with looking for a friend who promised to join you on the beach. No reason to hide.

When no one had arrived at Purcell's by nine-thirty, I plopped down on the dune, wiggled a butt-shaped seat into the warm sand, and began to sort my sticks by size and color. It was stupid, but no one would be looking that hard. And, even if they did, people do stupid, slow-motion things on the beach. *The poor fella's on vacation, Marge. Let him play with his sticks in peace.*

A black Chrysler pulled up and parked next to Purcell's Caddy. *Okay. Now what? How do I get close enough to do anything?* I picked up the carefully sorted sticks in my left hand and cringed to think I was leaving my "gun hand," for God's sake, empty and ready to shoot.

I tried to look relaxed, to look like a tourist, to look proud of my sticks.

I was near the cars now, and the Browning's heft and its steel ridges chafed my side. Loutie materialized around the front corner of the house. She didn't look relaxed. She looked ready to kill someone. The car door opened. Tim, Sonny's painting partner at See Shore Cottage, stepped out of the driver's door and slammed it shut as the passenger door swung open. An enormous man stepped out and gaped at his monied surroundings like a Baptist in a titty bar. He had dark Mediterranean skin and hair and, judging from a distance, looked to be maybe six four and close to two eighty. He looked like more of Purcell's muscle, but something about the guy bothered me. Something about him tugged at a memory.

I waited. Carli had to be in the backseat or maybe in the trunk. The men went inside, but I knew there could be someone else hiding in back, someone holding my client hostage and waiting to shoot anyone who came near.

Loutie approached a ground floor window of Purcell's mansion and peered inside. Then she motioned me forward with her hand and pointed at the Chrysler. I nodded and trotted over next to the trunk. I glanced back at Loutie. She gave me a thumbs-up. I peeked inside at empty seats and then pushed the door release button and eased open the back door. My phone vibrated. The backseat and the floorboards were indeed empty, and my phone vibrated. I opened the passenger door, found the trunk release, pushed it, and my phone vibrated. Carli was not in the trunk. I raised my shoulders and shook my head at Loutie, and my phone vibrated.

Loutie motioned for me to follow her, but I shook my head and walked back out onto the beach and sat on my dune, all the while wondering who was vibrating my hip. Of course, it was Susan.

"What is it?" I may have sounded a little terse.

Susan said, "You didn't answer."

"Bad timing. I'm fine. What is it?"

"They're not bringing Carli here. They don't even have her."

And I had it. I said, "That's her father, isn't it? That's Rus Poultrez."

"How'd you know?" I didn't answer. I was trying to think this through. Susan went on. "I heard them over Loutie's equipment. They brought him in to help find Carli. They're talking money now. Sounds like they had some kind of agreement, and now Poultrez is trying to squeeze more money out of Purcell. I've heard the numbers thirty thousand and fifty thousand."

I felt sick. "Who would sell his own daughter for thirty thousand dollars?"

Susan said, "The same guy who would rape and abuse his daughter instead of protecting her or even ignoring her. Someone disgusting and worse. Someone evil."

I cussed and kicked some sand into the air that blew back in my face. I told her I was returning to the house.

For most of the next hour, Susan, Loutie, and I listened over hidden mikes as Poultrez bitched about how much money he was losing by sitting around Seaside instead of staying home to work the seas off New England for cod. Every now and then, as Poultrez paused to savor a particularly salient argument, Purcell would say, "If you don't want the thirty thousand, go back home."

Purcell didn't get to be king redneck just by being the biggest nut on the tree. As Poultrez tried to work him for more money, Purcell was demonstrating surprising control and even glimmers of limited intelligence. He knew Poultrez had put his fishing business on hold and flown all the way to Florida based on an offer of thirty thousand. The fisherman would take more if he could get it. But Poultrez had come for thirty, and, in the end, he would happily sell his daughter's life for that amount.

In contrast to his host, Carli's father kept pushing after all hope and most of Purcell's patience had evaporated. Poultrez proceeded from financial arguments to threatening to get on a plane, and Purcell told him to do what he thought best. Poultrez tried anger, and Purcell gave the same answer. Finally, Poultrez tried threatening Purcell, and the football-hero leader of the Bodines offered to kill Poultrez, chop him into edible chunks, and leave his butchered carcass scattered over a saltwater marsh for the crabs and alligators. That was pretty much the end of that.

Poultrez still tried to sound tough, but he mostly just sounded defeated. "This is bullshit. Over the phone, you said thirty for sure and probably more if I came. That's what you said. 'Probably more.' And now that I hauled my ass down here to the middle of nowhere, you just say take the thirty. Shit. I lost my temper threatening you the way I did before, but . . . shit."

A feminine voice with a heavy Latin accent announced lunch. Joey's bugs were so good we could hear the springs on the sofa creak as someone stood. A few seconds later, Purcell's voice said, "Sit over there," and we could hear even better than before.

I whispered to Loutie, "This is amazing."

Loutie said, "They're not two-way mikes, Tom. You don't have to whisper."

Of course I knew that. It just seems like you should whisper when you're eavesdropping. But explaining would have been worse than nothing, so I said, "Oh," and Susan pretended not to notice.

Chewing, slurping, and swallowing sounds emanated from Purcell's and Poultrez's mouths and buzzed into our rented kitchen through black-screened speakers.

Loutie said, "There's a bug under the table and one in the light over it."

More masticating filtered through the speakers, and Purcell said, "Thirty's all you get for Carli. You wanna make more, you gotta do more. There's a lawyer named McInnes, Tom McInnes, who's mixed up in this. I personally took the time to try and reason with him, but the guy's a prick. Attacked one of my men by throwing food at him like some dumb-ass kid and then stabbing his tire and running away like a chicken shit." Purcell paused to gulp something and emit a barely stifled belch. "Like I said, I gave him a chance to be smart. He screwed it for hisself. So, here's the deal. I want you spending your time looking for the girl. That's first. But, if you come across McInnes while you're doing it, and if you put a bullet in his head, I'll add twenty thousand to the thirty thousand finder's fee I'm offering for Carli."

Poultrez's greed had new legs. "Twenty's not much for killing somebody. Hell, back home, up in Boston . . ."

Purcell said, "Do I look like somebody who gives a rat's ass what people in Boston-fucking-Massachusetts do?" Poultrez didn't answer. "Twenty's the same deal I'm giving my own men. One of

’em nails McInnes, I’ll pay the twenty. You nail him, you get the twenty.”

The room swirled—just a little—and I realized I was breathing too fast. Shallow gusts filled the top shelf of my lungs and gushed out again under their own power. I blinked and focused on breathing deeply and slowly. Two strong hands squeezed my shoulders, and I jumped—again, just a little. Susan was standing behind me, meaning to comfort me.

I said, “That’s interesting.”

Loutie looked unfazed. She said, “Yeah. It is.”

chapter twenty

SUSAN TRIED TO put the best face on my impending death. "Tom. In a way, this is good. Isn't it? I mean, we've got Leroy Purcell on tape." She looked at Loutie. "It is on tape isn't it?" Loutie nodded, and Susan turned back to me. "So, we've got him on tape taking out a contract on your life. We can take that to the police and get them to do something."

I said, "Do what?"

"Arrest him or something."

"We illegally bugged Purcell's house, Susan. Down the road somewhere, the tapes may or may not be admissible in court, if we get that far. But, for now, we've got all kinds of problems with them. Just to start, Joey and Loutie committed breaking and entering, which is a felony, to hide the bugs. Joey would lose his investigator's license, he and Loutie might do some jail time, and I'd expect the State Bar to question my fitness to continue practicing law, since Joey and Loutie planted the bugs at my direction."

Susan said, "But if it'll save your life."

"Susan, if I knew turning over the tapes would save your life, Carli's life, or mine, I'd turn them over to the cops today. But it wouldn't work. It's only our word that that's actually Purcell on the tapes. He'd claim we manufactured them. And he's connected down here and we're not. Who do you think they're going to believe? The guy's scum, but he's still a hero to a lot of people in Florida because of his football days."

Susan's eyes scanned the room, lingered on the window, and came to rest on the listening equipment. She was completely focused, trying with everything she had to find the good in what we had heard. I was touched by how hard she was working not to think about what it really meant.

I said, "We're a long way from dead, Susan. The tapes aren't important. What is important—the good part—is that we know about Purcell's plans ahead of time."

Susan brightened. "Yes, that is good. Now you know to stay out of his way and not to go wandering around his house again like you did this morning. Now we can figure out what to do."

I've always read about people in danger smiling bravely. That's what I tried to do.

While Susan rummaged in the refrigerator and began putting out cold chicken salad and sliced fruit for lunch, I trotted upstairs and packed. Purcell's conversation with Poultrez had let me know one thing. It let me know to get as far as possible from anyone I cared about; it let me know that Susan's dyed hair wouldn't do much good if I was around to be seen and shot at and, more or less, murdered. Purcell had never seen Susan—particularly outfitted with her new brunette persona. My presence in the house would be a neon sign for Purcell and his tattooed toadies.

The phone rang as I was packing my razor and other bathroom stuff. Someone downstairs answered. I tossed the small toilet kit into my duffel and carried my little hobo bundle down the rented teak stairs and put it next to our canary-yellow door. Susan glanced at the duffel and looked confused. Loutie held out the telephone receiver and said, "It's Joey. I filled him in. He wants to talk to you."

I put the phone against my ear and said, "It's been a fun morning."

Joey said, "Sounds like it. You get a look at Rus Poultrez?"

"Yeah. He's big. Not as tall as you, but he weighs more. I thought he was some of Purcell's hired muscle when he went in, if that tells you anything."

The line was quiet for a few beats. Joey said, "I hear somebody wants you dead." I didn't say anything. "I wouldn't worry too much about it, Tom. But I do think you ought to come down here with me. We can watch each other's back."

"Not to mention that Susan and Loutie will be safer with me gone."

"Not to mention that." Joey said, "Listen, the reason I called is our buddy, Thomas Bobby Haycock, looks like he's getting ready to do a little smuggling. Maybe commit a felony or two."

"How can you tell?"

"Just been watching him so much I guess. I don't know if there's a list of reasons I think he's going out, but I think he is. You know, he doesn't have any of that swamp trash nookie hanging around. He gassed up the truck. And hell, I don't know, he just has the look about him."

"I'll call Billy Teeter and see if I can rent his boat."

"I'm thinking I should come with you on the boat. You could run into some trouble out there."

"No." I said, "I want you to get over to the mainland and be ready to follow Haycock's truck when he goes over tomorrow morning." Joey started to argue. I said, "We can tiptoe around protecting each other, or we can figure this mess out and maybe bury Purcell and his people."

"I don't like it."

"But I'm right."

"Yeah," Joey said. "I guess." And he hung up.

I placed the receiver in its cradle, and Susan's voice, unnaturally quiet, came from behind me. "Where are you going?"

I turned to face her. Loutie said, "He's not running away, Susan."

Susan said, "I know," but it sounded like a question.

Loutie said, "Tom's the only one of us Purcell and his men have seen, Susan. If he's here and they want to kill him, then . . ." Her voice trailed off.

I said, "Joey says Haycock's getting ready for another shipment tonight. I'm going back down to the island and get Billy Teeter to take me out and have a look around."

Susan said, "You packed before Joey called about Haycock." I was stunned. Susan really did think I was running out on her. Loutie quietly left the room. I walked over and put my arms around Susan's waist. She placed her hands on my shoulders but not around me. She felt stiff in my arms.

I asked, "Do you really think I'd run out on you because I'm scared?"

Susan said, "I've been dealing with a lot by myself for a long time, Tom. I kind of thought that was over." I said her name. She shook her head and kept talking. "I'm not eighteen. I know that just because we feel the way we do . . . Well, I know lust, or whatever this is, doesn't always last. But I care about you, and I thought you'd be someone to get through the bad stuff with even if we didn't last as lovers."

"I thought the same thing, Susan. But I can't stay here like some kind of murder beacon to bring the Bodines down on you and Loutie."

Susan said, "I don't think you're running out and leaving me at Purcell's mercy. I think you're being a noble ass. You're going to leave here and get killed, and I'll get to go through another six months of guilt and misery and hell like the ones after Bird died."

I said, "Oh."

Twin crescents of tears filled Susan's lower lids above the uncharacteristic, spiky shelves of dark mascara. Loutie and I had both read her wrong. Susan wasn't upset because she thought I was a coward. She was getting mad at me in advance for getting killed.

I smiled. "Jeez, Susan, just go ahead and kill me off, why don't you?" I kissed her and tasted salt. She pushed away, then stood on her toes and put her arms around my neck. I said, "I'm kind of a resourceful guy. I'll be fine. And remember, Joey will be around, and I'm not sure Joey's someone who can actually *be* killed. And, as for you, you couldn't ask for better protection than that scary chick in the other room."

From the living room, Loutie said, "I heard that."

Susan laughed, and I kissed her again. This time, she kissed back.

Loutie Blue and I walked outside and, after I opened the trunk of my rented, silver-blue Bonneville and tossed my duffel inside, we stood by the car and talked. Loutie wanted to follow Rus Poultrez when he left Purcell's place. I wanted her to stay in Seaside, keep an eye on Purcell, and keep Susan safe.

The bottom line was that Joey worked for me and Loutie worked for Joey. So, in the end, I more or less insisted, and she stayed with Susan.

I cruised into Appalachicola a few minutes before four. A soft breeze ruffled the fronds of tall palms lining the main drag; housewives steered station wagons and four-by-fours in and out of the Piggly Wiggly parking lot; a boney-tailed real estate type taped new listings on a plateglass window; and twenty or thirty cars and pickups cruised the streets with aimless intent. I curved hard in the air, circling the marina, and followed the suspended pavement over the bay and out of town. Fifteen minutes later, I turned right toward St. George and then left onto the narrow county road leading into Eastpoint. I had called ahead. I was expected.

Billy Teeter's partner-in-seafood, Julie, was planted in the same porch chair she had occupied the last time I was there. I parked and stepped out onto the narrow, sandy parking area. I said, "Hello," and she nodded. She just nodded. Julie's features stayed noncommittal. I asked, "Where's Mr. Teeter?"

"Around back."

"I need to park off the street." Julie just looked at me. I added, "You know, out of sight."

She said, "Drive around back," as if any fool would have known to do that.

I steered over faint wheel tracks leading across the ragged yard and around the left side of Teeter's Seafood and pulled in close to the back of the shack. A sandy pathway led down the shoreline past a series of commercial docks where blue-gray pelicans perched atop two of the creosote pilings that stuck up above concrete walkways. Diving bunches of ugly, mottled gulls picked at mounds of discarded shellfish that held just enough decaying flesh to keep the birds interested and to fill the air with the bitter stink of sea animals dying on land. Twenty yards west of the shack, Billy Teeter's bear-like form rose above the deck of a shrimp boat so perfectly maintained that it looked like it had just come out of dry dock. I waved, and Billy parted his scruffy, bearded face into a surprisingly welcoming smile full of nicotined teeth.

Down the path and out on the dock next to the *Teeter Two*, I called out. "Hello!"

Teeter said, "You gonna need a coat out on the water." I told him I had one and went back to the rented Pontiac to get it out of the duffel. Back on the dock, I said, "Am I supposed to ask permission to come aboard?"

Billy Teeter smiled, put one foot on the gunwale, and reached out a hand. "Get on up here, boy." Most white-collar types would never believe a human hand could get that hard. I thought about what my own soft lawyer's hand must have felt like to Billy as he pulled my hundred and ninety pounds over the gunwale and into the boat with no more effort than most men would expend pulling a child into the family van. Billy said, "It's good to see you again, Tom." I reached into my pocket and came out with two hundred fifty dollars, and Billy shook his scruffy brown and gray chin. "No, sir. I ain't done the work yet. You pay when we get back."

I held out the money. "You better take it. If I fall in the water out there and drown, you may not get paid."

The old man looked into my eyes before shifting his glance to my hand as he took the money and pushed it deep inside his hip pocket. In a matter-of-fact voice, he said, "You think you're kidding."

I smiled. He didn't. Billy turned and called out, "Willie!"

A nineteen-year-old version of the captain emerged from the tiny bridge. Billy's namesake stood about five ten. He had a football player's overdeveloped neck and the thick back and shoulder muscles of a shrimper. Brown hair stood erect on the boy's tanned head in an old-fashioned crew cut, and his square chin and jaws were smudged with a dark stubble of Teeter family whiskers. If young Willie had grown a seaman's beard, his resemblance to old Billy Teeter would have been almost comical.

Captain Billy said, "This here's Mr. McInnes." Willie didn't speak. I reached out and shook a limp, calloused hand; and I was struck, not for the first time, by how softly most men who work with their hands shake hands with other men. Maybe it's just something that people outside the white-collar world don't do in the ordinary course of their lives, so they never get very good at it. Or maybe they're just afraid they'll hurt you.

"Call me Tom."

Billy said, "Get Tom a life jacket. He's gonna be wearing it soon as we leave the dock." I doubted that the Teeters bothered with life jackets while shrimping, and that doubt was verified by young Willie's amused expression. Billy saw his grandson's face too. He said, "Straighten up, Willie. Tom's a paying passenger. It's gonna be your butt gets kicked if I see him with that jacket off."

Willie said, "I'll keep an eye on him, Granddaddy," but he kept smiling.

Over the next two hours, the three of us talked over the best way to proceed. Billy sat on a crate, Willie sat on the gunwale, and I sat cross-legged on my bright orange, oddly emasculating life jacket. I described the location on Dog Island where I thought the smugglers would land around midnight. Billy and Willie discussed channels, oyster beds, and other things I didn't know a lot about. Finally, Billy said he knew all he needed to know. He said we would wait until nine to leave. "Be black dark by then. And we don't want to be floating around out there too long without putting nets in the water. It'd look wrong if anybody cared enough to pay us any attention."

With three hours more to kill, Willie found a deck of cards and we played stud poker to pass the time. The kid had grinned a little too broadly about Billy sentencing me to spend my hours on the water in a life jacket, so I played a little harder than I should have against a nineteen-year-old and ended up with eighteen dollars of his money. It was not a mature exhibition. My only saving grace was that I let his grandfather win most of it back. By 8:40, my playground honor felt mostly restored, and we were ready to get under way. I walked back to the stern, away from the shrimpers, and placed a call to Susan. There was no news of Carli.

Willie cast off while Captain Billy fired the diesels. As we nosed away from the dock, young Willie walked up holding my orange flotation device by one finger like it was a dainty thing disdainful to his gender.

I took it and tied it on.

chapter twenty-one

INSIDE APPALACHICOLA BAY, black water chopped against the hull in jarring stutters. Captain Billy moved west along the buoy-marked intracoastal waterway, steering a course parallel with the shore before turning toward the dark silhouette of an ancient lighthouse on Little St. George Island.

A fine, stinging rain began to fall as we cruised through the mouth of Bob Sikes Cut a few minutes after nine. Gray boulders held the edges of the narrow passage between St. George Island to the east and Little St. George to the west. Both islands are long, narrow strips of land, especially thin near the cut, and a strong man could come close to throwing a rock from one end to the other and from one island to the next. Inside the cut, stuttering chop turned smooth and then rose to a deep, steady roll as the boat pushed out into the Gulf.

Our bobbing bow cut a line to the moonlit horizon, which seemed to roll up and down and side to side in an ever changing figure eight with no sense of balance or equilibrium. It was fascinating to watch until I felt the queasily familiar pressure on the sides of my throat, the beginning flow of saliva, and the thick ropes of nausea crawling inside my stomach. I stepped outside the bridge cabin and washed away most of the nausea by leaning my head back, opening my mouth, and letting rain pellets splatter my face and neck and tongue.

Captain Billy called out. "Boy, you gonna get cold later with that rainwater down your shirt."

I decided I'd worry about later when it came. I hadn't had dinner, and the thought of dry heaves made a little freezing rain seem comforting by comparison.

I yelled over the engines. "How far?"

"Be there in thirty minutes or so. Taking the long way around. We got plenty of time."

The shore was a dotted line of lights now, and, in the distance, lightning began to splinter the horizon. Slowly, the ropes of nausea uncoiled and settled, almost comfortingly, into one small corner of my stomach. Then Billy turned east toward Dog Island. Heading directly into the waves had provided me with one sort of challenge, but now we steered a course parallel to the shore and the rolling swell gave the boat a whole new disconcerting movement and personality. As we moved back and forth, side to side, up and down, and sometimes, it seemed, round and round in a horizontal kind of way, my mind searched desperately for distraction, and I thought of an old joke about a young boy who married an older woman. After his honeymoon, the boy's father asked if the girl had been a virgin. The boy responded that he thought the up-and-down had come naturally but the round-and-round must have been learned. I smiled, then leaned out over the gunwale and emptied Susan's chicken-salad-and-sliced-fruit lunch into the Gulf of Mexico.

The rest of our trip to the waters off Dog Island proved to be personally difficult, gastronomically repetitive, and a source of genuine amusement to the Teeter men. But, at first, it appeared to have been worth it. As we neared the island, Captain Billy called out my name. I loosened my death grip on the railing that had seen so much of my inner workings and looked up. He pointed at a short row of white lights suspended beneath a bright blue dot in the distance.

I yelled, "What is it?"

"Big pleasure boat."

"How can you tell?"

Billy looked concerned about my faculties. He yelled, "'Cause it looks like one."

Obviously he saw something I didn't, but that wasn't surprising. Billy Teeter had spent the better part of fifty years on those waters, much of it shrimping at night. I had to assume that he knew what he was talking about.

It was close to ten. Billy cut the engines to an idle and came out to stand beside me. He was wearing full yellow rain gear like a fisherman in a children's story. "Whatcha wanna do?"

I asked, "How suspicious would it look for us to just sit here and watch them for a while?"

"Probably be fine. Depends on how jumpy they are. The captain's gonna know shrimpers set still all the time to rig nets or check the water or just decide where to head next. With this rain comin' down, anybody who knows boats is likely gonna figure we're tryin' to figure whether to head back in."

"So we're fine here for a while."

"Yep."

At exactly 11:00 P.M., a blue spotlight flashed three times on the deck of the yacht. Young Willie had joined us; he was outfitted in a green plastic poncho. I told the Teeter men about the signal Joey and I had seen a week earlier at midnight on a deserted stretch of beach on Dog Island. And we waited. Willie said, "I reckon they're not too worried about us if they're givin' the same signal."

Through silver streaks of rain, a pair of headlights flashed three times on shore, and I said, "It doesn't look like it. It looks like they're going to go ahead with the drop-off."

Young Willie was jumpy. I could almost hear the adrenaline pumping inside his poncho. A smaller blue light flashed midway between the yacht and the shoreline, and Willie pointed and said, "Look! Look at that. What're they doing?"

I said, "That's the drop-off boat. They're taking whatever they're smuggling to shore."

Willie said, "Cool," and Captain Billy shook his head.

Another set of blue flashes were answered by headlights. I said, "The men in the drop-off boat are armed. We better cruise over now and check out the yacht. I'm guessing there'll just be one or two men left onboard. They've got to be figuring that any trouble is going to come onshore."

Billy climbed into the bridge cabin and eased the engines into gear. We had started our rolling approach when a loud hum approached the stern out of the night. I called Billy and pointed into the dark rain. Billy squinted at me and then at the piece of night I had pointed into and then at me again. I stepped up next to the small door leading into the covered bridge. "Somebody's out there. I hear a loud motor, like a speedboat or something."

"Whatcha wanna do? It's your dollar."

I said, "Keep moving as fast as you can."

Just as Billy pushed the throttle wide open, a spotlight swept a silver path through the rain and came to rest on the bridge. A twenty-foot cigar boat pulled up alongside. Billy called out. "We ain't gonna outrun that."

I said, "Turn away from them," and Billy spun the chromed wheel. The speedboat shot past us and quickly began to circle back.

I pulled the 9mm out of my back waistband, and Billy said, "Whoa. I didn't sign up to shoot nobody. Put that thing back where you got it."

"What if they shoot at us first?"

"Then you can take it out." He reached up to pat a twelve-gauge pump hung from two brass stirrups above the front glass. The rear stock had been sawed off and shaped into a pistol grip. "Somebody points a gun at this boat, and I'll blow their ass out of the water. You don't worry about that."

Billy was a tough old bird, but I held on to my Browning. The cigar boat was alongside again. Its narrow spotlight swept the deck, stopping on young Willie who gave them a one-finger salute through pouring rain that shone like tinsel in the light's beam. A loud, sharp crack cut the night air, and Willie went over the side. I screamed at Billy. "Stop! Stop this thing. Willie's in the water." Billy yanked down on the throttle arm. The shrimp boat dropped its nose into the surf, and, once again, the cigar boat shot past. I shouted, "I'll go after Willie. Use the shotgun."

As I turned to run, Billy's leathery hand closed painfully on my bicep. "Stay still. You get out in the water, and they'll run you down or shoot you too. We can't do nothin' for Willie till we take care of that boat." We could hear the speedboat coming back. Billy said, "Get down. I'll try to hit the spotlight. You unload that pistol into whoever's drivin'." I nodded and wondered if I'd have that much sense, that kind of balls, if someone I loved was flailing around in the night ocean with a gunshot wound.

The speedboat revved and then cut to idle as it came near. A yellow beam hit the bow, and Billy waved me back. I ran doubled over to the stern and hunkered down behind a pile of nets. The light swept back over the deck and then forward again to the bridge cabin. Without warning, automatic gunfire splintered Billy's bridge into bits of glass and wood that spun and flashed across the light like lethal fireflies. *Shit.* I popped up and put three shots as close to the light as I could, considering that I was firing from the deck of one rolling boat to another. The light spun toward me, and I hit the fiberglass-coated metal deck just before automatic gunfire made the netting pop and dance above my head.

A loud boom interrupted the fast crack of automatic fire, and the spotlight blew, spewing electric sparks into the night. Two more booms came in quick succession. Billy was unloading on the boat. I rolled away from the netting and jumped up. Two dark bodies moved inside the cigar boat. I took aim at the form behind the wheel and had fired six jarring shots before the shadow jumped and fell sideways. Two more booms echoed across the water, and flames shot out of the oversized motor next to the larger man who had fired the automatic weapon. The big man dove forward. I pumped three rounds into the speedboat and the windshield fell and twisted like a gleaming mirror reflecting fire from the engine. Something heavy splashed, and the big man was in the driver's seat. The torched engine roared. The boat hooked hard to port, and its bow shot out of the water as the stern scraped the hull of the *Teeter Two*.

I was on my feet screaming into the night, emptying my clip into the flaming cigar boat. I stared hard through the rain to see who had done this, to see who Billy Teeter and I would have to kill when we got home. The bullet-shaped boat skipped down the larger boat's hull and, just before roaring away, the driver looked across the gunwale directly into my face. Then Carli's father, the New England cod fisherman, literally fired off into the night.

Billy stood beside me. I cussed. Billy grabbed my arm. He said, "He's going the wrong way. Watch him. He's gonna hit."

Poultrez zoomed toward shore trailing flames and thick smoke like a jet afterburner. I said, "It's going to blow."

"Won't need to. Watch."

A loud, mechanical ripping noise echoed across the water, and Poultrez's flaming bullet boat shot into the air, tucked its fiery tail under, and slapped top down into the surf sending a gush of black seawater into the air.

I said, "What the hell?"

"Oyster beds." Billy said, "Let's go find my grandboy."

While Billy cleared broken glass off the bridge and got the boat going, I found a flashlight and examined the hull section scraped by Purcell's cigar boat. It was going to need some woodwork and paint—and I was going to pay for it—but, as far as I could tell, we weren't in any danger of sinking.

Billy was working his spotlight back and forth across the water, steering carefully toward the place where Willie went over. The old man was slowly and rhythmically clenching his jaw with each swivel of the lamp. I moved up to the bow. I heard Billy using his radio, calling for help. Then I heard something else—a voice, thin and distant. I held up my hand. Billy pulled back on the throttle and stepped out to look.

I said, "Cut the engine. I think I hear something." The old man reached inside the bullet-riddled bridge cabin and twisted a key, and the Gulf fell silent. I said, "Move the light. See if you can see him." The spot swept across rolling waves, and the thin voice came again. "He's seeing the light. Stop!"

Sixty yards off the starboard bow, an eerily white head bobbed in the waves. I pointed, and Billy turned over the engines and moved the right way. I lost Willie twice in thirty yards. Then we were on him, and I dropped over the side.

The Gulf in March was still cold enough to take my breath when I hit the water. Willie's pale head seemed to float toward me as I paddled in place. His eyes were open, his lips blue and trembling. I managed to slide my arm under his and grip him across the chest. I kicked hard and seemed to paddle in place again while, this time, the boat floated toward me. Billy had a ladder over the side. I perched Willie on the bottom rung, held on with my left fist, and pushed his hypothermic mass up into Billy's strong arms with my right hand. I hung there trying to catch my breath and quickly realized the water was sapping my breath and my strength. I made it up the ladder alone.

On deck, Captain Billy had Willie on his stomach, alternately pressing his upper back and lifting his underarms. It's what the United States Marines taught in 1942, and it works, just not that well. I said, "Move," and was surprised when Billy complied. I flipped Willie onto his back and checked his pulse and breathing. The first was strong. The second was weak and shallow. I put a hand under Willie's neck to cock his head back and swept the back of his tongue with my fingers to check for blockage. Then I placed my lips over his clammy, whiskered mouth and pushed a lung full of air into his chest. Willie gurgled and choked the air back out. Again, I breathed deeply into the young man's lungs; and he vomited violently into my mouth. Reeling backward, I spit out Willie's mess and then puked the last few morsels of my lunch across Willie's chest and onto the deck.

He was breathing strongly on his own, so I began checking for gunshot wounds. There weren't any. I looked up at Billy. "He's not shot. He got some water in his lungs when he hit the water. You got any blankets?" Billy immediately pulled off his coat and put it over his grandson. A few seconds later, he was back with a silver emergency blanket and two large sheets of opaque plastic. I got Willie as comfortable as possible on the rolling, rain-soaked deck while the old man throttled up and headed for shore.

God and nature protect teenage boys. Willie began to come around before we hit the bay. Captain Billy had radioed ahead for help, and an ambulance met us at the dock. Willie, complaining loudly now, got lifted onto a stretcher and loaded into the ambulance. Billy climbed into the front seat next to a paramedic, and the white van screamed off into the night.

I was left standing on the dock, checking the lines, surveying the damage, and generally feeling like a complete asshole for involving the Teeters in a death match with Carli's father and the Bodines. I would pay for the damage. I would give Captain Teeter one hell of a bonus. I'd even pay for Willie's medical bills. But none of that was going to make me any less of a prick for having involved them.

It was past midnight and cold. My saltwater-soaked clothes felt hard and rough on my skin. I opened the trunk and pulled out my duffel. No one was around. I found clean underwear, a shirt and chinos. I had stripped and, thankfully, pulled on dry boxers when Billy's partner, Julie, came around the corner of the shack. I started to apologize; then I saw the two men behind her. They wore dark suits and ties, and they had the look of men you run from in the night.

I pulled on my pants. I smiled. I spun on the balls of my feet and ploughed into the widest human being I have ever had the displeasure of meeting.

chapter twenty-two

THE HUMAN WALL looked like an Hispanic Odd Job, minus the decapitating bowler. This one just had a gun, which he used to tap me on the head until he had my complete attention. He didn't say much. One of the other men, one of the ones with Julie, spoke.

"Come with us, please."

"Where?" It seemed a reasonable question.

Odd Job said, "Move," and gave me a shove. I turned and looked for my 9mm inside the Bonneville's open trunk. It was there, no more than a foot from the bumper where I could easily grab it as I walked by and, if I were really lucky, click off the safety, chamber a round, and shoot one of these guys before the other two pumped me full of little pieces of metal. And, at that moment, standing in the shadows behind a shrimper's shack at midnight with a twenty-thousand-dollar bounty on my head, it didn't seem like a particularly bad idea. Fortunately, Julie saw me look. She stepped forward into pale yellow light from inside the trunk, picked up the Browning, and fixed me with a look of such hatred that I thought she was going to shoot me herself. Instead, she turned and handed my gun to one of her escorts. Odd Job bumped me on the head again and repeated, "Move."

"Mind if I get a shirt?"

He pushed me aside, rummaged in my duffel while keeping his narrow black eyes trained on my face, and handed me a sweatshirt. More precisely, he shoved the wadded shirt against my chest with enough aggression to leave no doubt that he enjoyed his work, and, as he manhandled me, Odd Job repeated his last instruction. "Move."

I wanted to stick a fist in one of his nasty little porcine eyes—eyes that looked like someone had slit his dark meaty face with a razor to reveal onyx marbles—but the man had a gun and he outweighed me by a hundred pounds, so what I did was move.

The two suits led the way. Julie followed them. I followed her, and Odd Job brought up the rear. We circled Teeter's Seafood, mounted the porch, and walked in through the front room where, during the daytime, customers bought shrimp and fish and frozen crab cakes so good they "taste like something that came off a menu at a restaurant." We walked through a doorway into a back room that looked like an old, single guy's idea of a den. A wood-burning stove squatted in the back right corner beneath a crooked length of stovepipe that angled out through the rough paneled wall. The front right corner held an abused television in a stained and chipped wooden cabinet. Opposite the stove and the television, antlered deer heads, plaster-filled fish with lacquered scales, and worn fishing tackle hung from the walls. Below the trophies and spinning rods, a collection of upholstered chairs and sofas waited in varying states of distress.

As we entered, a dark, slender man in a two-thousand-dollar suit rose effortlessly out of an orange Naugahyde chair and stepped forward.

"You are Thomas McInnes?"

I was a little overwhelmed and more than a little afraid, and I didn't answer right away. Odd Job took offense and tapped me once again on the crown with the barrel of his automatic. I found my voice, "You want to talk to me, tell Odd Job to quit hitting me on the head."

The dark man held up his palm at Odd Job, and, with the quiet authority of someone who was used to being obeyed, he said, "Please." Then he nodded at the door and my head tapper walked out, turning sideways to navigate the opening. The dark man turned back to look into my eyes. "I apologize, señor. Please sit down." He motioned at a used-up La-Z-Boy upholstered in mustard hopsack and punctuated with exposed tufts of almost matching foam rubber.

I sat. One of the suits, the one who had spoken, moved to the far wall and watched. He held what appeared to be an UZI in one hand. At least, it looked like what I imagined an UZI would probably look like. The second suit left the room, I assumed to help Odd Job secure the perimeter or some such thing.

The dark man was attired with the formality expected of a business executive in Europe or Latin America. Thick black hair swept back from a narrow forehead and would have curled if he had been the sort of man to allow such lack of control.

He said, "Are you comfortable?"

"No."

He smiled. "No, señor. Yours is not a comfortable situation." He sat back and studied me. "You like cigars?"

"Sure."

He reached inside his coat and produced a black alligator cigar case. As he opened it, he said, "Would you like one?"

"No."

He didn't appear surprised or offended. He pulled a huge, unwrapped cigar from the case, glanced at the foot, which had already been cut, and put it in his mouth. The UZI guy walked forward, reaching into his pocket with the obvious intention of lighting the cigar. The dark man held up his palm, just as he had earlier, and the UZI guy stopped and returned to his corner.

I said, "Got 'em trained with hand signals."

"Señor?"

"Nothing."

He lit his cigar with a match, and he took a while doing it. When he had it going, he said, "My name is Carlos Sanchez."

"Nice to meet you. I'm John Smith."

Once again, he smiled. "Yes. I see what you mean. But it is something to call me. We have business to discuss."

A.k.a. Carlos Sanchez smoked his Havana the way only Central and South Americans smoke them, drawing the thick, pungent smoke deep into his lungs and then letting it out through his mouth and nostrils. He said, "You are an intelligent man. Or, more precisely, you are 'smart.' That is the word we hear about you. 'Tom McInnes is smart.' "

"I feel so good about myself now."

"Señor?"

"What do you want?"

"We want you to leave Leroy Purcell and his group alone."

I said, "What?" and he started to repeat. "No, I hear you. I just don't believe what I hear. Your buddy, Leroy Purcell, has taken out a twenty-thousand-dollar contract on my life. He's trying to kill a young girl who's a client of mine, and, I'm not certain, but he's probably got a contract out on another woman who's a better person than you and me put together."

Sanchez simply said, "Susan Fitzsimmons."

I looked at him.

"And Carli Poultrez. Daughter of Russell Poultrez of Gloucester, Massachusetts."

I kept looking at him and thought some more before I spoke. "Are you offering an end to this? Can you guarantee the safety of Susan and Carli if we agree to walk away from Purcell and his people?"

"I can try to arrange these things. I cannot guarantee. Señor Purcell is an unpredictable and dangerous man. But I believe I can arrange for your safety and that of Señora Fitzsimmons."

"And Carli?"

Sanchez shook his head.

"Are you saying Carli's not part of the deal?"

"I'm afraid she is not. That part has gone too far. But I can arrange . . ."

I interrupted. "Who are you? I've been sitting here talking with you, basically humoring you, because there's a guy with a gun over there. But it looks like you know everything about me and my clients and . . . Who the hell *are* you?"

Sanchez rolled his cigar between a manicured thumb and a set of fragile-looking, tanned fingers, then raised the moist foot of the Churchill to his lips and turned the ash red as he pulled smoke into his lungs. He was thinking. Considering. He reached inside his tailored coat, once again pulled out the alligator case, removed the cap, and held out the cigars. "Please."

This time I took one—maybe I needed a prop too—and he lit it for me with a wide, flat match.

As he replaced the case in his inside pocket, Sanchez said, "I work with a group of Cuban patriots who are pursuing a number of goals. None of which are in any way contrary to the interests of the United States. Please understand that. It is most important. We have great respect for the United States and wish to see many, if not all, of its ideals emulated in a free and democratic Cuba." He stopped to smoke and look at the UZI guy. Some unspoken communication passed between them. He went on. "You, Señor McInnes, and your two clients have become involved, through no fault of your own, with something that could become quite . . . unmanageable."

He paused to give me a chance to comment on that. I didn't.

He said, "I am told that either Susan Fitzsimmons or Carli Poultrez witnessed a murder last Wednesday night on St. George Island. Is that correct?" I looked at him some more. Sanchez said, "We have a problem. Your clients are in danger because of what one or both of them saw, and, of course, because they want to go to the police and see justice done. Unfortunately, I cannot allow them to take that action."

"You can't allow that, huh?"

"No. I'm afraid I cannot. You see, Leroy Purcell did kill someone that night."

"Who?"

"Señor?"

"Do you know who he killed?"

"Not that it should matter to you, Señor McInnes, but no. I do not. It was, as they say, an internal matter."

"Is that what Purcell says?"

"That is precisely what he says. So, you see, other than the understandable shock of witnessing such an, ah, event, it was a bad ending between two men who both worked in the kind of business where such things are, if not foreseeable, at least they are not unexpected. In any event, you will never prove that anyone died inside that cottage. All evidence has been obliterated, and, if it becomes necessary, your clients will disappear along with the rest of the evidence."

"Is that how Cuban patriots do business?"

"We will protect our interests. It is that simple. We will take any and all necessary actions, however distasteful, to pursue and protect our interests. As far as 'doing business,' as you put it, we do business with Mr. Purcell and his organization because, at this time, it serves those interests."

"With the Bodines."

He smiled. "Yes. I believe that is how they are known by the police. In any event, they perform essential services for me and my organization. And I cannot allow you to cause the authorities to investigate the murder on St. George Island."

"How do you plan to stop us? I mean, other than killing me, which, just so you'll know, won't stop anything."

"It is very simple, Mr. McInnes. If you cannot promise to cease your attempts to jail Mr. Purcell and guarantee that you can control your clients, then we will kill you and everyone else who is involved." He paused, and then said, "Tonight."

"But Carli's not part of the deal, right? Keeping a teenage girl alive isn't something that serves your 'interests.'"

He shook his patrician head. "Señor McInnes, we are interested. The Bodines are not. They do not trust the girl—this runaway who works as a waitress—to keep silent."

"And if I can't agree to that . . ." I needed to think, to stretch out the conversation and run Sanchez's offer around in my head. I said, "These are decent people you're talking about murdering."

"That is why we are talking."

"And I think I should point out that I have a few friends who are kind of hard to kill."

Sanchez said, "The white giant and his associates? Yes. That is another reason we are talking."

"Well, that's honest." Sanchez struck another wide match and held it out toward me. I hadn't realized my cigar had gone out, since I hadn't really wanted the damn thing to begin with. I leaned forward and let him relight the ash. I said, "The family on the beach on Dog Island the other night. They were some of your people, weren't they? Purcell smuggles in illegal immigrants. People fleeing Cuba? Hot people from other places?" He didn't answer, but then I really didn't expect him to. I was thinking out loud. "Whatever. The guy who came in with his family is kind of famous, I guess."

Again, Sanchez didn't respond, but he couldn't stop a small ripple of surprise, maybe even panic, from moving across his handsome features. And I thought, not for the first time, that there seemed to be much more to the chubby illegal immigrant with the pretty wife and the cloned son than just another "patriot" seeking a better life in Los Estados Unidos. I registered Sanchez's discomfort and made a mental note to remember the tender spot. I said, "I guess South Florida has gotten too hot. So now you're bringing in warm bodies through the Panhandle. And nobody does illegal business on the Panhandle without going through the Bodines."

Now Sanchez spoke. "We do business where we please."

"But it's easier to work with an existing operation than to set up your own from scratch."

Sanchez was letting me think. He nodded slowly. "It is easier."

I decided to float some of Squirley McCall's information and see if I could get a reaction. "Is it easier to do business with an arms smuggler?" Sanchez didn't answer. I took a different tack. "And is it easier to work with someone who wants to kill three or four innocent people than it is to get rid of one criminal who's turned a spotlight on your group? And he'll do it again. Leroy Purcell is a bomb waiting to explode in your face."

Sanchez said, "I'm sure you are a talented lawyer. But we are not bargaining."

"Then explain about Carli. You said she's not part of the deal. Why is that? Why is it you can't protect a teenage girl who's more willing to forget all this than I am?"

"It has gone too far. Arrangements have been made. Payments have been accepted, and, unfortunately, emotion is involved. Arguments from you will not help. I have made those same arguments to no avail. The feeling is that a point, an, ah, example, must be made. Too many of the Bodines know of her involvement. This problem, señor, has digressed into notions of honor and control in . . . in some minds."

"That doesn't make any sense. Why do I get to walk away? Why does Susan get to walk away? They've already tried to kill her once at her beach house."

"First of all, you, Señor McInnes, did not actually witness anything. You are an attorney, a professional, and, in Leroy Purcell's view, something of a mercenary. He, therefore, believes that your actions are motivated by considered self-interest. He believes that if it is better for you to keep quiet, then that is what you will do."

"That's funny. I thought he wanted me dead."

"He and I engaged in discussions this evening that I am certain have influenced his view."

"What about Susan?"

"Señora Fitzsimmons is an adult. She is well-off and has much to protect. Also, Purcell is aware of a long-term relationship between the señora and yourself. He believes that your silence will be guaranteed by including her in the offer." Sanchez paused to relight his cigar and fill his chest with smoke. He said, "Which brings us to the issue of Carli Poultrez. She is young. She is frivolous, and she is from the peasant classes. Even I would not expect her to control her tongue. Purcell, of course, feels even more strongly on this point. And, as I have said, he believes an example must be made. It is, he believes, important to his position with the Bodines. In his mind, the Poultrez girl is the obvious choice for that example."

"And I'm expected to just turn my back on her and walk away?"

"Señor McInnes, that is exactly what Purcell expects you to do. In your place, he would do so without a second thought."

My mind raced. I could, I thought, react loudly and emotionally and get myself and a handful of my favorite people killed, or I could accept Purcell's deal—protecting Susan's life and my own—and take steps to find Carli and get her to safety, assuming I could find her before the Bodines did. But that option, while immeasurably superior to the first, still left Carli with a lifetime of looking over her shoulder, waiting for a bullet or a knife or just a quick shove at a busy intersection.

His quiet voice startled me. "You are thinking."

It was a statement. I nodded. "Do you care what I do, so long as my actions do not expose your operation or bring the authorities into the equation?"

Sanchez just smiled at me through a curtain of cigar smoke.

I said, "I will not go to the police. Neither will Susan Fitzsimmons."

Sanchez stood and walked to the door. He stopped and said, "You have chosen a proper path, señor. Thank you for your time and for . . . the intelligence of your response." I studied his spare, intelligent features. He said, "Be careful, Señor McInnes. We have, for many reasons, gone to great lengths to avoid bloodshed. It is the right thing to do, and it is the smart thing to do. But, please make no mistake, just causes such as ours produce zealots—useful men who believe the greater the violence, the greater their commitment to the cause. So, as I said, please be most careful." He paused, and, as if mentioning an afterthought, said, "And you should know that a deputy sheriff in Appalachicola, a Mickey Burns, has been asking questions about you."

Sanchez turned to leave. I said, "One more thing," and he paused in the doorway. "Your buddy Purcell threatened me with, in his words, 'a crazy, mean-ass spic' who likes to cut people up and play with their guts. Purcell said all he'd have to do is make a phone call." Sanchez's eyes narrowed, and small muscles knotted in his slender jaw. "That wouldn't be the kind of 'zealot' you're so proud of, would it?"

Sanchez opened his mouth to answer, then closed it again without emitting a sound. He cocked his head to one side as if physically rolling thoughts around in his skull. Finally, he said, "I will control my people, and I think Leroy Purcell can control his. But," he hesitated, "some people, some . . . forces are beyond reason and control."

"And one of these forces—one who likes to play with knives and other people's guts—just may turn up if I don't walk away. Is that the bottom line?"

Sanchez met my eyes and held them before turning and walking out of the room, followed closely by the UZI man.

I looked around the room at the decapitated deer and glass-eyed fish and felt a certain kinship.

Sanchez's cigar tasted heavy and bitter. I stood and walked over to poke it through the mouth of the cast-iron stove before leaving. In the front room, perched on a red commercial cooler with *Coca-Cola* written on the front, sat Julie the seafood woman. I stopped to look at her. She looked back.

I put two dollars on the counter and said, "I'd like a beer."

She said, "I ain't giving you nothing."

I walked around the counter and stood in front of her. She sat on one of the cooler's two chrome doors. I opened the other one and found a cold Coors. Julie looked furious but didn't move to stop me. I asked, "What did I do to you?"

"You come close to getting Willie killed tonight for one thing."

"What's the other thing?"

"Huh?"

"What else have I done to get you so mad?"

"You done enough. You mess with one of us down here and you messed with all of us."

"Is Captain Billy one of you? Is Peety Boy?"

Julie's face flushed. She looked at the floor and muttered, "You messed with Sonny." Now, she had my full attention. "Made him look bad to his boss. We ain't gonna put up with that."

"What's Sonny to you?" Julie didn't answer. I said, "He's on his way here, isn't he?"

Now she smiled. Sonny was coming to kill me.

chapter twenty-three

"I KNOW YOU want me to stick around and get dismembered by Sonny, but I'm leaving. Sorry." As I spoke, Julie put her right foot against the counter, blocking my path by creating a bridge with her leg between the red cooler and the Formica counter. I said, "You've got to be kidding," and turned to put my left buttock on the counter to swivel my legs over and leave.

But Julie really had not been kidding. I glimpsed an amber flash just in time to dodge an unopened bottle of Budweiser swung hard at my left ear. A violent breeze swept the tip of my nose as I jerked my head back and pivoted over the counter. Julie seemed to feel deeply about not wanting me to leave. I, on the other hand, felt just as deeply that rolling around the floor trading punches with a female fishmonger would irreparably damage my self-image—particularly if she won. So, as soon as my bare feet hit floorboards, I sprinted through the open front door and into the night. Julie's longneck exploded against the door frame behind me, but I was gone. Not only did Julie decline to chase me, which would have been undignified for both of us, but she also confounded expectations by failing to pelt my windshield with bottled beverages as my rented Pontiac spun around the front corner of the shack and screeched onto the road. I could only guess that she was busy calling Sonny or maybe looking for one of Captain Billy's old shotguns.

This, I thought, is not why I went to law school.

A mile or two west of the causeway to St. George, a speeding Appalachicola Sheriff's Department cruiser met me on Highway 98, going, I suspected, where I had come from. I couldn't tell for sure whether the uniformed driver was my old compatriot Mickey Burns, since, speeding at eighty miles an hour through the night, one black-and-white looks pretty much like the next. I watched the deputy's red taillights recede in my rearview mirror until they faded from sight; then I reached over to switch on the radio and noticed my Browning 9mm on the passenger seat. Bless Carlos Sanchez. The clip was full and the chamber was empty, just as they had been when Julie lifted it out of the trunk.

Following a quick stopover in Panama City at an all-night truck stop with a Hertz franchise, I pulled into Seaside a few minutes after sunrise in a newly rented, dark-blue Taurus. I parked in back, stepped out of that peculiar rented-car smell, and walked around to the front of the cottage. Loutie Blue answered the door.

I said hello and searched her face. "Can you tell me what's going on with Carli?"

Loutie shook her head. "Sorry, Tom. There's nothing to tell. As far as we know, they're just still looking."

When we were seated in the kitchen, she said, "Purcell's gone. He left late yesterday to meet with 'the Cubans,' whoever they are. Susan's fine. She's still asleep. Kelly's been calling you. Three times last night. She said she needs to talk to you as soon as possible."

I stood and walked to the refrigerator. "*The Cubans* are a group of self-described 'patriots' who waylaid me last night to give us our lives back. According to their leader—at least I think he's their leader. Anyway, I wouldn't bet my life on it, but it's possible that Purcell no longer longs for my demise. I'll fill you in on the details later." I looked inside the fridge at eggs and cinnamon rolls and bagels and realized I was too tired to eat. I closed the door. "I'm going to bed. If anything happens, come get me."

"Kelly found out something about that yacht's ownership. The one the Teeter guy told you about seeing the other night when you and Joey were on Dog Island. It belongs to some corporation in Tampa."

"Would you mind calling her for me? Ask her to check out the company. Find out if there's any Cuban-American management or ownership."

"There's Cuban-American owners or managers in just about everything in South Florida, Tom."

"I know. Just ask her. And call Joey and ask him if he can turn loose and meet us here . . . What time is it? Six-twenty? Ask him if he can make it around three or four this afternoon."

"No problem." Loutie said, "Go to bed. You look like hell."

I trudged up the stylish staircase and hesitated outside the room where Susan slept. It was the same room where she and I had made love two nights before.

I liked her. She liked me. We had slept together and liked that too. But climbing into her bed at daybreak to catch up on lost sleep, that—I don't know why—but that seemed too intimate, as if I would be taking too much for granted. Maybe it was the way we had parted. Maybe it was the fear that her idea of us was different than mine. Maybe it felt too, almost, married. Maybe I was just tired.

I walked a few steps farther down the hall and found a room no one was using. The mattress was bare. I spied a yellow blanket with satin trim stuffed onto a shelf in the closet. I put my head on a purple, ruffly pillow, pulled the nubby blanket up to my chin, and felt sleep soak into my body like a warm bath.

Someone sat on the bed. A woman's voice said, "Tom, Joey's here now, and Kelly's been here for a couple of hours. They're waiting downstairs." It was Susan's voice. And I felt no ambiguity whatsoever about how glad I was to hear it.

I pushed the twisted blanket away, rolled onto my back, and said, "Nice to see you."

Susan smiled. "You too. Wash your face and come on down. Everyone's waiting." And she left the room.

I walked out into the hall and through Susan's room to the bath, where I had a look in the mirror and was greeted by swollen eyes, red pillow marks on one cheek, and, I was pretty sure, breath that would melt paint. I turned on cold water in the shower, took off my shirt, and leaned over the tub and let the frigid spray run over my face, neck, and hair. I needed a real shower, but people were waiting, so I did what I could. After toweling and combing my hair and making vigorous use of a toothbrush, I felt more or less like myself again, and I headed downstairs.

Once again, everyone had congregated in the kitchen. I said, "I'm getting tired of looking at this kitchen. Can we do this in the living room?"

Joey said, "Did we wake up grouchy from our nap?"

I said, "Bite me," and walked into the living room. Joey, Susan, Loutie, and Kelly followed. Loutie came in carrying something that looked like the kind of miniature radio my father used to listen to at football games. As she walked, she worked at poking a tiny black foam knob into her ear.

I looked at her. She said, "Mobile monitor," and sat on the sofa next to Joey. Susan sat in an upholstered chair next to mine, and Kelly came in a few seconds later and put a glass of Coke on the table next to my chair. I said, " Bless you," and drank half of it right away. "Who wants to start?"

Susan said, "Loutie says you said something about Leroy Purcell not wanting you dead anymore."

"That's what this Cuban guy wants me to think."

My stomach felt queasy, and I realized I hadn't eaten in almost thirty hours. I took another swallow of Coke. Joey said, "You trying to be dramatic? Tell us the frigging story."

"Oh. Sorry." I said, "Actually, I'm trying not to throw up again. It's been a while since I ate. Yesterday at lunch. And I managed to lose most of that on Billy Teeter's boat last night." I looked at Susan. "I'll back up and fill you in later on Teeter's boat and the yacht off Dog Island and all that, but the bottom line is that Carli's father, Rus Poultrez, is dead."

All Susan got out was, "How?"

I told her.

Susan said, "I can't believe how happy I am that another human being is dead."

"Something else," I added. "I met with some kind of Cuban revolutionary last night who claims to do business with Purcell and the Bodines. He also claimed he's convinced Purcell to leave you and me alone. He didn't offer the same deal for Carli."

Joey said, "Why the hell not?"

"He said Purcell wants to make some kind of example out of her. You know, 'don't fuck with Leroy Purcell' or some equally eloquent sentiment."

Susan stood. "Kelly, tell Tom what you told us about the yacht. I'm going to get this poor guy something to eat. Don't let him say anything else until I get back."

I said, "Thanks. Just not that chicken salad and fruit we had for lunch yesterday. I saw a little too much of that on the boat."

Susan said, "Yuck," and left the room. I picked up my Coke and turned to look at Kelly.

She said, "The yacht Billy Teeter spotted the night you and Joey saw the drop-off is registered to a corporation in Tampa called Products Americas, Inc." Just as a good legal secretary should, Kelly pronounced Inc. "Ink," rather than saying "incorporated," as most people would—a distinction that matters only to people who try lawsuits or draft contracts for a living. She said, "They are sort of an import-export business. I called around and found out they sell American machinery in half a dozen South American countries, and I guess they buy mostly agricultural stuff down there and sell it here.

"Anyway, after Loutie called this morning and said you wanted to know about Cuban owners or managers, I started calling again, and you were right on the money. The chairman and the president and three other senior officers are 'of Cuban descent,' as they put it. I found that out from the company itself. The investor relations department. Apparently, I wasn't the first person to ask. I guess other Cubans like to invest in Cuban enterprises or something. Whatever the reason, they weren't shy about telling me."

Joey interrupted and said, "Tell him about the guy in Tallahassee, Kelly."

Kelly said, "Okay. So, after I got as much as I could from the investor relations woman, I asked who I could talk to about this yacht the company owned. That kind of rattled her. Not, I think, because some manager in investor relations would know about illegal activity on the company yacht. What I think was that she didn't want to catch a lot of grief from an investor about expensive perks for the president or something like that. Anyway, she said she didn't know anything about any boats the company might own, and she referred me to their outside PR guy."

Joey was literally on the edge of his seat. He said, "Listen to this," as if I might have been napping through the rest of it.

Kelly said, "Be quiet, Joey. It's not that dramatic. I just called the guy. It's a man named Charles Estevez. 'Charlie,' he says. He's one of those guys who wants everyone to call him by his first name. This Estevez has a lobbying and PR firm in Tallahassee, and I found out before I called him that he has a pretty good reputation. I also found out that he is *the* point man in the Florida legislature when it comes to lobbying for anything having to do with Cuban refugees, or like relations and trade with Cuba, that kind of stuff.

"So, I get him on the phone and ask about Products Americas, and he starts babbling a mile a minute about what a great company it is and how wonderful and civic minded the management is.

"Then I ask about the yacht, and suddenly Estevez just doesn't have that kind of information about his clients. So I give him the registration number and tell him the Coast Guard has verified that the boat belongs to Products Americas. And, guess what. He seems to remember something about the yacht. Suddenly, he even remembers being on it one time for a cocktail party or something. Then, get this, he just volunteers that the boat is, quote, 'really just a marketing tool for the company.' He says the thing is used mostly for entertaining customers who are in Tampa on business, and that it, quote, 'hardly ever leaves the Tampa Bay area.' Which, I don't know about you, but I thought that seemed like kind of a strange thing to just volunteer out of the blue. So Tom, you weren't around to ask, so I just told him the yacht was spotted in Appalachicola Bay on such and such a date, just to see what he'd say. I hope that was okay."

"That was fine. This isn't a walk-on-eggshells kind of case anymore. What did he say?"

Kelly smiled and looked endearingly proud of herself. "He said he had another call coming in, and he'd have to call me back." Joey and I laughed as Susan came in the room and put a plate with two sandwiches and a handful of chips on the table next to my Coke. I thanked her, and she got comfortable in her chair.

Loutie frowned at the floor and pressed the foam knob further into her ear. I ate some sandwich. Kelly said, "A little over an hour went by, and the phone rang. All of a sudden, Estevez knows *all* about you and wants you to call him. 'Personally.' I tried to get more information, but he insisted on talking to you."

I asked, "When was this?"

"I called Products Americas yesterday. My conversation with Estevez was this morning."

"This *is* getting interesting," I said. "Last night I get briefly kidnapped by a Cuban revolutionary who knows all about Carli and Susan and Joey and, especially, me and Purcell. And the discussions he said he had with Purcell took place yesterday morning. I guess after you called Products Americas. I wondered why Sanchez showed up out of the blue last night."

Everyone seemed to pause and think about that for a beat or two; then Susan said, "Okay. Now tell us about the Cubans and Purcell not wanting you and me dead and why he won't leave Carli alone."

So I did. I started with chugging out into the bay with Willie and Captain Billy and finished with every detail I could remember about my forced meeting with Carlos Sanchez. When I was done, I asked Joey, "How close are we to finding Carli?"

"We're not."

I said, "Damn."

"Yeah. I know. Randy Whittles is killing himself, and I've got a couple of guys helping him. But, like you said, damn." Joey shook his head and went on. "I did find out where our buddy Thomas Bobby Haycock has been taking his illegal shipments, though."

I asked, "Where?"

Joey said, "You're not gonna believe this shit, either."

Loutie Blue interrupted. "Joey. Come in the kitchen. I've got a female voice at Purcell's place."

chapter twenty-four

SUSAN ASKED THE question. "Is it Carli?"

Loutie pressed the tiny foam knob against her ear and waved Susan off as she left the room. We all hurried into the kitchen where Loutie turned up the volume on the speakers. A feminine voice said, ". . . not that hungry. Sorry I'm late. I thought Jim was never going to leave."

"That's not Carli," Susan said. "Sounds like little Leroy has a hot date."

Loutie agreed. "Sounds like it. I'm going to stay in here and listen." We looked at her, and she explained. "If there's any kind of conversation, we need to listen. You never know what might come out." She looked around. "And it would be easier if the rest of you went somewhere else."

Back in the living room, Joey returned to his story. "So, getting back to Haycock. I followed him this morning from the ferry landing in Carabelle. He headed west up 98 and then hung a right on 65 toward Tallahassee, and I figure he's planning to fence the stuff in the city. But just a few miles up, he turns off into a place called 'Tate's Hell Swamp.' No shit. That's actually the name of this frigging place on the map."

Joey looked at Susan and Kelly and then at me. I was anxious for less color and more useful facts, and I think it showed.

He said, "So anyway I follow Haycock into the woods. About four miles in, the woods turn into swamp, and it's just this one pissant logging road. And if somebody decides to come out, there's not much I can do but try to get out of their way. So I'm getting pretty nervous about being able to keep tailing him without anybody seeing me.

"About that time, I come around a curve and Haycock's truck is stopped dead in the middle of the road. So I slam on the brakes and damn near wreck sliding into a little gully there."

I said, "Joey, this is a fascinating travelogue. But you're here, so we know you got away. Can we cut to what you found at the end of the road?"

"I'm getting there, but you gotta hear this. I'm off in the gully where Haycock can't see me, and I can't see him. I roll down the windows and hear his truck start up again, and I'm hoping he hasn't turned around. But, if he has, I don't wanna get caught like a sitting duck, so I pull back up on the road. And, guess what, Haycock's gone. Disappeared."

Susan asked, "Where'd he go?"

I said, "Don't encourage him."

Joey smiled. "Took a while to figure it out. Haycock had driven off through this tall grass next to the road. Stuff's like rubber. Just pops back up after you drive over it. But he just had turned off, so I could still see his tracks. I followed 'em three or four hundred yards across this field and then hooked a left into some trees. And I'm telling you, he took me through some of the nastiest-looking shit I've ever come across. Black, scummy water up to my axle most of the time.

"I could see on the trees where the way was marked with cuts in the bark, like somebody marking a land line. A few hundred yards of that and I'm back on a road that just picks up in the middle of nowhere.

"I follow the road up around this little curve where the road rises up to a bridge over a creek, and I can see up ahead. About two hundred yards off, there's four metal buildings, and Haycock was just pulling up to 'em.

"I shit you not. These guys got a frigging compound out in the middle of the swamp. Like an island or something. It's this piece of solid ground slap-ass in the middle of Mosquitoville. I'm telling you, the place is nothin' but mile after mile of fuckin', I mean friggin', snake heaven. I saw four alligators on the way in. No shit. Four alligators."

I tried to get him back on point. "You said you could see Haycock pull into the compound?"

"Yeah. Haycock's unloading his truck and taking the stuff into this big warehouse-looking building. And there's a guard. The guy just stands there holding some kind of short weapon—it was too far away to tell what kind of firearm it was—and he spends his time watching the road for trouble."

"Did you see anything else?"

Joey said, "I sure as hell did," and paused for dramatic effect. "I saw that dark, chubby guy Haycock picked up on the beach the other night. You know, the Carpintero guy they smuggled in with his wife and kid."

I asked, "What was he doing?"

"Just talking with Haycock. Looking through the boxes and stuff in the truck, and, it looked like, maybe telling Haycock where to put the stuff he was unloading."

"Anything else?"

"Nope. That's about it. I needed to get out ahead of Haycock. So, after I checked things out and made a little map and a diagram and took some pictures, I got the hell out of there."

For a few seconds, I wasn't sure I'd heard right. "You took some pictures?"

"Sure." Joey grinned. "When Carpintero came out, I went back to the car and got my camera and popped a three-hundred-millimeter lens on it. I clicked off a roll of film, mostly of Carpintero, but I got the buildings and Haycock and the boxes and stuff too."

I said, "You're a genius."

"Ain't that the truth. I haven't gotten it developed yet. Overnighted it to a guy in Mobile. He'll turn 'em around in an hour, once he gets 'em."

"Good." I said, "Let me ask you something. Did the chubby guy from the beach—Carpintero—did he look familiar somehow? I mean, familiar from somewhere besides Dog Island."

Joey stopped and looked at the floor for a second or two and said, "Nope. Why?"

I shrugged.

Joey looked amused. "Did he scare you?"

"He gave me the creeps, is what he did."

I turned to Kelly. "Have you got Charles Estevez's number?"

She said, "Sure," reached down to get her purse, and fished out a thick Day-Timer bristling with business cards, pink phone message slips, and a couple dozen yellow and pink Post-its.

I said, "Come on. Let's go give Charlie a ring."

Kelly tagged along as I used the phone in Loutie's bedroom. Estevez had gone home for the day. I left my cell phone number with his answering service, and less than five minutes later, he called. He admitted "knowing *of* Carlos Sanchez." I felt him out, discussed the various uses of beachfront properties, dropped a name or two, and got off the phone.

Kelly said, "What did he want?"

I said, "He wanted to make sure that I'm more afraid of Sanchez than I am Purcell, which I am. And he wanted to, quote, 'open up the lines of communication.' No kidding. That's what he said."

Kelly smiled and asked, "Well, are they open?"

I said, "I think maybe a little more open than he had in mind."

The weather had become less fickle outside our aggressively cute beach house, and bright spring sunshine glinted off sand and water in one direction and white impatiens, pink and purple azaleas, and faux-Victorian gingerbread in the other. Susan opened the blinds to let in the late afternoon sun, and, for the next two hours, we rehashed stories and theories.

I still had a young client with a death sentence, and even if we did find her first I'd have to figure out what to do about Purcell. Carli was a juvenile with little education and fewer skills, and we weren't going to be able to simply send her to Europe or South America and expect her to fend for herself. Carli would want to stay in this country. And, sooner or later, she was going to call her mother, if she had one, or her sister, if she had one of those, or her best friend from junior high. And, when she did, Purcell would have her.

Around seven, I drifted into the kitchen. "What's Purcell up to?"

Loutie said, "Screwing."

It was not an answer I had expected. So I said, "What?"

Joey said, "Screwing, Tom. You know, rubbing uglies, choking chubby, grounding the gopher . . ."

Loutie sounded like a disappointed mother. "Joey?"

". . . bumping monkeys, pounding the puppy, squeezin' squigley, polishing the Jag . . ."

Loutie sounded, at once, amused and exasperated. "Shut up, Joey."

Joey grinned. "I know a lot more."

Loutie said, "We don't care."

While my giant friend wasn't exactly drunk, he wasn't exactly sober either. But after long days and sleepless nights of crouching between a pine tree and a gritty sand dune forcing himself to focus on every insipid detail in the life of an eighth-grade dropout turned criminal, Joey was entitled.

I looked at him, and he grinned some more. I turned to Loutie. "Have you heard anything useful?"

Loutie said, "Other than entertaining Joey? No. Some doctor's wife came over when her husband left to take their kids back to Atlanta. Apparently, she wanted to stick around for a few more days of sun, and whatnot."

I wandered back into the living room and plopped down on the sofa next to Susan. Kelly sat on the carpet. She had pulled down a seat cushion and leaned it against the front of her chair to make a floor-level lounger. The two women were watching an attractive female anchor on CNN who looked disturbingly like a vampire. A report on one of Princess Grace's randy kids ended just as I was snuggling my backside into the linen cushions. The vampire anchor rearranged her smiling eyes and glistening red lips into a somber expression as a photo of a petite, bookish woman appeared over her shoulder, and she began to read a story about an Iraqi physician with an almost Teutonic genius for exploiting horrific diseases.

A few minutes of that was more than enough reality, and we switched over to HBO and watched a Bruce Willis, everything-gets-blown-up movie until we were bleary-eyed. Kelly got up to go to bed, and Susan went with her to help find sheets and blankets. When Susan came back, she said, "I'm tired, Tom. I'm going on up."

And, suddenly, I didn't quite know what to say. It occurred to me that the problem with having avoided Susan's bedroom earlier in the day was that my actions might have damaged the *assumption* that it was still my room too. In other words, now that I had gotten out, I wasn't quite sure how to get back in. I said, "Where's Kelly sleeping?"

Susan said, "She's in the yellow bedroom."

"The yellow bedroom? Is that the one I took a nap in today?"

"I'm not sure I'd call seven hours a nap, but, yeah, that's it. It's the only empty room we've got. Joey will stay with Loutie, assuming she ever goes to bed. She's listening to that black box every night when I go upstairs and every morning when I wake up. So I'm just assuming she actually goes to sleep at some point." Susan yawned and stretched her arms over her head and arched her back in a maneuver that caused her knit shirt to pull across her breasts in an interesting way. Of course, it would have been hard for me to imagine anything about Susan's breasts that wasn't deeply and profoundly interesting. She said, "Good night."

"Susan?"

She said "Huh?" And I hesitated. Actually, I choked. Susan smiled and said, "You're still invited. Is that what you're hemming and hawing about?"

"I wouldn't exactly call it hemming and hawing."

She rolled her eyes and said, "Come on. Let's go to bed."

A blinding light filled the room. "Tom! Susan! Get up." It was Loutie. "They've got Carli."

I bolted up in bed. "Where? Where is she?"

Loutie said, "I don't know where. But she's still alive. Purcell got a call from some guy named Rupert about five minutes ago saying they found her. We gotta move. Joey's downstairs listening. Get up. We've got to be ready to follow Purcell when he leaves his house."

A thought hit me. "You sure Joey's ready for this?"

"Joey's fine. The man's got the metabolism of a racehorse. He sobers up like nothing I've ever seen." Loutie said, "Now, come on. Move it."

Susan was already on her feet and dressing while I was sitting on the bed talking to Loutie. She went into the bathroom while I got dressed, and, as we hurried downstairs, I noticed that she had run a wet comb through her hair.

I glanced at my watch. It was seven-fifteen. We had gotten more sleep than I thought.

Down in the kitchen, Joey's massive frame was perched on one of the fragile-looking chrome and leather chairs that seemed to have been designed more for looking at than sitting on. He said, "Go brush your teeth and get dressed for some outside work. Purcell's not going. Not now anyhow. He's got that little doctor's wife in his bed, and he ain't going anywhere anytime soon. He told this Rupert guy who called to just hold on to Carli, quote, 'on the island,' and he'd meet them there around noon."

Susan said, "Do you think they're talking about St. George, or did they actually bring Carli to Dog Island on the one night you weren't there?"

Joey and I together said, "Dog Island."

Susan looked confused. "How do you know?"

Joey said, "Makes sense."

"Why?"

Joey looked pleadingly at me. I said, "I guess they could mean any island within driving distance, Susan. But Dog Island is hard to get to; they've got an isolated cottage there; they're used to doing business there; and there aren't any cops on the island."

Susan said, "Okay."

"None of that means we're right. But I think we are." I looked around. "Where's Kelly?"

Loutie said, "Still asleep. She hasn't got any business in this. She works for you, Tom. But that's what I thought."

"You thought right. Kelly needs to get back to Mobile. And I guess Joey and I need to head for Dog Island. Try to beat Purcell there."

Joey said, "Yeah. And Loutie, you get on over to Purcell's place. Hang around outside. Don't let him out of your sight."

Joey turned to me. "Tom, did you get that tracker box stuck under Purcell's Caddy?"

"Yeah, the first day here."

Joey caught Loutie's eye to make sure she'd heard me and then looked at Susan. "Can you handle the listening equipment?" Susan said yes. "Okay, then you stay here and listen and work the phones. Tom and I will keep you up on what we're doing. Loutie, you do the same. I mean, you keep in contact with Susan to let her know what you're doing." He stopped and looked around the room and smiled. "I never been around such a bunch of gloomy people. We know where she is. This is the good part."

chapter twenty-five

AFTER TWO DAYS without a decent bath, one of which was spent hurling digestive juices on a rolling shrimp boat, a hot shower was not a luxury. I made a quick job of it, left Susan upstairs getting dressed, and met Joey downstairs. He had loaded his Expedition with guns, blankets, and food—what he described as his "rescue kit." Loutie would stay by the listening equipment until Susan came down; then she would head over to watch Purcell.

By eight, Joey and I left the strained charm of Seaside behind.

Neither of us spoke much. Joey pulled out a paper sack of Dolly Madison cinnamon rolls and canned drinks, and we made a breakfast of that as we listened to the news on NPR. On the eastern side of Port St. Joe, as we neared Appalachicola, Joey said, "I called about a boat while you were in the shower. Susan knew somebody. We don't need to be trying to ride a ferry with all these guns in the car, and we sure as hell don't need to be standing around waiting for the ferry after discharging firearms into the locals."

I asked, "You really think that's going to be necessary?"

"Never know. I sure as hell hope not. We have to kill a couple of those Bodine boys, and you're gonna have to take up the life of the hunted again."

I said, "The life of the hunted?" And Joey smiled.

He drove straight through Appalachicola and Eastpoint to a marina called "The Moorings" in tiny Carabelle, Florida. It was where we had caught the ferry when we went out to watch Thomas Bobby Haycock.

As Joey put his vehicle in park and pulled the key, he said, "Why don't you wait in the car? After your adventure with the Teeters, you're probably a minor celebrity around here." And he closed the door.

So I hunkered down in the seat feeling a little embarrassed to be left behind but lucky not to be going—like a child waiting for his father to come out of the liquor store. Four interminable minutes passed, and the door locks snapped as Joey shot them with his remote. He opened the door and stepped in. He said, "Got it," and backed the Expedition out and pulled around the side of the marina.

Dozens of luxury sailboats and motor yachts were huddled so tightly around a maze of concrete docks that it looked as though the first guy in would never leave again. But then, no one seemed to be leaving. Retired couples in baggy shorts and slouch hats polished brass or coiled ropes between trips to other boats to talk sailing or diesel motors or maybe a little fishing with someone from Wilmington or Bar Harbor or some other place where money intersected with seacoast.

Our little Boston Whaler was tied up among the working boats, which were kept well away from the yacht trade, and we had clear access to the waterway leading out into the bay. Joey popped the hatch on his Expedition. The food was in a cooler; the blankets were loose; and the firearms were discreetly zipped inside a fatigue-green duffel bag. As we loaded the blue-and-white Boston Whaler, Joey and I looked like nothing more than a couple of friends out for a day of fishing, except maybe for the complete absence of fishing equipment.

Joey said, "You know how to drive one of these things?"

"Well, yeah. On a lake. I thought you were in the Navy."

"We didn't spend a lot of time tooling around in pissant fishing boats in Naval Intelligence." I looked at him. He said, "How hard can it be? Crank it up. The guy in the marina told me how to get to the island. Hell, it's just over there. Soon as you pull around that place there where the land boops out you can see the damn thing."

"Boops out, huh?"

Joey ignored me.

I asked, "Did he tell you where all the oyster beds are too?"

"I asked about that."

"That was nice of you."

"He said they're not too bad between here and Dog Island. Just don't drive too fast."

"Like Rus Poultrez did?"

"Just like that."

While Joey rummaged in the cooler for additional sustenance, I puttered the boat away from the dock. Then, ever so gently, I steered a course in the general direction of Dog Island. The sour-sweet, almost carnal scents of the coast swirled in the spring air as a persistent chop paddled the hull and sprayed us with salt mist. Thirty minutes out of Carabelle, I judged that we were not quite halfway there. I asked, "How far is it supposed to be out to the island?"

"The guy in the marina said seven miles."

"It didn't look that far when we came out into the bay."

"You can't tell lookin' over water. Everything looks closer. The way to tell is you gotta turn around and bend over and look across the water through your legs."

I said, "Uh-huh."

"No shit. It works. An old forester taught me that. One summer in high school, I worked on a survey crew cutting land lines through the woods. We'd hit a stretch of swamp every now and then. The only way to tell how much wading you were gonna have to do was to bend over and look through your legs."

I said, "Uh-huh."

Forty minutes later, we were maybe a hundred yards off the narrow strip of island, and Joey said, "Hook around the left end of the island there."

It took another half hour to putt around the tip of the island and land the boat on the same desolate stretch of beach where I had parked my Jeep a week earlier as we hunkered in the dunes watching Haycock's place.

I had been working at keeping things light—trying to behave as though none of this bothered me. But, as Joey unzipped the green duffel and pulled out some kind of machine pistol, I could feel the morning grow cooler as light perspiration covered my face and neck and hands. Acid churned my stomach and adrenaline fogged my mind, and I had to concentrate to follow what Joey was saying.

"This is a Tech 9. It holds twenty rounds in the clip, plus one in the chamber. This is the safety. Up is on. Down is off. Push it down to fire."

"I've got my nine millimeter."

Joey said, "That's fine. You're used to shootin' it, so you should stick to it if you can. But we don't know what or who's waitin' for us. If six guys come around a corner with guns, you're gonna get your ass shot off if you count on that Browning. The Tech 9 is automatic, or at least the way I've got it set up it is. Pull back like this to chamber the first round and then just hold down the trigger. It'll squeeze out four rounds a second. So don't waste 'em all on one guy. Spread it around if you have to use it." Joey pulled out two black shoulder bags and tossed one to me. "Put it in there till you need it. We could run into somebody." Then he pulled out an identical weapon for himself, which he put in his black nylon bag. He also dropped in a Glock 9mm before zipping it up. Finally, he produced a tiny Walther PPK .380 and put it in his hip pocket.

As Joey worked at readying assault weapons in the morning sun, knot-kneed sandpipers scurried in and out with the surf, poking spindly beaks into quartz-white sand in search of sand fleas and baby shrimp. Above our heads, black-headed laughing gulls spiraled in the air, begging frantically for food. The gulls' shrill calls sounded in sporadic bunches, and with each shriek the abdominal muscles south of my navel clenched my gut like a nervous fist.

I said, "Somebody's been feeding them bread or something."

Joey glanced up at the birds and then back at me. "You ready?"

"Not really."

Joey looked at me for a second or two and said, "Look, why don't I just go in by myself? It's probably just Haycock and the Rupert guy watchin' Carli and waitin' on Purcell. Tell you what. Let me go look around. If it's bad, I'll come back for you."

"Nope."

Joey shrugged.

I took in a deep breath and said, "Let's go."

"Okay, hot dog. But as soon as we take the first step, I'm in charge. You do what I say. You got it?"

I nodded.

We moved crouched over, running awkwardly across dry sand, filling our shoes with grit and our pant legs with cocklebурs, and finding inadequate cover first behind one sand dune and then another. When we were about two hundred feet from Haycock's cottage, Joey waved me toward the trees we had used for shelter on stakeout. I turned and trotted to the scraggly clump of wind-tortured pines. Joey waited. When I got there, he made a hand motion that usually means "Hold it down." I dropped to one knee. He nodded and moved behind a dune. Minutes dragged by, and I saw him near the house on his stomach. Joey was crawling commando-style toward the back window, and he looked like he knew what he was doing. I watched him crawl, and I watched too long.

Tim the painter was only thirty feet from the front door when I saw him. Adrenaline flushed through my brain and muscles with such violence that I almost yelled out to Joey. *Think.* Joey was out of sight in back, and, so far, Tim seemed oblivious to our presence. Then he seemed to hear something. The man stopped, and I fell onto my stomach as he turned to survey the dunes and trees and scrub. I could just see his head. He was very still and seemed to be listening, more so than watching, for trouble. Then he swiveled his head toward the cottage. Now, he knew Joey was there.

I moved. Keeping low and quiet, I circled behind the painting Bodine and watched as he unclipped a small walkie-talkie from his belt and spoke quietly to someone. *Shit.* Joey was coming around the back corner, shaking his head and looking for me among the pines. Tim was too close to the cottage to see Joey—the angle was wrong—but he heard him. In one efficient movement, Tim gently dropped the radio to the ground and pulled a machine pistol from a shoulder holster. He dropped to one knee and waited. The Tech 9 was still zipped inside my shoulder bag. The zipper would make noise, and I didn't really know how to use the damn thing anyhow; so I eased it onto the sand and reached back inside my windbreaker and pulled out the Browning and clicked off the safety.

Joey was going to walk around the corner and get shot in maybe two seconds. I tried to sound official. "Hold it right there, asshole."

Tim froze. Slowly, he began to raise his hands, and I began to breathe again. Joey was still out of sight. I said, "Drop the gun."

The gun moved and, for one fleeting instant, I thought he was putting it on the ground. Then he spun on his knees and landed on his back. The man took aim with both arms stretched out toward me in a rigid wedge and both hands steadying the pistol. I fired. Tim's pant leg popped out at the knee as if some unseen hand had snatched the cloth, and a second shot from the other direction followed so quickly that it sounded like an echo of the first. Tim the painter's face exploded with his eyes fixed on mine.

Joey was standing next to the house, holding the Glock on the man whose face he had just blown off. I called out, "He's dead," and Joey and I began to approach the body from opposite sides. Joey's hollow-point had entered through Tim's crown and blasted out through some part of his face. Standing over the body in a kind of fascinated and repulsed shock, I couldn't tell much more than that. There wasn't enough face left to tell exactly where Joey's mushroomed bullet had exited.

I managed to say, "He had a walkie-talkie," and to point at the tiny communicator where Tim the painter had dropped it.

Joey leaned over and picked it up. He said, "Let's get the hell out of here."

"What about Carli?"

"Get your bag." I looked at him. He snapped, "Get the goddamn weapons bag you dropped back there."

I ran back and retrieved the shoulder bag with the Tech 9 inside. As I returned, Joey grabbed my jacket and pulled me roughly along as he retreated behind the house. As I stumbled behind him, Joey said, "Carli's not here. Nobody's here. We're in the wrong place. Or somethin' worse." I looked at him. He said, "Let's get to the boat. Keep your eyes open. That guy wasn't talkin' to himself." Joey took off toward the beach, running in his tucked-over stance, and I followed.

Voices floated across the sand. Joey kept moving. I sprinted to catch up and slapped him on the back. As I did, I said, "Down," and Joey dropped even before I did. "You hear that?"

Joey moved his chin from side to side and sat still. The only sounds were the surf and the wind and the sporadic, shrill cackles of laughing gulls as they fished the waves and fought for trash along the shoreline. Then the human voices came again. Joey turned and pointed at my chest and then at the ground. I nodded, and he left me there sitting on one knee in the sand between a grassy dune on one side and a gnarled clump of brown and green brush on the other.

Male voices ebbed and flowed among the sounds of surf and wind, and Joey reappeared and motioned for me to follow. We moved away from the beach. A hundred feet in, Joey stopped and spoke quietly. He was breathing heavily, more, I thought, from fear or excitement than effort. He said, "One man at the cottage. Two on the beach. Spread out. They're watching the boat. Waiting."

I asked a stupid question. "For us?"

Joey nodded. And he looked scared, which was one of many emotions I had never seen on his face. I tried to think, to concentrate, and then wished I hadn't. I said, "They knew." My oversized friend didn't answer. He was scanning the beach.

Then he whispered, "Call Susan," and my breathing turned fast and shallow.

I found my cell phone and punched in the number of the beach house. No one answered. I asked Joey how to get Loutie and punched in her number. She answered on the second ring. I said, "Where are you? Are you at the beach house?"

Loutie sounded surprised. "No. I'm in Mobile. Purcell's taking the doc's wife to some kind of party here. Brunch or something."

I interrupted. "Susan's not answering."

"Maybe she's . . ."

Again I cut her off. "Carli's not at the house on Dog Island. They may have been waiting for us."

Loutie said, "How would they . . . ?" And her voice trailed off.

I said what she was thinking. "Purcell may have found the bugs. We're on the island, and you're following him around Mobile. And Susan's not answering."

Joey reached for the phone, and I let him take it. He said, "Loutie? Haul ass back to Seaside. Keep trying Susan. The Bodines have got our boat staked out, and Tom and I are gonna have to find another way off the island." He stopped to listen and said, "Call the goddamn second you know something."

chapter twenty-six

BRIGHT SUNSHINE RADIATED across blue sky, glinting off sugar-white sand and suddenly consuming the world in blazing light that blocked out everything except the tiny black cell phone in Joey's hand and the tortured thoughts racing through my mind. I grabbed the phone from Joey and once again dialed the beach house in Seaside. Still no one answered. I hit the *end* button and punched *redial*, and Joey said my name. I listened to the phone ringing in our whimsically sterile Seaside cottage, and Joey said my name again. Finally, I said, "What!"

"That's not doing any good, Tom. You're just gonna use up the battery."

"I don't really give a shit if I use up the battery."

"Loutie's calling. She's in her car. So she can call all day without running out of juice. If we run out, Loutie's not even gonna be able to call and tell us if there is news."

I could feel my heart thumping against my sternum, and coursing blood sounded inside my ears like boots running in mud. I tried to control the erratic rhythm of my breathing. Slowly, shapes began to emerge from the blinding glare, and other sounds floated back to me. Wind sighed across the island, and gulls filled the air with shrill chatter.

Joey looked out across glowing sand dappled green and brown with undulating sea grass and streaks of coarse underbrush. He said, "You see what I mean, don't you? We gotta stay calm and wait on Loutie. She's as good as they get, Tom. You couldn't ask for somebody better if—and I'm just saying *if*—Susan's gotten in trouble."

I flipped the phone shut and pushed it inside the pocket of my windbreaker. I looked out at the idyllic landscape, searching now for human shapes, and asked, "You said the men are spread out?"

"The two at the beach are spread out maybe a hundred feet apart hiding in that tall grass and stuff between the dunes."

"What about the guy at the cottage?"

"Standing around cussing about the one we shot when I saw him. Could be hidden by now. Or I guess he could be down at the beach with the others."

I stopped to think and said, "But he's probably covering the road between here and the ferry."

Joey said, "Yeah. I guess. I hadn't thought of that, but it makes sense."

"Because their job is not to let us get out of here alive."

"That would be it."

"So, can we take out the ones watching the boat? I mean, if they're spread out, couldn't we just take them out one at a time?"

Joey stopped scanning the land between us and the Bodines and looked at me. "You okay with killing two more men?"

"I didn't say kill anybody. We could just knock them over the head or something, couldn't we?"

Joey returned to scanning the surrounding countryside as he spoke. He said, "Not unless you know something I don't. And I *know* how to take somebody out without making a sound. That's something I *did* learn from the Navy. But you don't do it by 'knocking 'em on the head or something.' You do it with a knife."

"That's not an option. I shot the guy back there because he was trying to shoot me. We are not going to start cutting throats."

Joey said, "It's not really a cut. It's actually more of a stab and twist thing."

"Joey."

"I know. I wasn't arguing to do it. I'm just explaining that you can't sneak up and bop a man on the head with the butt of a gun like on *Mission: Impossible* and expect him to fall over without a sound and wake up later with a bump and tiny little headache. You hit a guy hard enough to knock him unconscious and you're probably gonna kill him anyway. And if you don't hit him pretty much hard enough to kill him, he's gonna squawk and bring in his buddies, who will shoot you full of little holes."

"I got it, Joey. The horse is dead and beat to hell."

"Just trying to be helpful." Joey said, "So, what now? You're supposed to be the smart one."

Joey was talking too much, and he was doing it for a reason. He was—none too subtly—trying to keep my mind off Susan, and, even though some part of my brain was able to analyze the conversation and realize what he was doing, it was still kind of working.

I said, "Well, I'm not an old Naval Intelligence man or an ex-cop, but it seems pretty obvious to me that the Bodines are going to be watching the road *and* the ferry. If we wait until dark, we can probably get by whoever's watching the road. By then, though, the ferry will quit running. Which doesn't really matter, since, like I said, they'd be watching it anyway. And we can't just run into the motel and scream for the cops, either. First of all, there aren't any. Second, we're the ones who killed someone out here today. These guys haven't done anything but look for us. All of which means we wait until dark, head toward the other end of the island, and see if we can find an unguarded boat along the way." I paused. "At least, that's what I think. You got a better idea, I'm all for it."

Joey said, "You're a very analytical person." I looked at him. He said, "And you're probably right."

An hour passed. The sun shone directly overhead now, and Joey trotted off to check out the beach while I did reconnaissance on the road and Haycock's cottage. It wasn't easy, and, if I hadn't grown up hunting in the tangled forests along the Alabama River, I might never have picked out the outline of a lone man crouched in thick cover along the roadside. But I did pick him out, and I started to feel pretty confident that Joey and I could circle around him and get out well before sunset. And since it was just past noon, that was not an inconsequential discovery.

A little over thirty minutes after we split up, I returned to our hiding place nestled between a tall sand dune and a cluster of wild azaleas. Joey was waiting. I told him about the man guarding the sandy road leading away from Haycock's cottage and how I thought we could circle him in daylight. He agreed. Then the phone vibrated in my pocket.

I flipped it open and said, "Loutie?"

"Yeah. It's me. Let me talk to Joey."

I asked, "Are you in Seaside?"

She said, "It'd be better if I talked to Joey, Tom." And my face turned cool and clammy just as it had earlier when we were stuffing automatic weapons into little black bags.

"What happened?" She didn't answer. I said, "Goddamnit, Loutie. What happened?" Joey reached for the phone but took his hand back when I met his eyes.

Loutie said, "It's Susan, Tom. Looks like they waited till we were all gone and sent somebody in here."

"She's gone. Is that what you're saying?"

Loutie paused, and I listened to three or four seconds of mild static. Then she said, "I'm sorry, Tom. Yes, Susan's gone, and it doesn't look good. The house was shut up. I could still smell gunpowder when I came in. And, I'm sorry, Tom, but somebody lost a lot of blood in the kitchen." She paused again and said, "There are drag marks, like feet or legs, from the blood in the kitchen to, well almost to, the front door."

My face and hands felt sleep-dead, and I lowered the phone. Joey pulled it from my hand, and, as if from a distance, I could hear him talking with Loutie. My cheeks pricked with numbness, and a cruel claw began to stir my guts.

I felt movement and looked up to see Joey walk away to leave me to grieve in private. Time passed, a lot of time, and sickness turned to anger and then quieted into stunned withdrawal, and I came to realize that Joey had been gone a very long time.

I was just rising to go in search of my friend when he stepped into view. Joey walked toward me, standing straight now, and said, "Let's go to the boat."

I looked at him without comprehending.

He said, "Come on, Tom. Let's go."

I asked, "What about the men? Are they gone?" Joey was silent, and I looked into his face. Surface calm masked pure rage.

Joey said, "They're dead."

I studied his face. "How many?"

As Joey turned in the direction of the beach, he said, "All of 'em."

This time Joey drove the open boat, and he gave me some time before he spoke again. We were a hundred yards off Carabelle when Joey said, "Just so you'll know. I paid cash for the boat, but the guy at the marina knows we took it out and were headed for Dog Island. Not much we can do about that." I didn't feel like talking, and I didn't. He went on, "Not much to worry about, though. There's just one cop in Carabelle. They don't even have a police station. The place is kinda famous for that. This cop just hangs around a phone booth and waits for it to ring." I looked at him. "No shit. The town was famous for about five minutes twenty years ago when Johnny Carson talked about it on *The Tonight Show*."

Joey was trying, once again, to make me think about something other than Susan. I said, "You think we could talk about this later?" He gave up and concentrated on steering a course to The Moorings, which was fine with me.

The marina was open. We did not go back inside. We tied up the boat, loaded the Expedition, and left. Two hours later, as we cruised through the unsightly jumble of Panama City, Joey turned north onto Highway 231 and drove away from the coast.

I asked, "Where are we going?"

"Mobile. But right now, we're making a big damn circle around Seaside."

Until then, I had thought of nothing but loss. Now, my mind conjured the too-vivid image of Susan lying in a pool of blood in that tacky designer cottage. I asked, "What about Susan and Loutie and the cottage?"

"Loutie's taking care of everything. By tonight, nobody'll ever know we were there. Rented under an alias. Loutie's doing cleanup."

Cleanup. What a nice, descriptive term. I said, "Why don't we just call the cops? As far as I'm concerned, all bets are off. Sanchez didn't protect anybody. What's he going to do? Threaten to kill me? The hell with him."

"We don't need to do anything right now, Tom. We gotta get somewhere and think this mess out. You gotta realize, it ain't Sanchez or Purcell killing you I'm worried about. I mean, you know, that wouldn't exactly make me happy, but we got other problems too. We just left four dead guys piled in a beach house on Dog Island. What're we supposed to tell the cops? We were in a shoot-out, and they lost? Hell, three of 'em aren't even shot. How do you figure we're gonna explain two guys with their jugulars knifed open and one with a broken neck?" He turned to look at me, then turned back to watch the road. "Shit. I don't know. Maybe that is what we wanna do. But I'd kinda like to think about it before we volunteer for the electric chair."

I thought out loud. "Second degree or manslaughter. Wouldn't be the electric chair."

"Huh?"

I said, "Nothing," and closed my eyes. "Turn around."

"Why?"

I opened my eyes and looked out at the strip-mall and fast-food mess scattered across the north side of Panama City. "I want to go to Seaside."

Joey slowed, but he didn't stop. "That's a bad idea, Tom. You sure you wanna do it? 'Cause some major-league bad shit has happened today, and we need to put some space between us and . . ."

"You going to turn around?"

Joey mumbled, "Well, just fuck me," but he pulled into the parking lot of a Chevron station and circled back out heading south. Less than an hour later, we pulled up next to Loutie's car outside the rented beach house in Seaside.

I knocked on the canary door. No one answered. Joey called out, "It's us, Loutie. Open the door."

Immediately, the door swung aside, and Loutie motioned for us to hurry inside. She said, "You're not supposed to be here."

Joey looked down and shook his head from side to side. "Tell *him* that."

Loutie said my name, but I had already walked out of the room. In the kitchen, the gray metal boxes full of eavesdropping equipment had vanished. Our food was gone. Our presence had been erased, and so had Susan's—or, hopefully, someone else's—blood. I turned around and saw Joey and Loutie standing in the doorway, watching me.

Joey said, "There's nothing to see, Tom. We all need to get out of here fast."

I looked at Loutie. "Is Purcell still in Mobile?"

Joey cussed. Loutie didn't answer.

"Answer my question, Loutie. Where's Purcell?"

Loutie sighed and said, "He got back a little over an hour ago. I heard him come in before I unhooked the equipment."

I started out of the room, and Joey stepped in front of me. "Tom, let's talk about this a minute."

"Move."

Joey put his hand on my shoulder. He did it in a friendly way, but it was meant to stop me. "Let's just sit down . . ."

I looked up and met his eyes. "Get your hand off me, Joey." He smiled, but he didn't move the hand. "You can move, or I can move you."

Joey's eyes narrowed. "You sure you can do that?"

My hands trembled with adrenaline and rage. None of it was aimed at Joey, but he was in the way. I said, "Step aside, Joey."

Joey dropped his hand from my shoulder and surrendered with a grin. "Be a hell of a fight. I'll say that much." He stepped to one side. "If you're gonna go, mind if I go with you?"

I said, "That's up to you," and walked through the living room and out through the front door.

I didn't look at beaches or birdhouses or pastel architecture. I watched my feet strike sand for a hundred yards, and I was on Purcell's front stoop. The knob twisted easily in my hand. The door swung open, and I stepped inside. The huge beach house was quiet. I pulled the Browning from my waistband, chambered a round, and clicked off the safety; then I started in. Purcell's living room, dining room, and kitchen were all clean and cool, well-lighted and empty. The last room on the ground floor was his study, which was where I finally found what was left of the former University of Florida football great.

Closed blinds blocked out the afternoon sunshine. The only illumination was a cone of yellow light radiating from a brass ship's fixture suspended over the desk. Beneath the fixture, Purcell's lifeless form and the attendant handiwork of a deeply sadistic person stood out in sharp relief beneath the single lightbulb.

chapter twenty-seven

PURCELL HADN'T BEEN dead long, so the smells inside his air-conditioned study were the slaughterhouse odors of fresh blood and butchered meat. Whatever horrible things the man had done during his first forty years on the planet, he had paid for many times over during his last hour.

The heavily muscled ex-jock lay spread-eagle across a cherry partners' desk that had been cleared off and used like an operating table. Yellow seams of fat and jagged clumps of gray muscle protruded from a gaping incision extending across his belly; thick ropes of intestines had been pulled from the wound and draped over his sternum where they lay in a mass of thickening fluids. A blood- and saliva-soaked hand towel had been stuffed inside his mouth to muffle his screams.

Even as I wondered if the killer was still in the house, I found myself edging closer. Strange. The corpse was empty and flattened somehow, like a snakeskin nailed to a board to dry in the summer sun. And I could see now that that was close to the truth of it. The tortured body had been restrained by forty or fifty tenpenny nails driven through the skin of his arms and legs and through the outside of his rib cage. Under the glow of the overhead light, his thick neck shone like melted wax where the skin had been stretched out like gills on either side and nailed to the desktop. I gagged and gagged again as I stepped back away from the blood-soaked carpet. Stomach acid burned in my chest and against the sides of my throat.

I heard footsteps on the carpet behind me. I turned and saw Joey spin Loutie around and shove her out the door before closing it tight. He came up beside me. All he could say was, "What the . . ."

"I guess he didn't take Susan."

"I guess not." Joey took a tentative step forward before recoiling. "Shit, Tom. They even nailed his nutsack to the desk. Who would do that?"

Joey didn't expect an answer, but I said, "He called him a 'mean-ass spic.'"

"Huh?"

"Nothing. I don't know."

Joey raised his voice. "Well, can we please get the fuck out of here *now*?"

"Let's go."

Joey moved out ahead of me, pushing Loutie ahead of him and pausing only twice to wipe two doorknobs clean of our fingerprints on the way out.

Back inside our rented beach house, we stopped in the living room to catch our breath. I was numb. Loutie looked like she was going to be sick. Joey's face had grown pale and hard, and his hands trembled at his sides.

Loutie said, "I've never seen anything like that." It was a stupid comment—none of us had ever seen anything like that—but stupid is what shock does to you.

Joey walked into the kitchen and came back with a glass of water for Loutie. She took a small sip.

Joey looked at me. "We need to go."

I asked, "Is the place clean?"

Loutie nodded.

I looked at the tough ex-stripper and asked, "Are you going to be okay? Can you drive?"

She nodded.

I said, "Joey. Drive her. I'll see you back at Loutie's house in Mobile."

Loutie shook her head as if trying to shake off the image from Purcell's study. "No. My car's jammed full of equipment and stuff. There's no room for Joey even if I wanted him to come with me, and I don't. I'll be fine. You two get out of here. I'm going to give the place a final once-over and I'll be right behind you."

Joey said, "We're not leaving you here."

"Fine. Then wait. I'll be done in three minutes."

And she was. Loutie turned the key in the lock, climbed into her car, and pulled out ahead of us. Joey and I climbed into his Expedition, and he steered back onto Highway 98.

Miles of scruffy beach vegetation droned by, and exhaustion poured over me. I was drifting into unconsciousness when the phone began vibrating against my hip. I reached into the windbreaker's side pocket, fished out the phone, and handed it to Joey. It was probably Loutie.

Joey said, "Hello," listened some, and handed the phone back.

I looked at him and put the tiny gray receiver against my ear. "Hello?"

"Mr. McInnes, this is Charlie Estevez in Tallahassee. We must talk."

"No shit."

"There has been a death."

My stomach tightened, and I prepared to hear the worst about Susan. "Who is it?"

"Leroy Purcell."

I let out a breath I didn't know I was holding. "How do you know?"

"I don't understand. Were you involved? We believed you weren't. If you were, then we have nothing else to discuss."

"What the hell are you talking about?"

Estevez said, "I'm calling on behalf of Mr. Sanchez. He wanted to warn you. One of our people found Leroy Purcell murdered not five minutes ago. Mr. Sanchez was concerned that certain people in Purcell's organization might suspect you."

I tried to sound a little more surprised. "What happened?"

"Somebody knifed him. He was . . . I'm sorry, but I don't know how else to put this. As it was described to me, Purcell had been . . . well, gutted. And, ah, something worse than that."

Estevez wanted to tell me the lurid details. But he wanted me to ask. Instead, I asked about the doctor's wife from Atlanta who had been with Purcell that morning in Mobile for brunch.

Estevez said, "She's fine. Reports are that there was some kind of argument, and Purcell walked out and left her at the party."

I thought it was kind of soon to already have "reports" on Purcell's date that morning. I said, "Well, that's good," and decided it was time for an awkward pause.

I was getting on Estevez's nerves. He wanted to tell me about Purcell's death, and I wanted to get off the phone.

Almost five seconds passed before Estevez said, "Purcell had been . . . Our man found him spread-eagle on the top of his desk with a bunch of nails hammered through his wrists and the skin on the sides of his neck and, pardon the detail, but . . ."

I interrupted. "I got the picture." Once again, Estevez paused. I asked, "Anything else?"

"That's not enough?"

I said, "More than enough."

Joey slowed to a respectable speed as we crossed the state line and followed Highway 331 through the fruit-stand-lined streets of Florala. Just a couple of car lengths ahead, hard tropical sunshine bounced off the back window of a red Saturn, partially obscuring our view of four sun-streaked ponytails that bobbed and bounced with animated conversation. The Greek letters for *phi mu* clung to the red, rear-window brake light, and one of the girls had draped a shapely, suntanned leg out of the front window on the right side. The leg's owner wiggled her toes in the warm wind as she sipped dark cola from a liter bottle and adjusted her sunglasses.

Joey said, "That's what Carli ought to be doin' at her age."

I looked over at him and nodded.

He said, "It's not gonna happen, is it? We get her out of this, and—after what her father did to her and everything else—she still ain't ever gonna be like those little sorority girls."

The scene back at Seaside had gotten to him. For Joey, this was pouring his heart out. I put my hand over the cell phone mouthpiece and said, "Not like them. No. But one day she'll make it. Look at Loutie."

Joey was through talking. He was studying the girls. I refocused my attention on the cell phone and on Charlie Estevez, who had been patiently waiting for me to respond to his news about Purcell.

I said, "Tell Sanchez I need to see him right away."

Estevez cleared his throat. "Mr. Sanchez is a very busy man. I'm not even sure where he is, ah . . ."

"There have been other, connected deaths today. Do you understand?" Estevez didn't answer. I said, "And that's all I'm saying over the phone about that. Sanchez needs to know, though, that somebody's making a move on everyone involved, and up until now I thought it might be him. That's why I wasn't real polite when you told me who you were. But, if it's not your *patriots*, you better tell Sanchez to call me in a hurry. This is all spinning out of control, and somebody's going to pay. You got that?"

Estevez let a few seconds pass before answering, but when he spoke he sounded more thoughtful than irritated. "I have it. Will you be at this number?"

"Yeah. Unless my battery gives out. If it does, I'll call you back in one hour." I said, "By the way, we learned something interesting today about who my client actually saw with Purcell in See Shore Cottage that night. One of Jethro's cousins—if you follow me—told my partner that all this started over some Cuban, in his words, some 'Castro' getting whacked." Estevez was quiet. I said good-bye and pushed the *end* button.

Joey said, "By any chance, am I the partner who heard about the murder?"

"Yeah. You are."

"Just when exactly did I hear this?"

I said, "I haven't decided yet," then tossed my phone on the seat and pulled Joey's out of the clip on his dash and called Kelly. I explained to her, somewhat cryptically since we were talking over airwaves, what had happened, and told her to check into a hotel or go visit her mother for a few days. Kelly promised to get out of town.

When I finished, I filled Joey in on Charlie Estevez's side of our phone conversation, and Joey said, "Gimme that," and took his phone out of my hand. He called Randy Whittles, Navy SEAL and loser of lost girls, and checked on his progress finding Carli. Joey filled Randy in on what was happening and told him to be available in Mobile that night for a meeting.

Joey put the phone back in its dashboard holder and said, "We gotta get everybody together tonight and figure out what to do about all this."

I said, "I'm not going to vote on it, Joey. I'm going to find out who took Susan and . . . and cause somebody some pain."

Joey looked miserable. "I know it doesn't look good, but we don't know *what* the hell happened with Susan today. And, Tom, I like Susan too. Not like you do. But she's my friend too. Believe me, if we find out somebody hurt her, I'm gonna skip the pain part and go right to killing the sonofabitch."

Bright sunshine glinted off the hood and burned a fiery oval into my retina. I closed my eyes and rubbed hard at them with the heels of my hands. I could still see the blazing dot. Joey said, "There's a pair of sunglasses in the glove box."

I put them on.

I said, "You remember telling me about that dagger tattoo on the arm of one of the guys who jumped you outside the bar the first night you were in Appalachicola?"

"Outside Mother's Milk. Yeah. I remember."

"You said there were initials over and under it."

Joey rubbed his jaw. "Yeah. I remember it said R.I.P. Rest in Peace, I guess. And it had something like initials too."

"R.E.T."

"I'd have to check my notes."

"It's R.E.T. I remember. And I saw the tattoo myself on Sunday." Joey glanced over. I said, "Sonny. Purcell's guy who was one of the painters. It's the same asshole who burned Susan's painting."

Joey smiled a little for the first time since leaving Seaside behind. "The one you threw grits at."

I nodded. "And the one Billy Teeter's partner, Julie, called to come kill me after Willie fell in the water off Dog Island. Look, I was thinking. There are obviously a hell of a lot of names that start with T, but the arm stamped with this particular T is tied to Julie and the Teeters. So, I was thinking that maybe we could make another donation to your friends on the Panama City force and find out if they have any record of a convicted felon named R. E. Teeter. You said it looked like a prison tattoo."

Joey sat and thought about that for a few seconds. "It was definitely one of those shitty homemade jobs *like* people get in prison. Can't be sure, though. Nowadays, street punks give themselves fake prison ink to try and look tough, but . . ." He picked up his cell phone and dialed up Detective Coosa in Panama City. When the conversation ended, Joey put his phone back in its clip on the dash and said, "He'll call back."

Twenty minutes later, the phone rang. It was Sanchez. We set up a meeting at my office that night in Mobile; then Joey called Randy to make arrangements for that evening.

An hour went by before Detective Coosa called. Joey listened, made phone noises, and hung up. He said, "Rudolph Enis Teeter."

I said, "Not a really dangerous-sounding name."

Joey grinned. "Damn if I wouldn't wanna be called Sonny too."

"What did he do time for?"

"Assault with a deadly weapon, attempted murder, and resisting arrest."

I said, "Tough guy."

Joey said, "Or just a dumb-ass."

chapter twenty-eight

WE PULLED INTO Mobile at rush hour and slowly made our way to Loutie's house. As we turned down her comfortable, tree-lined street, Joey said, "You sure this is a good idea? Your buddy Carlos could be behind this whole thing."

"Maybe, but I don't think so. I think he's the catalyst."

"What's that mean?"

"A catalyst is . . ."

"I may not be a lawyer, Tom, but I'm not a moron. How is Sanchez a catalyst?"

"I'm not sure yet."

Joey said, "Thanks. I'm glad I asked."

"But it's got something to do with the fat guy on the beach and whether somebody thought Leroy Purcell stepped outside his territory or overstepped some kind of bounds when he started smuggling and shooting people on the islands."

Petite, dangerous, and nervous, Randy was waiting inside when we arrived. Two of his men kept watch on the street and the alley. Loutie Blue wasn't home yet, and Joey was having a hard time hiding his concern. Finally, he called her and found out she was caught up in traffic.

Randy had picked up Chinese takeout, but I skipped the egg rolls and rice and found a bottle of Dewar's. After two whiskies, I thought I was better. After the third drink, I could feel the tense tingling pressure that, since I was a child, has always closed in on the sides of my throat when I'm going to lose it, and tears began to fill my eyelids. Without excuse or explanation, I left Joey and Randy in the kitchen shoveling Mongolian beef into their mouths and pretending not to notice that there was another grown man in the room who was crying—sort of. I walked through the house to the room where Susan and I had made love while panic had gripped Carli and sent her climbing through a window to escape into the night.

Inside the bathroom, I twisted the shower's ceramic crosses and stripped and stepped into the steaming spray. Hot water poured over my face and scalp and shoulders, and I tried to think. If Susan really was dead, well, there would be time to grieve. But, right now, I had to work on the premise that she and Carli were alive and well and out there somewhere in desperate need of help.

I stood there beneath the stinging spray until it turned warm and then cold, and I stood there some more to let the frigid water run over my face. It didn't help. I checked my reflection in the mirror while drying off, and I still looked awful. I didn't necessarily look like I had been crying, which, I admit, was what I was worried about, but I still, unarguably, looked, as Joey would say, like shit on a lollipop.

When I was dressed, I took a deep breath—and a lesson from Loutie Blue—and pushed the hurt and anger down deep where, I hoped, I could use them when the time came.

Back downstairs, Randy and his men had left to recon my office building and take up positions. Joey and I climbed into his Expedition and followed. Twenty minutes later, we pulled into the deck of the Oswyn Israel Building and stepped out into the oppressively dark concrete structure. As we walked toward the entrance to my building, I whispered. "Somebody's here."

Joey spoke even more quietly than I had. All he said was, "Yeah."

"Is it Randy's men?"

Joey shook his head and whispered. "No idea," but I noticed the Glock 9mm had moved out of his shoulder holster and into his hand.

I used my key card to open the double glass doors and work the elevator. The hall was lighted, and my office door was open. Odd Job waited, appropriately enough, in the waiting room. As we entered he tried to pat me down. I pushed him away, and, with surprising speed, Odd Job pulled a gun from inside his coat. But before he could level it, something white flashed across his face and he hit the floor shoulders first. I looked over and saw Joey massaging his right fist with his left hand. His gun was on the floor.

Joey said, "I figured you didn't want him shot."

I said, "Knocked on his ass is good."

We found Sanchez waiting in my office. He stood and nodded. "Good evening."

Joey said, "Not for Sumo Joe out there."

Sanchez looked puzzled and stepped out of the office. We followed. Sanchez very nearly tripped over his three-hundred-pound bodyguard, who lay unconscious on the floor opposite the front door. Odd Job, a.k.a. Sumo Joe, was breathing heavily, and a small rivulet of blood trickled from the corner of his mouth. Sanchez asked, "What is this about?"

I said, "He behaved badly at the end of a bad day."

Sanchez looked a little disgusted, but I couldn't tell with whom. He turned and walked back into my office and sat in the upholstered guest chair he had been using when we came in. Then he casually, almost gracefully, crossed his legs and said, "It also was a bad day for Leroy Purcell."

Joey said, "We don't really give a shit about Leroy Purcell's day."

Sanchez shrugged and turned to me. "I cannot sympathize with whatever difficulties you encountered today because I do not know what you are talking about. On the telephone, you told Señor Estevez that there have been other deaths. That is all I know."

I looked at Joey, and he raised his shoulders. *Tell him if you want to.*

So I leaned back in my chair, put my feet on the desk, and told Carlos Sanchez about our day on Dog Island.

As I talked, Sanchez pulled out his cigar case and placed a long, thin Montecristo between his small, white teeth. As he put the match to the end, he said, "They knew about the listening devices."

I said, "Yeah. It looks that way."

He said, "I am sorry about Señora Fitzsimmons, uh, missing. As you know, I wanted very much to avoid anything like this."

I looked at him. "Actually, you assured me that Purcell would leave me and Susan alone."

He held up open palms. "We did all we could to control the situation. Leroy Purcell is . . . *was* too ambitious for his own good. I imagine his death was no great loss to anyone."

"No shit."

He paused. "You said there was an attempted ambush. People died."

"We had to kill them to escape."

"Where are the bodies?"

I said, "In a house used by the Bodines on Dog Island. A man named Thomas Bobby Haycock has been living there."

He said, "Do you expect me to clean up your mess? Is that why you are telling me this?"

I said, "Yep."

Sanchez said, "No," and Joey's Glock 9mm appeared. Sanchez said, "Do you plan to kill me also?"

Joey shrugged.

I said, "If I thought you had anything to do with Susan, you'd already be dead. But I don't think you would have come here if you had. So we have to decide how we're going to move forward. Joey and I are working on the assumption that you and your group are either going to be with us or against us. In other words, we don't see you sitting on the sidelines while we get slaughtered. And if you're not willing to help, that means—and I'm just guessing here—that you will probably try to kill us to keep this mess from getting any messier and to keep the cops out of your business. And Mr. Sanchez, or whoever the hell you are, if you're going to try to kill us, well, we have to figure we've got a better chance of staying alive long enough to find Susan if we shoot you right now."

Sanchez let thick, gray smoke drift out through his nostrils. He said, "I could simply lie and kill you later."

"That's true. But I don't think you will. Something's going on with the Bodines, and I think you need to know what it is. Your contact man, Leroy Purcell, just had his guts cut out by someone." I said, "The man had a long list of enemies, but it's too much to believe it's a coincidence that he got killed the same afternoon when someone was busy kidnapping Susan and trying to kill Joey and me. It's all connected somehow. And since you didn't do it, and since Joey and I don't have a frigging clue, it stands to reason that killing us isn't going to solve the problem." I paused, and Sanchez remained quiet. I said, "So, in short, someone's drawing a lot of attention to the Bodines in a way that's bad for you and for us. We don't want to go to jail for defending ourselves on the island, and you don't want your fellow patriots to rot in South America while you try to set up a new operation. And you sure as hell don't want to get yourself in the newspaper or on the evening news."

Sanchez looked from me to Joey and back again. He said, "I expected more. That is a weak argument, Señor McInnes." This time, I shrugged. He inhaled deeply from his Montecristo, blew a long, narrow plume of smoke at the ceiling, and said, "If the bodies have not already been discovered, we can take care of the cleanup on Dog Island." My stomach tightened as I heard *cleanup* used the same disturbing way for a second time that day. "But understand that I am making what I believe is the logical choice under the circumstances. Please do not fool yourself that you can deal with us through threats." And he rose to leave. As he passed Odd Job, he stopped and looked down.

Joey said, "I got 'im," and walked over to drag the unconscious bodyguard outside.

Sanchez turned back to look at me. "You told Charlie Estevez that one of the Bodines you saw today said something about your client seeing Purcell kill a Cuban."

"Nope. He said, as nearly as Joey could remember, that, quote, 'all this mess started over a fucking Castro getting whacked.' "

Sanchez said, "What else did he say?"

I said, "As far as I know, nothing." I hesitated and said, "There was something else, but it didn't make much sense."

"What was that?"

"This guy, I think it was the one who ended up with a broken neck, tried to bargain with Joey. He said he could tell us about 'the fat spic in the swamp.' " I stood and looked at him. "Does that make any sense to you?"

A.k.a. Carlos Sanchez looked at the floor and shook his head as if giving the question great thought and coming up empty; then he walked out the door.

When Joey came back in, I asked if Sanchez had tried to talk to him in the hallway. He shook his head and said, "You think you talked him out of killing us?"

"I don't know. I think, probably yeah, for the time being."

"It was kind of a weak-ass argument."

"Yeah. Well, you'd be right except for one thing."

Joey looked puzzled.

I said, "Sanchez's front group owns the house on Dog Island where you just left a pile of dead guys. And he's scared to death somebody's going to find out."

chapter twenty-nine

WE HEADED BACK to Loutie Blue's house, making sure, we thought, that no one was tailing us. As we came through the front door, Loutie came downstairs, and I heard the back door close a few seconds before young Randy Whittles strode into the room. He said, "We made two in the alley and two on the street."

Loutie nodded. "That's what I saw. There's probably at least one more waiting with their car, wherever that is, but two and two is all I could see."

I asked, "Who are they?"

Randy said, "No way to be sure. But probably the Cubans. They're not doing anything. Just watching the house, and my men are watching them."

Loutie glanced at me and said, "Let's go talk in the kitchen. Tom needs to eat something."

I said, "I'm not hungry," and everyone walked out of the room in the direction of the kitchen and left me sitting alone. My choices seemed to be either to sit in the living room by myself or to go in the kitchen and let Loutie shove food at me.

 Randy's take-out feast was spread out across the kitchen table in little white boxes with red pagodas printed on the sides and wire handles looped across their tops. I sat at the table, and Loutie put a clean plate in front of me.

I said, "I don't want anything," and she started piling steamed rice on the plate. I said, "Damn it, Loutie, I told you I don't want this stuff," and she began to spoon Mongolian beef over the rice. I gave up and turned to Randy. "What have you found out about Carli? Do you think she's still on the Gulf somewhere?"

Randy managed to look both embarrassed and a little impotent. He said, "Loutie says we can't talk until you eat something."

I exploded. "This is childish bullshit. Susan may be dead. Carli's missing and God knows in what kind of trouble." I turned to look at Loutie. "We do not have time for this crap."

Loutie said, "Then I guess you better eat something."

I looked at Joey with the intention of reaming him out. But he just grinned and raised his shoulders as if to say, "Whatcha gonna do?" So I picked up a fork and ate a mouthful of lukewarm beef and onions and rice. Loutie smiled and walked to the refrigerator, where she poured a glass of iced tea and put it down next to my plate.

I said, "You going to burp me when I'm done?"

Loutie looked unfazed. She said, "If you need it," and sat down.

Now that I was actually eating, I was kind of hungry. I chewed while Randy talked. "Carli went from here to a bus stop three blocks east. Around five A.M., she caught a bus to the main terminal downtown and left there for Biloxi at seven-twenty. She got off the bus in Biloxi at *their* main terminal and was spotted later in the day, just after lunch, hitchhiking about forty miles northeast of there on the road to Meridian." Randy looked down at the table and flexed his jaw. He said, "That's it. That's all we know."

Joey said, "Tom. I don't wanna sound like an insensitive prick here, but now that Purcell and Rus Poultrez are dead, how much difference does it make that we can't find her? I mean, I know it's bad for any fifteen-year-old to be out running around the countryside by herself, hitchhiking and all, but . . . Hell, you know what I mean."

I said, "You're right. At least, you probably are. Some of Purcell's boys may still be out looking for her, but I'm guessing they're more interested in finding who killed their boss. Not to mention jockeying around to see who's going to be the next King of the Jethros."

Randy said, "Don't you think they're gonna blame you for killing Purcell?"

"Probably."

Randy was not a complex personality. He said, "What're you gonna do?"

I stood and raked half the food Loutie had given me into the garbage disposal and put my plate in the sink. My bottle of Dewar's was on the counter. I found a glass, put some ice in it, and poured some whiskey over the ice. Loutie wrinkled her nose a little, but didn't say anything. I sat down and said, "Randy. I'm going to have to think about that. But right now I'm thinking that we're going to need almost an army to get the Bodines off our backs."

Randy chuckled. "We don't exactly have an army, Tom."

I said, "No. But Carlos Sanchez does."

At 11:47 that night, the hero of New Cuba knocked on Loutie's door. This time, Odd Job had been replaced by the UZI man who had guarded Sanchez in Captain Billy's trophy den in Eastpoint. Now, he seemed to have lost interest in me. Joey's fame had preceded him, and the UZI man made a point of staying close to Sanchez and watching Joey the way a rattler watches a king snake.

I said, "I guess those are your men outside."

Sanchez said, "They are."

"Planning to hurt somebody?"

Sanchez walked over and sat in an upholstered chair. He said, "The matter on Dog Island has been taken care of. The men are buried, and the house has been cleaned and stripped of fabrics."

"Sounds like you've done this before." Sanchez just looked at me and waited. I said, "Thank you."

"You still have problems," he said. "The Bodines do, indeed, believe you killed Purcell."

"They think I slaughtered him like that?"

"The Bodines know about your brother's criminal activities before he died. And I am told that you personally and violently drowned the person responsible for his murder."

I was getting angry. "It was . . . not how it sounds."

Sanchez nodded. "I am sure."

He was working me, probing the ragged edges of my guilt to maneuver me into doing something—much the same way I was doing my best to maneuver him by feeding him small bites of information, mixed with out-and-out lies, designed to drive a wedge between his group and the Bodines. I just didn't know yet what he wanted me to do, and it was becoming clear that, whatever it was, he wasn't going to just come out and tell me. I asked, "What do they want?"

Sanchez said, "They *claim* to want you dead."

"Claim?"

"Well, there is a man—very young, very ambitious—who is not unhappy that Purcell is out of the way. The problem is that he sees killing you as the final step in becoming the new leader of their organization. You see, he feels that avenging the death of their football-hero leader will make him something of a hero to his unwashed brethren."

"Then I guess I better find out who really killed him."

Sanchez looked off into the distance. After a time, he said, "I'm not sure that would make much difference. Your death would be symbolic. This is not a court of law. It's not justice he wants. It is the appearance—or, I should say, the reputation, if you will, for violence and revenge that is important here."

"So this new wanna-be leader doesn't really care who killed Purcell?"

"No."

"He just wants to be known as the man who took out *somebody* for doing it?"

"Yes."

I looked over at Joey and asked, "You got anything to say?" Joey had locked eyes with Sanchez's bodyguard, and he didn't speak. He just slowly shook his head. I looked at Sanchez. "I don't think they like each other."

Sanchez smiled. "They are a different sort of man than you and I."

I said, "You think you and I are alike?"

"No. Or I should say, I do not know you well enough to have formed an opinion." He motioned to Joey and his bodyguard. "Except that I suspect we are alike in that—while we are capable of violence if provoked—we are not drawn to the sort of primitive, visceral violence that comes so easily to men like these."

Joey said, "You might wanna watch your mouth, Carlos."

Sanchez smiled and continued to look at me. "My people have done enough. I do not wish to adopt you, Señor McInnes. So I would like to know how you are going to handle your problem with the Bodines *without* going to the authorities."

"I'm a lawyer. You're going to tell me who this new leader is, and I'm going to find out something he wants and make a deal."

Sanchez shook his head.

"You're not going to tell me ?"

Sanchez said, "No. At least, not now. There are many people watching or, I should say, looking for you. My group, we are watching. The rest look. And I have no plans to turn you over to anyone. But, Señor McInnes, I quite frankly do not expect you to make it."

I said, "And you're not interested in tying yourself to a dead man."

"No." Sanchez stood and said, "By the way, what has become of your young client?"

"I wish I knew." I asked, "Have they found Rus Poultrez's body?"

"Señor?"

"After the crash the other night off Dog Island. I thought you knew. Rus Poultrez flipped a speedboat over an oyster bed and slammed upside down into the water."

"I knew of the accident, but Poultrez is not dead."

I felt sick. "How do you know that?"

As Sanchez walked toward the door, he said, "We know. You do not need to know how." He turned and looked into my eyes. "Who do you think killed Leroy Purcell?"

I said, "Are you saying that. . . ?"

He answered before I finished the question. "I am saying *only* that Purcell is dead and Russell Poultrez of Gloucester, Massachusetts, is alive. The rest is simply what I think, what I . . . surmise." And he walked out the door followed by the UZI man.

I looked at Joey. "Do you think Poultrez killed Purcell?"

He said, "Yep."

"Why?"

"Beats me. I guess I *surmised* it."

chapter thirty

I STOOD IN the living room and felt pure exhaustion soak into my muscles and begin a warm ache in my neck and shoulders and back, even in the tiny joints of my fingers. I didn't sit for fear that I wouldn't want to stand up again. So Joey and I stood there looking at each other, at the floor, at whatever until Loutie and Randy appeared and informed us that Sanchez had departed, taking his business-suited soldiers with him.

I said, "I'm about to drop, and I know the rest of you probably are too, but we've got a lot to do. I'm sure as hell open to suggestions, but I can't see us waiting until morning to get started. With Rus Poultrez out there, we all know he could find Carli any minute. And I don't even want to think about what she might be going through while we're catching up on sleep."

Loutie said, "And there's Susan. It's been about, what, twelve hours since she came up missing?"

"Close to that."

"Well, we may not want to think about it, but if that blood on the floor was hers, she needs somebody to find her fast and get her to a hospital."

I said, "Even if it wasn't her blood . . . ," and my voice trailed off as images of Purcell's tortured and mutilated body flashed through my thoughts and I left the obvious unspoken. "Anyway, Randy, I'd like you to split up your people—hire somebody if you need to—and put at least one good man looking for Carli and another looking for Rus Poultrez. And I'd like *you* to concentrate your own time on the father. That's the key with Carli. She's a tough kid. We can deal with her living on the road. She's done it before. The danger to Carli is her father." I turned to Loutie and said, "I'd like you to find Susan." And I knew any further instructions or suggestions would be pointless. With Loutie, the thing to do was just point her and pull the trigger. Everything else was self-guided.

Loutie said, "It might help if you told us what's going on."

"What do you mean?"

Joey said, "Loutie thinks you're smarter than the rest of us." He looked from me to Loutie. "She's probably right."

I said, "Loutie, I'm not even sure I know what I know. I'm mostly still guessing." Loutie put her hands on her hips and locked eyes with me. I gave up. "Okay. I haven't wanted to waste time on theories, but . . . here's what I *think* I know." Against my better judgment, I walked over and sat on the sofa. "The murder that started all this took place in a house called See Shore Cottage, and that house is owned by a group called ProAm Holdings Corp. I found that out pretty early. Then the name came up again when Joey and I were trying to get information out of a snitch in Appalachicola called Squirley McCall."

Joey interrupted. "Said it was the name used by a bunch of what he called 'cigar spics,' who are buying property on the coast. He claimed Purcell brought them into the area."

I said, "So we know that ProAm is buying land, that it's a Cuban-American enterprise, and that they owned See Shore Cottage. Also, I checked, and the same company owns the house on Dog Island where Haycock was staying."

Loutie said, "Products Americas. ProAm for short, I guess."

I said, "Holding company."

"Oh. Okay. That's the company Kelly found out about that owns the yacht they used to smuggle in the fat guy and his family."

"Yep. L. Carpintero." I said, "What's the name sound like?" Joey shrugged. "Think about it. Change the 'L' to 'E- L' and it literally means 'the carpenter.' I didn't get it either until Squirley said one of the Cubans' leaders was called Martillo and the other one was nicknamed 'Carpet Hero.' "

Loutie said, "Carpintero."

"Uh-huh. When Squirley mentioned the name along with Martillo, it finally rang a bell. A couple of Mexican-American carpenters remodeled my new office when I left Higgins & Thompson last year, and I was in there trying to work while they were still nailing up molding. They learned 'hold it down' from me and I learned, among other things, that *martillo* is Spanish for hammer."

Loutie said, "The fat guy killed Purcell."

"Looks like it."

Randy said, "I'm not following."

I said, "*El carpintero* is 'the carpenter.' *Martillo* is hammer, and Purcell was . . ."

"Nailed to his own desk," Randy said. "But that doesn't make sense. You're saying that Purcell brought the Cubans, including this Hammer guy, into Appalachicola. Why would he turn around and kill Purcell?"

"I don't know. But I do know that Purcell threatened me early on with a 'mean-ass spic,' who he said would do something like slice me open and play with my guts while I was alive and watching. I thought he was just making up a scary story—and not a very realistic one—to get me to turn over Susan and Carli."

Loutie said, "Purcell probably just pissed this crazy guy off. Somebody psychotic enough to do something like that I'm guessing isn't really weighted down by normal human emotions like loyalty or gratitude."

I said, "Yeah, and Purcell could piss off the pope."

Joey looked confused. "I thought we thought Rus Poultrez murdered Purcell."

I took a deep breath and stood up. "As far as we know now, he did. This hammer stuff may be reaching. We're just guessing it's some kind of street name for a sadist with a nail fetish. For all we know, the guy's last name is Carpintero or Martillo or Hammer, and they're just playing word games with aliases. Poultrez may still be the killer." I looked around. "But, I don't think so. Poultrez hated Purcell. But—unless somebody else made Poultrez a better offer—Purcell getting dead means Poultrez has lost any chance of making money on Carli, which is all he cares about. And earlier tonight Carlos Sanchez made a not-very-subtle point of trying to point us at Poultrez for Purcell's murder."

Joey said, "He *surmised* it."

I ignored him. "It just doesn't make sense for Poultrez to kill the golden goose. No, I think all this is happening because Carlos Sanchez, Charlie Estevez, and Products Americas are throwing *way* too much money around, and we've blundered into a gang war over control of the smuggling trade in and around Franklin County, Florida. And I think that Carpintero, or whatever his name is, killed Leroy Purcell mostly because he needed to and—considering what he did to him—at least partly because he enjoyed it."

Everyone was quiet for a few beats.

I said, "I guess the only other thing is about Susan. There's no reason I can think of why somebody would want to kill her, except maybe to get to the rest of us. Or I guess she could have surprised someone."

Joey cut in. "She ain't dead. We don't need to stop pressing now."

"I know. You're right, and it's what makes sense. If the Bodines killed her by mistake or on purpose they would've left her there. Think about it. There was too much blood for them to think they were covering something up. No. No, I think somebody *took*

Susan, and they took her for one of two reasons. Either we're going to get a 'leave-us-alone-or-we'll-kill-her' call *or* somebody out there needs her help with something—and, as far as I can see, the only thing she could help with is finding Carli or finding us."

Joey said, "And nobody's called any threats in or dropped by to shoot at us."

"Yeah. So, I'm thinking that somebody—Sonny or Poultrez or some other asshole—grabbed her to help find Carli."

Joey reached up and scrubbed at his scalp with both hands and then looked off into the distance. No one spoke for a few seconds until Joey said, "Okay. Tell me if I got it. Purcell was connected with both the Cubans and this sick Carpintero bastard. The Bodines are smuggling for the Cubans, and one of the things they smuggle is the fat guy and his family, who are holed up in the middle of a swamp. So, both the Cubans and Purcell know about the fat guy, and it looks likely that the fat guy is this nail-hammering asshole."

I said, "Yeah, it looks like it. I guess we can't be sure, but when there's a guy around named El Carpintero and somebody gets nailed to a desk . . ."

Loutie said, "And it looks like Carli's father—this Rus Poultrez—was busy grabbing Susan . . ."

I said, "*If* he's the one who did it."

Loutie nodded. "Yeah, well, bear with me a second. Let's say Poultrez took Susan 'cause he needs her to help find Carli. He was grabbing Susan at pretty much the same time this Hammer guy was wailing on Purcell. So, unless it was one hell of a coincidence, it looks like there was some coordination there between Carpintero and Rus Poultrez."

I said, "And even if it wasn't Poultrez, the fact that Susan's kidnapping and Purcell's murder happened the same afternoon leads us right back to Carpintero."

Joey said, "So, if Poultrez took Susan, looks like he was working with—or at least coordinating with—Carpintero. And if

Carpintero took Susan . . . Well, shit, it all leads back to the fat prick with the hammer, doesn't it?"

I said, "Yeah. It looks like it. Of course, as logical as it sounds plotted out like this, it could all still be wrong."

"Yeah," Joey said, "but it makes sense."

I said, "And it gives us a place to focus."

Joey flipped his head to one side and cracked the tension out of his neck. "Damn right. We focus on finding this Carpintero asshole and see how bad he is with his hammer stuck up his ass."

Vertical lines formed between Loutie's eyebrows as she processed the conversation. When the room grew quiet, she asked, "Is that it?"

I said, "That's all the facts and most of the guesses," and she left the room.

Randy hung around for another minute or two, staring into space and working it out in his head, before leaving by the front door.

Joey and I were the only ones left.

I didn't know what I looked like, but he looked beat. His tanned complexion had gone pale except for dark smudges over his cheekbones. Everyone involved was tired, but it was Susan's blood-trailed disappearance that was devouring Joey and me.

I asked, "Did your people get a good picture of Sanchez tonight?"

"They got him. We gotta wait to see how good they are, but we took a shitload of shots."

"What about the shots of Carpintero?"

"A buddy of mine at the ABI has already got 'em. He's checking Carpintero's shots against their files." Joey stopped to rub the back of his neck. "Randy'll send over the shots of Sanchez when they're ready."

I thought for a minute. "That's just a criminal check though, right?"

Joey nodded.

I said, "Well then, get a set of prints to Kelly too, with a message to run them by somebody at the newspaper. That's not a problem is it?"

Joey said, "That is not a problem," and walked over to Loutie's phone. After conveying instructions to Randy, Joey replaced the headset. He tilted his head back and looked up at the ceiling. "So this Carpintero or Hammer or whoever he is is the key."

"Looks like it."

"I guess you and me are going to Florida."

"Yeah." I said, "Tate's Hell Swamp."

I hadn't been home for a week, and I needed clothes and waders, a flashlight and field glasses. Our choices for procuring these things at two in the morning were to either stop by my beach house on Point Clear or burglarize a sporting goods store. Joey had a pair of binoculars, camera equipment, and camouflage clothing—your basic private investigator stuff—for himself. But I needed my things, things not made for the big and tall.

My white gravel driveway shone like snow in the moonlight. I rolled to a stop a hundred feet from the front steps and shoved the rented transmission into park. Joey had disconnected the Ford's interior lights, which was one of his private investigator stealth specialties, and we were able to leave the car with minimal fuss. With the empty car left idling on the driveway, Joey moved quietly toward the front of the house, while I trotted around to the bay side and stopped short of the open beach to look and to listen for something wrong or different.

Deep purple clouds with silver edges sped across the sky, and warm breezes flowed across the choppy, charcoal bay, rustling sea grass, and sharp black pine needles. On the house, squares of white trim floated, suspended in air, as cloud cover rendered weathered siding invisible. I closed my eyes because I once read that assassins wait outside dark rooms with their eyes shut so their vision will be adjusted to the dark when they go in to kill. And I listened. Closing one's eyes in a dangerous place is unnatural; so I listened hard during the long seconds I was able to last. And when I reopened my eyes, I actually could see a little better in the night.

I watched the home where, for six months of endless nights, I had tossed and turned and wandered the beach, and I began to make sense of the shadows, separating shades of charcoal into familiar shapes and objects. I knew every sound and smell and look of that fragment of the world—even at 2:00 A.M. And there *was* something wrong.

I crouched closer to the sand and flipped open my cell phone and punched in Joey's number. Somewhere on the front of the house, his pocket vibrated, and I put the phone away and waited. He did not respond, which meant either his side was clear or he was incapacitated. But, inasmuch as I hadn't heard a cannon go off, the likelihood of his incapacity was, I thought, pretty close to nil.

I studied shadows because those were what bothered me. Everything looked fine. Only it didn't look the same, and I wasn't really sure why that was. I jogged across the beach, sending little half-circles of powder puffing out in front of each foot as it struck dry sand. Ten yards in, I stopped by a clump of tall, black grass that I hoped would break up my silhouette. And again something was out of place, something near the first-floor deck in back. Then he moved. Too small and too thin at the waist to be Poultrez, the man had thick shoulders, and he was holding a long weapon. He was waiting inside a deep shadow beside the deck. He was just waiting. Maybe he understood now that no one was inside the idling Taurus, and he was scared. Maybe he was just patient.

I decided to test my virtue against his and settled in for a long wait that wasn't. No more than three minutes passed, and he couldn't stand it. The strong man with the narrow waist had to have a look around, and he moved left toward the near corner of the house. As he moved, I saw new movement at the other, far corner and recognized Joey's hulking shadow. I circled left, matching my pace with the armed man's, then stopped and waited some more when he halted two paces from the corner and, it seemed, turned to look out at the beach. Shadows from the eaves blanked out his head and body, but now the moonlight found his arms and the tip of his nose, and I knew he had seen me. The long gun came up to his shoulder, and I dove into the sand as the hollow boom of a shotgun blast pounded the beach. And then nothing. Nothing but wind and the redundant sigh of water lapping sand. I rolled onto my back and pointed the Browning with both hands the way Tim the painter had done just before he died, and I waited for the shotgunner to come inspect his kill.

Phantom boots jogged through wet sand inside my head; the hard tang of copper flooded my mouth; and Joey called out my name. I waited. If the shotgunner was near, answering would give him a target. Then Joey's voice came again. "Tom! Answer me. I got the guy. Answer me!"

I called out, "I'm here," and got to my feet, dusting sand out of my shirt and pants.

"You okay?"

"Yeah. Fine." I could see Joey now, standing near the spot where the shotgun had gone off. I shouted, "Who is it?"

"Don't know. Never seen him before."

As I approached, I saw Joey standing over a vaguely familiar form lying prostrate on the sand. I asked, "Is he alive?"

Before Joey could answer, a voice said, "Mr. McInnes, it's me." And young Willie Teeter sat up and looked at me with the moonlight now full on his face.

"What the hell are you doing here?"

Willie sounded scared. "Granddaddy sent me. Julie said you and her had a run-in, and Granddaddy couldn't get you on the phone, and he sent me up here to find you. Make sure you're all right."

I said, "Stand up," and Joey reached down and lifted the nineteen-year-old shrimper by one arm. The boy's feet actually dangled in the air for a second before Joey put him down. Willie seemed impressed. When Joey released his arm, the boy turned and studied the big man's face. I asked, "Did your Granddaddy tell you to come up here and blow my head off too?"

"No, sir. No, sir, he didn't. I was supposed to wait around for you and let him know, you know, whether you're okay. But I heard the car and got scared and hid around back here."

Joey said, "You bring that shotgun along to shoot possums while you were waiting?"

Willie turned to Joey and looked up into his face. "No, sir. We knew Sonny was pissed off at Mr. McInnes. And you don't know Sonny, but he's crazy. Been in prison half his life. Kill anybody. No shit. He'd just as soon kill you as look at you. I thought that's who I was shooting at. I seen a shadow, and I could see what looked like a gun, you know, kind of outlined against the beach. And I shot." He turned back to me. "I'm sorry as hell, Mr. McInnes. I was scared."

I looked into the boy's face but couldn't read anything there. Maybe it was the dark. Maybe not. I asked, "Have you checked out the house?"

Willie said, "Just through the windows, but I been here a long time. I'm pretty sure there ain't nobody in there."

Willie waited in the yard while Joey and I went in fast. The alarm was set. Everything was just as I had left it. I punched in the alarm code, called Willie, and told him to go in the kitchen with Joey. I ran upstairs, pulled together a loose stack of clean clothes, and located my fishing gear. Joey would be amused. I laid out a pair of Orvis Gor-Tex waders with inflatable suspenders and a pair of Russell Moccasin custom wading boots with felt soles. None of which was exactly what one might call swamp gear, but they were what I had and they fit. I emptied out an old nylon dive bag, put my clothes and gear inside, and threw a pair of quick-focus Nikon binoculars and a black-rubber Mag-Lite flashlight on top.

When everything was packed down and zipped up in the dive bag, I closed the door to my bedroom and made two phone calls. The first, which took less than a minute, was to the information operator for the area code covering Florida's Panhandle. The second was to a number in the quaint fishing village of Eastpoint, and that one lasted much longer.

Joey and Willie were drinking from glasses filled with something clear and carbonated when I came into the kitchen. I looked at Joey—he was holding Willie's shotgun now—and said, "Let's go."

Willie's eyes perked up. "Where are you goin'?"

Joey caught my eye and, almost imperceptibly, shook his head.

I said, "We've got business to take care of. Sorry, but if you want that drink, you're going to have to take it with you."

Willie put his glass on the kitchen counter. "Alright then." He turned to Joey. "I need my shotgun back."

Joey just said, "Nope."

The young shrimper flushed red. "That's an expensive gun. It's mine and I want it back now."

Joey glanced at me. He'd had about all he wanted of Willie Teeter. I said, "Willie, I'll get the shotgun back to your grandfather. You already tried to shoot one person tonight. I don't think we'd be doing you or Captain Billy a favor to let you leave here with that thing."

Willie glared at the floor; then he said, "Well, fuck both of you," and walked out.

Joey said, "Somebody ought to explain to that kid that the innocent good-old-boy routine don't exactly fly if it's sandwiched between shooting at you and telling you to fuck off."

"Who's going to go get him."

Joey sighed and walked outside.

The muffled sound of Joey calling Willie's name floated in on the night air. I set my duffel on the floor and fished keys out of my pocket as I walked through the living room to my study. Inside the study, I unlocked the dead bolt on the heavy closet door and stepped inside to retrieve my Beretta Silver Pidgeon over-and-under and an old humpback Browning twelve-gauge. I heard Joey and Willie come in the front door and called out for them. They entered the study just as I was emerging from the closet with an armful of fly rods.

Joey said, "I told Willie we changed our minds about sending him off by himself."

Willie smiled and tried to look appreciative.

As I dropped the tackle on a leather sofa, Joey said, "Tom, you got everything you need out of there?"

I said, "Everything that's worth anything."

A dim bulb seemed to light in Willie's eyes, and he just managed to get out, "What the . . . ," before Joey clamped one hand on the back of Willie's neck and another on the boy's belt and sent him hurdling into my gun closet. Joey slammed the door and wedged a foot against the bottom to keep it shut. I walked over and turned the key in the lock.

I looked at Joey. "Not very smart is he?"

Joey said, "Doesn't look like it."

And Willie started screaming a furious line of insults, curses, and threats, the gist of which was that he wanted out of the closet. Joey and I left the room. I retrieved my duffel while Joey went outside to get the car. But when I stepped onto the porch and closed the door, the car was there and Joey wasn't.

Before I had time to worry, I heard what sounded like the roar of a race-car engine coming from the beach, and Joey came tearing around the side of my house in a mud-splattered four-by-four pickup mounted on elephantine circus tires. He skidded a little when he stopped; then he rolled down the window.

I said, "What are you doing?"

"We're headin' into the swamp. That little Ford over there might make it where we're going, and, then again, it might not. This thing was built for it. Get in."

I tossed my dive bag into the truck bed and stepped up and

slid onto the passenger seat. I noticed a couple of spliced wires hanging down next to Joey's right knee. I said, "I guess you didn't ask Willie for the keys to his truck."

As Joey backed around to head down the gravel driveway, he said, "Didn't see where I needed 'em."

Minutes later, as we swerved onto Highway 98, I asked, "Have you got a good friend in the Baldwin County Sheriff's Office?"

Joey said, "How good?"

"I don't want Willie breaking out of that closet and trashing my house. If you know somebody who could go by and pick him up, the key's on the kitchen counter."

Joey nodded and fished a phone out of his pocket. As he punched in the number and then cajoled some deputy into picking up Willie, I rolled down the window and reached out to adjust the oversized outside mirror so I could watch the road behind us.

When Joey ended his call, I said, "Do you believe his grandfather got him out of bed or maybe even out of the hospital to come up here and check on me?"

I noticed Joey was also keeping an eye on the rearview mirror. He said, "Nope."

"You think someone else we didn't know about could have been back at the house?"

Joey looked again at the rearview mirror. "Nope."

I said, "But you're not sure there's not someone following us, are you?"

Joey concentrated on the road ahead. "No," he said, "I'm not."

chapter thirty-one

A GRAY RIBBON of pavement unwound beneath the yellow wash from our headlights as Joey sped toward Tate's Hell Swamp and a confrontation with a refugee sadist. He pushed Willie's ridiculous, steroidal truck hard, anxious to confront Carpintero and squeeze the truth out of him. I, on the other hand, wasn't much looking forward to meeting the man who had tortured and eviscerated Leroy Purcell. I was doing what I had to do to find Susan and Carli Poultrez.

Joey interrupted my thoughts. "The shotgun was kind of a giveaway."

"What?"

Joey motioned over his shoulder with his thumb, pointing at the window rack where he'd hung Willie's shotgun. "The kid—Willie Teeter—he screwed up bringing the gun to your house. It's kinda hard to believe his granddaddy sent him up to check on you armed with a shotgun."

"He didn't plan on having to explain it. He could have killed both of us." I said, "We were lucky."

"That's the trick in this business. Don't let anybody kill you, and stay lucky. Something usually turns up." Joey scratched his jaw. "I guess that's two tricks."

Relieved to think about something—anything—other than Carpintero, I said, "You know, Willie does have the same last name as *Rudolph Enis* Teeter."

"Huh?"

"Sonny."

"Oh, yeah."

"And one of the guys who came after Susan and Carli on St. George—the one who blasted out the picture window downstairs—used a shotgun."

Joey flicked on the high beams. "Be hard to find a house on the Panhandle that doesn't have two or three shotguns. Something to think about though. Most men who wanna kill you from close up tend to bring a pistol. Not many professionals use a shotgun, but the ones who like 'em won't use anything else. Course, as far as we know for sure, the only profession Willie's got is shrimping."

I turned to study the shotgun Joey had lifted from Willie. "What kind of gun is that? It looks like it's made out of plastic."

"The stock's some kinda polymer. It's a Benelli. Loutie's got one at her place."

"Isn't that a riot gun?"

Joey said, "Can be. Some people use 'em for hunting. With interchangeable chokes, it's a pretty good all-around shotgun. They use 'em in Mexico and down in South America where doves are so thick they don't have any limits on how many you can kill. You can run forty boxes of shells through one of these things without it jamming. Regular hunting guns like a Remington or a Browning aren't made for that." He looked at me. "But, a Benelli like this one is really *designed* to be an assault weapon."

I said, "Oh," and reached down to feel the outline of a switchblade in my hip pocket. It was the yellow-handled knife Joey had taken from Haycock at Mother's Milk, and it's sharp outline imparted a strange sense of comfort as we sped over that lonely, dark strip of highway. I leaned against the door and closed my eyes.

Some time later, a bump or turn or maybe nothing at all jerked me out of a deep sleep. My legs jumped; my chin bounced off my chest; and I said something along the lines of "Ooobah."

"Huh?"

I looked around. "Where are we?"

"Just passed the turnoff to St. George."

A few miles past Eastpoint, Joey hung a left on 65. Minutes later, he pulled off onto a strip of sand next to a sign that read *North Road*.

We were five miles into the swamp, still on solid logging roads, when Joey accelerated around a curve, cut his lights, and turned into a side road.

I started to speak, and Joey said, "Wait."

Fifteen or twenty seconds passed, and one set of headlights passed by on the road behind us.

I asked, "Were they following us?"

Joey shrugged. "I'm not sure. People do live up in here. Not many, though." I noticed his hands twisting nervously on the steering wheel.

I smiled. "I thought you were good at this."

Joey turned the truck around and pulled back onto the road. He said, "I am good at it. But I'm a hell of a lot better in daylight. Out here at night, one set of headlights half a mile back look pretty much like the rest of 'em. Just keep your eyes open."

More than an hour after leaving the blacktop, Joey stopped the truck. "We gotta turn over that way through that field for a pretty good ways. Three or four hundred yards."

I asked, "Is there a road?"

"You see the grass?"

I said that I did indeed see the thousand or so acres of grass extending out in front of us.

"That's all there is. Saw grass. And it's not like a field, really. The stuff grows in mud. And the mud can be a couple inches deep or it can be deep enough to swallow your ass up. Like quicksand."

"You've driven over it before. Right? When you spotted Carpintero at the compound."

"Yeah. That was daytime, and I was followin' somebody, but . . . When you don't have a choice, you just do it, right?"

The ground wasn't a problem. Finding the turnoff through the brackish water surrounding the field was. But an hour later, as the first rays of sunlight preceded the sunrise, Joey spotted the machete marks on a pair of ancient cypresses that marked the entrance to the invisible road beneath the swamp.

As we moved from the field to the thick swamp, the beginning glow of sunlight we had been enjoying disappeared and was replaced by almost total blackness. Fifty yards in, the road descended into two feet of brackish water and disappeared from sight, and the machete marks on cypress trunks that Joey had followed in daylight were now invisible. The trees themselves were almost invisible.

I grabbed a flashlight and tried using it from the window. Twenty yards later, I crawled out through the passenger door and into the truck bed, where I moved the flashlight's beam back and forth like a poacher spotlighting for deer. When I managed to find a machete mark high up on a tree, I'd bang on the top of the cab.

It worked pretty well—right up until the truck pivoted right as if sliding on oil, and the rear axle dropped into four feet of water.

A loud thump echoed across the swamp, and I realized the sound was my back pounding into the metal truck bed. The jolt sent me rolling into the tailgate, where I did a one-eighty into the swamp. I was under. Cool, black water engulfed me. The fall had knocked the wind out of me, and I could feel my diaphragm spasming. Seconds passed when I couldn't tell which way was up, until my feet hit the quicksand bottom. I pushed hard and felt the mud take hold of my feet and suck me down as I pushed away.

I pushed harder, and the cold suction of sludge reached up to my calves. Blood thumped in my ears, and I concentrated on choking off the hard spasms in my chest. I reached down to pull at my knee, and only pushed the other foot deeper. Mud and algae leaked into my mouth, and I gagged and gagged again.

Stretching to reach high over my head, I felt my fingers break the water's surface. I turned my palms out and pulled two handfuls of water in hard, downward arcs, and my legs came free. Another sweep, and my head popped through the surface. I kicked hard and clamped one hand over the tailgate.

Joey was standing inside the truck bed. Black mud covered him from chest to toe, and the giant man's eyes were bright with fear. He reached over the tailgate, and pulled me into the bed. I scrambled to my knees and sucked in a lung full of air; then I bent double and honked. Breathe, honk. Breathe, honk. And, all the while, Joey just stood there looking at me.

Finally, he said, "I couldn't see where you went in."

I nodded and breathed deeply. "How long was I down there?"

"I don't know. As soon as we stopped, I jumped out on the roadbed and lost my feet and fell into this shit up to my armpits. I got up and climbed back here as fast as I could. You came up seven or eight seconds after I got back here and started looking."

I said, "It feels longer when you're drowning."

"Yeah. I guess it would." He turned around to survey our mess. "You okay?"

"I'll live."

"You ready to get out of here?"

I stood next to Joey. "The engine's still going. It's a four-wheel-drive, and two tires are still on the roadbed. It's worth a try."

Joey reached forward and grasped the open driver's door. As he stepped over the side of the truck bed and swung a leg inside the cab, he said, "Get your ass inside."

And I thought that sounded like a hell of an idea.

While I scrubbed dark swamp mucus out of my eyes, Joey dropped the transmission into low and revved the engine. The roar choked and caught and the back bumper eased out of the muck, sending an oily gray cloud of exhaust into the still, dank air. Joey yanked on the parking brake to hold his ground while he spun the steering wheel to get us off a diagonal and headed back in the direction of the road. With the clutch engaged and the transmission in low, he gunned the engine again to build up torque and reached for the parking brake release as exhaust fumes billowed across the black water and the roar of the engine echoed through thick stands of cypress.

And if it hadn't been for the fumes and the roar—if Joey hadn't been looking back at the submerged rear tires and I hadn't been rubbing muck out of my eyes and trying to shake off the delayed confusion of nearly drowning—we might have heard the growing rumble of another monster truck hurling toward us like a freight train.

chapter thirty-two

I HEARD JOEY shout and cuss, and the world exploded into swirling bits of glass and flying metal. Every bone and joint, every muscle and organ seemed to smash in one crashing millisecond of pain, and I was flying against the open passenger door and somersaulting once again into the swamp. Penetrating cold enveloped me, and I fought against the black ooze like a drowning animal. This time, I came up fast and banged the top of my head on the truck's undercarriage. I hooked throbbing fingers over rusted steel and hung on, not out of conscious thought but in the way a drowning man will grab another swimmer and pull him down with him into death.

So strong was my need for something solid to hold on to, if the truck had gone under in that hurt and dazed second after the crash, I would have held on and gone with it. But it stayed. It stayed bottomed out across the submerged roadbed with just enough air between the swamp and the rear axle for one scrambled head and ten locked fingers. I blew the swamp out of my nose and mouth and let go with one hand long enough to wipe at my eyes and face. And the world fell back into place.

Muffled voices carried across the water. I was on the left side of the roadbed, and my feet could touch something more solid than quicksand. My arms and hands worked; my legs and ankles ached but moved freely enough to rule out fractures or puncture wounds. I moved my neck to see if I could. And the voices came again, and I thought of Joey.

Using Willie's oversized rear tire for cover, I moved hand over hand to the side of the truck facing the vehicle that rammed us. An old, two-tone Chevy Blazer, mounted, like Willie's truck, on tractor tires, sat solidly on the roadbed. Its grill was smashed and separated by three or four feet from the decimated, left front quarter-panel of Willie's truck. Above the Blazer's buckled hood, two men were visible inside the cab. And they were screaming at each other.

The larger man sat in the passenger seat but had turned and leaned in toward the much smaller driver, whose shirtfront was gathered inside the big man's fist. The windows were up, and the words inaudible. But the sounds of the two contrasting voices were fury answered with fear.

Turning away from the Blazer, I slid my hands along the rear axle to the other side to put the truck between me and what I assumed were a couple of homicidal Bodines. The passenger door I had shot through like a stream of tobacco spit was still open, and, if it hadn't been spun into the swamp by the collision, my Browning was on the seat or in the floorboard or somewhere inside the cab. Moving around the right rear tire, I crawled up onto the roadbed and had raised up onto my knees in the shallow water when I heard one of the Blazer's doors open.

Up on my toes and staying low now, I scurried to the open passenger door of Willie's wrecked truck and popped my head up over the seat.

Joey sat crumpled against the steering wheel. Blood covered the side of his face and neck and ran in a viscous stream from his right ear, and shiny bits of glass stuck to the splattered blood covering his head and shoulders.

I whispered his name. "Joey?"

Nothing.

His left arm appeared to be wedged between his ribs and the driver's door; his right was tucked in front of him, pressed between his stomach and the steering wheel.

Water splashed as one of the Bodines stepped out onto the roadbed, and I could hear his voice clearly. "Okay, damnit. I'm going."

Feet sloshed through water, and I began frantically scanning the inside of the cab for my Browning automatic. But nothing was where it had been. The seat where I had been was clear, except for thousands of diamond-sized shards of windshield glass. The floorboard was strewn with shattered bits of plastic and metal, with fragments of electronics and heating and air-conditioning parts. Even Willie's riot gun was gone—shot through the rear window, taking the gun rack with it.

A door slammed, and I pulled up onto the side of the truck bed and peeked inside. Willie's twelve-gauge Benelli lay propped against my dive bag like the hand of God had placed it there for me. All I had to do was get to it without catching a bullet in the process.

I caught a flash of color and dropped down as the smaller Bodine came around the front of his smashed grill and approached Joey's window.

"This one, the driver, looks dead."

I heard another door open, and the larger man's voice came from inside the Blazer. "Which one is it?"

"It's the big sonofabitch."

Water sloshed as the bigger Bodine stepped out onto the road and then slammed his door shut. "What about the lawyer?"

The little man said, "He ain't here. Looks like he got slung out when we hit 'em."

"No sign of him?"

"None I can see. Probably on the bottom of the swamp."

"I told you to slow down. We didn't need to wreck both goddamn trucks to stop 'em."

The little one wanted to argue some more. "You said ram 'em. You didn't say bump 'em a little, and I'm tired of you riding my ass about it."

The big man cussed and said, "Well pull him out of there, and let's get the road cleared."

"The hell with that. This guy's bigger than you are. You come up here and pull his big ass out."

I heard the big man sloshing toward the truck. "You're a useless little shit. You know that?" The water sounds stopped. "He is big, though, isn't he?"

"I told you."

The mechanical click of the door handle being lifted sounded unnaturally loud in the still swamp, and a deep moan came from inside the cab.

The small man yelled, "Shit! He's alive."

I reached up and grabbed the top edge of the truck bed and sprang up out of the water with all the power left in my aching legs. My knees caught on the side, and I spun into the truck bed and scrambled for the twelve-gauge.

One of the men screamed like a woman. My hands found the shotgun, and I jumped up to see the big man spinning my way with a short double-barrel. I lowered the Benelli to fire, but the double-barrel exploded first as Joey's door flew open and slammed into both men, sending a load of buckshot straight up and knocking both men over backward into the water. The big man managed to lift up his shotgun and blindly blast one of Willie's tractor tires before he sank out of sight.

I stood in the truck bed with the Benelli trained on the swirling water. I called out, "Joey?"

"Yeah." His voice sounded tight and strained.

"You okay?"

"I'm not dead."

Seconds passed before the two men surfaced ten or twelve feet from where they'd gone in. They had been trying to swim away underwater. Now they gasped in air and spun in the muck looking for me and the shotgun. I called out. "Where the hell do you think you're going?" They didn't answer. "You've got nowhere to go."

The smaller man yelled, "Help."

Joey's strained voice came again. "Help yourself, you little prick."

I said, "I'm not going to shoot you. Swim to the road."

The smaller man almost cried. "I can't make it."

I said, "Then don't," and jumped down out of the truck bed and sloshed up to Joey's open door.

Joey was sitting back now. His pale gray eyes shining through a mask of blood and windshield glitter.

I said, "I thought you were dead."

"Thought same thing about you." He spoke with his teeth clenched. "Better keep watchin' the water."

I nodded and turned to watch the two men flail around in the swamp. I asked, "How bad are you? Looks like a broken jaw."

Joey's voice sounded even weaker than before. "Yeah. And something's wrong with my left leg. Can't move much."

I nodded. "We'll take the Blazer. Get you to a doctor."

"You gonna drive right over Willie's truck?"

Willie's monster truck was completely blocking the only way out. I said, "We could try to push it out of the way with the Blazer, but we could end up with both trucks underwater." Joey was quiet. "I guess there's probably somewhere to turn around along here, but . . ."

I looked back, and Joey just shrugged.

I went on, ". . . we don't know where it is."

"And we been having enough trouble just staying on the road in here."

"So, I guess we load you into the Blazer. And, since the road's underwater and we don't know anywhere to turn around, I get to try to drive backward through this mess until we hit dry land."

Joey tried to smile and grimaced instead. All he got out was, "Sounds pretty stupid."

"Yeah."

Joey motioned toward the Bodines, who had made it up onto the road and were sitting in water up to their chests and catching their breath. "What're we gonna do with those two?"

I said, "I thought I'd tie them up and toss them in the back of Willie's truck and leave them here."

Joey said, "Now *that's* a good idea."

Three hundred yards and thirty minutes later, I backed the Bodines smashed and smoking Blazer onto dry land. After pulling up onto the sandy roadbed, I put the Blazer in park and turned to check on Joey, who was laid out on the backseat. When I turned, Joey had his hand down the front of his pants.

I said, "Bored?"

Joey just unzipped his pants and said, "Turn around."

"Would you two like some privacy?"

"Fuck you. Something's trying to hook on to my unit."

"Leech?"

"Yeah."

"You okay?"

"Do I fucking look okay?"

"I don't know. You made me turn around. Not that I really want to get a good look at this." I heard Joey roll down the window and flick something out. "You get it?"

"Yeah."

I was laughing. "Well, can I turn around now."

Joey said, "You know, it really ain't funny."

I turned around and said, "Actually, it kind of is."

"You know," Joey said, "you were in the water a lot more than I was."

I stopped laughing and got out of the Blazer. After a short inspection, I climbed back in and said, "I tried the flip phone. It's a goner. I don't know what else to do but try to get to a phone or maybe a CB at Carpintero's compound and see if I can get a Lifesaver Helicopter or a boat to come out here and get you."

Joey just nodded.

"You got a better idea?"

Joey reached up to rub at his eyes. "Nope."

"How far is it to the compound?"

"Not far. You can keep driving until just before you get to this little bridge. There's a place there you can pull off and hide the Blazer." I guess he saw the worry on my face because he added, "I ain't gonna be any safer here than I am there, and you'll have the vehicle close by."

I turned around in the driver's seat and maneuvered the rickety gearshift into first. "So," I said, "I guess it's time to meet the Hammer."

chapter thirty-three

IT WAS ALMOST eight o'clock when the little bridge came into sight. I pulled off into a stand of scrub pine, and Joey told me as much as he could about the compound's layout. I left my cut, bruised, and broken friend stretched out on the backseat of a stolen vehicle with Willie's Benelli twelve-gauge across his chest.

I took Joey's little Walther PPK and started out through the underbrush to the camp's perimeter. Joey told me there would be one guard at the entrance. So I circled around to the side of the compound and, keeping a huge Butler Building between me and the road, moved into the clearing.

Running low and feeling ridiculous, I checked out the buildings for communication equipment. One warehouse was just that—full of machinery, firearms, and rum and more cigars than I thought were in the world. The cavernous metal building was stuffed with all the things the Bodines had been smuggling in, things in demand on the black market. The second warehouse was the weird one. Padlocks secured both doors, but large windows had been mounted in opposite walls, and morning light flooded the place. It looked like a high school chemistry lab full of long tables with beakers and test tubes and electronic machinery. From the window, I could see three desktop computers.

Besides the warehouses, there were two smaller buildings. One looked like a makeshift home, with a porch across the front and a vintage Mercedes and a new Explorer parked out front. An old air-conditioning unit droned in a side window.

The other smaller building had a porch, too, but looked empty—if it's possible for a building to look empty from the outside. But that's how it looked; so that's where I went. And that's where I found an unlocked door, four filing cabinets, a metal desk, and one beige telephone.

I placed a long-distance call to Loutie in Mobile and made sure the first words out of my mouth were that Joey was going to be fine. As I was downplaying his injuries, Loutie interrupted. "Tom. I know you'll take care of Joey, but you need to know something. Joey's buddy at the Baldwin County Sheriff's Office called."

"About Willie?"

Loutie sounded scared. "Don't interrupt, Tom. Somebody could be after you right now. When the deputy got to your house, Willie was gone. And he didn't break out. Somebody had used your key to let him out."

I said, "So he wasn't there alone."

"Doesn't look like it."

"And they could have been behind us all the way. Is that what you're saying?"

Loutie said, "I'm saying they could be watching you right now."

I said, "Loutie. About Joey. We need to get somebody out here . . ."

I froze in midsentence as the door to the shack swung open and Willie Teeter pointed an autoloading shotgun at my gut.

I put the phone back in its cradle and said, "Hello, Willie. I was just talking about you."

Then a strange thing happened. Willie pulled a silver whistle from his hip pocket and blew a shrill, piercing blast.

Through the door over Willie's shoulder, I saw three young men—all about Willie's age—sprint out of the woods and onto the cleared grounds of the compound, where they dropped to their stomachs and pointed guns at nothing in particular.

I asked, "Playing army?"

Willie was back to his tough-guy mode. "Let's go outside."

I said, "There's a guard out there."

Willie smiled. "Not anymore. Move."

As we passed through the doorway, a big, baby-faced, football-player-looking kid stepped up onto the porch. I said, "So. I guess you're the young Turks."

Willie smiled again. "No. We're 'The Sequel.' You know, better, bigger, even more explosions."

"Cute."

The pie-faced football player said, "Cute ain't the word for it, asshole. The Sequel is your worst fucking nightmare."

"My worst nightmare is about getting lost in a department store."

Pie Face looked puzzled.

Willie said, "Let's go," and stepped up to take the gun out of my hand.

I walked out into the yard ahead of Willie. "Where are we going?"

Willie just said, "Stop." So I stopped.

"Down on your stomach. Hands behind your head."

This was not going well. I said, "You going to shoot me in the back of the head, Willie?" And he hit me in the stomach with the butt of his new shotgun.

I lay on my stomach and laced my fingers behind my neck.

Willie stepped a few feet away and blew three sharp blasts on his whistle. Seconds later, three more men—college age but not exactly college material—came running.

Willie said, "Simon and Rooter?"

One of the boys, a thin kid with acne scars on his cheeks, said, "Got 'em set up north and south."

"Okay. Good. Looks like the only people here are in that house over there with the Mercedes parked in front. The two big buildings are like warehouses. One's got whiskey and cigars and other stuff Purcell smuggled in. The other one may be a meth factory."

Pie Face spoke up. "They're ours now."

The others guffawed and said things like, "Bet your ass," and "Fucking A."

Then I heard Willie blow his whistle again. One long blast.

Nothing happened.

Willie cussed and blew again. Still nothing. He said, "Don't those morons know the signal?"

Pie Face said, "Maybe they see something. They ain't gonna come if they're watching somebody."

Willie said, "Go see," and Pie Face trotted off in search of Simon and Rooter.

Minutes passed during which the grumbling from Willie's posse grew louder. Finally, he blew his whistle again. And, once again, nothing happened.

I had seen Willie and Pie Face and two others. Two more, Simon and Rooter, had been standing watch on the north and south ends of the compound. Now, the lookouts were unaccounted for, as was Pie Face. There were three left, including Willie, and they were all standing over me.

I said, "Something's wrong, boys."

Willie said, "Shut up."

Two rifle shots split the air, and I heard the soft thuds of bodies hitting dirt. I eased my hands to the ground and looked up. Willie's two buddies squirmed in the grass. One cussed. The other sobbed like a child. Each boy gripped his thigh and tried to keep blood from pumping out.

A voice came from the trees. "Put your gun down, Willie."

Willie stood his ground. "Granddaddy?"

"Put the shotgun on the ground, boy."

Willie hesitated before answering, and the cussing and sobbing of the two leg-shot boys filled the air.

"Granddaddy, what're you doing? Mr. McInnes is fine. We didn't hurt him. We just stopped him. They're working with Purcell. Come on out here where we can talk about it."

I yelled out. "Don't do it, Billy."

Willie lowered his voice. "You wanna get shot in the back of the head? Shut your mouth."

"You going to shoot your own grandfather, Willie?"

"Shut up."

"You can still walk away from this. Put the gun down. Let your grandfather come up here and take care of you."

Willie said, "I can take care of my . . ."

An engine roared. Willie spun around, and I sprang to my feet as the Mercedes that had been parked outside the only occupied house in the compound threw a cloud of dust into the air as it rounded the small warehouse and headed for the road.

I ran for cover behind the empty shack and felt the first shotgun blast in my chest, but it was the percussion I felt and not the load. I glanced back and saw Willie firing at the speeding car, leading the driver's window the way you lead a dove flying over a field of Egyptian wheat. Three more explosions shattered the morning air, and the car swerved and burst into flame and crashed into the porch. I dove to the left to avoid the car and any shots that might be coming my way.

I landed and rolled in the sand and sat up facing Willie. He was reloading. Without thinking, I jumped up and ran hard at him. Willie saw me when I was ten yards away.

The swamp was silent except for the wind gushing in my lungs and the blood pulsing inside my chest. The barrel arced slowly upward from the ground to point at my stomach, and what Willie's hands were doing became very important to me. The blunt, gnawed fingertips of his left hand gripped the front stock. His right fingers flipped out and away from his body like someone slinging water off his hands, and Willie tossed three red spinning shells into the air. His right fingers moved back to the checkered lever on the side of the housing, and he pumped the first round into the chamber. I dove under the barrel at his ankles and found nothing.

Willie still moved like the high school jock he had been. And I skidded across clipped saw grass as he skipped out of reach. I rolled onto my back and looked up. Willie smiled. He had seated the stock against his shoulder and just taken aim at my face when a rifle shot from the brush snapped Willie's head forward and dropped him face first into the dirt.

For a time, I could see only the boy's face pressed into soft earth; I could hear only my own breathing. Then conscious thought floated back and brought with it the soft whimpering of leg-shot teenagers, the muffled pump of running feet in sand, and the hiss of fire.

Peety Boy reached me first. He held a carbine in his left hand. He used his right to pull me to my feet. "You all right, son?"

I didn't answer, and he repeated the question while shaking me by the arm.

"Yeah. Yeah, I'm okay. Who shot him?"

"I did. Didn't figure his own granddaddy ought to have to do it. Somebody had to." Peety Boy looked over at the flaming car. "Who's that?"

I looked over at a curly black, lifeless head hanging from the side window. I said, "It's L. Carpintero. The Hammer."

Peety Boy seemed to think about that for a few seconds. His leathery forehead wrinkled, and he worked his nearly toothless jaw. Then he said, "Who's that?"

While Captain Billy stood watch, Peety Boy and I loaded Joey into the cab of his truck and tossed the four hurt members of The Sequel into the bed alongside the two Bodines that Peety Boy had already retrieved from the wrecked truck in the swamp. The old fishmonger headed out for the hospital emergency room in Appalachicola.

Back in the compound, Captain Billy crouched on one knee beside his dead grandson and wept.

I walked over to examine Carpintero and the wrecked Mercedes. On the leather seat beside him were an automatic pistol, a black leather briefcase, and a nail gun with a portable compressor next to it.

I walked back and stood over Captain Billy Teeter. The old man got to his feet.

I said, "I never meant for anything like this to happen."

Billy looked up at the sky with pale wet eyes. "When you called me last night, I knew it was gonna get bad. The boy took a shot at you then, and he was gonna kill you just now. I reckon I didn't know the boy, 'cause the one I knew couldn't a done this." Then he added. "Didn't have no daddy and not much of a mother."

"I'm sorry, Billy. But I've got to get moving. The young girl I was trying to help is missing now. And a woman, a good friend, is missing too and may be hurt."

Billy wiped tears from his eyes with the veined back of a calloused hand. "The house over there where the car come from, that the only one with anybody in it?"

I nodded.

"Better check it over again. We could still get shot out here."

And the old man picked up his carbine and started off. I retrieved a thirty-thirty that one of the leg-shot boys had dropped and followed Billy's path. When I arrived, the old man had his back pressed flat against the outside wall next to a window.

He held up a palm to stop me. Then he pointed at the house, nodded his head, and made an opening-and-closing motion with his thumb and fingers to indicate someone was talking inside.

I retreated around the corner of a warehouse.

Minutes passed. Billy listened, and I waited. Finally, the old shrimp boat captain waved me over. "There's a woman and a little kid in there. Maybe somebody else. But, if there is, he ain't saying nothing. You think you can kick open that door?"

"You cover me through the window, and I'll kick it in."

The old man had aged a decade since Peety Boy, his childhood friend, had shot his grandson and namesake in the back of the head. Tears still clung to his gray eyelashes, his wrinkled-leather face had turned sallow, and his thick hard hands trembled on the stock of his carbine. But Captain Billy Teeter was functioning. He was still helping a man who was arguably responsible for getting his grandson killed because it was the right thing to do.

He said, "Go."

chapter thirty-four

THIS WAS NOT an oak security door on a million-dollar beach house. One hard kick buried my shoe in the veneer surface and sent the door hurling inward. I jumped inside, minus one shoe that now hung from a footprint-shaped hole in the open door, and pointed my gun at nothing.

The room was empty. I snatched my shoe from the door and pulled it on.

A single door led to a back room. I walked toward the door, being careful to stay to one side, and tried the knob. It turned. Keeping to one side, I pushed it wide. Three shots spit through the opening and splintered wood across the room. *Shit.*

I tried, "You're surrounded," and realized it sounded even dumber out loud than it had in my head.

No answer.

"You've got nowhere to go. Toss out the gun. We don't want anyone else hurt here today."

Three more shots hit the other side of the wall that my back was pressed against. One blasted out a light switch and snapped my shirt against my ribs. *The hell with this*. Lots of handguns are six-shooters; a lot aren't. I took off my shoe and flipped it into the room.

I heard the *clack* of a firing pin striking a spent casing, and I went in fast. So fast and so scared that I almost shot the dark pretty woman from the beach on Dog Island. She was fumbling with the cylinder of a snub-nosed revolver.

I yelled, "Stop!"

She didn't. Trembling fingers with manicured nails pulled spent rounds from the chamber and reached for a box of cartridges on the bed beside her.

"What are you doing? Stop, damnit. Uh, alto. Alto!"

She had a fresh bullet now, but she was fumbling as frightened eyes darted from me to the empty chamber of her revolver.

"Shit! What's the word?" My mind raced back fifteen years to Señora Stippleman's Spanish I. Some half-forgotten vocab test floated in. "Pare!"

She glanced up at that one. She glanced up as trembling fingers clicked the bullet home. I raised my carbine. "Pare, goddamnit. Pare!"

The dark beauty had one bullet and five empty chambers. She swung the cylinder into place, and I tightened my finger against the trigger.

I couldn't do it. "Shit!" I let go of the front stock and whipped the carbine at the wall to divert her attention. Before the gun hit, I was moving. Three steps and I dove as Señora Carpintero leveled the snub-nose at my chest and pulled the trigger.

I heard the metallic *clack* of the firing pin snapping an empty chamber as I hit her full force and jammed the gun into the air with my right hand. She fought, and I had to twist her wrist harder than I wanted to wrest the gun from her grip. I plucked the revolver off the bedspread where it had fallen and scrambled to my feet.

The señora rubbed her wrist and watched me with narrow wet eyes. I popped open the cylinder on her handgun and let the one good bullet drop to the floor. When I did, she sprang off the bed and ran for my discarded rifle. She almost made it. I got a handful of blouse and spun her back onto the bed.

"Stop! Jeez, lady, it's time to give up. I'm not going to hurt you. It's okay. You understand? It's okay."

She sat and watched. I called out for Captain Billy before realizing he was standing four feet behind me. He said, "You okay?"

I was trembling as much as the tiny woman on the bed. "I'm not shot. Do you speak Spanish?"

"Nope. She think you were gonna rape her or somethin'?"

I looked around. "We just killed her husband."

"Oh."

"And she's got a kid around here somewhere. That's who she's trying to protect."

Billy walked up to stand beside me. "Want me to have a look in the closet?"

"No. I want her to calm down first. If she thinks we're looking for the boy to hurt him, I'm afraid we'd have to shoot her to keep her from scratching our eyes out."

Billy was quiet for a few beats; then he said, "I seen what you done. Been easier to shoot her. Didn't want to, did you?"

"Would you shoot her for defending herself and her kid?"

Billy said, "Might. If it was me or her."

"Bullshit. Come on, let's get her out of here. See if we can get her to calm down some."

Captain Billy handed me his gun and walked over to the bed. He held out his hand and parted his Brillo-pad beard into a brown-toothed smile. Señora Carpintero didn't take his hand, but she did stand and walk toward the door. She was leading us away from her child. We let her.

Unfortunately, just down the road, her husband lay dead in a wrecked Mercedes, which didn't seem to be a recipe for either calm or cooperation. I stopped her in the outer room, which was kind of a living room, dining room, kitchen combination. I pointed at a green sofa, and she sat down.

I said, "Billy, go stand by the front door," and I walked to the sink. On the plywood counter, four glasses had been left upside down to drain on a red striped washcloth. I picked one up, turned it over, and filled it with water from the tap. After handing the glass to Señora Carpintero, I pulled over a folding director's chair from next to the dining table and sat down.

"Do you speak English?"

She sipped the water and searched my face with her black eyes.

I repeated my question.

"Sí. *Un poco*. A little." *Ah leetle*.

"Good. We do not want to hurt you. Do you understand that?"

She said, "I understand the words."

I smiled. "You have a son, uh, *hijo*. Sí?"

The señora's eyes grew large and her arms tensed. Then, just as suddenly, the muscles in her face and arms relaxed a little, "You are the man from the beach? *La isla*?"

"The island. Yes. I am the man who spoke to your son on the island."

She said, "There were shots." And she pointed at the open door leading outside.

"Yes."

"The doctor, ah, he is the dead?"

"You mean your husband?"

She nodded her head.

"Yes. He's dead."

Now all the tension seemed to drain from her body. "You kill him?"

I said, "No," and she simply nodded her head.

"It was, *como se dice*? *Destino*?"

"Destiny?"

"Sí. *Destino*. My husband, he go with violent men."

I watched her eyes. She seemed neither happy nor sad that her husband was dead. She accepted it the way people accept the death of the old and sick. She seemed to say, *Perhaps it's better*.

"We know your son is here. Do you want to bring him out?"

She looked less-than-genuinely surprised. "*Que?*"

I smiled. "Fine. Can we take you somewhere?"

"The four-wheel. It is outside still?"

I nodded.

"You will leave it for me?"

I nodded again.

A weak smile turned the corners of her full lips. She saw hope for her son.

I asked, "Can you help me? I'm looking for a friend. I believe your husband knew where she is. Now he cannot tell me."

"No. Now he cannot."

"Can you?"

"I am the wife. My husband did work not . . . I have no understanding of his work."

"My friend will die. She does not deserve to die."

"My husband, he deserved to die?"

I didn't answer. Seconds ticked by. Señora Carpintero said, "Your friend, she is *granjero?*" I raised my palms in the air and shook my head. Her face brightened. "Farmer. She is farmer?"

"Yes. She has a farm."

"Then she is with a man who is the fisherman. That is all I know."

"Is anyone else with them? A young girl? A teenager?"

She repeated, "That is all I know."

"What do you know about why your husband, the doctor, was here?"

She went back to, "I am the wife."

"Yeah. I got that. You are the wife. But I don't think even a South American wife boards a boat with smugglers and lands in a new country in the middle of the night without a pointed question or two for her husband."

"*Que?*"

Wonderful. We were back to Spanish again. I tried a more direct path. "Is that your husband's laboratory out there?"

"Yes."

"What's he been cooking up? Meth? Coke?"

The señora's high cheekbones burned red. "My husband was a medical doctor, expert in tropical disease. He was not the drug lord."

I started to ask more, but decided it was a lost cause. Or maybe I was a little afraid of Señora Carpintero.

Billy Teeter and I left dark, beautiful, dangerous Señora Carpintero—or whatever her name was—sitting on the green sofa in the living room of a metal house deep in the bowels of Tate's Hell Swamp.

After taking a cursory look into the doctor's lab, I retrieved Joey's Walther PPK from Willie's corpse. Captain Billy and I loaded his grandson's body onto the air boat that The Sequel had used to tail us to Carpintero's compound. Billy climbed into the high chair in front of the fan. I sat at his feet as he steered away from the compound and skidded across miles of flooded saw grass.

We didn't talk.

I didn't kill Willie. I hadn't even gotten him killed. Not really. Willie got killed playing tough guy. It was his choice. If it hadn't been that day, it would have been another. Sooner or later, he would have met up with men who don't play tough, the kind who make money by taking it away from wanna-bes.

Billy Teeter and I would not be friends. And, from that day on, neither would he and Peety Boy—the childhood friend who had fought Hitler in France. And won.

Marina was too complimentary a term. It was a gray-weathered shack with sodas and bait inside and a ragged dock outside. Billy was using the pay phone. I waited with Willie's corpse.

A bass boat pulled up and two men climbed out and walked over to look at Willie's body. "Goddamn. What happened? Who is that?"

I looked at the men, who looked excited. To them, this was a story to tell, something to spread around work the next day.

I said, "Show some respect." They ignored me, so I tried another tack. "Get the fuck out of here."

One of the men—he wore a slouch hat with fishing flies stuck in the sweatband—said, "What's your problem?"

I stepped into the boat and picked up one of the carbines. The men moved off. When he thought he was out of earshot, the one with the flies called me an asshole.

Captain Billy walked out onto the small dock. "Ambulance is on the way. I talked to the other boys who got shot. Told 'em to say somebody shot them and Willie from a bridge. Told 'em which one."

"Cops going to buy that?"

The old fisherman shrugged.

"Thank you."

Billy sat on the dock with his feet hanging off the side and rubbed at his eyes with the thick muscles at the base of his thumbs. "Way I see it. You didn't kill Willie. You might've got him killed a little sooner than he should've been. But you called me up on the phone last night to tell me what'd happened, and I told you me and Peety Boy'd cover your back." The old man wiped his palms on his pant legs. "Naw. You didn't kill him, Tom. But my grandboy did try to kill you. Twice. I owe you something for that."

I said, "You didn't owe me anything. But I appreciate what you did."

Billy looked out across the water. "Yep."

"I don't guess you want to see me again, though."

"No, Tom. I don't."

chapter thirty-five

THE AMBULANCE BEARING Willie Teeter's young body pulled into the emergency entrance of Appalachicola Memorial Hospital more than an hour after Captain Billy placed the call. No need to hurry. The EMTs off-loaded the gurney with its lumpy, sheet-covered cargo and wheeled it inside. Billy followed along to the morgue, and I went in search of Joey. I found him in a private room on the third floor. A clear bag of something dribbled through a tube into his arm; silver wires peeked out through his lips; and he was seriously sedated.

I went in search of a doctor, then a nurse, then another living soul. Lots of patients, but no healers in evidence. Finally, I just reached over the nurses' station and helped myself to Joey's file, which was hanging on a rack with the rest of the patient histories. I had just hooked the file folder and flipped it open when a nurse appeared as if by magic.

"What are you doing?"

"Trying to find you."

She said, "Did you think I was hiding inside that *private* folder," and took Joey's chart out of my hand.

I smiled. "It was the last place I looked." She didn't return my smile, which was kind of a shame. Nurse Ratched wouldn't have been a bad-looking woman if she smiled or maybe just quit looking quite so pissed off. "The patient is a friend of mine. I wanted to find out how he is."

"Are you family?"

"If I were family, I would have used that word. I just want to know how he's doing." So much for charm.

She flipped open Joey's chart. "Your friend has a fractured nose, multiple hairline fractures of the left orbital globe, and a dislocated jaw. His left shin has been fractured." She skimmed the page. "He also has a minor concussion. He has been sedated."

I said, "Thank you," and turned to walk away.

Nurse Ratched said, "This is a hospital. The way you live is your business, but you shouldn't come in here covered in filth."

Nice lady.

I found Joey's room again and placed a credit card call to Loutie. She promised to be in Appalachicola as soon as possible, and I promised not to leave Joey's side until she got there.

I sat down in the hospital's idea of an easy chair—a metal frame holding foam rubber cushions covered in tan plastic—and tried to get comfortable and think. The swamp water had evaporated out of my clothes, leaving my pants and shirt, even my underwear, crisp with dry sand and sludge. My mouth tasted like mud; my hair felt like steel wool; and, in every little out-of-the-way, never-seen crevice of my body, I could feel small, crusty remnants of my morning dip in the swamp each time I moved.

Two long nights had gone by now without sleep. I put my head back and tried to concentrate.

Somewhere, buried deep in the foggy recesses of my mind, I knew that I knew where Carli was, if only I could reach in there and pull it out. I started with her good-bye note and tried to work forward. The room got kind of shifty. Shadows floated and blurred, invisible weights pressed on my eyelids, and I fell into a dark pit of unconsciousness. When a woman's hand finally shook me awake, I was vaguely aware that I hadn't dreamed or turned or even moved my hands for more than four hours.

"Tom?" It was Loutie Blue's voice.

I think I said, "Umphum."

"You okay?"

I sat up and moved my head around, trying to roll the crick out of my neck. "Fine. Just tired."

Loutie stepped into the bathroom. I heard water running, and she came back out with a wet washcloth. She wiped my face with the warm cloth, like a mother waking a toddler from a nap. She asked what had happened and I told her, starting with Joey's condition and then looping back to our encounter with Willie at my beach house and coming forward.

When I was finished, Loutie said, "We have news about Carli, but we haven't found her yet."

"What news?"

"She's back in the state. A pulpwood-truck driver reported seeing her either yesterday or the day before, hitching outside a little town called Pine Hill. There's a big pulp mill there . . ."

"Yeah. I know." And there was the thought again.

Loutie had moved over by Joey's bed and was squeezing his huge thumb in her hand. She cocked her head at me. "What is it?"

I reached back to massage the stiffness from my neck. "It's just . . . I keep thinking I know where she is. It's in the back of my mind somewhere, and I can't get to it."

Loutie looked down at Joey. "Go grab a quick shower. I've got clean clothes for you and some for Joey when he needs them." I stood there trying to think. She said, "Go! I'm here with Joey now, so you're free to go find Susan. Get in the shower. Wake up. It'll come to you."

And fifteen minutes later, as I toweled the water out of my hair, it did.

With more than three hundred dollars in her pocket, why hadn't Carli grabbed the first bus or plane to Denver or Tucson or Los Angeles? Why head west and then turn back toward the northeast?

And why, in the first place, did she write a cryptic good-bye note on the bottom of a sheet of notebook paper where she had sketched Susan's old Ford pickup sitting in a hay field with rosebushes covering the front wheel?

Simple. But everything seems simple after you finally get it. I should have had it sooner. On some level, Carli had wanted to be found even before she dropped out of Loutie's guest-room window.

Susan's farmhouse—a place set among rolling hay fields and nestled inside swirls of holly and boxwoods and rosebushes—was empty. And Carli knew it. She had traveled to Biloxi by bus to throw off her father. Then she had started her real journey when she began hitchhiking northeast toward Meridian. And that's when I really did have enough information to have found her, if I had just been able to put it all together.

My father owns a sawmill just outside a small town on the Alabama River called Coopers Bend, which, as it happens, is about two hours drive due east of Meridian, Mississippi. If you drive to the side of town opposite the mill, cruise a few miles up a county highway called Whiskey Run Road, and turn down a narrow dirt road and follow that for four or five hundred yards through cow pastures and stands of loblolly pine and water oak, you will come to a mailbox that marks the entrance to the farm that Susan Fitzsimmons had shared with her crazy artist husband before he was murdered. It was where I first met Susan, and I was now sure that it was where Carli had been headed the minute she climbed out of the window in Loutie Blue's guest room.

I should have had it figured out a second time back in Tate's Hell Swamp when Señora Carpintero had asked if Susan was a *granjero*—a farmer, and then said Susan was with "the fisherman." My third bite at the apple came when Loutie reported that Carli had been spotted in Pine Hill, which is almost dead center between Meridian and Susan's farm in Coopers Bend.

The only question now was whether Rus Poultrez—"the fisherman," as the señora had called him—had both women, or only

Susan. It was possible that Carli hadn't yet made it to Coopers Bend. It also was possible that Poultrez was holding Susan somewhere else and that Carli would find the safe haven she had been seeking at Susan's farm. These things were unlikely, but still possible, which is why I didn't call the state police, the FBI, or even a few bad-ass boys I went to high school with to rush out there and take care of Poultrez. Instead, I pulled on clean clothes and went out to hurriedly explain things to Loutie. Then I placed a call to the Sheriff's Department in Coopers Bend and spoke at length with local law enforcement.

As I replaced the receiver in its cradle, Nurse Ratched came in. "What are you doing in here?"

I wasn't in the mood. "What is it?"

The nurse looked like she had just sucked a crawfish head. "Are you Tom McInnes?"

"Yep."

"Then you have a phone call at the desk."

Nurse Ratched turned and marched out, and I followed. A beige receiver was lying on a raised, white-Formica platform on the horseshoe-shaped nurses station. I picked it up.

"Hello?"

"Hi. How's Joey?" It was Kelly's voice.

"He got smashed in the face, and he's got a broken nose, a dislocated jaw, and some hairline fractures. But he's going to be fine. They've got him doped up for the pain." I was glad to hear Kelly's voice, but I also wanted to get off the phone and get on the road to Susan's farmhouse. The sheriff was checking it out, but . . . "Thanks for calling, Kelly. Sorry, but I've got to go. Call back later if you want. Loutie's in Joey's room with him."

"I found out something about L. Carpintero."

I said, "He's dead. Is it something that still matters?"

Kelly hesitated. "I'm not sure. I just kind of know who he is, or I guess who he was." I didn't speak. She went on. "The reason you thought his face looked familiar but you couldn't place it was that he looks like someone else. A lot. His uncle was the military dictator of Panama. He's in prison here in the states now. His name . . ."

"Yeah, I know who he is. Damn, it's obvious once you know it. Take away the general's acne scars and about thirty years and they're twins."

"Yeah. I didn't get it. The lady in the newspaper morgue saw the resemblance, and once we had that we were able to find out who he is. He's got the same last name as his uncle. And he was mixed up in his uncle's drug business."

"Which, I remember, was supposed to have a Cuban connection."

"That's it."

Nurse Ratched walked over and glared at me. "That is not a public telephone."

I turned my back. "And that's everything you found out?"

Kelly said, "That's all so far. Nothing, by the way, about him having any nicknames like Carpintero or hammer or anything like that. I'll keep looking, though. But," and Kelly paused for effect, "I did find out Carlos Sanchez's real name."

"Who is he?"

"We found a picture of him at a Republican fund-raiser in Mobile. The paper ran the shot a few months ago because the picture also included the son of a former president. Sanchez was kind of looking down and holding a glass in front of his face, but you could tell it was him."

"Kelly!"

"Okay, okay. You know how you never see Superman and Clark Kent in the same place? Well, guess who Carlos Sanchez really is."

I said, "Charlie Estevez."

"You're no fun at all. How in the world did you figure that one out?"

"I had a suspicion."

"Well, so much for my bombshell. That's all I've got."

I thanked her and got off the phone.

Ten minutes later, I was speeding north in Loutie's cherry-red GTO convertible.

Four hours of road time stretched out ahead, and my contact with the world—my little Motorola flip phone—was a goner. Slopping through Tate's Hell had taken care of that. I stopped at a quick mart in Panama City and called Sheriff Nixon in Coopers Bend. Deputies had been dispatched to check out the farmhouse. No report. An hour later, I stopped in Florala and got the same message. A little over an hour after that, I pulled over in Monroeville and made the same call. This time Nixon was in.

"Nobody's there."

I had been scared and nervous, worried about what might be happening to Susan and Carli while I was on the road. Now I was just scared. If they weren't at the farm, if all the clues I had stringed together were nothing but snippets of a larger picture that I was missing . . .

Nixon's hard voice cut my thoughts short. "You hear me? Are you still there?"

"Yes, I'm here. I was thinking. Are you sure no one was there?"

"Well, I didn't go out there myself. But two deputies did and said they looked around pretty good. Looked for cars, knocked on the door, even looked in the windows as best they could."

"They didn't go inside, though?"

"Hell, Tom. We can't just break in to somebody's house without a reason."

I grasped at straws. "Did they check out the barn in back?"

Nixon sounded like he'd had enough of this. "They checked the place out. You want to go out there and look some more, help yourself. I got other things to do." And he hung up.

Nice guy.

I climbed into Loutie's classic convertible and pulled back onto the blacktop. Before I had just been worrying. Now I was driving slower and thinking more, and I wondered if I had imagined all the clues and coincidences pointing to the farm. I ran everything over in my mind, turned it around, and pulled at it from as many different sides as I could find. The bottom line was that Carli had to be either at the farm or damn close to it. Susan—if the dark and dangerous Señora Carpintero could be believed—was with Rus Poultrez . . . somewhere.

I jammed down the accelerator. Either I was right about everything *and* everyone coming together at Susan's farm, or I didn't have a frigging clue.

chapter thirty-six

ACCORDING TO THE fluorescent lines on my diving watch, I turned onto the dirt road leading to Susan's farm a few minutes after 7:30 that evening. The sun had fallen beneath the horizon, but the western sky still glowed with sunset colors that cast long shadows across new-green hay fields. Pecan trees, post oaks, and cedars grown from bird droppings interrupted kinked lines of barbed wire that stretched along both sides of the right-of-way. Susan's mailbox came up on the right, and I clicked off the headlights. I pulled off onto the gravel shoulder and stepped out.

The shrill of crickets filled the fields and woods, and a bullfrog on one of Susan's ponds bellowed at whatever they bellow at. I turned down the gravel driveway and found myself trotting then jogging then running full out. I forced myself to stop. With my back pressed against the thick trunk of a pine, I got quiet and tried to listen. Crickets made music. A light wind rustled the pine needles and oak leaves overhead, and my heart thumped like a fist on the inside of my sternum. I breathed deeply, forcing my mind to calm, and started once again down the driveway.

Staying close to cover along the roadside, I walked slowly around the last small curve of gravel and dropped to one knee when the house came into view. Susan's classic white farmhouse seemed to float above the ground on a soft black cloud of shrubbery. No lights showed through the dark-shuttered windows in front. To the right of the house, the small, whitewashed barn Susan used for a carport seemed empty, but inside the barn was shadowed black, and I knew that a car or even Rus Poultrez himself could be hidden deep inside.

I had a choice to make.

The driveway leading to the farmhouse passes between two ponds. One is higher than the other, and water pours from the higher pond to the lower through large white pipes beneath the roadbed. I could reach the house in less than a minute, maybe thirty seconds, if I stayed on the road and crossed between the ponds. And, if I did that, I would make one hell of a nice target. On the other hand, I could circle one of the ponds, stay in thick cover, and get to the house in ten or fifteen minutes. No question about it. Circling made more sense. But on the other hand, I thought . . . *Screw it.* I crept to the pond's edge, took three deep breaths, and sprinted across the roadbed in full sight of God and possible killers and anyone else who wanted to watch.

Joey's Walther PPK was in my right hand, and I used it to pump as I raced into the night. Ten seconds of eternity passed as it felt as though my knees were flying up to my chest and my heels brushed the back of my head. Ten seconds, as it turned out, of nothing—nothing but running and breathing and terror. The far bank of the lower pond passed by on my left, and I dove off the driveway and landed in a base runner's slide, tearing down the bank with my right knee tucked under and my left toe pointed. Gravel ripped my pants, and I felt the sharp sting of small stones grinding away at flesh. It was a shallow ditch, and I hit bottom quickly. I tried to hold very still and listen for sounds other than my own heavy breathing.

I clicked off the Walther's safety and eased back up to the roadbed on my belly. The house was still dark. The carport was dark. Nothing moved. But there was *something*. In back, just visible through thick azaleas and boxwoods and holly trees, a pale light framed a porch swing hung from the limb of an oak tree. It could have been a security light or the reflection of moonlight off a second-story window. It could have been a lot of things.

I made another quick scan of the house and the carport and the grounds; then I worked my way through the ditch to a row of thick brush lining the fence. Minutes later, I was pressed against the wall of the huge red barn in back of the farmhouse, and I was looking up at the lighted shade of a bedside lamp in one of Susan's upstairs bedrooms.

Okay. Now what?

I watched. I watched for what seemed a very long time. And nothing happened. But finally I did notice something new. Through one of the back windows on the ground floor, I could just see the top of a doorway that I could have sworn led into Susan's study. And, I realized, there was no reason on earth that I should have been able to see the outline of an open door inside a dark house. The opening seemed to be lighted by a faint glow from the other side, from inside the study.

I needed a better view. Circling around the back of the barn, I made it to the other side of the yard and paused to pick out a shadowed path to Susan's wide, wraparound porch. Another quick look around the moonlit yard, and I took off, staying low and silently cringing as each footfall crunched through dried layers of leaves and pine needles that had accumulated while Susan was away.

Next to the back edge of the banistered porch, I had just hooked left to head for the side steps when my left foot struck something that felt like a sack of loose dirt. My front foot faltered and twisted as the other foot slid backward across loose leaves. I lost balance and hit the ground chest first. Something dull and hard gouged the side of my neck. Wind rushed out on impact, and I made an involuntary "Oomph" sound.

I grabbed for the stick that had gouged my neck and pushed. It moved, but in a strange, organic, rolling motion. It was attached to something, and that something was a leg. My hand was wrapped around the dirt-caked toe of a cowboy boot. And I was lying full across someone's corpse.

Shuddering and rolling, I cleared the lump of flesh and pressed my back against the porch. I held the Walther automatic against my chest and listened. But I looked at nothing but the dead body at my feet. It was a man. *Thank God.* He lay on his back with one narrow cowboy boot pointing up and the other lying flat. His head was twisted at an unnatural angle that buried his face in grass and leaves. But I knew who he was. I recognized the short, light hair; I recognized the build and even the clothes. I reached down and yanked up his left sleeve and found the tattoo: an ugly blue dagger with *R.I.P.* over it and *R.E.T.* underneath. Rudolph Enis Teeter, a.k.a. Sonny, had a bullet hole through his left side and, from the looks of it, a broken neck to boot.

I had just leaned forward to check his neck when I saw the shadow. A shovel with a tombstone-shaped head smashed into my right wrist, and the Walther PPK spun off into the dark. The giant black shadow of Rus Poultrez loomed over me. He didn't speak. He didn't laugh. He just raised the shovel back up over his head and aimed the metal spade at the top of my head.

I was crouching. I came up fast, burying my head in his gut, clamping his legs with my forearms, and driving with my legs. Poultrez managed to bring the shovel down in an excruciating blow to my lower back that shot hot waves of pain from my butt to my shoulder, but I had him off balance. The big man went over on his back as I jammed my head and all the weight behind it into his belly. I somersaulted over his chest and landed just over his head. My right hand was numb. I jammed the fingers of my left hand into my hip pocket and came out with the switchblade that Sonny Teeter had donated to Joey in the parking lot of Mother's Milk.

Poultrez was big, even bigger than Joey, but he didn't have Joey's speed. My fingers found the chrome button on the side of the yellow knife handle, and I felt the blade click open as I spun around and slammed my right elbow into the big man's face. In the same instant, the long thin blade protruding from my left fist found the soft flesh of his neck. And, just as Joey described on Dog Island, I jammed it in up to the hilt and twisted with all my strength. Hot blood gushed over my fist and down my forearm. Rus Poultrez shuddered and fell limp.

In an old cattle trough next to the barn, I washed off Poultrez's blood in a shallow pool of rainwater. The feeling started to return to my right hand, and with the feeling came searing pain. I could use my thumb and two of my fingers, but my index and middle fingers hung like dead tubes of meat.

I went back to check Poultrez. He was extremely dead.

It took a minute or so to find Joey's handgun. I picked it up in my left hand and mounted the porch. No one was moving inside the house.

I circled the house, found the front door unlocked, and stepped inside. The only sounds were the ticktock of Susan's antique grandfather clock and the periodic hum of the refrigerator's ice maker cycling on. I knew the house, so I left the lights out as I conducted a search of every room on the ground floor. Upstairs, only one person was in residence. And it was my client, Carli Poultrez.

Carli jerked and made a yelping sound when I opened the bedroom door. She said something like, "No." Her wrists and ankles were bound with shaggy twine and lashed to a four-poster bed. Her slit-up-the-outside shorts were unsnapped and unzipped, but they were still on. Carli's shirt and bra had been torn or cut open at the front, and the white mounds of her breasts looked soft and vulnerable against the tanned muscles of her stomach and shoulders.

I said, "It's okay, Carli. It's me, Tom."

She lifted head off the bed and stared wildly in my direction. "Get out of here. Run. Run now. Get out of here, Tom. Get out of here."

"Carli, it's okay."

She screamed. "Don't you understand? He's here! He'll kill everybody."

I glanced down the hallway and closed the door before walking over to the bed. I reached down and pulled a spread over Carli's exposed breasts. "Who's here, Carli? Is it just your father?"

She started to cry and spoke between deep, wrenching sobs. "Yes. My father. He's here."

I dropped the Walther in my hip pocket and started picking at the knots on her left wrist. I could have cut them—if only my knife hadn't still been buried in her father's neck. "Is anyone else here? Anyone else who wants to hurt you?"

"No. Just him." She looked at what I was doing and seemed to find herself a little. "Hurry. He'll be back. You need to hurry. We gotta find Susan."

I had one wrist free now, and Carli reached across to claw at the twine binding her other arm while I moved down to untie her ankles. "It's okay, Carli. Your father's dead. He tried to bash my head in with a shovel, and I had to kill him. I'm sorry."

Her wrists were free now. Carli sat up and looked at me. "He's dead? You sure? He's really dead?"

"Yes, Carli. He's really dead."

She squeezed shut her eyes and began to cry again. The spread had fallen away when she sat up, and each sob made her young breasts tremble. All she said was, "Good."

I was untying the last piece of twine. She looked down and pulled the covers up to her neck. I said, "Do you have any other clothes here?"

She seemed to be coming into the present. "Yeah. In my bag. It's over in the closet there." I walked over and opened the closet. As I bent over to pick up her backpack, she said, "I put it in there yesterday when I first got here. You know, before I knew Susan and my . . . before I knew *he* was here."

I dropped the backpack on the bed. "Susan's here?"

Carli came a little unfocused, then said, "She *was* here. He couldn't handle her and me at the same time. He said . . . he said he was gonna shut her up and save her for later. He said she was gonna be dessert." She started to cry again.

"Is she okay?"

"I don't know. I guess."

"Carli. Was Susan hurt? We found a lot of blood in the room where they kidnapped her."

The girl's eyes focused. "No. Susan wasn't hurt when I got here. Unless, since then . . ."

"Did he leave the farm with her?"

Carli stopped to think. "No. I don't think so. He wasn't gone long enough. At least, I don't think he was." She gazed off at the wall. "He tied me up before they left. He was gone awhile, and I heard him downstairs. Banging around the kitchen, fooling with the TV and stuff. Some time went by. I heard him come up the steps and open the door. That's when he tore up my clothes and got his hands in my pants."

"Carli, don't."

She shrugged and reached for her bag, but it was feigned callousness. "He's done worse."

"I know he has, Carli. But he won't anymore. I promise, nobody's ever going to hurt you like that again." I patted her calf. "Get dressed. Take a shower if you need to. I've got to find Susan."

As I turned to leave, Carli said my name. "Tom? The first time we met you told me it'd be easier to just walk away and forget about the murder on St. George. You know, not go to the police." She looked down at the bedspread. "When it came to it, though, *you* didn't walk away."

I didn't know what to say.

I was opening the door when she said, "I knew you'd come help me."

And I left my young client sitting on the bed, staring at the little collection of possessions in her backpack.

I trotted downstairs and walked quickly through each room, flipping on lights and checking closets as I went. Susan was not in the house.

Like most Americans, Susan had a flashlight in a drawer in the kitchen. I found it rolling around among batteries and matches and scissors and tape. I clicked it on and left through the back door. No one had disturbed the barn that had been Bird Fitzsimmons' studio, and the carport was empty. I could think of only one other place to lock someone up. At the rear of the house, I found four fifty-pound bags of fertilizer stacked on top of the door to Susan's bomb shelter. Susan had shown it to me six months before when I needed a place to store my dead brother's stolen money. Some prior owner had built it during the 1950s atomic-bomb scare. Susan had used it as a root cellar.

I tossed the bags aside and yanked open the door. "Susan!"

"Tom?" She walked forward into the flashlight's beam.

"Are you okay?"

Susan squinted into the light. "Poultrez is here."

"Not anymore."

Susan is tough, and she seemed unhurt. I told her Carli was inside the house, getting cleaned up and changing clothes.

"What did he do to her, Tom?"

"Maybe she should tell you about that." Susan looked scared, so I added, "He didn't rape her. Just, you know, ripped her clothes and touched her, I think."

We were up on the porch now. Susan reached over and rubbed her hand over my back and said, "Thanks." I cringed. She had managed to rub over the imprint of the business end of Poultrez's shovel on my lower back. She stopped and faced me. "What'd he do to you?"

I smiled. "Hit me with a shovel."

"God. Is that why you're holding your hand funny?"

"Yeah."

"Is it broken?"

"Well . . . yeah."

Susan pushed open the door. "Go in the kitchen and put some ice on that. I've got to go check on Carli. I'll come tend to you when I'm done." She looked at me. "Go!"

So I went. And, as I went, I was all but certain I heard mumbled words, containing, among other things, the words "ridiculous" and "macho," coming from Susan's direction.

In the kitchen, I found a family-size bag of Green Giant LeSeur Early Peas in the freezer, bopped it on the counter to break up the frozen peas a little, and draped the bag over my broken hand. Then I walked over to the little built-in, kitchen desk, picked up the phone, and punched in *911.* I relayed my predicament to a bored municipal employee and hung up.

Not five minutes later, I heard a loud knock on the front door.

Susan was still upstairs with Carli. I wandered through the house to the entry hall, pulled open the door, and found myself face-to-face with Deputy Mickey Burns of the Appalachicola Sheriff's Department.

chapter thirty-seven

"YOU GET A transfer?"

Deputy Mickey smiled. But then, he pretty much always did. "I heard the call go out about the murders on the way in. I was already headed up here to get you." He stepped forward with the obvious expectation that I would react normally and step aside. I didn't. He stopped and said, "May I come in?"

"I'm still thinking about it."

Deputy Mickey actually stopped smiling. "I'm here to take you back to Appalachicola for questioning in the murder of Willie Teeter."

This was not good. Either Captain Billy had changed his mind or the two boys who Billy and Peety Boy had plugged in their respective legs had started talking. I decided to do innocent. "What are you talking about?"

I should have been paying closer attention to his hands. I knew he had stepped back. I just hadn't noticed the service revolver in his meaty, freckled paw. "Turn around and put your hands against the door." I hesitated, and he raised his revolver level with my chest and brought up his left hand to steady the gun in firing position. "Do it!"

So I did. At least, I leaned with my left hand and kind of propped against the door with my right elbow.

"Get your feet back."

I managed to put one foot back a little and say, "My hand's broken." I listened for Susan and Carli, hoping they were locked in a bathroom upstairs taking care of each other. *Just stay upstairs. The sheriff's coming. An ambulance is coming.*

The deputy patted me down, lifted Joey's Walther PPK out of my pocket, and said, "Oh. Okay, turn around. I'll cuff you in front."

I pushed away from the door and turned to face him. "Cuff me? What the hell for? Am I a suspect or something?"

His only answer was to slap cuffs on my wrists in that quick, clip-on way cops have of doing it. It hurt, and I wondered how much time he'd spent practicing that cute move on his bedpost or maybe a girlfriend.

I let the bag of frozen peas drop and said, "Can you hand me that? It's the only thing that's helping the pain."

My plan was, first, for him to bend over to pick up the peas and, second, for me to kick him as hard as I could in his friendly freckled face. But apparently he'd heard of that plan because, before he bent over to get the frozen veggies, Deputy Mickey jammed the barrel of his revolver into my stomach and kept it there until he had placed the bag back over my wrist and stepped away.

He said, "Move," and I thought I could see panic creeping into his eyes.

I had a new plan: kill time. "Look, you and I both know you don't even have jurisdiction here, and the local cops are on the way. Let's just sort this out when they get here. I grew up in this town. You probably don't know that but . . ."

He *was* panicked, and the veneer of polite professionalism disappeared. Deputy Mickey Burns reached out and clamped his gun-free hand over my broken hand and gave it a sharp squeeze and a yank. I yelped a little, which wasn't particularly dignified, and he said, "I told you to move. Now."

Another change of plans: I decided that getting the deputy away from Susan and Carli wasn't the worst thing I could do. And since I didn't have a hell of a lot of choice, I might as well find something good about being hauled off into the night by a Florida deputy with no jurisdiction, authority, or good reason.

Deputy Burns maintained a death grip on my arm as we hurried across the porch and down the front steps. When we reached the cruiser, he pulled open the back door, put his hand on the back of my head, and shoved me inside.

Peering out through the steel screen separating the back seat from the front, I could see the flash of moonlight on the deputy's equipment belt as he sprinted around the front of the vehicle. He literally jumped inside. The motor roared, and I fell sideways as the grinding noise of tires spinning through loose gravel filled the air. I righted myself in time to see Susan's twin ponds streaming by the side windows. The trees across the way were coming too fast, and the cruiser fishtailed through a small curve as it left the ponds behind. We spun and swerved over another quarter mile of dirt road. But the deputy never lost control, and he had made it out to the highway and covered another three miles toward town before the sweeping red lights of the ambulance met us. The deputy slowed, and a quarter mile later representatives of the Coopers Bend Sheriff's Department appeared over a hill in a wash of swirling blue light. Unfortunately, they weren't interested in us. They were speeding toward the charming country farmhouse where I had just discovered one corpse and deposited another.

We had been riding for a little more than an hour. I had been trying to think. I guessed my captor had been doing the same. I decided to try a little conversation.

"Where are we going?"

"Where do you think?"

"I mean, are we going straight to the Appalachicola Sheriff's Office? Or are we going to the hospital, or what?"

He didn't answer. I was beginning to feel ignored.

A minute or two passed. Deputy Mickey plucked his mike off the dash, looked at it like it was something he'd never seen before, and put it back. Then he reached over and punched the button on the glove box. The door fell open and a little bulb lighted a haphazard collection of maps and what looked like paperback field manuals. Burns shoved a freckled hand under the maps and stuff and came out with a thick mobile phone that had a coiled wire hanging from it like an oversized tail.

I said, "Who are we going to call?"

The deputy glanced back and forth from the road to the phone as he pulled the cigarette lighter from the dash and replaced it with the phone's adapter.

I decided to try again. "You think I could use that thing to call a lawyer? It'll make things go faster when we get there."

Again, he didn't answer, and it was becoming clear that we were not going to be friends.

Instead of engaging me in dialogue, the good deputy punched a long series of numbers into his phone and then pressed it against his ear. "This is Burns. I got him." Silence. "No. No problem. We oughta be there in three hours or less." Silence. "Yeah, okay."

He punched a button and put the phone on the seat beside him.

I leaned up close to the metal screen separating me from the front seat. "What's wrong with your radio?"

"Shut up, McInnes."

"I was just wondering . . ."

"You want a drink of water, you can get one when we get there. You need to take a leak, you can piss your pants. You want to use the phone, well, you're shit out of luck. Now. That's all the conversation we're gonna have. Any more questions and I'm gonna pull over on the side of the road and cuff your hands and feet together and stick a rag in your mouth. You got that?"

I said, "Got it," and lay back against the seat. Might as well get comfortable.

Three hours later, when we cruised straight through the municipality of Appalachicola, Florida, without stopping, I got a lot less comfortable. After Deputy Mickey Burns turned north on 65 and hung a right into Tate's Hell Swamp, I felt downright miserable.

Burns followed the same route Joey had taken the night before. We were going to Carpintero's compound. I thought about the dead nephew of a Panamanian dictator—the corpse we had left in a smoldering wrecked car—and I thought about the pretty young wife who I hoped had gotten far away with her fat little kid.

I wondered how Deputy Mickey planned to get his patrol car across the submerged road that led through the swamp without either drowning out the engine or sliding off into the ooze the way Willie's truck had. But, as we rounded a curve and approached the saw grass field, that question was answered with the headlights of half a dozen pickups and 4x4s.

We had a welcoming committee. And I didn't feel a damned bit welcome.

Bumping across miles of field and marsh and swamp while lying in the bed of a truck tied to a metal cleat, nursing a broken wrist, and trying to avoid any contact with the black-and-blue imprint of a shovel on your back . . . Well, it sucks is what is does.

Deputy Mickey Burns had departed, leaving me in the care of eight guys with long hair, multiple tattoos, and expensive jewelry. And it quickly became obvious that the caravan of 4x4s was indeed headed for Carpintero's compound.

With each new jolt of hot pain in my wrist, my breathing grew more erratic and another ounce of hope floated away and drowned itself in the slimy black water that surrounded us.

I tried to think. I couldn't. I was too damn scared.

Even with jarring pain, even lashed to the cleat of some redneck criminal's truck, being alive was better than what waited at the compound. So I felt no relief when the six-car caravan entered the compound and parked in perfect order beside two more off-road vehicles.

For some reason, I glanced at my watch. It was close to midnight, and the swamp was full of the sounds of crickets and frogs and night birds. I could hear the metallic clicks and thuds of truck doors being opened and closed. Someone opened the gate on the truck I was tied to and stepped into the bed. The back end sank under his weight, and the truck made creaking, complaining noises of metal against metal.

A knife clicked open. The ropes pulled against my wrists sending an electric jolt of pain shooting up to my shoulder, and I looked at the man standing over me. He wore cowboy boots like the ones Sonny Teeter's corpse was wearing that night. The ropes popped loose under the pressure of his knife blade, and he jerked me to my feet. He wore a white, western-style shirt with pink stripes and starched blue jeans with sharp creases down the front. His bald head shone in the night above a curtain of shoulder-length hair that hung from his temples and the back of his head. He looked like a malnourished Benjamin Franklin.

I asked, "What do you want?"

Ben spun me by one shoulder and shoved me over the side of the truck. I managed to spin and get my feet under me but then misjudged the ground and landed on my shovel-imprinted back.

Bald Ben hand-sprinted over the side and landed next to me. Another man joined him. They snatched me up, and each man picked an elbow and clamped down. We headed into the large warehouse structure that I had searched earlier that same day—although it seemed days now, maybe weeks, since I had watched Peety Boy shoot Willie Teeter and since I had disarmed Señora Carpintero and helped Captain Billy take his dead and dishonored grandson to the morgue.

Inside, overhead fixtures flooded the warehouse with yellow light. Shipping crates lined the walls. Ten feet up on a storage area that looked like a barn loft, brown cardboard boxes were stacked head high.

My escorts walked me to the middle of the wooden floor and left me.

My shattered hand shot hot jolts of electricity up my arm. My back throbbed, and the bright light stung my eyes. I looked around the warehouse. I was surrounded by cowboy boots and Air Jordans, printed T-shirts and tank tops, blue jeans and cut-offs, and, everywhere, tattooed arms and hands.

A man I recognized stepped forward. He was the on-duty deputy who had pointed his gun at Susan and me the night Purcell's killers had broken into Susan's beach house.

"This is the man who killed Leroy Purcell." He spoke like a senator addressing Congress, like a man giving a speech, except that his voice came out in a high-pitched, bluegrass twang.

I decided to speak up. "That's not true."

The orator was quicker than he looked, or maybe I was deeper in shock than I thought. He spun on his heels and popped me across the mouth with a backhand before I saw it coming. The blow scattered my thoughts for a few seconds and the deputy resumed his speech.

"This man's name is Tom McInnes. Yesterday afternoon, he killed Tim and Elroy, Johnny and even little Skeeter out on Dog Island. He rented a boat at The Moorings, floated out there with this big white-haired asshole, and they killed all four of 'em. Then he come back in and drove up to Seaside and killed Leroy." The deputy swept his open hand around the room, motioning at the rogues' gallery. "You heard about it. It ain't no secret. This rich asshole lawyer from up at Mobile killed Leroy and then used a hammer to nail his ball sack to a table."

The deputy was doing a good job, and, with the mention of Purcell, murmuring began to fill the warehouse. When he reminded them of the nails, the threats became audible and graphic.

"Mickey promised you he'd bring in Purcell's killer. He done it. Mickey said he'd let all of us get a chance to question the bastard that done it. He done that too. And—as much as Mickey Burns wanted to take this piece-of-shit bastard and nail his balls to a table—he promised to bring him here and give us the pleasure of fuckin' him up any way we want before we bury him in the swamp. And Mickey done that too."

It was pretty obvious that Deputy Mickey Burns was the ambitious young man Carlos Sanchez had mentioned who wanted to replace Leroy Purcell as the head Jethro. It was also obvious that Deputy Mickey had a hell of a campaign manager in his fellow deputy.

Now or never. "I did not kill Leroy Purcell. He was killed by a man named Carpintero. A man called 'the Hammer.'" My voice sounded hollow.

The speaker spun and slung another backhand at my mouth, and I tasted blood.

The deputy said, "Who's got theirself a question?"

The skinny Ben Franklin who had pushed me out of his truck bed spoke up. "Fuck that. Only question I got is who gets to kill him."

My voice came again, almost without my knowing it would. "Listen! Listen to me, damnit!"

The skinny speaker stepped toward me and threw a fist this time. But I saw this one coming and slipped the punch. When his hand had swung around and he was off balance, I stepped forward and kicked him in the balls with every ounce of strength left in my body. A thick groan came from deep in his chest as his legs lifted off the ground and he fell facedown on the floor, squirming and puffing and making the same guttural sound over and over.

I heard running, and a strong hand grasped my arm. Half a second later, a fist slammed into my left kidney, and I fell to one knee.

Legs and fists swirled around me as more men rushed forward. I caught a flash of cowboy boot, jerked my head back, and felt the wind from a hard kick aimed at my mouth. A knee hit and pain exploded in my chest, and I went down in a hailstorm of pounding boots.

Automatic gunfire shattered the air inside the metal building.

"Stop!" An accented male voice boomed above the celebration.

There was a pause as murmuring filled the space above my head.

Again automatic gunfire crackled throughout the warehouse, and pieces of the boxes lining the walls spun and danced under the floodlights.

"Step away from Mr. McInnes." The Bodines looked for the disembodied voice, but they didn't move. The unseen man shouted, "Now!"

Jean-clad legs had just begun to back away when a pair of creased and starched jeans walked past and swung a cowboy boot into my stomach. A single, penetrating explosion echoed inside the warehouse, and skinny Ben Franklin fell backward and landed perpendicular to my prostrate body. A ragged, bloody hole poured blood from the place where his left eye had been.

I pushed my chest up off the floor just as another shot echoed inside the metal walls, and I glanced over to see a man in a tank top fall to his knees with a hole in his chest. He looked surprised; then he fell dead.

The voice came again, and I was sure I could hear echoes of an equatorial accent. "Mr. McInnes, you may leave."

A quiet mumbling started again.

"Mr. McInnes! Get up and get out of here!"

I was on my feet and moving fast through the outside door. I ran out past the trucks and looked for whatever help was there. A soft, familiar voice came out of the darkness. "Over here, Señor McInnes." And Carlos Sanchez stepped out of the night. At his side was Deputy Mickey Burns.

I said, "What's going on?" It was a stupid question, but I wasn't really in a smart mood.

Sanchez said, "You are safe."

I nodded at Burns. "I was safe before he brought me here."

Sanchez puffed on his ever-present cigar. "Actually, no. You weren't. There was a price on your head. Those men inside wanted you dead."

"And now they don't?"

Sanchez shrugged.

In the distance, I could hear helicopter blades beating the night air. I pointed at the sky with my good hand. "Is that yours?"

He nodded.

"Was Deputy Mickey here in on this all along?"

The deputy spoke up. "That's Deputy *Burns*. And what I've been doing is none of your business."

The freckle-faced deputy was puffing himself up to fill Leroy Purcell's shoes; he was ready to don the Caterpillar-cap crown of the next King Jethro. And he seemed a lot surer than I was that there would still be a few Bodines around to follow him after tonight.

As I stood there thinking about all that, I heard running and turned to see a dozen men in black clothing round the corner of the warehouse and disappear inside. Each man had an angular automatic weapon suspended from a shoulder strap and secured by one hand.

I asked, "What's going to happen in there?"

Sanchez drew again on his thin cigar, making the red tip glow like a hot coal in the night. "Do you really want to know?"

"Yeah. I do."

"There will be a boating accident. A chartered fishing vessel has already left the marina in Carabelle. The names on the charter will match those of the men inside."

"Am I safe?"

He nodded.

"What about my clients?"

"You and they have nothing else to fear from Leroy Purcell's branch of the organization." Sanchez turned to Deputy Burns. "Go see what's happening."

The deputy squared his shoulders and said, "I don't want no part of this."

Sanchez turned to face Burns and simply said, "Now."

Two seconds passed while the deputy tried to think of a way to salvage some dignity, and he turned toward the warehouse.

I looked up to search the stars for the helicopter, and a pistol fired next to my ear. I fell to one knee and froze. Deputy Mickey Burns of the Appalachicola Sheriff's Department lay dead on the ground. I turned to see if Sanchez was still alive. He was. And he was sliding what looked like Joey's Walther PPK into a hiding place inside his coat.

Suffering a broken wrist, a shoveled back, and multiple kicks and stomps had taken a lot out of me. It took some effort to get back on my feet. I asked, "Am I next?"

Sanchez just said, "No," and then paused to look at the blanket of stars spread overhead. "The helicopter will be here soon. It will take you to only one place. Dog Island. I am sorry about your hand. You hold it as though it is broken."

I nodded.

"Too bad. There is no medical help on the island. In any event, you will check into the inn and stay there until morning. At that time, you may take the ferry to Carabelle. After that, you are free to go wherever you please."

"Except the police."

"Yes. Except the police."

"Why Dog Island?"

"Arrangements have been made. It is the island or, well, nothing. Perhaps, so you will understand, *nothingness* would be a better word."

"Why are you doing this?"

Sanchez paused to look at one of his men who had exited the warehouse. The night-clad soldier nodded at Sanchez, who shook his head in response. The soldier went back inside the building. The two-named patriot turned back to me. "Your young client deserved none of this. You are in trouble only because you tried to help." He paused. "We are not criminals. We are soldiers. This mess was, in some ways, our doing. I have decided to set it right, to the extent that that's possible."

I studied his aristocratic features in the moonlight. I said, "And Purcell got out of line." He didn't answer, so I repeated the same words and added, "*And* it's as good a reason as any to take the Bodines out of the picture once and for all."

Sanchez smiled. "As I said, we heard you were smart."

Suddenly the helicopter appeared over the treetops and dropped its tail as it began its descent into the compound.

I yelled over the blades. "One more thing." Sanchez looked at me. "Whose idea was it to bring a dethroned Panamanian dictator's nephew into the country?"

Carlos Sanchez rolled his cigar between manicured fingers. A few seconds passed before he said, "We did. And we knew the dangers associated with his family's presence. But he was well connected in Castro's government, and we thought his contacts would be worth the risk."

I shouted. "And was it? Was it worth all this?"

His only answer was to point at the helicopter and say, "Go."

I ran to the chopper and climbed inside. The helmeted pilot lifted off as I watched Sanchez walk to the warehouse door, speak with one of his soldiers, and then hurry to a waiting Hummer. As the helicopter climbed into the night sky and leveled out over the black mass of oak and cypress treetops, I could have sworn I heard the jarring staccato pops of automatic gunfire echoing inside the warehouse and splintering the night air.

epilogue

BRIGHT SUNSHINE FILLED the bedroom. A cool spring breeze floated through open French doors, softly ruffled the sheets, and lifted me out of a deep, satisfying sleep. I smiled and reached over for Susan. She was gone, and my heart missed a beat before I realized Carpintero, Leroy Purcell, and—thanks to New Cuba—the rest of the renegade Bodines had gone on to their rewards, if the kind of afterlife that was likely to greet them could be called a reward. I plumped my pillow and leaned my back against it. I didn't look at my watch or the clock on the bedside table. Judging from the sun, it was somewhere around midmorning, and that was close enough.

Sounds of Susan piddling in the kitchen drifted up the staircase.

I rolled out of bed, and, after brushing my teeth and splashing a little water on my face, I lifted the terry cloth robe off the hook on the bathroom door and wandered out onto my second-floor deck. And that's where I was, leaning against the railing and watching a tanker headed for the Port of Mobile, when Susan appeared in the doorway with a large glass of orange juice in each hand. And, only two days after being rescued from root-cellar imprisonment, she looked pretty damned good.

Lying in bed last night, Susan and I had talked long past midnight, and now I understood most of what had happened.

It looked as though Purcell had dispatched Rus Poultrez and Sonny Teeter to grab Susan from Seaside while Joey and I were busy on Dog Island looking for Carli. Purcell had wanted Susan as a hostage. Poultrez, on the other hand, wanted Susan to help him find Carli. What neither of them counted on was Susan plugging Sonny with her little snub-nosed .38 when he broke into the Seaside cottage where she was manning our listening equipment. That's where the hole in Sonny's side and the blood at the Seaside cottage had come from. Unfortunately, Susan only got off one shot before Poultrez grabbed her from behind after coming in the back.

Apparently, Poultrez and Sonny had spoken freely in front of Susan—probably because they planned to kill her later. Susan heard Poultrez say that he knew Carli had headed for Meridian, and, after finding Susan's address in her purse, Poultrez and Sonny just sat Susan in the backseat and headed for the farm. She had waited for a chance to get away, but none came.

When they arrived, the house was empty. So, Sonny—just having been gut shot and all—decided that killing Susan right then was a hell of an idea. Poultrez disagreed and finally snapped Sonny's neck to drive home his point.

What I didn't know and couldn't figure out was the sequence of events at the farm. When did Carli get to Coopers Bend and why was Susan in the root cellar unhurt . . . ?

"Hello?"

I came back into the present. "Oh, hi."

Susan smiled. "I'm here bearing gifts."

I took a glass in my good hand; my right fist was locked in plaster and suspended from a sling. "Orange juice is a gift?"

"Yes. From Minute Maid. What were you thinking about?"

"Poultrez and Sonny and the rest of it."

Susan set her glass on the railing and plopped down in a redwood deck chair. "You're not still worried are you?"

"Oh. Hell, no. I'm just trying to piece it all together. You mind if we talk about it a little?"

"I told you last night. I'm fine."

I thought maybe she was a little testy about the subject for someone who was fine, but I let it go. I said, "I just didn't know if you wanted to mess up a great morning like this by talking about it." Susan looked at me, then picked up her glass and sipped some juice. So much for my stab at sensitivity. "Okay. Here's what I don't understand. I know Carli didn't get to the farm until after you and Poultrez and Sonny were already there. But I don't know how long Carli was there with her father before I showed up."

Susan rose out of her chair and came to stand beside me. "I guess a couple of hours. Poultrez locked me in the bomb shelter just after Carli got there. I didn't have a watch, but about two hours or so is my best guess. And Poultrez killed Sonny before I went in. So . . ." Susan put her elbows on the railing and leaned out to look down the beach. "In case you're wondering, you probably saved Carli from being raped by showing up when you did. She told Sheriff Nixon in Coopers Bend that, when her father heard you outside, he had just 'started on her.'" Susan made a face. "God, what a way to put it."

"Better than most of the alternatives."

"I guess. Anyway, he's gone and she's going to make it." I shrugged, and Susan said, "Really. I believe that. Loutie's going to take care of her for a while. Get her some counseling, whatever she needs. Like I told you from the first, there's more to Carli than meets the eye."

"What about her mother?"

"It's pitiful. Carli says not to worry. Apparently, the mother's kind of . . . well, she's just about what you'd expect to be married to her father."

I drank some orange juice and said, "Oh."

I was thinking about Carli and watching three slack-jawed pelicans drift over the bay when the phone started ringing. I set my juice back on its round wet spot on the railing.

Susan said, "Let the machine get it."

"Turned it off."

"Well, then just let it ring."

As I turned to walk inside, I said, "I stabbed a guy in the throat two days ago. They know it was self-defense, but it wouldn't be a great idea for the cops to think I had sneaked off somewhere. I'll be right back."

I walked around and sat on the bed before picking up the receiver.

"Hello?"

"Tom?" It was Carlos Sanchez—known in political circles as Charlie Estevez—and he apparently had decided that we were on a first-name basis.

Unfortunately, I wasn't sure which name to use. So, all I said was, "Yes?"

"Carlos Sanchez."

That answered that. "Good morning, Carlos." Two could play at that game.

"How's your friend? The giant with white hair."

"The giant with white hair is fine. He's back in Mobile, and he's got a beautiful woman to nurse him back to health. The doctors say a few weeks and he'll be back to normal."

"That *is* good to hear." Sanchez hesitated just as Susan walked into the room.

She whispered, "Who is it?"

I put my hand over the mouthpiece. "Carlos Sanchez."

Susan whispered again. "Did you tell him you know his real name?"

I kept my hand over the phone. "Hell, no." Susan laughed, and I realized that Sanchez had been saying something. "I'm sorry Carlos, someone just came in. What were you saying?"

"I was asking about your young client."

"Carli's doing about as well as I guess anyone could under the circumstances."

"Yes. It is very sad."

As far as I was concerned, Carlos Sanchez was a pretty good guy. I formed this opinion after he rescued me from being kicked to death in the swamp by a bunch of tattooed, redneck smugglers. But I did not believe he had called my home to check on my friends' health and well-being. He wanted something.

"Why'd you call?"

"Ah, we have a problem, and it could turn out to be your problem too." He had my attention. "Someone is missing."

"Who?"

"The Carpenter. With what happened to Leroy Purcell, well, I don't need to tell you what kind of attention such a psychopath could focus on my organization."

"Then I take it Carpintero's done this before."

Sanchez hesitated before answering. "Yes. I am afraid 'the Hammer,' 'the Carpenter,' whatever name you want to use, is quite famous among former political interrogators in Central America."

"I didn't think that kind of thing went on down there anymore."

"Well, with the spread of democracy, it is certainly not accepted practice anymore, which is one reason El Carpintero was looking for a new, ah, venue."

"And you were going to supply one?"

"What? No. No, señor."

I decided I had jerked him around enough. "Carpintero is dead."

"You have seen the body?"

"Sure. He crashed into a building out there in the compound. He was trying to make a run for it in an old Mercedes and one of the young Bodines, a guy named Willie Teeter, either shot him or just shot *at* him and made him crash. Whichever, he was dead."

Sanchez was silent long enough for me to wonder if we had lost the connection. Finally, he said, "You said Señor Carpintero died in a crash?"

"That's right."

"And his wife. What happened to the señora?"

I could feel hair prickling on the back of my neck. "We found her in a cabin. She tried to shoot me. I managed to disarm her and ask a few questions. Then an old man and I left on an airboat. We left Señora Carpintero and her son—who she had hidden somewhere in the bedroom—we left them in the cabin. There was a four-wheel-drive parked outside with the keys in it."

Sanchez laughed, but there was no humor in it. "And you North Americans say Latinos are chauvinists. The man you call Señor Carpintero was an overweight, undisciplined political hack with a rich uncle and family connections. His wife, the mother of that chubby little boy, was a prison physician who was brought in years ago to revive political prisoners after torture. She developed a taste for it. And a specialty. In addition to her scalpel, she liked to use nails."

I opened my mouth to speak and nothing came out. Susan sat on the bed beside me and put her hand on my leg. "What's wrong. What is it, Tom?"

I shook my head at Susan and spoke into the phone. "Why did she kill Purcell?"

"We don't know the details, but it appears Leroy Purcell treated Carpintero and her husband like employees. I expect it doesn't take much to set her off. Anyway, they were setting up some kind of lab out there in the swamp. And the word is that a disagreement arose."

"A disagreement." It wasn't really a question or a statement, and Sanchez let it lie there. I said, "What was it, a meth lab?"

"I'm afraid not. As far as we can tell, it was some kind of biological hazard setup. That's something this woman has tried her hand at before. I can only guess that Purcell planned to enter the weapons trade." I cussed, and Sanchez added, "We burned her laboratory to the ground."

"If you didn't, I'll make sure someone else does."

"We set fire to the whole complex. Feel free to ride out there and check, but it shouldn't be necessary. The fire rangers were all over it an hour after we pulled out. I'm sure there's a report."

Pictures of Leroy Purcell's corpse flashed through my mind, and one stuck. I couldn't shake the image of his thick jock-neck spread out and nailed to the desk, the skin glistening like melted wax where it was stretched tight across his throat from neat rows of nail holes on each side.

And, I thought, I had let the person who did that loose on America. I could almost see the señora, riding down a highway somewhere in the heartland in that harmless-looking, soccer-mom four-wheel-drive—a raven-haired beauty with a chubby little boy and a taste for evisceration.

Sanchez was waiting for me to say something about the fire. I managed to say, "Okay. Fine."

"Tom, are you all right?"

"No."

Some time went by, and he said, "So. If nothing remains to be handled, we will put this behind us."

I looked at Susan. All the color had drained from her face. She was suddenly frightened, and she didn't even know why—except that she had seen the terror in my eyes.

I said, "One more thing. Who was the poor bastard who started all this? Who *did* Leroy Purcell shoot in the mouth in See Shore Cottage while Carli was peeking in the window?"

"Tom," Sanchez said, "I have absolutely no idea."